KING SOLOMON'S

MINES

H. Rider Haggard

edited by Gerald Monsman

broadview literary texts

National Library of Canada Cataloguing in Publication Data

Haggard, H. Rider (Henry Rider), 1856-1925
   King Solomon's mines / H. Rider Haggard ; Gerald Monsman, editor.

(Broadview literary texts)
Includes bibliographical references.
ISBN 1-55111-439-9

   1. Quatermain, Allan (Fictitious character)—Fiction. I. Monsman, Gerald, 1940- II. Title.
III. Series.

PR4731.K5 2002   823'.8   C2002-902937-6

Broadview Press Ltd. is an independent, international publishing house, incorporated in 1985. Broadview believes in shared ownership, both with its employees and with the general public; since the year 2000 Broadview shares have traded publicly on the Toronto Venture Exchange under the symbol BDP.

We welcome comments and suggestions regarding any aspect of our publications–please feel free to contact us at the addresses below or at broadview@broadviewpress.com.

North America
PO Box 1243, Peterborough, Ontario, Canada K9J 7H5
3576 California Road, Orchard Park, NY, USA 14127
Tel: (705) 743-8990; Fax: (705) 743-8353
email: customerservice@broadviewpress.com

UK, Ireland, and continental Europe
Thomas Lyster Ltd., Units 3 & 4a, Old Boundary Way
Burscough Road, Ormskirk
Lancashire, L39 2YW
Tel: (01695) 575112; Fax: (01695) 570120
email: books@tlyster.co.uk

Australia and New Zealand
UNIREPS, University of New South Wales
Sydney, NSW, 2052
Tel: 61 2 9664 0999; Fax: 61 2 9664 5420
email: info.press@unsw.edu.au

www.broadviewpress.com

Broadview Press Ltd. gratefully acknowledges the financial support of the Government of Canada through the Book Publishing Industry Development Program for our publishing activities.

Series editor: Professor L.W. Conolly
Advisory editor for this volume: Professor Eugene Benson

Text design and composition by George Kirkpatrick

PRINTED IN CANADA

Contents

Appendix D: Historical Documents: Spoils of Imperialism: Gold, Diamonds, and Ivory

Preface

In numerous instances unfamiliar terms, figures, and territories are explained in the primary text by the author, but those not so explained are annotated at their first appearance in the main text and again at their first appearance in the appendices. I omit the annotative clutter of further repetition and of notes for insignificant figures and districts for which data are inexact. The appendices vary in length. Reactions to Haggard's novel are represented by short critical "takes" that cut to the heart of lengthier analyses; on the other hand, one of Haggard's essays (difficult of access) is reprinted in full and another at length because they are indispensable evidence of his political and aesthetic attitudes at the time he composed *King Solomon's Mines*.

I wish to thank Robert Langenfeld, Editor of *English Literature in Transition*, for permission to include parts of my essay "Of Diamonds and Deities: Social Anthropology in H. Rider Haggard's *King Solomon's Mines*," *ELT* (43:3 2000): 280–297, in my Introduction. I wish also to thank my colleague, Vic Baker of the University of Arizona Department of Hydrology, for confirmation that Haggard's episode about the presence of water on a desert koppie (hill) is perfectly in accord with scientific fact.

A map of South Africa by John Arrowsmith (1857) with the routes of David Livingstone, a missionary whose explorations provided a foundation for Haggard's geographical knowledge. A note on this map indicates that rivers and lakes delineated by dashed lines "are from Oral information, generally."

Introduction: Of Diamonds and Deities in King Solomon's Mines

H. Rider Haggard's early manhood was the stuff of fiction—quite literally. Whatever praise or blame his many novels may deserve, one fact is indisputable: when he wrote of Africa, he wrote of what he had seen, done, or heard from eye-witnesses, although he also deliberately intermixed with his facts elements of the fantastic, of the supernatural, and of fictional history to give his tales an aura of exoticism. Certainly no one would have predicted literary fame for young Haggard. He was born in 1856 in Norfolk, England, sixth son (eighth of ten children) of William and Ella Haggard. His father was a barrister and country squire who seems either not to have recognized his son's abilities or to have tired of paying for Rider's older brothers' university education. At any rate, after Ipswich Grammar School, Haggard did not prepare to enter the university. He failed an army entrance examination, studied for the Foreign Office examinations, experimented with spiritualism, and fell in love with Lilly ("Lilith") Jackson.

But when Sir Henry Bulwer, Squire Haggard's friend, was newly named Lieutenant-Governor of Natal Colony, Haggard's father wrote to inquire if Bulwer could somehow make use of Rider in Africa.[1] The answer was positive; and Haggard, duties undefined, embarked for South Africa with Bulwer in 1875 for what became the defining half-dozen years of his life. Africa galvanized him, awakened his latent abilities. He became the governor's trusted aide, hobnobbed with the imperial elite, learned to speak Zulu, negotiated with African chieftains, and hunted from galloping horses.

In 1877, a hundred thousand Zulus began massing on the borders of the Boer Republic of the Transvaal to attack five thousand armed Dutch. Spear against rifle, it would have been a bloodbath

---

1 At that time, present-day South Africa consisted of independent territories, among them the Cape Colony and Natal (chiefly British), the Orange Free State, and the Transvaal (Boer, i.e., Dutch), Zululand, and Basutoland (tribal).

destabilizing native-imperial relations in the surrounding territories, including Natal. Because at that moment the Zulus respected the British, if the Transvaal became a crown colony, the threatened bloodbath would be averted. (Gold and diamonds in the Transvaal provided incentive for British intervention.) Haggard, among others, was recruited by the charismatic chief of native affairs, Sir Theophilus Shepstone, for this diplomatic mission, and a small group trekked to Pretoria, the capital, to inform the Dutch that the British were taking over their Republic. Standing in front of an armed, ominously silent crowd of Dutchmen, Haggard personally hoisted the Union Jack over Pretoria and, he recalled, "when the late Sir Melmoth Osborne grew nervous in reading the proclamation, I took it from his hand and finished the business,"[1] thereby claiming for his Queen (on her birthday) a territory as big as Great Britain itself. For a young man, all but a boy, that certainly compensated for bypassing *Literae Humaniores* at Oxford! On the way back to Natal the small group escaped a night ambush by the Boers only because Haggard had convinced his companions to take the scenic moon-lit route.

Haggard later served as assistant to the Transvaal colonial secretary and was appointed as Registrar and Master of the Transvaal High Court. But news of Lilly Jackson's marriage in England devastated him. He travelled briefly to England to marry a Norfolk heiress with whom he returned to Africa to take up ostrich farming on the border of Natal and the Transvaal. Then political trouble loomed. The Boers wanted their country back, and in 1881 they defeated the British at Majuba Hill (properly Amajuba, Zulu for "the hill of doves"). Because Haggard's farm was on the border, his kitchen was used to negotiate the treaty reestablishing Dutch independence. Having escaped one ambush in 1877, Haggard thought it safest to return to England with his wife and child to study law and write—at first with only modest success. What Haggard needed to do was harness the tremendous potential of his experience of Africa—its gold, diamonds, natives, warfare, magic and ritual—in an exciting adventure narrative.

---

1   Haggard, *The Private Diaries of Sir H. Rider Haggard* (London: Cassell, 1980) 33-34, 111.

Roger Lancelyn Green describes this turning point best:

> Stevenson's *Treasure Island*, recently published, was attracting considerable attention, and to while away dull evenings in London lodgings, Haggard wrote *King Solomon's Mines*: "it was written out of a bet with his brother. The bet was made casually, to prove it possible for someone, not at all known in authorship, to do a 'thriller' as successful as *Treasure Island*." The book was a complete novelty, and publisher after publisher refused to undertake it. Finally it came into the hands of W. E. Henley, who showed it to Andrew Lang, between whom and Haggard a firm friendship soon sprang up. Either Henley or Lang recommended it to Cassells, who agreed to publish it on a small copyright basis. On the eve of publication, so Sir Max Pemberton recalls, he was sitting next to a well-known London publisher at a dinner table, who remarked to him: "There's a silly story of a diamond mine published today. It's by a man named Rider Haggard. They offered me this book six months ago, and I declined it. Some fool has bought it as you will see—and I'm sorry for him." "I have often wondered," Sir Max goes on, "how sorry he remained when Cassells were at their wits' end to bring the book out fast enough and it remained easily the best seller of the year." (145)

King Solomon's Mines was published in September 1885 by Cassell & Company in a binding designed to make it look like a companion volume to Stevenson's *Treasure Island*. With a flair for advertising, Cassell's plastered large posters all over London announcing "King Solomon's Mines—The Most Amazing Book Ever Written." Richard Dalby notes that

> in spite of this apparent confidence in the book's potential, Cassell's printed only a modest 2000 copies of the first edition, of which only one thousand were bound up in September (the first issue with a catalogue at the rear dated 5G.8.85). Five hundred more were bound up in October

with a catalogue at the end dated 5G.10.85 (the second issue), and the remaining five hundred were shipped to New York and bound up there in November.[1]

The cover was in red cloth on which was imprinted its title and author's name, with a design (called a "trophy" by bibliographers) of a Zulu shield, weapons, and elephant tusk. The popularity of Haggard's tale quickly eclipsed even that of *Treasure Island*. Because Haggard's romance spoke of a reassertion of British masculinity and of exploits utterly foreign to nineteenth-century drawing rooms, the novel sold 31,000 copies in its first year, an enormous number for that time.

Haggard described his method of romance-writing as "swift, clear, and direct," purged of "dark allusions": "such work should be written rapidly and, if possible, not rewritten, since wine of this character loses its bouquet when it is poured from glass to glass."[2] Haggard's writing has powerful affinities with dreams or even with such early psychoanalytic devices as Rorschach tests, tapping lapsed memories and subliminal impressions. At the climactic moment in *King Solomon's Mines*, the trio is illuminated in the dimming lamp: "Presently it flared up and showed the whole scene in strong relief, the great mass of white tusks, the boxes full of gold, the corpse of poor Foulata stretched before them, the goat-skin full of treasure, the dim glimmer of the diamonds, and the wild, wan faces of us three white men seated there awaiting death by starvation." Quatermain observes that "wealth, which men spend all their lives in acquiring, is a valueless thing at the last." Despite Haggard's predilection for "grip" in romance writing, one cannot dismiss this scene as simply the climactic moment of suspense before the escape. Nor is Quatermain's observation on the valuelessness of diamonds merely a conventional response.

---

1   "*King Solomon's Mines:* A Centenary Remembered," *Antiquarian Book Monthly Review* (October 1985): 391-392.
2   *The Days of My Life: An Autobiography* (London: Longmans, Green, 1926) 2:92. In *Private Diaries*, Haggard does remark, a propos of Kipling's appreciation of *Yva* (*When the World Shook*), still in manuscript, "he (Kipling) has imagination, vision and can *understand*, amongst other things that Romance may be the vehicle of much that does not appear to the casual reader" (101).

In a 1905 Canadian speech, Haggard cited this specific passage to assert that the commercial and technological wealth of urban life is valueless apart from an Antaeus-like contact with the land and its fertility. Like the native, the European must go to the land, must discover the natives' wealth, not in the form of diamonds but as a source of rebirth and renewal. This is the fundamental mythopoeic hook on which Haggard hangs his heroic quest.

When Haggard returned from Africa to England after the retrocession of the Transvaal, which he felt to be a "great betrayal" of settlers and natives alike by the Gladstone government,[1] he found England by comparison a spiritually barren society spawning a crude mass of worthless fiction. After the success of *King Solomon's Mines*, he observed in "About Fiction" (1887) that contemporary Anglo-American writing was either dreary and insipid or decadently naturalistic. Haggard invited his reader to

consult his own mind, and see how many novels proper among the hundreds that have been published within the last five years, and which deal in any way with every day contemporary life, have excited his profound interest. The present writer can at the moment recall but two — one was called "My Trivial Life and Misfortunes," by an unknown author, and the other, "The Story of a South African Farm," by Ralph Iron. (See Appendix B, "About Fiction.")

---

1 Haggard, *Life*, 2:262-3; 1:194; see also "The Transvaal," *Macmillan's Magazine* 36 (May 1877): 70-79. Among the political ramifications of Haggard's "Transvaal," the incredible prize of diamonds is hidden in his understated locution, "mineral resources"; and his metaphor of the new colony as the unpolished jewel in the crown poeticizes and veils the economic motivation for intervention — the very real diamonds with which the new colony is filled. Only in London will Africa's "unpolished" jewels be sold, their commercial value seemingly unknown until, as in the romance, "Streeters" definitively pronounces them "of the finest water." Haggard probably downplayed the economic motivation because for him diamonds *were* less precious than the powers in the land itself. Though the land belongs by "birthright" to the "natives" (the root *nasci*, to be born, grounds that principle), the unfurling of the Union Jack allows the British colonists to be naturalized in the Transvaal by giving birth or rebirth to themselves as Anglo-African "progeny," the last word in Haggard's essay. For Haggard, this possibility of rebirth into a more vital mythopoeic primal unity with the land ended when the Transvaal was returned to the Boers in 1881.

According to Haggard, who cited Olive Schreiner's male pseudonym and got the title wrong, *The Story of an African Farm* (1883) is a notable contemporary narrative of "spiritual intensity"; Haggard also valued tales of "pure imagination."[1] Among such "purely romantic fiction," he implicitly included his own recently-published romance. Haggard sought to blame a British ethos of gentility for turning him away from the novel of "life as life is, and men and women as they are" and towards romance ("About Fiction"). This attack on contemporary fiction produced a backlash that inflicted lasting damage on his reputation; for a century, he was ostracized by the literary establishment as little more than a writer of juvenile action-fantasy who got his start imitating *Treasure Island*. Certainly Haggard's dedication of *King Solomon's Mines* "to all the big and little boys who read it" suggests an obvious marketing strategy to piggyback on Stevenson's success; but dark and bloody adventure also released Haggard's imagination in ways that were neither puerile nor prurient. Haggard's earlier attempts at realistic fiction had aspired to something like Schreiner's entangled, tragic relationships; but only in romance was he able to capitalize on mythic and visionary patterns, to give full rein to the longing of unrequited desire and "the soul and the fate of man" in a modern, hellish world.[2]

Sitanda's Kraal, the trio's last outpost before the desert, is on old maps of Rhodesia, located in present-day central Zambia; but beyond this point Haggard's topography becomes mythopoeic. Graham Greene, the novelist and dramatist, testifies in *The Lost Childhood and Other Essays* (1951) to Haggard's impact on his imagination:

---

1 In *Life*, Haggard described *King Solomon's Mines* as "a work of pure imagination" because in its time "very little was known of the region wherein its scenes were laid" (2:96; also 1:233, 264).

2 Haggard, *Private Diaries*, 135-37. Though Haggard's (and on this occasion also Rudyard Kipling's) sense of the hellishness of modern existence may be due partly to the infirmities of two old men intensified by the mood of the First World War, Haggard's despairing vision was also for Andrew Lang a key trait: "Men brood on buried loves, / and unforgot, / Or break themselves on some divine decree, / Or would o'erleap the limits of their lot"—as Lang phrased it in "*She*," his poetic tribute to Haggard's second romance. (Green, R.L. *Andrew Lang: A Critical Biography* [Leicester: E. Ward, 1946].)

If it had not been for that romantic tale of Allan Quatermain, Sir Henry Curtis, Captain Good, and, above all, the ancient witch Gagool, would I at nineteen have studied the appointments list of the Colonial Office and very nearly picked on the Nigerian Navy for a career? And later, when surely I ought to have known better, the odd African fixation remained. In 1935 I found myself sick with fever on a camp bed in a Liberian native's hut with a candle going out in an empty whisky bottle and a rat moving in the shadows. Wasn't it the incurable fascination of Gagool with her bare yellow skull, the wrinkled scalp that moved and contracted like the hood of a cobra, that led me to work all through 1942 in a little stuffy office in Freetown, Sierra Leone? ... Yes, Gagool has remained a permanent part of the imagination, but Quatermain and Curtis—weren't they, even when I was only ten years old, a little too good to be true? ... Sir Henry Curtis perched upon a rock bleeding from a dozen wounds but fighting on with the remnant of the Greys against the hordes of Twala was too heroic. These men were like Platonic ideas: they were not life as one had already begun to know it. (188)

But were Homeric heroes any less ideal? It was precisely that mythic dimension—including those "too heroic" archetypes— that fed the imaginations of young Greene and his generation and made *King Solomon's Mines* a profound work of literature.

Diamonds and Deities

Contemporary interpretations of *King Solomon's Mines* characterize it either as an adventure across psychological terrain into unknown and tabooed frontiers of the unconscious or as a journey of exploration, capitalist conquest, and the establishment of a colonial patriarchy. Without discarding psychological and cultural readings, an interpretation that combines diamonds and deities— Victorian imperial politics and the world of magic and religion— best explains the relevance and context of this novel. Every reader now knows that the central characters of *King Solomon's Mines* travel to Kukuanaland for its diamonds; their avowed aim to rescue Sir Henry's brother serves only as a convenient pretext for recovering Solomon's treasures, the original objective of the lost George Curtis. The wisest and richest of biblical rulers, Solomon would have provided the strongest moral sanction for the Victorian resumption, as it were, of mineral extraction on the dark continent. When Haggard's adventurers arrive at "a vast circular hole with sloping sides, three hundred feet or more in depth, and quite half a mile round," Quatermain asks:

> "Can't you guess what this is?" I said to Sir Henry and Good, who were staring in astonishment down into the awful pit before us.
>
> They shook their heads.
>
> "Then it is clear that you have never seen the diamond mines at Kimberley. You may depend on it that this is Solomon's Diamond Mine; look there," I said, pointing to the stiff blue clay which was yet to be seen among the grass and bushes which clothed the sides of the pit, "the formation is the same."

His allusion to the Kimberley "Big Hole" — Anthony Trollope had called it "the largest and most complete hole ever made by human agency" — connects mining activities in southern Africa in the 1870s and 1880s to a biblical antecedent in the mythopoeic Africa of Solomon's legend. Although the setting of Solomon's mines derived from nineteenth-century maps showing stone ruins near Victoria in Mashonaland (Zimbabwe), discovered and explored 1868-71 by Renders and Mauch, contemporary exploration and the politics of diamond mining were not the only formative influences on Haggard's romance.

The expansion of exploration, trade, and empire in the late nineteenth century stimulated a curiosity about primitive peoples, an interest first provoked by colonial contacts going back at least to the Spanish conquest of the Americas and by the writings of Hobbes, Rousseau, and Montaigne (on cannibals). Because imperial rule had opened primitive societies to investigations of their cultural history, *King Solomon's Mines*, although set in a strange land where the marvelous abounds, is directly influenced by Victorian anthropological ideas as well as its politics. Haggard transposed not only his personal experiences with African colonial politics (the contemporary issues of "diamonds") into a tale of magic and religion (an adventure into a land of strange "deities"), but also contributed to an emerging aesthetic indebted intellectually, thematically, and formally to "the primitive." The *Popular Magazine of Anthropology* (inaugurated 1866) and the public meetings of the Ethnological Society (founded 1843)—from which sprang the Anthropological Society of London (1863)—signaled a strong Victorian interest in this area. The societies' lectures and such enthographically oriented fiction as that by G.A. Henty on Ashanti warfare reveal a fascination with primitive man that grew into what by the century's end Andrew Lang termed a new "exotic" literature.[1]

After Darwin's *On the Origin of Species* (1859), widely-accepted anthropological theories (by no means empirically grounded) maintained that primitive peoples were evolutionarily arrested and that such inferior races should not intermarry with Europeans (See Appendix C, Schreiner, *Thoughts on South Africa*, for an alternate theory). In the popular literature of imperialism such ideas often combined with the belief that the annihilation of aboriginals was justified by natural selection and the survival of the fittest. With their sense of racial superiority, the British applied Hobbes' phrase to describe the natives' lives as "nasty, brutish, and short" — though one wit has remarked that native life in pre-independence times was, more accurately, "nasty, British, and short." Certainly not all popular nineteenth-century writers endorsed racist views. In the opening pages of H. G. Wells's *The War of the Worlds* (1898), he writes:

---

1 In connection with the rejuvenation of British masculinity, Katz quotes from *Allan Quatermain* the eponymous hero's disgust with the primness of British life vis-à-vis the ethos of the Zulu warrior (*Rider Haggard*, 31); and Patrick Brantlinger notes Haggard's preoccupation with "the diminution of opportunities for adventure and heroism in the modern world" (*Rule of Darkness: British Literature and Imperialism, 1830-1914* (Ithaca: Cornell UP, 1988) 230. Sir Henry is a sort of Nordic "white Zulu," the epitome of military masculinity (much like Charles Kingsley's Hereward the Wake).

we must remember what ruthless and utter destruction our own species has wrought, not only upon animals, such as the vanished bison and the dodo, but upon its own inferior races. The Tasmanians, in spite of their human likeness, were entirely swept out of existence in a war of extermination waged by European immigrants, in the space of fifty years. Are we such apostles of mercy as to complain if the Martians warred in the same spirit?[1]

And despite Chinua Achebe's indictment of Joseph Conrad as a "bloody racist," Conrad in *Heart of Darkness* (1899) did pose the difficult moral issue of the legitimacy of *any* colonial intrusion— even a well-intentioned enhancement of "waste spaces" as ostensibly benign as that envisioned by Ruskin. (See Appendix C, Ruskin, Rhodes, and Schreiner.)

More than a dozen years before Wells and Conrad, Haggard's distrust of missionary zeal (which he puts into the mouth of Ignosi) and of the colonial practices of the Boers (if not the native policies of Shepstone, his mentor) constituted an indictment of the imperial mentality. Far from reluctantly conceding that African behavior and ritual epitomized an earlier, primitive stage of European cultural development, Haggard extolled its natives as closer to humanity's primal springs of being. If, in the unreflective imperialism of the "penny-dreadfuls," the "noble savage" is displaced by the virtuous imperial hero, in *King Solomon's Mines* this is not so. Umbopa tellingly remarks to Sir Henry, "'We are men, thou and I'"—and throughout Haggard's narrative a Berserker/Zulu knighthood (epitomized by mail shirts and oxtails) imbues *both* European and African. (Likewise in "The Sagas" Andrew Lang had called the Zulus "a kind of black Vikings of Africa" because of their warlike ways.) Although the provincial Quatermain disapproves of Good's affair with Foulata, which colonials referred to as "going native," Haggard's sympathy with Foulata and her fate, while obvious, could not extend to advocating in print an affair between a white man and a black woman. This attitude reflects the paradoxical nature of Haggard's

---

1   H.G. Wells, *The War of the Worlds* (New York: Random House, 1960) 14 (bk. 1, chap. 1).

own personal position—he was in Africa as a colonial administrator, and although (as writer) he presents Africa (and Foulata) as
symbols of profound female love, he returns to England to find a
wife. Like Olive Schreiner, he did not question the morality of
colonization per se—they both believed in the possibility of a
non-exploitative, Anglo-African settlement. That Haggard's
fiction transcended the dominant imperial mind-set of newspapers, schools, and missions is due in part to the fact that, as with
Richard Burton, a knowledge of African history and ethnography
enriched his writing. Haggard also quickly discovered that the
exoticism of this new ethnographic fiction could successfully
challenge the popularity of both the domestic novel and the naturalism of Zola. In "About Fiction" Haggard contrasted his artistic
ideal with contemporary fiction:

> Art in the purity of its idealized truth should resemble some
> perfect Grecian statue. It should be cold but naked, and
> looking thereon men should be led to think of naught but
> beauty. Here, however, we attire Art in every sort of dress,
> some of them suggestive enough in their own way, but for
> the most part in a pinafore. The difference between literary
> Art, as the present writer submits it ought to be, and the
> Naturalistic Art of France is the difference between the
> Venus of Milo and an obscene photograph taken from life.
> (Appendix B, "About Fiction")

The primness and feminization of English domesticity, Haggard
argued, must be fired by the elemental facts of life, by the ambiguous, mystical Venus or the goddess Ashtoreth of the novel, "nude"
but "of great though severe beauty." This rejection of the materi-
alism of Victorian society in favor of a mystic life in nature is the
ideology behind *King Solomon's Mines*—this, despite Quatermain's
ingrained impulse to stuff his pockets with Solomon's booty.

Victorian scholarship in comparative mythology owed much to
F. Max Müller (1823-1900), a linguistic ethnologist, who hypoth-
esized that the origin of culture lay in a "mythopoeic age" in
which the diurnal and seasonal "solar drama" was re-enacted by a
young hero whose death is "suggested by the Sun, dying in all his

youthful vigor, either at the end of a day, conquered by the powers of darkness, or at the end of the sunny season, stung by the thorn of winter."[1] However, not only were the gods and heroes of myth already established for Haggard as solar or vegetation figures, but even the sort of literary relevance that T. S. Eliot, W. B. Yeats and James Joyce later found in Frazer's *The Golden Bough* (1890–1915) had been anticipated by the liberal Bishop of Natal, J. W. Colenso, a friend of Haggard's father. The crucial anthropological implication of Colenso's biblical scholarship "was the relevance of so-called uncivilized thought and lower cultures to the most cultivated and sophisticated theological, philosophical, and historical viewpoints. Thus, in a modest and oblique way he adumbrated the shattering implications later thinkers were to find in *The Golden Bough*."[2] Haggard's novel appears both to have anticipated the modernist's fantasy of Africa as the locale for a recovery of spiritual vitality and to have foreshadowed T. S. Eliot's interpretation of modernism's handling of myth as "a continuous parallel between contemporaneity and antiquity."[3]

From boyhood, years before his discussions of comparative mythology with Andrew Lang, Haggard had been a keen student of ancient Egyptian and Teutonic customs and religion.[4] As a

---

1 Müller, "Comparative Mythology" [1856] in *Chips from a German Workshop* (New York: Scribner, Armstrong, 1876) 2:107, 140; see also his *Lectures on the Science of Language* [second series, 1864] (London: Longmans, Green, 1885) 565. Brian Street, *The Savage in Literature*, 168, asserts that Sir Henry's speculation on Ashtoreth, Chapter 16, derives from Max Müller, *Introduction to the Science of Religion* (1870).

2 Haggard, *Life*, 1:56; John B. Vickery, *The Literary Impact of The Golden Bough* (Princeton: Princeton UP, 1973) 17. Haggard does not acknowledge specific anthropological indebtednesses, but the names that crisscross Tylor's references to travellers, historians, and missionaries amply document a plethora of contemporary observations of primitive myth and ritual. The emergent friendship with Andrew Lang (see note 4, below) indicates Haggard's parallel preoccupations and knowledgeability.

3 T. S. Eliot, "*Ulysses*, Order, and Myth" (1923) in S. Givens, ed., *James Joyce: Two Decades of Criticism* (New York: Vanguard Press, 1948): 201; Marianna Torgovnick, *Gone Primitive: Savage Intellects, Modern Lives* (Chicago: U of Chicago Press, 1990) 275.

4 "From a boy ancient Egypt had fascinated me, and I had read everything concerning it on which I could lay hands.... I love the Norse people of the saga and pre-saga times.... I have a respect for Thor and Odin, I venerate Isis, and always feel inclined to bow to the moon!" (Haggard, *Life*, 1:254–55). Haggard began his life-long personal acquaintance with Lang when he was seeking a publisher for *King Solomon's Mines*. At that time, Haggard could have been familiar with Lang's earliest work on myth in the periodicals (*Frazer's*, *Fortnightly*, *Academy*) or, possibly, in his first book on the subject,

young man preoccupied with thoughts of death and toying with religious skepticism, he had been drawn to pagan notions of reincarnation as an alternative to orthodox belief. This was perfectly in tune with an agrarian, Romantic mythopoesis and with Haggard's instinctive rejection of the social values emerging from the shift to an industrial society. Thus when Quatermain announces that he is "going to tell the strangest story that I know of," Haggard may well be hinting at a narrative that replaces the "petticoat" culture of the British drawing-room with the worship of ancient deities and their rites of death and rebirth. Quatermain begins his account of Solomon's treasure by pretending to ignore Sheba and claiming that his story has "'no woman in it—except Foulata. Stop, though! there is Gagaoola, if she was a woman and not a fiend. But she was a hundred at least, and therefore not marriageable, so I don't count her. At any rate, I can safely say that there is not a *petticoat* in the whole history.'"[1] However, various critics (Bunn, McClintock, and Scheick) have pointed out that the landscape the adventurers cross is visualized as the female body, in which the treasure map read upside down shows Sheba's breasts, navel, and pudendum.

Sheba as Africa's Body

Haggard expands this image of Sheba into an icon of the African landscape in its fertility and death. The "big and little boys" to whom Haggard's narrative is dedicated undoubtedly were titillated by "Sheba's breasts," but Victorian schoolboys were unlikely to see the novel's extended pattern of sexual imagery. What Haggard

---

Custom and Myth (1884); but most likely their instant bonding was based on a common interest in folklore, dreams, and ghosts (the young Haggard had attended London spiritualist séances with nearly the same credulity as the youthful Yeats a generation later). In the 1870's, Lang undertook to refute Müller's narrowly-based philological explanations and argued that survivals from savage myths still persist in modern life, their basic themes and symbols refined variously in differing cultures. In later years, Lang also responded to Frazer's work.

1   Of course, the fabled Zulu maiden, Umkxakaza-wakogingqwayo, is described "*e bincile umuntsha wezindondo.*" But as a chief's daughter (unlike Foulata, who is not quite the "Kukuana Pocahontus" of Andrew Lang's phrase) one might expect to see Umkxakaza on festive occasions in a brass-beaded "petticoat." Henry Callaway, *Nursery Tales, Traditions, and Histories of the Zulus* (London: John A. Blair, 1868) 193, 201.

draws upon for his legend of Solomon and the Queen of Sheba comes from sacred sources, both 1 Kings 10:1 *et seq.* and chapters 27 and 34 of the Koran, "The Ant" and "Sheba," as well as later Islamic tales and medieval European art. The tradition of Sheba as African (the country and, metonymically, the woman) is at least as old as the historian Flavius Josephus (AD 37-100) who calls her the "Queen of Egypt and Ethiopia." She is a Moorish, mythopoeic figure from the city of Ophir, to whom in the Song of Solomon 1:5 the words, "I am black but comely," traditionally are ascribed.

While current criticism suggests that Haggard's Sheba is representative of the rapist-imperialist's sexual oppression of women, native or otherwise, it is not so; and the patriarchal connections within modernist expressions of the primitive—the landscape as female, sexual, and deadly—would have been seen by Haggard and Victorian anthropologists as a "survival" from ancient myth. Haggard understands human identity and its relation to nature in terms of a mother/mistress analogue in which birth and death are expressed by a female landscape, both generative and fatal. Within this mythic drama, Sheba and Solomon are mutually restorative figures, whose union is productive of the interval in which life supplants death. A mythic potency flickers across the form of Sheba because, like the animistic Venus, she too expresses the procreative force. The novel's earthy allusiveness to breasts and pudendum is a strike at Mrs. Grundy's strait-laced abhorrence of the natural and the erotic, Haggard's assertion that neither social conventions nor literary art can or should suppress passion and beauty. The Victorian urge, in the genteel, mid-century tradition of Thomas Bulfinch or Charles Kingsley, was to refine and classicize away the violence and sexuality of myth (in contrast to the anthropological realism of E.B. Tylor's shocking account of primitive behavior in *Primitive Culture*, 1871). Both Haggard and the major modernists deplored the disruption of a primal connection between man and nature, and the consequent impoverishment of mystery and wonder; but whereas Frazer, the Cambridge Anthropologists, and Jung (writing on racial memory) are all seen as contributing to the modernists' mythic imagination, Haggard in 1885 had only Tylor to inspire his fictional use of elemental and regenerative archetypes.

The Solomon-Sheba legend is Haggard's literary presentation of those primal interrelations of love, pain and death; and his trio of nineteenth-century adventurers themselves confront this mythic fertility pattern in the witch hunt, the battle, and their entrance into the place of death. Haggard explicitly opens the door to such an anthropological interpretation when he describes the austere goddess of the Silent Ones (manifestly a feminine double of Sheba) as having on her head "the points of a crescent." She and her companions are: "'Ashtoreth the goddess of the Zidonians, Chemosh the god of the Moabites, and Milcom the god of the children of Ammon'"—heathen or biblically "false divinities." (Their silence signifies an archaic fatality and is rooted in such biblical passages as Jeremiah 8:14 and Psalms 94:17 and 115:17.) Solomon, doubtless under the influence of his thousand wives, had built a high-place for Ashtoreth at Jerusalem (1 Kings 11:5; 2 Kings 23:13). Ashtoreth-Astarte is the Mesopotamian mother-goddess, the personification of life itself, the female principle of fertility, both of the reproduction and growth of plants and trees and of sexual love. She is the female counterpart of the sun-god Baal; and because she was represented with horns, she was formerly assumed to be a lunar goddess. In the Mesopotamian astral-theological system, not only the moon but the planet Venus was identified with Ashtoreth in her variant guises.[1] Thus when the trio announces they are from the "biggest star," they align themselves (dishonestly and ominously) with this goddess since after the sun and moon, Venus, the morning and evening star, is the most brilliant body in the sky.

In Greek mythology, Demeter gives birth, fertilizes the fields, and clothes nature; but she is also a grim goddess, cruel and destructive, who revokes her life-giving power and brings barrenness and death. Her cyclic pattern was personified by her daughters, Kore the goddess of summer and Persephone the goddess of

---

1   "Now Astarte, the divine mistress of Adonis, was identified with the planet Venus, and her changes from a morning to an evening star were carefully noted by the Babylonian astronomers, who drew omens from her alternate appearance and disappearance. Hence we may conjecture that the festival of Adonis was regularly timed to coincide with the appearance of Venus as the Morning or Evening Star." Sir James Frazer, *The Golden Bough*, abr. ed. (New York: Macmillan, 1922) 402.

winter. Hades, seeing Kore-Persephone gathering flowers, abducts her to his gloomy palace under the earth; only when she returns to the sunshine do flowers spring up again. In the Mesopotamian variant, as midsummer approaches (Haggard's adventurers predict the eclipse in June, a date that coincides with the Kukuana ritual of sacrifice), the springtime consort of the goddess is slain. She then enters the nether world to rescue him; and at each of the seven gates through which she passes, some of her clothing and adornments are removed until she passes through the last gate naked. The earth continues infertile until the goddess reemerges, arrayed again like nature in her full splendor. The strikingly different phases of the summer and winter Venus reflect this cyclic aspect of the goddess.

In Haggard's text, Ashtoreth as astral-lunar goddess finds her counterpart in Milcom and Chemosh, aspects of Baal the sun-god. Here, too, the "silent ones" represent not only a mythic pattern of thesis-antithesis (moon-death-nakedness in strife with sun-life-raiment) but also a synthesis, the mother-goddess personifying all three of nature's life-forces — moon against sun and, taken together, earth's ceaselessly interacting antinomies of generation and decay: "'What is the lot of man born of woman?' Back came the answer rolling out from every throat in that vast company: 'Death!'" This chorus swells to recount "various phases of human passions, fears, and joys. Now it seemed to be a love song, now a majestic swelling war chant, and last of all a death-dirge ending suddenly in one heartbreaking wail that went echoing and rolling away in a volume of blood-curdling sound." When we first encounter Foulata she is like Kore, the fairest maiden gathering flowers, "flower-crowned." As the summer goddess, she nurses Good, her consort, back to health. Foulata, marked out to be killed by the Gagool-Twala-Scragga cohort, embodies with her antagonist, Gagool, the darker aspect of the earth-mother's cycle of death that precedes renewal.

Demeter, as Walter Pater describes her, is "the wrinkled woman," who "grows young again every spring yet is of great age."[1] Gagool, the "mother, old mother," is Demeter in her cruel

---

1 Pater, "Demeter and Persephone," *Greek Studies* (London, Macmillan, 1910) 105.

phase who slays her child but is concurrently mourning her loss; thus, as Pater describes her, she is the "mistress and manager of men's shades."[1] (Gagool's origins initially were historical: she is an intensified version of the "witch-finder." See Appendix B, Haggard, "Zulu"; Appendix C, Fynney, *Zululand*.) Repulsive, Gagool nevertheless correctly sees an imminent bloody cataclysm and warns of a new colonialism in pursuit of diamonds. As winter goddess, Gagool brings her slain consort Twala to the Place of Death, like a Valkyrie to Valhalla. Her hall is a sort of Westminster Abbey in Kukuanaland where the famous dead are enshrined not in marble but in calcium carbonate—as Haggard condoned "a little crudeness" in characterization so he condoned the high kitsch of this visual setting.[2] In life, Twala is honored as "the One-eyed, the Black, the Terrible" and is a student of Gagool's "black arts," a necromancer whose malevolent magic discloses the future by consulting the dead. He is allied to the one-eyed Norse deity Odin, god of the dead—his single eye is the sun, his lost eye the moon, according to Tylor.[3] But in death, Twala becomes the vassal of the huge skeleton who presides, like Odin, over the banquets of slain heroes.

Gagool's and Twala's cruelty has placed the land under a curse, in "trouble" and "darkness," until the king, "languishing in exile," restores fertility: "So, O king! then is a curse taken from the land." Umbopa's birthright, proven by his secret snake tatoo, is confirmed by the transfer of the great uncut diamond from Twala's decapitated head to his, marking a national regeneration linked to the vegetation cycle: "The winter is overpast, the summer is at hand." Like Jacob-Israel, who wrestled with the angel and was renamed because he had "striven with God and with

---

1   Ibid., 94.

2   Haggard, *Life*, 92; Appendix B, "Zulu"; *Cetywayo and His White Neighbours* (London: Trübner, 1882) 3. In his *Private Diaries*, Haggard mentions an old explorer who told the story of a ring found in an Inca burial chamber "wherein, round a stone table, sat a dead and mummified man at the head and about a dozen other persons ranged round the table.... The tale made a deep impression on my youthful mind and, in fact, first turned it towards Romance. I used it in *King Solomon's Mines* when I depicted the White Dead sitting round the stone board under the presidency of the White Death" (209).

3   Tylor, *Primitive Culture*, 1:351-52.

men, and ... prevailed" (Genesis 32:29), Umbopa becomes Ignosi. Umbopa-Ignosi is the new Solomon, an African ruler whose principles of kingship are British (in point of fact, they double Sir Theophilus Shepstone's Zulu reforms[1]), but whose religion is mythic, and whose foreign policy is isolationist: Ignosi decrees a Kukuanaland uncontaminated by the socio-economic structures of the West; "traders" and "praying-men" who "make a path for the white men who follow to run on" will be repulsed, and total demolition of the quarry will greet those who "come for the shining stones."

Haggard's essay on the Zulu war-dance (see Appendix B, "Zulu") had described the warrior who served as a model for Sir Henry as a Kukuana general. But the warrior in Haggard's essay was emasculated and did not know it. In Zululand, the imperialist had annihilated the native's game and rendered his primitive weapons obsolete. Sir Henry's hand-to-hand combat implicitly restores the potency of the chieftain's weapons at the climatic moment and so suggests a different native-foreign power balance in Kukuanaland from that of the Boers and English in the land of the Basutos and Zulus. Unlike the Transvaal, governed by ambitious Europeans, and unlike Zululand, partitioned among British puppets, Kukuanaland will be ruled by an ancient-modern African chieftain who holds his ground not on "sufferance," war-dancing for entertainment, but as the "rightful lord" of a region closed to the enterprise of European settlers. Here the native ways of life and African herds of game survive untouched by capitalist development. Clearly, Haggard's blueprint for a restored Kukuanaland repudiated the Victorian imperial stereotype of subjugated tribes, and especially notions of wealth created by trade.[2]

In Haggard's mythic potpourri, Sir Henry, not Umbopa, defeats Twala in single combat to win the kingdom, suggesting that Sir Henry is the double of Ignosi. When Umbopa arises as Ignosi, Sir

---

1 Haggard, *Cetywayo*, 9-10.
2 Criticizing British middle-class crowd behavior, he observed: "The average European, especially if he be English, looks down upon Easterns and natives of all sorts whom he names 'niggers'. But would savages behave in such a way as this? So far as my rather extended experience of them goes, I should say 'No!' At any rate they have culture of a sort, they have manners — often quite distinguished manners — they have breeding and they have traditions. Lastly they are not vulgar" (*Private Diaries*, 202).

Henry goes into exile like the yearly wounded vegetation god Adonis-Tammuz. But unlike Ignosi, the adventurers are not mythically reborn from this shadowland. To explicate the narrative's sexual innuendo further, one may observe that "Kukuanaland," parsed as low slang, becomes "cuckoo" (the cuckoo lays its eggs in other birds' nests; thus, in slang usage the cuckoo is the penis and the cuckoo's nest the female pudendum) followed by "anal" with the copula "and." This crude pun of "cuckoo-anal-and" is less indicative of schoolboy prurience than of the biological-mythic structure that the adventurers enter at the mine-pit and the political question: will the British rehatch themselves in Africa's nest? Will they fulfill Haggard's aborted Anglo-African ideal for the Transvaal of 1877? In the romance, their entry into the chamber of the mine-pit may be a sexual penetration (Boccaccio's gates of hell or the devouring female pudenda), but the trio's exit is certainly earthy. Haggard's phallic and anal amalgamation, together with his multiple references to the "bowels" of the earth, clearly indicate that whatever sort of symbolic engendering their entrance into the cave may be, the trio is sexually devoured and shat out like lumps of excrement. This is an ironic rebirth at best, a parody of renewal.

Imperial Impotence

Although the adventurers claim to be gods, all have been injured in the leg—before, during, and after their quest: Allan Quatermain has been mauled by a lion and his leg continues to pain him; Good's leg has been badly wounded by a native tolla; and Sir Henry is accidentally shot in the leg by Quatermain's son while hunting. Even the leg of the lost George Curtis has been crushed by a boulder. The dandaical Good with his monocle, false teeth, gutta-percha collars and so on is quickly established, by virtue of his "beautiful white legs," as the most unlikely of sex objects, contributing its quota of humor to the plot. The nearly idolatrous farewell to Good's legs by "a pretty young girl, with some beautiful lilies in her hand" (Foulata rejuvenated for the Kukuanas but not for the English) suggests a phallic significance, as in nineteenth-century slang "leg-business" ("leg-lifting" meaning sexual intercourse): "'Let my lord show his servant his beautiful white legs, that his servant may look on them, and remember them all her days, and tell of them to her children; his servant has travelled four days' journey to see them, for the fame of them has gone throughout the land'" (p.236, this edition). The lame white gods become the nineteenth-century version of Frazer's sexually impotent deities. But the wounded leg that denotes the mortality of Sir Henry and his companions, and even Ignosi's patriarchal prototype Jacob, does not defile the Kukuana or their new king. Ignosi is the regenerative consort of Kukuanaland-as-Sheba. In Solomon's legend in the Koran and in medieval art, Sheba is lame in one foot (or suffers from hairy legs or ass's hooves) and undergoes a conversion and cure by Solomon. In the final analysis, Sheba is one of those ambiguous females who attempts, like Gagool, to subvert masculine power; she is Solomon's dark double, at first challenging and impeding the king's claim to power and freedom, but finally rejoicing in his revitalization of the sacred cosmic (and patriarchal) order. In a strange and surreal way, the goddess-queen-sorceress, appearing to do evil, ends by doing good.

But unlike Solomon with Sheba, the trio achieves no mystical interplay of sun and moon, and thus no cure attends their ordeal and escape. No less than the broken promises of the British government in the Transvaal, the trio's misrepresentation of their motives and identities in Haggard's tale corrupts Solomon's wisdom, the wisdom of a king who speaks to birds and animals and commands demons and jinn. Thus when the natives beg to be pardoned for mistaking the trio as mortal, Quatermain continues the deceit.

> "It is granted," I said, with an imperial smile. "Nay, ye shall know the truth. We come from another world, though we are men such as ye; we come," I went on, "from the biggest star that shines at night."
> "Oh! oh!" groaned the chorus of astonished aborigines.
> "Yes," I went on, "we do, indeed;" and I again smiled benignly as I uttered that amazing lie. "We come to stay

with you a little while, and bless you by our sojourn."
(p. 112)

Later, when Good hoodwinks the natives with the prediction of an eclipse, Quatermain calls out: "'Look, chiefs and people, and women, and see if the white men from the stars keep their word, or if they be but empty liars!'" In creating their own eclipse myth, the trio's imperial ambition is symbolized in recurrent imagery of the moon eaten or swallowed, given resonant concreteness in "Zulu" by the European's depletion of the native's game.[1]

When Ignosi invites the trio to remain and marry native wives (repeating Twala's offer), they choose instead the recovered diamonds causing Ignosi to curse the stones that have bereaved him. He says, "'your names, Incubu, Macumazahn, and Bougwan [their Zulu agnomens] shall be as the names of dead kings, and he who speaks them shall die.'" Haggard footnotes this Zulu custom of tabooing names, later explicitly documented by Frazer, not just for reasons of anthropological curiosity but to emphasize that the trio has entered a ghostly existence, like the calcified kings who guard Solomon's treasure.[2] Dying, Foulata had asked Quatermain to tell Good that "'I love him, and that I am glad to die because I know that he cannot cumber his life with such as me, for the sun cannot mate with the darkness, nor the white with the black.'" She then imagines a reunion in the afterlife "in the stars," an impossibility because the cosmic interplay between black and white, moon and sun remains arrested: "'I will search them all, though perchance I should there still be black and he would— still be white.'" On the mythic level, Haggard implies that Foulata

---

1 Tylor inventories eclipse myths in *Primitive Culture*, 1:328–35. In "Zulu," if one gets past Haggard's cliches, one realizes that Haggard's remarkable detail of the silence is the outcome of Gagool's prediction that the "white people ... shall eat ye up" —an eventuality as yet unrealized in the panoramic scene-painting from *King Solomon's Mines* which includes "countless herds of game or cattle" and "groups of dome-shaped huts ... whilst over all was the glad sunlight and the wide breath of Nature's happy life."

2 Frazer, *The Golden Bough*, 300. Tylor noted that the natives, impressed with the white man's "pallid deathly hue combined with powers that seem those of superhuman spiritual beings, have determined that the manes of their dead must have come back in this wondrous shape" (*Primitive Culture*, 1:5).

is forever separated from her revitalizing consort because, owing to the trio's return to England with the diamonds, Good will not pursue her from the underworld to the stars. Quatermain priggishly considers her death "a fortunate occurrence" that avoids the complications of racial miscegenation; and Foulata's corpse is borne into the treasure chamber of the underworld, thenceforth always to be associated with its attendant diamonds like the pomegranate seeds that seal Persephone's presence in Hades. Years later, Haggard singled out this scene in the infernal halls of the kingdom of the dead to condemn the choice of wealth by trade rather than an adoption of the land's mystic plenitude.

Though a "lady" is the suspected cause of the quarrel over inheritance between Sir Henry and his brother George, and thus at the root of the adventure, by narrative's end the brothers are reunited while the contested "lady" is abandoned like Foulata or Sheba-as-Africa. George, after his rescue and reconciliation, no longer uses his alias Neville, a feeble echo of Ignosi retaking his kingly name. Good himself becomes the laughing-stock of society papers, a most unheroic apotheosis, and cannot find among English petticoats a mate as attractive as Foulata. And how meaningful is the wounding and healing of Sir Henry precipitated by Quatermain's son, the future doctor, compared to the wounds of native battle and Foulata's mythic ministrations? Although Quatermain will arrive just at Christmas to publish his novel, a drizzly London Christmas pales in comparison to the *dies natalis solis invicti* or the seasonal rituals of Kukuanaland. The quest that began over a contested inheritance, doubled in Twala's and Umbopa's disputed kingdom, ends with riches in London but, in contrast to the national restoration of Kukuanaland, with no recovery by modern man of his original birthright in nature. Perhaps this trio of social misfits has not escaped from Valhalla but has arrived in London at Hela's moldering realm of the unheroic, spiritually dead. This loss of the heroic in England, including the truth of human destiny, and its replacement with the material comforts of a spiritually arid society became, of course, Haggard's target in "About Fiction." In *Allan Quatermain*, the continuation of this saga, the burial of Quatermain's son opens the narrative; seeking heroic closure, Quatermain there decides to return to

Africa to "die as I had lived, among the wild game and the savages."[1]

Haggard's narrative, despite its ostensibly juvenile audience, is a notable instance of Victorian romanticism, perfectly in tune with Wordsworth's declaration in "The World is Too Much with Us" that ancient paganism is preferable to his urbanized, secularized culture.

> More and more, as what we call culture spreads, do men and women crave to be taken out of themselves. More and more do they long to be brought face to face with Beauty, and stretch out their arms towards that vision of the Perfect, which we only see in books and dreams.... Here we may even—if we feel that our wings are strong enough to bear us in that thin air—cross the bounds of the known, and, hanging between earth and heaven, gaze with curious eyes into the great profound beyond. ("About Fiction")

---

1 Haggard, *Three Adventure Novels*, 419.

H. Rider Haggard: A Brief Chronology

1856 Born 22 June in Norfolk, England.

1862-74 Early schooling by private tutors; from 1869 to 1872 at Ipswich Grammar School.

1875 Embarks for South Africa as secretary to Sir Henry Bulwer, newly named Lieutenant-Governor of Natal.

1876-77 Goes with a small party to negotiate with Chief Pagate; recruited by Sir Theophilus Shepstone for a diplomatic mission to the Transvaal.

1877-78 Serves as assistant to the Transvaal colonial secretary; appointed Registrar and Master of the High Court in the Transvaal.

1879-1880 News of his inamorata Lilly Jackson's marriage devastates him; leaves government service and purchases a farm; returns briefly to England and marries a Norfolk heiress, Mariana Louisa Margitson.

1880 Sails again for Africa with his wife to take up ostrich farming on the border of Natal and the Transvaal (basis of his 1887 novel, *Jess*); the so-called first Boer War begins.

1881 The Transvaal is returned to the Boers (retrocession treaty is negotiated in HRH's farmhouse); first child, son John "Jock" Rider born August 31; returns to England and studies law.

1882 Publishes *Cetywayo and his White Neighbours*, a prescient analysis of Zulu-British politics.

1883 Daughter Agnes Angela Rider born January 6.

1884 Publishes with only modest success the first two of what will be over fifty novels; daughter Sybil Dorothy Rider born in March; admitted to the bar of Lincoln's Inn.

1885 September 30, Cassell & Company publishes *King Solomon's Mines*, an enormous success.

1887 Publishes both *She*, a tale of an immortal white queen, Ayesha, "She-who-must-be-obeyed," who rules an isolated African tribe, and also *Allan Quatermain*, a sequel to *King Solomon's Mines*; both Quatermain and Ayesha also appear in numerous other romances; travels to Egypt.

1890 Publishes in collaboration with Andrew Lang, *The World's Desire*, a novel of Odysseus and Helen; visits Mexico.

1891 Death of his son Jock at age nine; devastated, Haggard sinks into a lifetime depression.

1892 *Nada the Lily*, the first in HRH's saga of the Zulu nation; followed by the trilogy *Marie* (1912), *Child of Storm* (1913), and *Finished* (1917), an epic history of fact and legend of the rise and fall of Chaka's Zulu dynasty; daughter Lilias Rider born, December 9.

1895 Narrowly loses election to Parliament.

1900 *A Winter Pilgrimage*, an account of HRH's travels through Palestine, Italy, and Cyprus.

1912 Knighted for his nonfiction studies of agricultural techniques, such as *A Farmer's Year* (1899) and *Rural England* (1902).

1914 Revisits South Africa and explores the Zimbabwe ruins; returns a second time in 1916.

1925 Dies May 14.

A Note on the Text

I have chosen the first edition of *King Solomon's Mines* for this Broadview edition. Changes made by Haggard between the first and revised new illustrated edition of 1905 are not significant. I amend the first edition only to correct typographical errors ("two" replacing "too"; "Bamangwato," instead of "Bamamgwato," and so on.) Variants such as "waggon" rather than "wagon" are retained as part of the text's 1885 flavor.

KING SOLOMON'S MINES.

BY

H. RIDER HAGGARD,

Author of "Dawn," "The Witch's Head," &c.

———•••———

CASSELL & COMPANY, LIMITED:

LONDON, PARIS, NEW YORK & MELBOURNE.

1885.

Fold-out frontispiece in sanguine (i.e., the color of dried blood) in the first edition. The "translation" appears in this edition on page 55.

Dedication.

THIS FAITHFUL BUT UNPRETENDING RECORD
OF A REMARKABLE ADVENTURE
IS HEREBY RESPECTFULLY DEDICATED
BY THE NARRATOR,

ALLAN QUATERMAIN,

TO ALL THE BIG AND LITTLE BOYS
WHO READ IT.

INTRODUCTION.

Now that this book is printed, and about to be given to the world, the sense of its shortcomings, both in style and contents, weighs very heavily upon me. As regards the latter, I can only say that it does not pretend to be a full account of everything we did and saw. There are many things connected with our journey into Kukuanaland which I should have liked to dwell upon at length, and which have, as it is, been scarcely alluded to. Amongst these are the curious legends which I collected about the chain armour that saved us from destruction in the great battle of Loo, and also about the "silent ones" or colossi at the mouth of the stalactite cave. Again, if I had given way to my own impulses, I should have liked to go into the differences, some of which are to my mind very suggestive, between the Zulu and Kukuana dialects. Also a few pages might profitably have been given up to the considera- tion of the indigenous flora and fauna of Kukuanaland.* Then there remains the most interesting subject—that, as it is, has only been incidentally alluded to—of the magnificent system of mili- tary organisation in force in that country, which is, in my opinion, much superior to that inaugurated by Chaka[1] in Zululand inas- much as it permits of even more rapid mobilisation, and does not necessitate the employment of the pernicious system of forced celibacy. And, lastly, I have scarcely touched on the domestic and family customs of the Kukuanas, many of which are exceedingly quaint, or on their proficiency in the art of smelting and welding metals. This last they carry to considerable perfection, of which a good example is to be seen in their "tollas," or heavy throwing knives, the backs of these knives being made of hammered iron,

---

* I discovered eight varieties of antelope, with which I was previously totally unac- quainted, and many new species of plants, for the most part of the bulbous tribe. — A.Q.

1 Chaka] (otherwise Shaka, Tyaka, T'shaka; names are often spelled with confusing pho- netic variation) a Zulu warrior (1780s-1828) who united the South-Eastern African tribes under his chieftanship, making the Zulu a powerful nation. Chaka massed his troops in a crescent formation, with reserves in the shape of a parallelogram able to reinforce the vulnerable points. For close combat, he lengthened the blade and short- ened the shaft of the spears (stabbing assegais) and increased the size of the shield. Warriors were allowed to marry only after distinguishing themselves in battle.

and the edges of beautiful steel welded with great skill on to the iron backs. The fact of the matter is, that I thought (and so did Sir Henry Curtis and Captain Good) that the best plan would be to tell the story in a plain, straightforward manner, and leave these matters to be dealt with subsequently in whatever way may ultimately appear to be desirable. In the meanwhile I shall, of course, be delighted to give any information in my power to anybody interested in such things.

And now it only remains for me to offer my apologies for my blunt way of writing. I can only say in excuse for it that I am more accustomed to handle a rifle than a pen, and cannot make any pretence to the grand literary flights and flourishes which I see in novels—for I sometimes like to read a novel. I suppose they—the flights and flourishes—are desirable, and I regret not being able to supply them; but at the same time I cannot help thinking that simple things are always the most impressive, and books are easier to understand when they are written in plain language, though I have perhaps no right to set up an opinion on such a matter. "A sharp spear," runs the Kukuana saying, "needs no polish;" and on the same principle I venture to hope that a true story, however strange it may be, does not require to be decked out in fine words.

ALLAN QUATERMAIN.

KING SOLOMON'S MINES.

CHAPTER I.

I MEET SIR HENRY CURTIS.

It is a curious thing that at my age—fifty-five last birthday—
I should find myself taking up a pen to try and write a history. I
wonder what sort of a history it will be when I have done it, if
I ever come to the end of the trip! I have done a good many
things in my life, which seems a long one to me, owing to my
having begun so young, perhaps. At an age when other boys are
at school, I was earning my living as a trader in the old Colony.[1] I
have been trading, hunting, fighting, or mining ever since. And
yet it is only eight months ago that I made my pile. It is a big pile
now I have got it—I don't yet know how big—but I don't think
I would go through the last fifteen or sixteen months again for it;
no, not if I knew that I should come out safe at the end, pile and
all. But then I am a timid man, and don't like violence, and am
pretty sick of adventure. I wonder why I am going to write this
book: it is not in my line. I am not a literary man, though very
devoted to the Old Testament and also to the "Ingoldsby
Legends."[2] Let me try and set down my reasons, just to see if I
have any.

---

1 old Colony] the Cape Colony on the most southern part of Africa, first settled by the
   Dutch in 1652.
2 "Ingoldsby Legends"] a popular work of humorous verse (1840), particularly treating
   medieval legends comically, by Richard H. Barham.

First reason: Because Sir Henry Curtis and Captain John Good asked me to.

Second reason: Because I am laid up here at Durban with the pain and trouble in my left leg. Ever since that confounded lion got hold of me I have been liable to it, and its being rather bad just now makes me limp more than ever. There must be some poison in a lion's teeth, otherwise how is it that when your wounds are healed they break out again, generally, mark you, at the same time of year that you got your mauling? It is a hard thing that when one has shot sixty-five lions as I have in the course of my life, that the sixty-sixth should chew your leg like a quid of tobacco. It breaks the routine of the thing, and putting other considerations aside, I am an orderly man and don't like that. This is by the way.

Third reason: Because I want my boy Harry, who is over there at the hospital in London studying to become a doctor, to have something to amuse him and keep him out of mischief for a week or so. Hospital work must sometimes pall and get rather dull, for even of cutting up dead bodies there must come satiety, and as this history won't be dull, whatever else it may be, it may put a little life into things for a day or two while he is reading it.

Fourth reason and last: Because I am going to tell the strangest story that I know of. It may seem a queer thing to say that, especially considering that there is no woman in it—except Foulata. Stop, though! there is Gagaoola, if she was a woman and not a fiend. But she was a hundred at least, and therefore not marriageable, so I don't count her. At any rate, I can safely say that there is not a *petticoat* in the whole history. Well I had better come to the yoke. It's a stiff place, and I feel as though I were bogged up to the axle. But "sutjes, sutjes," as the Boers[1] say (I'm sure I don't know how they spell it), softly does it. A strong team will come through at last, that is if they ain't too poor. You will never do anything with poor oxen. Now to begin.

I, Allan Quatermain, of Durban, Natal, Gentleman, make oath and say—That's how I began my deposition before the magis-

---

1   Boer] a white Afrikaans-speaking farmer of Dutch descent, as in the nineteenth century in the Transvaal republic between the Vaal and Limpopo rivers. See Introduction, pages 9-10.

trate, about poor Khiva's and Ventvögel's sad deaths;[1] but some-how it doesn't seem quite the right way to begin a book. And, besides, am I a gentleman? What is a gentleman? I don't quite know, and yet I have had to do with niggers—no, I'll scratch that word "niggers" out, for I don't like it. I've known natives who *are*, and so you'll say, Harry, my boy, before you're done with this tale, and I have known mean whites with lots of money and fresh out from home, too, who *ain't*. Well, at any rate, I was born a gentle-man, though I've been nothing but a poor travelling trader and hunter all my life. Whether I have remained so I know not, you must judge of that. Heaven knows I've tried. I've killed many men in my time, but I have never slain wantonly or stained my hand in innocent blood, only in self-defence. The Almighty gave us our lives, and I suppose he meant us to defend them, at least I have always acted on that, and I hope it won't be brought up against me when my clock strikes. There, there, it is a cruel and a wicked world, and for a timid man I have been mixed up in a deal of slaughter. I can't tell the rights of it, but at any rate I have never stolen, though I once cheated a Kafir[2] out of a herd of cattle. But then he had done me a dirty turn, and it has troubled me ever since into the bargain.

Well it's eighteen months or so ago since I first met Sir Henry Curtis and Captain Good, and it was in this way. I had been up elephant hunting beyond Bamangwato, and had had bad luck. Everything went wrong that trip, and to top up with I got the fever badly. So soon as I was well enough I trekked down to the Diamond Fields, sold such ivory as I had, and also my waggon and oxen, discharged my hunters, and took the post-cart to the Cape. After spending a week in Cape Town, finding that they over-charged me at the hotel, and having seen everything there was to see, including the botanical gardens, which seem to me likely to confer a great benefit on the country, and the new Houses of Parliament, which I expect will do nothing of the sort, I deter-mined to go on back to Natal by the *Dunkeld*, then lying in the

---

1 Khiva's and Ventvögel's sad deaths] see Haggard, "Notes on *King Solomon's Mines*," Appendix B.
2 Kafir] originally a Xhosa-speaking native, but the name came to be applied to any indigenous African.

docks waiting for the *Edinburgh Castle* due in from England. I took my berth and went aboard, and that afternoon the Natal passengers from the *Edinburgh Castle* transhipped, and we weighed and put out to sea.

Among the passengers who came on board there were two who excited my curiosity. One, a man of about thirty, was one of the biggest-chested and longest-armed men I ever saw. He had yellow hair, a big yellow beard, clear-cut features, and large grey eyes set deep into his head. I never saw a finer-looking man, and somehow he reminded me of an ancient Dane. Not that I know much of ancient Danes, though I remember a modern Dane who did me out of ten pounds; but I remember once seeing a picture of some of those gentry, who, I take it, were a kind of white Zulus.[1] They were drinking out of big horns, and their long hair hung down their backs, and as I looked at my friend standing there by the companion-ladder, I thought that if one only let his hair grow a bit, put one of those chain shirts on to those great shoulders of his, and gave him a big battle-axe and a horn mug, he might have sat as a model for that picture. And by the way it is a curious thing, and just shows how the blood will show out, I found out afterwards that Sir Henry Curtis, for that was the big man's name, was of Danish blood.* He also reminded me strongly of somebody else, but at the time I could not remember who it was.

The other man who stood talking to Sir Henry was short, stout, and dark, and of quite a different cut. I suspected at once that he was a naval officer. I don't know why, but it is difficult to mistake a navy man. I have gone shooting trips with several of

---

* Mr. Quatermain's ideas about ancient Danes seem to be rather confused; we have always understood that they were dark-haired people. Probably he was thinking of Saxons. —*Editor.*

---

1 Sir Theophilus Shepstone, Haggard's mentor and Natal Secretary for Native Affairs, was the "white chief" (literally and unironically) of the Zulu nation (see "A Zulu War-Dance," note 1, p. 268, Appendix B); see also Haggard's *Cetywayo and His White Neighbours* (London: Trubner, 1882), 9, 111, and the instance of John Dunn as a Zulu chieftain, 35; Haggard, *Days of My Life* (London: Longmans, Green, 1926) 1:71. "The idea of the Englishman who effortlessly and successfully rules over 'savage' people as a savage chief would recur again and again in Haggard's fiction. Haggard's most prominent fictional instance is Ayesha in *She*, the great white Queen in Africa" (Norman Etherington).

them in the course of my life, and they have always been just the best and bravest and nicest fellows I ever met, though given to the use of profane language.

I asked a page or two back, what is a gentleman? I'll answer it now: a Royal Naval officer is, in a general sort of a way, though, of course, there may be a black sheep among them here and there. I fancy it is just the wide sea and the breath of God's winds that washes their hearts and blows the bitterness out of their minds and makes them what men ought to be. Well, to return, I was right again; I found out that he *was* a naval officer, a lieutenant of thirty-one, who, after seventeen years' service, had been turned out of her Majesty's employ with the barren honour of a commander's rank, because it was impossible that he should be promoted. That is what people who serve the Queen have to expect: to be shot out into the cold world to find a living just when they are beginning to really understand their work, and to get to the prime of life. Well, I suppose they don't mind it, but for my part I had rather earn my bread as a hunter. One's halfpence are as scarce perhaps, but you don't get so many kicks. His name I found out—by referring to the passengers' list—was Good— Captain John Good. He was broad, of medium height, dark, stout, and rather a curious man to look at. He was so very neat and so very clean shaved, and he always wore an eye-glass in his right eye. It seemed to grow there, for it had no string, and he never took it out except to wipe it. At first I thought he used to sleep in it, but I afterwards found that this was a mistake. He put it in his trousers pocket when he went to bed, together with his false teeth, of which he had two beautiful sets that have often, my own being none of the best, caused me to break the tenth commandment. But I am anticipating.

Soon after we had got under weigh evening closed in, and brought with it very dirty weather. A keen breeze sprang up off land, and a kind of aggravated Scotch mist soon drove everybody from the deck. And as for that *Dunkeld*, she is a flat-bottomed punt, and going up light as she was, she rolled very heavily. It almost seemed as though she would go right over, but she never did. It was quite impossible to walk about, so I stood near the engines where it was warm, and amused myself with watching the pendulum, which was fixed opposite to me, swinging slowly backwards and forwards as the vessel rolled, and marking the angle she touched at each lurch.

"That pendulum's wrong; it is not properly weighted," suddenly said a voice at my shoulder, somewhat testily. Looking round I saw the naval officer I had noticed when the passengers came aboard.

"Indeed, now what makes you think so?" I asked.

"Think so. I don't think at all. Why there"—as she righted herself after a roll—"if the ship had really rolled to the degree that thing pointed to then she would never have rolled again, that's all. But it is just like these merchant skippers, they always are so confoundedly careless."

Just then the dinner-bell rang, and I was not sorry, for it is a dreadful thing to have to listen to an officer of the Royal Navy when he gets on to that subject. I only know one worse thing, and that is to hear a merchant skipper express his candid opinion of officers of the Royal Navy.

Captain Good and I went down to dinner together, and there we found Sir Henry Curtis already seated. He and Captain Good sat together, and I sat opposite to them. The captain and I soon got into talk about shooting and what not; he asking me many questions, and I answering as well as I could. Presently he got on to elephants.

"Ah, sir," called out somebody who was sitting near me, "you've got to the right man for that; Hunter Quatermain should be able to tell you about elephants if anybody can."

Sir Henry, who had been sitting quite quiet listening to our talk, started visibly.

"Excuse me, sir," he said, leaning forward across the table, and speaking in a low, deep voice, a very suitable voice it seemed to me, to come out of those great lungs. "Excuse me, sir, but is your name Allan Quatermain?"

I said it was.

The big man made no further remark, but I heard him mutter "fortunate" into his beard.

Presently dinner came to an end, and as we were leaving the saloon Sir Henry came up and asked me if I would come into his cabin and smoke a pipe. I accepted, and he led the way to the *Dunkeld* deck cabin, and a very good cabin it was. It had been two cabins, but when Sir Garnet[1] or one of those big swells went down the coast in the *Dunkeld*, they had knocked away the partition and never put it up again. There was a sofa in the cabin, and a little table in front of it. Sir Henry sent the steward for a bottle of whisky, and the three of us sat down and lit our pipes.

"Mr. Quatermain," said Sir Henry Curtis, when the steward had brought the whisky and lit the lamp, "the year before last about this time you were, I believe, at a place called Bamangwato, to the north of the Transvaal."

"I was," I answered, rather surprised that this gentleman should be so well acquainted with my movements, which were not, so far as I was aware, considered of general interest.

"You were trading there, were you not?" put in Captain Good, in his quick way.

"I was. I took up a waggon-load of goods, and made a camp outside the settlement, and stopped till I had sold them."

Sir Henry was sitting opposite to me in a Madeira chair, his arms leaning on the table. He now looked up, fixing his large grey eyes full upon my face. There was a curious anxiety in them I thought.

"Did you happen to meet a man called Neville there?"

"Oh, yes; he outspanned alongside of me for a fortnight to rest his oxen before going on to the interior. I had a letter from a lawyer a few months back asking me if I knew what had become of him, which I answered to the best of my ability at the time."

"Yes," said Sir Henry, "your letter was forwarded to me. You said in it that the gentleman called Neville left Bamangwato in the beginning of May in a waggon with a driver, a voorlooper,[2] and a Kafir hunter called Jim, announcing his intention of

---

1 Sir Garnet] General Sir Garnet Wolseley took the *S.S.Dunkeld* when he shipped out to South Africa to take command of the Army from Lord Chelmsford in 1879. When Sir Henry Bulwer took over the administration of Natal from Wolseley, the General observed in his diary (28 August 1875) that Bulwer's "only staff consists of a leggy youth not long I should say from school who seems the picture of weakness and dullness" (i.e., Haggard). In 1881 Haggard returned to England aboard the *Dunkeld*.

2 voorlooper] leads the team of oxen, holding a rope attached to the horns of the leading bullocks.

trekking if possible as far as Inyati,[1] the extreme trading post in the Matabele country, where he would sell his waggon and proceed on foot. You also said that he did sell his waggon, for six months afterwards you saw the waggon in the possession of a Portuguese trader, who told you that he had bought it at Inyati from a white man whose name he had forgotten, and that the white man with a native servant had started off for the interior on a shooting trip, he believed."

"Yes."

Then came a pause.

"Mr. Quatermain," said Sir Henry, suddenly, "I suppose you know or can guess nothing more of the reasons of my—of Mr. Neville's journey to the northward, or as to what point that journey was directed?"

"I heard something," I answered, and stopped. The subject was one which I did not care to discuss.

Sir Henry and Captain Good looked at each other, and Captain Good nodded.

"Mr. Quatermain," said the former, "I am going to tell you a story, and ask your advice, and perhaps your assistance. The agent who forwarded me your letter told me that I might implicitly rely upon it, as you were," he said, "well known and universally respected in Natal, and especially noted for your discretion."

I bowed and drank some whisky and water to hide my confusion, for I am a modest man—and Sir Henry went on.

"Mr. Neville was my brother."

"Oh," I said, starting, for now I knew who Sir Henry had reminded me of when I first saw him. His brother was a much smaller man and had a dark beard, but now I thought of it, he possessed eyes of the same shade of grey and with the same keen look in them, and the features too were not unlike.

"He was," went on Sir Henry, "my only and younger brother, and till five years ago I do not suppose we were ever a month away from each other. But just about five years ago a misfortune befell us, as sometimes does happen in families. We had quarrelled

---

1 Inyati] site of Robert Moffat's Christian mission, 1857; the Matabele (or Ndebele) in present-day Zimbabwe are of Zulu descent.

bitterly, and I behaved very unjustly to my brother in my anger." Here Captain Good nodded his head vigorously to himself. The ship gave a big roll just then, so that the looking-glass, which was fixed opposite us to starboard, was for a moment nearly over our heads, and as I was sitting with my hands in my pockets and staring upwards, I could see him nodding like anything.

"As I daresay you know," went on Sir Henry, "if a man dies intestate, and has no property but land, real property it is called in England, it all descends to his eldest son. It so happened that just at the time when we quarrelled our father died intestate. He had put off making his will until it was too late. The result was that my brother, who had not been brought up to any profession, was left without a penny. Of course it would have been my duty to provide for him, but at the time the quarrel between us was so bitter that I did not—to my shame I say it (and he sighed deeply)—offer to do anything. It was not that I grudged him anything, but I waited for him to make advances, and he made none. I am sorry to trouble you with all this, Mr. Quatermain, but I must to make things clear, eh, Good?"

"Quite so, quite so," said the captain. "Mr. Quatermain will, I am sure, keep this history to himself."

"Of course," said I, for I rather pride myself on my discretion.

"Well," went on Sir Henry, "my brother had a few hundred pounds to his account at the time, and without saying anything to me he drew out this paltry sum, and, having adopted the name of Neville, started off for South Africa in the wild hope of making a fortune. This I heard afterwards. Some three years passed, and I heard nothing of my brother, though I wrote several times. Doubtless the letters never reached him. But as time went on I grew more and more troubled about him. I found out, Mr. Quatermain, that blood is thicker than water."

"That's true," said I, thinking of my boy Harry.

"I found out, Mr. Quatermain, that I would have given half my fortune to know that my brother George, the only relation I have, was safe and well, and that I should see him again."

"But you never did, Curtis," jerked out Captain Good, glancing at the big man's face.

"Well, Mr. Quatermain, as time went on, I became more and more anxious to find out if my brother was alive or dead, and if alive to get him home again. I set inquiries on foot, and your letter was one of the results. So far as it went it was satisfactory, for it shewed that till lately George was alive, but it did not go far enough. So, to cut a long story short, I made up my mind to come out and look for him myself, and Captain Good was so kind as to come with me."

"Yes," said the captain; "nothing else to do, you see. Turned out by my Lords of the Admiralty to starve on half pay. And now perhaps, sir, you will tell us what you know or have heard of the gentleman called Neville."

CHAPTER II.

THE LEGEND OF SOLOMON'S MINES.

"WHAT was it that you heard about my brother's journey at Bamangwato?" said Sir Henry, as I paused to fill my pipe before answering Captain Good.

"I heard this," I answered, "and I have never mentioned it to a soul till to-day. I heard that he was starting for Solomon's Mines."

"Solomon's Mines!" ejaculated both my hearers at once. "Where are they?"

"I don't know," I said; "I know where they are said to be. I once saw the peaks of the mountains that border them, but there was a hundred and thirty miles of desert between me and them, and I am not aware that any white man ever got across it save one. But perhaps the best thing I can do is to tell you the legend of Solomon's Mines as I know it, you passing your word not to reveal anything I tell you without my permission. Do you agree to that? I have my reasons for asking it."

Sir Henry nodded, and Captain Good replied, "Certainly, certainly."

"Well," I began, "as you may guess, in a general way, elephant hunters are a rough set of men, and don't trouble themselves with much beyond the facts of life and the ways of Kafirs. But here and there you meet a man who takes the trouble to collect traditions from the natives, and tries to make out a little piece of the history of this dark land. It was such a man as this who first told me the legend of Solomon's Mines, now a matter of nearly thirty years ago. It was when I was on my first elephant hunt in the Matabele country. His name was Evans, and he was killed next year, poor fellow, by a wounded buffalo, and lies buried near the Zambesi Falls.[1] I was telling Evans one night, I remember, of some wonderful workings I had found whilst hunting koodoo and eland in what is now the Lydenburg district of the Transvaal.[2] I see they have come across these workings again lately in prospecting for gold, but I knew of them years ago. There is a great wide waggon road cut out of the solid rock, and leading to the mouth of the working or gallery. Inside the mouth of this gallery are stacks of gold quartz piled up ready for crushing, which shows that the workers, whoever they were, must have left in a hurry, and about twenty paces in the gallery is built across, and a beautiful bit of masonry it is.

"'Ay,' said Evans, 'but I will tell you a queerer thing than that;' and he went on to tell me how he had found in the far interior a ruined city, which he believed to be the Ophir of the Bible,[3] and, by the way, other more learned men have said the same long since poor Evans' time. I was, I remember, listening open-eared to all these wonders, for I was young at the time, and this story of an ancient civilisation and of the treasure which those old Jewish or Phœnician adventurers used to extract from a country long since lapsed into the darkest barbarism took a great hold upon my imagination, when suddenly he said to me, "Lad, did you ever hear of the Suliman Mountains up to the north-west of the Mashukulumbwe country?" I told him I never had. "Ah, well," he said, "that was where Solomon really had his mines, his diamond mines, I mean."

"'How do you know that?' I asked.

"'Know it; why what is "Suliman" but a corruption of Sol-

---

1   Zambesi Falls] probably Victoria Falls, so-named by David Livingstone in 1851.

2   Lydenburg ... Transvaal] see Andrew Lang, "King Solomon's Mines," Appendix A.

3   Ophir] I Kings 9:28, 10:11, 22:48; and Chronicles, Job, Psalms, and Isaiah; its exact location remains unknown; see Hugh Walmsley, *The Ruined Cities of Zulu Land*, Appendix D.

omon!* and, besides, an old Isanusi (witch doctor) up in the Manica country[1] told me all about it. She said that the people who lived across those mountains were a branch of the Zulus, speaking a dialect of Zulu, but finer and bigger men even; that there lived among them great wizards, who had learnt their art from white men when "all the world was dark," and who had the secret of a wonderful mine of "bright stones."'

"Well, I laughed at this story at the time, though it interested me, for the diamond fields were not discovered then, and poor Evans went off and got killed, and for twenty years I never thought any more of the matter. But just twenty years afterwards—and that is a long time, gentlemen, an elephant hunter does not often live for twenty years at his business—I heard something more definite about Suliman's Mountains and the country which lies beyond it. I was up beyond the Manica country at a place called Sitanda's Kraal,[2] and a miserable place it was, for one could get nothing to eat there, and there was but little game about. I had an attack of fever, and was in a bad way generally, when one day a Portugee arrived with a single companion— a half-breed. Now I know your Delagoa Portugee[3] well. There is no greater devil unhung in a general way, battening as he does upon human agony and flesh in the shape of slaves. But this was quite a different type of man to the low fellows I had been accustomed to meet; he reminded me more of the polite dons I have read about. He was tall and thin, with large dark eyes and curling grey moustachios. We talked together a little, for he could speak broken English, and I understood a little Portugee, and he told me that his name was José Silvestre, and that he had a place near Delagoa Bay; and when be went on next day with his half-breed companion, he said, 'Good-bye,' taking off his hat quite in the old style. 'Good-bye, señor,' he said; 'if ever we meet again I shall be

---

* Suliman is the Arabic form of Solomon.—EDITOR.

---

1 Manica country] Manicaland in Eastern Zimbabwe.
2 Sitanda's Kraal] a "kraal" is a village of huts surrounded by a stockade and occupied by the household of a chief. Haggard may be indebted here to Frederick Selous, *A Hunter's Wanderings in Africa*, Chapter XVIII.
3 Delagoa Portugee] Portuguese slave-traders since the sixteenth century from the coast north of Natal around Delagoa Bay.

the richest man in the world, and I will remember you.' I laughed a little—I was too weak to laugh much—and watched him strike out for the great desert to the west, wondering if he was mad, or what he thought he was going to find there.

"A week passed, and I got the better of my fever. One evening I was sitting on the ground in front of the little tent I had with me, chewing the last leg of a miserable fowl I had bought from a native for a bit of cloth worth twenty fowls, and staring at the hot red sun sinking down into the desert, when suddenly I saw a figure, apparently that of a European, for it wore a coat, on the slope of the rising ground opposite to me, about three hundred yards away. The figure crept along on its hands and knees, then it got up and staggered along a few yards on its legs, only to fall and crawl along again. Seeing that it must be somebody in distress, I sent one of my hunters to help him, and presently he arrived, and who do you suppose it turned out to be?"

"José Silvestre, of course," said Captain Good.

"Yes, José Silvestre, or rather his skeleton and a little skin. His face was bright yellow with bilious fever, and his large, dark eyes stood nearly out of his head, for all his flesh had gone. There was nothing but yellow parchment-like skin, white hair, and the gaunt bones sticking up beneath.

"'Water! for the sake of Christ, water!' he moaned. I saw that his lips were cracked, and his tongue, which protruded between them, swollen and blackish.

"I gave him water with a little milk in it, and he drank it in great gulps, two quarts or more, without stopping. I would not let him have any more. Then the fever took him again, and he fell down and began to rave about Suliman's Mountains, and the diamonds, and the desert. I took him into the tent and did what I could for him, which was little enough; but I saw how it must end. About eleven o'clock he got quieter, and I lay down for a little rest and went to sleep. At dawn I woke again, and saw him in the half light sitting up, a strange, gaunt form, and gazing out towards the desert. Presently the first ray of the sun shot right across the wide plain before us till it reached the far-away crest of one of the tallest of the Suliman Mountains more than a hundred miles away.

"'There it is!' cried the dying man in Portuguese, stretching out his long, thin arm, 'but I shall never reach it, never. No one will ever reach it!'

"Suddenly he paused, and seemed to take a resolution. 'Friend,' he said, turning towards me, 'are you there? My eyes grow dark.'

"'Yes,' I said; 'yes, lie down now, and rest.'

"'Ay,' he answered, 'I shall rest soon, I have time to rest—all eternity. Listen, I am dying! You have been good to me. I will give you the paper. Perhaps you will get there if you can live through the desert, which has killed my poor servant and me.'

"Then he groped in his shirt and brought out what I thought was a Boer tobacco pouch of the skin of the Swart-vet-pens (sable antelope). It was fastened with a little strip of hide, what we call a rimpi, and this he tried to untie, but could not. He handed it to me. 'Untie it,' he said. I did so, and extracted a bit of torn yellow linen (see *Frontispiece*), on which something was written in rusty letters. Inside was a paper.

"Then he went on feebly, for he was growing weak: 'The paper has it all, that is on the rag. It took me years to read. Listen: my ancestor, a political refugee from Lisbon, and one of the first Portuguese who landed on these shores, wrote that when he was dying on those mountains which no white foot ever pressed before or since. His name was José da Silvestra, and he lived three hundred years ago. His slave, who waited for him on this side the mountains, found him dead, and brought the writing home to Delagoa. It has been in the family ever since, but none have cared to read it till at last I did. And I have lost my life over it, but another may succeed, and become the richest man in the world—the richest man in the world. Only give it to no one; go yourself!' Then he began to wander again, and in an hour it was all over.

"God rest him! he died very quietly, and I buried him deep, with big boulders on his breast; so I do not think that the jackals can have dug him up. And then I came away."

"Ay, but the document," said Sir Henry, in a tone of deep interest.

"Yes, the document; what was in it?" added the captain.

"Well, gentlemen, if you like I will tell you. I have never

showed it to anybody yet except my dear wife, who is dead, and she thought it was all nonsense, and a drunken old Portuguese trader who translated it for me, and had forgotten all about it next morning. The original rag is at my home in Durban, together with poor Dom José's translation, but I have the English rendering in my pocket-book, and a fac-simile of the map, if it can be called a map. Here it is."

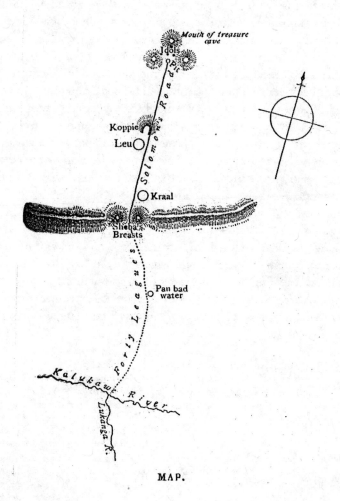

MAP.

"I, José da Silvestra, who am now dying of hunger in the little cave where no snow is on the north side of the nipple of the southernmost of the two mountains I have named Sheba's Breasts, write this in the year 1590 with a cleft bone upon a remnant of my raiment, my blood being the ink. If my slave should find it when he comes, and should bring it to Delagoa, let my friend (name illegible) bring the matter to the knowledge of the king, that he may send an army which, if they live through the desert and the mountains, and can overcome the brave Kukuanes and their devilish arts, to which end many priests should be brought, will make him the richest king since Solomon. With my own eyes have I seen the countless diamonds stored in Solomon's treasure chamber behind the white Death; but through the treachery of Gagool the witch-finder I might bring nought away, scarcely my life. Let him who comes follow the map, and climb the snow of Sheba's left breast till he comes to the nipple, on the north side of which is the great road Solomon made, from whence three days' journey to the King's Place. Let him kill Gagool. Pray for my soul. Farewell.

"José da Silvestra."[*]

When I had finished reading the above and shewn the copy of the map, drawn by the dying hand of the old Dom with his blood for ink, there followed a silence of astonishment.

"Well," said Captain Good, "I have been round the world twice, and put in at most ports, but may I be hung, if I ever heard

---

[*] Eu José da Silvestra que estou morrendo de fome ná pequena cova onde não ha neve ao lado norte do bico mais ao sul das duas montanhas que chamei seio de Sheba; escrevo isto no anno 1590; escrevo isto com um pedaço d'ósso n' um farrapo de minha roupa e com sangue meu por tinta; se o meu escravo dér com isto quando venha ao levar para Lourenzo Marquez, que o meu amigo (———) leve a cousa ao conhecimento d' El Rei, para que possa mandar um exercito que, se desfiler pelo deserto e pelas montanhas e mesmo sobrepujar os bravos Kukuanes e suas artes diabolicas, pelo que se deviam trazer muitos padres Fara o Rei mais rico depois de Salomão. Com meus proprios olhos vé os diamantes sem conto guardados nas camaras do thesouro de Salomão a traz da morte branca, mas pela traição de Gagoal a feiticeira achadora, nada poderia levar, e apenas a minha vida. Quem vier siga o mappa e trepe pela neve de Sheba peito à esquerda até chegar ao bico, do lado norte do qual está a grande estrada do Salomão por elle feita, donde ha tres dias de jornada até ao Palacio do Rei. Mate Gagoal. Reze por minha alma. Adeos.

José da Silvestra.

a yarn like that out of a story book, or in it either, for the matter of that."

"It's a queer story, Mr. Quatermain," said Sir Henry. "I suppose you are not hoaxing us? It is, I know, sometimes thought allowable to take a greenhorn in."

"If you think that, Sir Henry," I said, much put out, and pocketing my paper, for I do not like to be thought one of those silly fellows who consider it witty to tell lies, and who are for ever boasting to new comers of extraordinary hunting adventures which never happened, "why there is an end of the matter," and I rose to go.

Sir Henry laid his large hand upon my shoulder. "Sit down, Mr. Quatermain," he said, "I beg your pardon; I see very well you do not wish to deceive us, but the story sounded so extraordinary that I could hardly believe it."

"You shall see the original map and writing when we reach Durban," I said, somewhat mollified, for really when I came to consider the matter it was scarcely wonderful that he should doubt my good faith. "But I have not told you about your brother. I knew the man Jim who was with him. He was a Bechuana by birth, a good hunter, and for a native a very clever man. The morning Mr. Neville was starting, I saw Jim standing by my waggon and cutting up tobacco on the disselboom.[1]

"'Jim,' said I, 'where are you off to this trip? Is it elephants?'

"'No, Baas,'[2] he answered, 'we are after something worth more than ivory.'

"'And what might that be?' I said, for I was curious. 'Is it gold?'

"'No, Baas, something worth more than gold,' and he grinned.

"I did not ask any more questions, for I did not like to lower my dignity by seeming curious, but I was puzzled. Presently Jim finished cutting his tobacco.

"'Baas,' said he.

"I took no notice.

"'Baas,' said he again.

"'Eh, boy, what is it?' said I.

"'Baas, we are going after diamonds.'

---

1   disselboom] the shaft of an ox wagon's front wheels to which the after-oxen are yoked.

2   Baas] boss, master; a form of respectful address by blacks to whites, not likely to survive in South Africa much beyond the twentieth century.

"'Diamonds! why, then, you are going in the wrong direction; you should head for the Fields.'

"'Baas, have you ever heard of Suliman's Berg?' (Solomon's Mountains).

"'Ay!'

"'Have you ever heard of the diamonds there?'

"'I have heard a foolish story, Jim.'

"'It is no story, Baas. I once knew a woman who came from there, and got to Natal with her child, she told me: — she is dead now.'

"'Your master will feed the aasvogels (vultures), Jim, if he tries to reach Suliman's country, and so will you if they can get any pickings off your worthless old carcass,' said I.

"He grinned. 'Mayhap, Baas. Man must die; I'd rather like to try a new country myself; the elephants are getting worked out about here.'

"'Ah! my boy,' I said, 'you wait till the "pale old man" (death) gets a grip of your yellow throat, and then we'll hear what sort of a tune you sing.'

"Half an hour after that I saw Neville's waggon move off. Presently Jim came running back. 'Good-bye, Baas,' he said. 'I didn't like to start without bidding you good-bye, for I daresay you are right, and we shall never come back again.'

"'Is your master really going to Suliman's Berg, Jim, or are you lying?'

"'No,' says he; 'he is going. He told me he was bound to make his fortune somehow, or try to; so he might as well try the diamonds.'

"'Oh!' said I; 'wait a bit, Jim; will you take a note to your master, Jim, and promise not to give it to him till you reach Inyati?' (which was some hundred miles off).

"'Yes,' said he.

"So I took a scrap of paper, and wrote on it, 'Let him who comes ... climb the snow of Sheba's left breast, till he comes to the nipple, on the north side of which is Solomon's great road.'

"'Now, Jim,' I said, 'when you give this to your master, tell him he had better follow the advice implicitly. You are not to give it to him now, because I don't want him back asking me questions which I won't answer. Now be off, you idle fellow, the waggon is nearly out of sight.'

"Jim took the note and went, and that is all I know about your brother, Sir Henry; but I am much afraid——"

"Mr. Quatermain," said Sir Henry, "I am going to look for my brother; I am going to trace him to Suliman's Mountains, and over them if necessary, till I find him, or till I know that he is dead. Will you come with me?"

I am, as I think I have said, a cautious man, indeed a timid one, and I shrunk from such an idea. It seemed to me that to start on such a journey would be to go to certain death, and putting other things aside, as I had a son to support, I could not afford to die just then.

"No, thank you, Sir Henry, I think I had rather not," I answered. "I am too old for wild-goose chases of that sort, and we should only end up like my poor friend Silvestre. I have a son dependent on me, so cannot afford to risk my life."

Both Sir Henry and Captain Good looked very disappointed.

"Mr. Quatermain," said the former, "I am well off, and I am bent upon this business. You may put the remuneration for your services at whatever figure you like in reason, and it shall be paid over to you before we start. Moreover, I will, before we start, arrange that in the event of anything happening to us or to you, that your son shall be suitably provided for. You will see from this how necessary I think your presence. Also if by any chance we should reach this place, and find diamonds, they shall belong to you and Good equally. I do not want them. But of course the chance is as good as nothing, though the same thing would apply to any ivory we might get. You may pretty well make your own terms with me, Mr. Quatermain; and of course I shall pay all expenses."

"Sir Henry," said I, "this is the most liberal offer I ever had, and one not to be sneezed at by a poor hunter and trader. But the job is the biggest I ever came across and I must take time to think it over. I will give you my answer before we get to Durban."

"Very good," answered Sir Henry, and then I said good-night and turned in, and dreamt about poor long-dead Silvestre and the diamonds.

CHAPTER III.

UMBOPA ENTERS OUR SERVICE.

It takes from four to five days, according to the vessel and the state of the weather, to run up from the Cape to Durban.[1] Sometimes, if the landing is bad at East London, where they have not yet got that wonderful harbour they talk so much of, and sink such a mint of money in, one is delayed for twenty-four hours before the cargo boats can get out to take the goods off. But on this occasion we had not to wait at all, for there were no breakers on the Bar to speak of, and the tugs came out at once with their long strings of ugly flat-bottomed boats, into which the goods were bundled with a crash. It did not matter what they were, over they went slap bang; whether they were china or woollen goods they met with the same treatment. I saw one case containing four dozen of champagne smashed all to bits, and there was the champagne fizzing and boiling about in the bottom of the dirty cargo boat. It was a wicked waste, and so evidently the Kafirs in the boat thought, for they found a couple of unbroken bottles, and knocking the tops off drank the contents. But they had not allowed for the expansion caused by the fizz in the wine, and feeling themselves swelling, rolled about in the bottom of the boat, calling out that the good liquor was "tagati" (bewitched). I spoke to them from the vessel, and told them that it was the white man's strongest medicine, and that they were as good as dead men. They went on to the shore in a very great fright, and I do not think that they will touch champagne again.

Well, all the time we were running up to Natal I was thinking over Sir Henry Curtis' offer. We did not speak any more on the subject for a day or two, though I told them many hunting yarns, all true ones. There is no need to tell lies about hunting, for so many curious things happen within the knowledge of a man whose business it is to hunt; but this is by the way.

At last, one beautiful evening in January, which is our hottest

---

1   Durban] the principal seaport and largest city of Natal Colony, about 825 miles by sea from Cape Town, which (at that time) extended from a sandy spit on Durban Bay called the Point inland to a range of low hills called the Berea; East London is a port in the locale.

month, we steamed along the coast of Natal, expecting to make Durban Point by sunset. It is a lovely coast all along from East London, with its red sandhills and wide sweeps of vivid green, dotted here and there with Kafir kraals, and bordered by a ribbon of white surf, which spouts up in pillars of foam where it hits the rocks. But just before you get to Durban there is a peculiar richness about it. There are the deep kloofs[1] cut in the hills by the rushing rains of centuries, down which the rivers sparkle; there is the deepest green of the bush, growing as God planted it, and the other greens of the mealie gardens and the sugar patches, while here and there a white house, smiling out at the placid sea, puts a finish and gives an air of homeliness to the scene. For to my mind, however beautiful a view may be, it requires the presence of man to make it complete, but perhaps that is because I have lived so much in the wilderness, and therefore know the value of civilisation, though to be sure it drives away the game. The Garden of Eden, no doubt, was fair before man was, but I always think it must have been fairer when Eve was walking about it. But we had miscalculated a little, and the sun was well down before we dropped anchor off the Point, and heard the gun which told the good folk that the English Mail was in. It was too late to think of getting over the Bar that night, so we went down comfortably to dinner, after seeing the Mails carried off in the lifeboat.

When we came up again the moon was up, and shining so brightly over sea and shore that she almost paled the quick large flashes from the lighthouse. From the shore floated sweet spicy odours that always remind me of hymns and missionaries, and in the windows of the houses on the Berea sparkled a hundred lights. From a large brig lying near came the music of the sailors as they worked at getting the anchor up to be ready for the wind. Altogether it was a perfect night, such a night as you only get in Southern Africa, and it threw a garment of peace over everybody as the moon threw a garment of silver over everything. Even the great bulldog, belonging to a sporting passenger, seemed to yield to the gentle influences, and giving up yearning to come to close quarters with the baboon in a cage on the foc'sle, snored happily in the door of the cabin, dreaming no doubt that he had finished him, and happy in his dream.

---

1   kloofs] (Dutch) deep, usually wooded, ravines.

We all—that is, Sir Henry Curtis, Captain Good, and myself—went and sat by the wheel, and were quiet for a while.

"Well, Mr. Quatermain," said Sir Henry, presently, "have you been thinking about my proposals?"

"Ay," echoed Captain Good, "What do you think of them, Mr. Quatermain? I hope you are going to give us the pleasure of your company as far as Solomon's Mines, or wherever the gentleman you knew as Neville may have got to."

I rose and knocked out my pipe before I answered. I had not made up my mind, and wanted the additional moment to complete it. Before the burning tobacco had fallen into the sea it was completed; just that little extra second did the trick. It is often the way when you have been bothering a long time over a thing.

"Yes, gentlemen," I said, sitting down again, "I will go, and by your leave I will tell you why and on what terms. First for the terms which I ask.

"1. You are to pay all expenses, and any ivory or other valuables we may get is to be divided between Captain Good and myself.

"2. That you pay me £500 for my services on the trip before we start, I undertaking to serve you faithfully till you choose to abandon the enterprise, or till we succeed, or disaster overtakes us.

"3. That before we start you execute a deed agreeing, in the event of my death or disablement, to pay my boy Harry, who is studying medicine over there in London at Guy's Hospital, a sum of £200 a year for five years, by which time he ought to be able to earn a living for himself. That is all, I think, and I daresay you will say quite enough too."

"No," answered Sir Henry, "I accept them gladly. I am bent upon this project, and would pay more than that for your help, especially considering the peculiar knowledge you possess."

"Very well. And now that I have made my terms I will tell you my reasons for making up my mind to go. First of all, gentlemen, I have been observing you both for the last few days, and if you will not think me impertinent I will say that I like you, and think that we shall come up well to the yoke together. That is something, let me tell you, when one has a long journey like this before one.

"And now as to the journey itself, I tell you flatly, Sir Henry and Captain Good, that I do not think it probable that we can come out of it alive, that is, if we attempt to cross the Suliman Mountains. What was the fate of the old Dom da Silvestra three hundred years ago? What was the fate of his descendant twenty years ago? What has been your brother's fate? I tell you frankly, gentlemen, that as their fate was so I believe ours will be."

I paused to watch the effect of my words. Captain Good looked a little uncomfortable; but Sir Henry's face did not change. "We must take our chance," he said.

"You may perhaps wonder," I went on, "why, if I think this, I, who am, as I told you, a timid man, should undertake such a journey. It is for two reasons. First I am a fatalist, and believe that my time is appointed to come quite independently of my own movements, and that if I am to go to Suliman's Mountains to be killed, I shall go there and shall be killed there. God Almighty, no doubt, knows His mind about me, so I need not trouble on that point. Secondly, I am a poor man. For nearly forty years I have hunted and traded, but I have never made more than a living. Well, gentlemen, I don't know if you are aware that the average life of an elephant hunter from the time he takes to the trade is from four to five years. So you see I have lived through about seven generations of my class, and I should think that my time cannot be far off anyway. Now, if anything were to happen to me in the ordinary course of business, by the time my debts were paid there would be nothing left to support my son Harry whilst he was getting in the way of earning a living, whereas now he would be provided for for five years. There is the whole affair in a nutshell."

"Mr. Quatermain," said Sir Henry, who had been giving me the most serious attention, "your motives for undertaking an enterprise which you believe can only end in disaster reflect a great deal of credit on you. Whether or not you are right, time and the event of course alone can show. But whether you are right or wrong, I may as well tell you at once that I am going through with it to the end, sweet or bitter. If we are going to be knocked on the head, all I have to say is that I hope we shall get a little shooting first, eh, Good?"

"Yes, yes," put in the captain. "We have all three of us been accustomed to face danger, and hold our lives in our hands in various ways, so it is no good turning back now."

"And now I vote we go down to the saloon and take an observation, just for luck, you know." And we did—through the bottom of a tumbler.

Next day we went ashore, and I put Sir Henry and Captain Good up at the little shanty I have on the Berea, and which I call my home. There are only three rooms and a kitchen in it, and it is built of green brick with a galvanised iron roof, but there is a good garden with the best loquot trees[1] in it that I know, and some nice young mangoes, of which I hope great things. The curator of the botanical gardens gave them to me. It is looked after by an old hunter of mine, named Jack, whose thigh was so badly broken by a buffalo cow in Sikukunïs country,[2] that he will never hunt again. But he can potter about and garden, being a Griqua[3] by birth. You can never get your Zulu to take much interest in gardening. It is a peaceful art, and peaceful arts are not in his line.

Sir Henry and Good slept in a tent pitched in my little grove of orange trees at the end of the garden (for there was no room for them in the house), and what with the smell of the bloom and the sight of the green and golden fruit—for in Durban you will see all three on the tree together—I daresay it is a pleasant place enough (for we have few mosquitoes here unless there happens to come an unusually heavy rain).

Well, to get on—for unless I do you will be tired of my story before ever we fetch up at Suliman's Mountains—having once made up my mind to go I set about making the necessary preparations. First I got the deed from Sir Henry, providing for my boy in case of accidents. There was some little difficulty about getting this legally executed, as Sir Henry was a stranger here, and the property to be charged was over the water, but it was ultimately got over with the help of a lawyer, who charged £20 for the job—a price that I thought outrageous. Then I got my cheque

---

1 loquot trees] an asiatic ornamental tree with fruit like a yellow plum, astringent if plucked too soon but like a juicy apple when ripe.

2 Sikukunïs country] in the north-eastern part of the Transvaal.

3 Griqua] "By Griquas is meant any mixed race sprung from natives and Europeans" (Livingstone)—often Dutch fathers and KhoiKhoi (Hottentot) or aboriginal mothers.

for £500. Having paid this tribute to my bump of caution,[1] I bought a waggon and a span of oxen on Sir Henry's behalf, and beauties they were. It was a twenty-two-foot waggon with iron axles, very strong, very light, and built throughout of stink-wood.[2] It was not quite a new one, having been to the Diamond Fields and back, but in my opinion it was all the better for that, for one could see that the wood was well seasoned. If anything is going to give in a waggon, or if there is green wood in it, it will show out on the first trip. It was what we call a "half-tented" waggon, that is to say, it was only covered in over the after twelve feet, leaving all the front part free for the necessaries we had to carry with us. In this after part was a hide "cartle," or bed, on which two people could sleep, also racks for rifles, and many other little conveniences. I gave £125 for it, and think it was cheap at the price. Then I bought a beautiful team of twenty salted Zulu oxen, which I had had my eye on for a year or two. Sixteen oxen are the usual number for a team, but I had four extra to allow for casualties. These Zulu oxen are small and light, not more than half the size of the Africander oxen, which are generally used for transport purposes; but they will live where the Africanders will starve, and with a light load will make five miles a day better going, being quicker and not so liable to get footsore. What is more, this lot were thoroughly "salted," that is, they had worked all over South Africa, and so had become proof (comparatively speaking) against red-water,[3] which so frequently destroys whole teams of oxen when they get on to strange "veldt" (grass country). As for "lung sick," which is a dreadful form of pneumonia, very prevalent in this country, they had all been inoculated against it. This is done by cutting a slit in the tail of an ox, and binding in a piece of the diseased lung of an animal which has died of the sickness. The result is that the ox sickens, takes the disease in a mild form, which causes its tail to drop off, as a rule about a foot from the root, and

---

1   bump of caution] phrenology, as popularly understood, placed the cranial protuberances or "bumps" of cautiousness above the ears toward the back of the skull.
2   stink-wood] highly valuable timber (black, white, and red woods) from several indigenous trees, sometimes called the teak of South Africa; the red (bitter almond) is valued for wagons and smells of prussic acid when cut or bruised.
3   red-water] a parasitic cattle disease transmitted by ticks characterized by red blood cells in the urine.

becomes proof against future attacks. It seems cruel to rob the animal of his tail, especially in a country where there are so many flies, but it is better to sacrifice the tail and keep the ox than to lose both tail and ox, for a tail without an ox is not much good except to dust with. Still it does look odd to trek along behind twenty stumps, where there ought to be tails. It seems as though nature had made a trifling mistake, and stuck the stern ornaments of a lot of prize bulldogs on to the rumps of the oxen.

Next came the question of provisioning and medicines, one which required the most careful consideration, for what one had to do was to avoid lumbering the waggon up, and yet take everything absolutely necessary. Fortunately, it turned out that Good was a bit of a doctor, having at some period in his previous career managed to pass through a course of medical and surgical instruction, which he had more or less kept up. He was not, of course, qualified, but he knew more about it than many a man who could write M.D. after his name, as we found out afterwards, and he had a splendid travelling medicine chest and a set of instruments. Whilst we were at Durban he cut off a Kafir's big toe in a way which it was a pleasure to see. But he was quite flabbergasted when the Kafir, who had sat stolidly watching the operation, asked him to put on another, saying that a "white one" would do at a pinch.

There remained, when these questions were satisfactorily settled, two further important points for consideration, namely, that of arms and that of servants. As to the arms I cannot do better than put down a list of those we finally decided on from among the ample store that Sir Henry had brought with him from England, and those which I had. I copy it from my pocket-book, where I made the entry at the time.

"Three heavy breechloading double-eight elephant guns, weighing about fifteen pounds each, with a charge of eleven drachms of black powder." Two of these were by a well-known London firm, most excellent makers, but I do not know by whom mine, which was not so highly finished, was made. I had used it on several trips, and shot a good many elephants with it, and it had always proved a most superior weapon, thoroughly to be relied on.

"Three double .500 expresses, constructed to carry a charge of six drachms," sweet weapons, and admirable for medium-sized game, such as eland or sable antelope, or for men, especially in an open country and with the semi-hollow bullet.

"One double No. 12 central-fire Keeper's shotgun, full choke both barrels." This gun proved of the greatest service to us afterwards in shooting game for the pot.

"Three Winchester repeating rifles (not carbines), spare guns.

"Three single-action Colt's revolvers, with the heavier pattern of cartridge."

This was our total armament,[1] and the reader will doubtless observe that the weapons of each class were of the same make and calibre, so that the cartridges were interchangeable, a very important point. I make no apology for detailing it at length, for every experienced hunter will know how vital a proper supply of guns and ammunition is to the success of an expedition.

Now as to the men who were to go with us. After much consultation we decided that their number should be limited to five, namely, a driver, a leader, and three servants.

The driver and leader I got without much difficulty, two Zulus, named respectively Goza and Tom; but the servants were a more difficult matter. It was necessary that they should be thoroughly trustworthy and brave men, as in a business of this sort our lives might depend upon their conduct. At last I secured two, one a Hottentot called Ventvögel (wind-bird), and one a little Zulu named Khiva, who had the merit of speaking English perfectly. Ventvögel I had known before; he was one of the most perfect "spoorers" (game trackers) I ever had to do with, and tough as whipcord. He never seemed to tire. But he had one failing, so common with his race, drink. Put him within reach of a bottle of grog and you could not trust him. But as we were going beyond

---

1   armament] the elephant rifles are double-barrelled, eight-gauge (diameter of gun-barrel), breach-loaders (cartridge received at the rear of the bore in contrast to the older muzzle-loaders); an "express" rifle (the trio's are of half-inch caliber) is designed to be super-accurate, having high muzzle velocity, a flat trajectory, a light bullet with a heavy charge of powder (semi-hollows expand on impact to create a nasty "wound channel"), and fixed-sight range (in Chapter 12 we are told they are "sighted to three hundred and fifty yards"); the Winchester repeaters and the Colt single-actions (both "44-40 frontier" caliber-load) were of recent American production, suggesting the common aspect of frontier conquest.

the region of grog-shops this little weakness of his did not so much matter.

Having got these two men I looked in vain for a third to suit my purpose, so we determined to start without one, trusting to luck to find a suitable man on our way up country. But on the evening before the day we had fixed for our departure the Zulu Khiva informed me that a man was waiting to see me. Accordingly when we had done dinner, for we were at table at the time, I told him to bring him in. Presently a very tall, handsome-looking man, somewhere about thirty years of age, and very light-coloured for a Zulu, entered, and, lifting his knob-stick[1] by way of salute, squatted himself down in the corner on his haunches, and sat silent. I did not take any notice of him for a while, for it is a great mistake to do so. If you rush into conversation at once, a Zulu is apt to think you a person of little dignity or consideration. I observed, however, that he was a "Keshla" (ringed man), that is, that he wore on his head the black ring, made of a species of gum polished with fat and worked in with the hair, usually assumed by Zulus on attaining a certain age or dignity. Also it struck me that his face was familiar to me.

"Well," I said at last, "what is your name?"

"Umbopa," answered the man in a slow, deep voice.

"I have seen your face before."

"Yes; the Inkoosi (chief) saw my face at the place of the Little Hand (Isandhlwana)[2] the day before the battle."

Then I remembered. I had been one of Lord Chelmsford's guides in that unlucky Zulu War, and had had the good fortune to leave the camp in charge of some waggons the day before the battle. While I had been waiting for the cattle to be inspanned[3] I had fallen into conversation with this man, who held some small command among the native auxiliaries, and he had expressed to me his doubts of the safety of the camp. At the time I had told

---

1 knob-stick] (also knobkierie) a short, round-headed stick used as a club and a missile by the natives.

2 Isandhlwana] in January of 1879, a small band of British and native troops invading Zululand camped at the foot of this hill, were attacked by about 10,000 Zulus under Cetewayo (nephew of Chaka) and wiped out; thus began the Zulu War.

3 inspanned] harnessed or yoked up, as oxen to a wagon; outspanned is the opposite, the draft animals unhitched.

him to hold his tongue, and leave such matters to wiser heads; but afterwards I thought of his words.

"I remember," I said; "what is it you want?"

"It is this, 'Macumazahn'[1] (that is my Kafir name, and means the man who gets up in the middle of the night, or, in vulgar English, he who keeps his eyes open). I hear that you go on a great expedition far into the North with the white chiefs from over the water. Is it a true word?"

"It is."

"I hear that you go even to the Lukanga River, a moon's journey beyond the Manica country. Is this so also, 'Macumazahn?'"

"Why do you ask whither we go? What is it to thee?" I answered, suspiciously, for the objects of our journey had been kept a dead secret.

"It is this, O white men, that if indeed you travel so far I would travel with you."

There was a certain assumption of dignity in the man's mode of speech, and especially in his use of the words "O white men," instead of "O Inkosis" (chiefs), which struck me.

"You forget yourself a little," I said. "Your words come out unawares. That is not the way to speak. What is your name, and where is your kraal? Tell us, that we may know with whom we have to deal."

"My name is Umbopa. I am of the Zulu people, yet not of them. The house of my tribe is in the far North; it was left behind when the Zulus came down here a 'thousand years ago,' long before Chaka reigned in Zululand. I have no kraal. I have wandered for many years. I came from the North as a child to Zululand. I was Cetywayo's man in the Nkomabakosi Regiment. I ran away from Zululand and came to Natal because I wanted to see the white man's ways. Then I served against Cetywayo in the war. Since then I have been working in Natal. Now I am tired, and would go North again. Here is not my place. I want no money, but I am a brave man, and am worth my place and meat. I have spoken."

---

1 "Macumazahn"] Of his friend and business partner, Arthur Cochrane, Haggard noted: "It was his native name, by the way—Macumazahn—that I took for that of Allan Quatermain" (*Private Diaries*).

I was rather puzzled at this man and his way of speech. It was evident to me from his manner that he was in the main telling the truth, but he was somehow different from the ordinary run of Zulus, and I rather mistrusted his offer to come without pay. Being in a difficulty, I translated his words to Sir Henry and Good, and asked them their opinion. Sir Henry told me to ask him to stand up. Umbopa did so, at the same time slipping off the long military great coat he wore, and revealing himself naked except for the moocha round his centre and a necklace of lions' claws. He certainly was a magnificent-looking man; I never saw a finer native. Standing about six foot three high he was broad in proportion, and very shapely. In that light, too, his skin looked scarcely more than dark, except here and there where deep black scars marked old assegai wounds. Sir Henry walked up to him and looked into his proud, handsome face.

"They make a good pair, don't they?" said Good; "one as big as the other."

"I like your looks, Mr. Umbopa, and I will take you as my servant," said Sir Henry in English.

Umbopa evidently understood him, for he answered in Zulu, "It is well;" and then with a glance at the white man's great stature and breadth, "we are men, thou and I."

CHAPTER IV.

AN ELEPHANT HUNT.

Now I do not propose to narrate at full length all the incidents of our long journey up to Sitanda's Kraal, near the junction of the Lukanga and Kalukwe Rivers,[1] a journey of more than a thousand miles from Durban, the last three hundred or so of which, owing to the frequent presence of the dreadful "tsetse" fly,[2] whose bite is fatal to all animals except donkeys and men, we had to make on foot.

---

1 the Lukanga and Kalukwe Rivers] in present-day Zambia, west of Sitanda's Kraal.
2 "tsetse" fly] the insect which by its bite is almost always fatal to "unsalted" (not immunized) cattle and horses; can cause "sleeping sickness" in man.

We left Durban at the end of January, and it was in the second week of May that we camped near Sitanda's Kraal. Our adventures on the way were many and various, but as they were of the sort which befall every African hunter, I shall not—with one exception to be presently detailed—set them down here, lest I should render this history too wearisome.

At Inyati, the outlying trading station in the Matabele country, of which Lobengula[1] (a great scoundrel) is king, we with many regrets parted from our comfortable waggon. Only twelve oxen remained to us out of the beautiful span of twenty which I had bought at Durban. One we had lost from the bite of a cobra, three had perished from poverty and the want of water, one had been lost, and the other three had died from eating the poisonous herb called "tulip."[2] Five more sickened from this cause, but we managed to cure them with doses of an infusion made by boiling down the tulip leaves. If administered in time this is a very effective antidote. The waggon and oxen we left in the immediate charge of Goza and Tom, the driver and leader, both of them trustworthy boys, requesting a worthy Scotch missionary who lived in this wild place to keep an eye to it. Then, accompanied by Umbopa, Khiva, Ventvögel, and half a dozen bearers whom we hired on the spot, we started off on foot upon our wild quest. I remember we were all a little silent on the occasion of that departure, and I think that each of us was wondering if we should ever see that waggon again; for my part I never expected to. For a while we tramped on in silence, till Umbopa, who was marching in front, broke into a Zulu chant about how some brave men, tired of life and the tameness of things, started off into a great wilderness to find new things or die, and how, lo, and behold! when they had got far into the wilderness, they found it was not a wilderness at all, but a beautiful place full of young wives and fat cattle, of game to hunt and enemies to kill.

Then we all laughed and took it for a good omen. He was a cheerful savage was Umbopa, in a dignified sort of a way, when he

---

1 Lobengula] murdered Haggard's servants; see Haggard, "Notes," Appendix B.

2 "tulip"] (in Afrikaans "tulp") an *Iridaceae* with flowers, highly poisonous to grazing livestock after summer rains when it grows up with the grasses; used, however, as a medicinal herb by Foulata, Chapter 15.

had not got one of his fits of brooding, and had a wonderful knack of keeping one's spirits up. We all got very fond of him.

And now for the one adventure I am going to treat myself to, for I do dearly love a hunting yarn.

About a fortnight's march from Inyati, we came across a peculiarly beautiful bit of fairly-watered wooded country. The kloofs in the hills were covered with dense bush, "idoro" bush as the natives call it, and in some places, with the "wacht-een-beche" (wait-a-little) thorn, and there were great quantities of the beautiful "machabell" tree, laden with refreshing yellow fruit with enormous stones. This tree is the elephant's favourite food, and there were not wanting signs that the great brutes were about, for not only was their spoor[1] frequent, but in many places the trees were broken down and even up-rooted. The elephant is a destructive feeder.

One evening, after a long day's march, we came to a spot of peculiar loveliness. At the foot of a bush-clad hill was a dry river-bed, in which, however, were to be found pools of crystal water all trodden round with the hoof-prints of game. Facing this hill was a park-like plain, where grew clumps of flat-topped mimosa, varied with occasional glossy-leaved machabells, and all round was the great sea of pathless, silent bush.

As we emerged into this river-bed path we suddenly started a troop of tall giraffes, who galloped, or rather sailed off, with their strange gait, their tails screwed up over their backs, and their hoofs rattling like castanets. They were about three hundred yards from us, and therefore practically out of shot, but Good, who was walking ahead, and had an express loaded with solid ball in his hand, could not resist, but upped gun and let drive at the last, a young cow. By some extraordinary chance the ball struck it full on the back of the neck, shattering the spinal column, and that giraffe went rolling head over heels just like a rabbit. I never saw a more curious thing.

"Curse it!" said Good—for I am sorry to say he had a habit of using strong language when excited—contracted, no doubt, in the course of his nautical career; "curse it! I've killed him."

---

1 spoor] any vestige, such as footprint, scent, or broken plants, showing the path taken by man or beast.

"Ou, Bougwan," ejaculated the Kafirs; "ou! ou!"

They called Good "Bougwan" (glass eye) because of his eye-glass.

"Oh, 'Bougwan!'" re-echoed Sir Henry and I, and from that day Good's reputation as a marvellous shot was established, at any rate among the Kafirs. Really he was a bad one, but whenever he missed we overlooked it for the sake of that giraffe.

Having set some of the "boys" to cut off the best of the giraffe meat, we went to work to build a "scherm" near one of the pools about a hundred yards to the right of it. This is done by cutting a quantity of thorn bushes and laying them in the shape of a circular hedge. Then the space enclosed is smoothed, and dry tambouki grass,[1] if obtainable, is made into a bed in the centre, and a fire or fires lighted.

By the time the "scherm" was finished the moon was coming up, and our dinner of giraffe steaks and roasted marrow bones was ready. How we enjoyed those marrow-bones, though it was rather a job to crack them! I know no greater luxury than giraffe mar-row, unless it is elephant's heart, and we had that on the morrow. We ate our simple meal, pausing at times to thank Good for his wonderful shot, by the light of the full moon, and then we began to smoke and yarn, and a curious picture we must have made squatted there round the fire. I, with my short grizzled hair stick-ing up straight, and Sir Henry with his yellow locks, which were getting rather long, were rather a contrast, especially as I am thin, and short, and dark, weighing only nine stone[2] and a half, and Sir Henry is tall, and broad, and fair, and weighs fifteen. But perhaps the most curious looking of the three, taking all the circumstances of the case into consideration, was Captain John Good, R.N. There he sat upon a leather bag, looking just as though he had come in from a comfortable day's shooting in a civilised country, absolutely clean, tidy, and well dressed. He had on a shooting suit of brown tweed, with a hat to match, and neat gaiters. He was, as usual, beautifully shaved, his eyeglass and his false teeth appeared

---

1   tambouki grass] (or tambooki, tamboekie) any of several species of tall grasses used by South Africans for thatching; such tall perennial grasses easily burn during the dry sea-son.

2   stone] a British measure of the mass weight of a person; one stone equals 14 pounds.

to be in perfect order, and altogether he was the neatest man I ever had to do with in the wilderness. He even had on a collar, of which he had a supply, made of white guttapercha.[1]

"You see, they weigh so little," he said to me, innocently, when I expressed my astonishment at the fact; "I always like to look like a gentleman."

Well, there we all sat yarning away in the beautiful moonlight, and watching the Kafirs a few yards off sucking their intoxicating "daccha"[2] in a pipe of which the mouthpiece was made of the horn of an eland, till they one by one rolled themselves up in their blankets and went to sleep by the fire, that is, all except Umbopa, who sat a little apart (I noticed he never mixed much with the other Kafirs), his chin resting on his hand, apparently thinking deeply.

Presently, from the depths of the bush behind us, came a loud "woof, woof!" "That's a lion," said I, and we all started up to listen. Hardly had we done so, when from the pool, about a hundred yards off, came the strident trumpeting of an elephant. "Unkungunklovo! Unkungunklovo!" (elephant! elephant!) whispered the Kafirs; and a few minutes afterwards we saw a succession of vast shadowy forms moving slowly from the direction of the water towards the bush. Up jumped Good, burning for slaughter, and thinking, perhaps, that it was as easy to kill elephant as he had found it to shoot giraffe, but I caught him by the arm and pulled him down.

"It's no good," I said, "let them go."

"It seems that we are in a paradise of game. I vote we stop here a day or two, and have a go at them," said Sir Henry, presently.

I was rather surprised, for hitherto Sir Henry had always been for pushing on as fast as possible, more especially since we had ascertained at Inyati that about two years ago an Englishman of the name of Neville *had* sold his waggon there, and gone on up country; but I suppose his hunter instincts had got the better of him.

Good jumped at the idea, for he was longing to have a go at

---

1 guttapercha] an early synthetic, made from a rubber-like tree sap.
2 "daccha"] or "dagga," Indian hemp (cannabis) introduced by the Dutch colonists from the East.

those elephants; and so, to speak the truth, did I, for it went against my conscience to let such a herd as that escape without having a pull at them.

"All right, my hearties," said I. "I think we want a little recreation. And now let's turn in, for we ought to be off by dawn, and then perhaps we may catch them feeding before they move on."

The others agreed, and we proceeded to make preparations. Good took off his clothes, shook them, put his eyeglass and his false teeth into his trousers pocket, and folding them all up neatly, placed them out of the dew under a corner of his mackintosh sheet. Sir Henry and I contented ourselves with rougher arrangements, and were soon curled up in our blankets, and dropping off into the dreamless sleep that rewards the traveller.

Going, going, go—What was that?

Suddenly from the direction of the water came a sound of violent scuffling, and next instant there broke upon our ears a succession of the most awful roars. There was no mistaking what they came from; only a lion could make such a noise as that. We all jumped up and looked towards the water, in the direction of which we saw a confused mass, yellow and black in colour, staggering and struggling towards us. We seized our rifles, and slipping on our veldtschoons (shoes made of untanned hide), ran out of the scherm towards it. By this time it had fallen, and was rolling over and over on the ground, and by the time we reached it it struggled no longer, but was quite still.

And this was what it was. On the grass there lay a sable antelope bull—the most beautiful of all the African antelopes—quite dead, and transfixed by its great cursed horns was a magnificent black-maned lion, also dead. What had happened evidently was this. The sable antelope had come down to drink at the pool where the lion—no doubt the same we had heard—had been lying in wait. While the antelope was drinking the lion had sprung upon him, but was received upon the sharp curved horns and transfixed. I once saw the same thing happen before. The lion, unable to free himself, had torn and bitten at the back and neck of the bull, which, maddened with fear and pain, had rushed on till it dropped dead.

As soon as we had sufficiently examined the dead beasts we called the Kafirs, and between us managed to drag their carcasses up to the scherm. Then we went in and laid down, to wake no more till dawn.

With the first light we were up and making ready for the fray. We took with us the three eight-bore rifles, a good supply of ammunition, and our large water-bottles, filled with weak, cold tea, which I have always found the best stuff to shoot on. After swallowing a little breakfast we started, Umbopa, Khiva, and Ventvögel accompanying us. The other Kafirs we left with instructions to skin the lion and the sable antelope, and cut up the latter.

We had no difficulty in finding the broad elephant trail, which Ventvögel, after examination, pronounced to have been made by between twenty and thirty elephants, most of them full-grown bulls. But the herd had moved on some way during the night, and it was nine o'clock, and already very hot, before, from the broken trees, bruised leaves and bark, and smoking dung, we knew we could not be far off them.

Presently we caught sight of the herd, numbering, as Ventvögel had said, between twenty and thirty, standing in a hollow, having finished their morning meal, and flapping their great ears. It was a splendid sight.

They were about two hundred yards from us. Taking a handful of dry grass I threw it into the air to see how the wind was; for if once they winded us I knew they would be off before we could get a shot. Finding that, if anything, it blew from the elephants to us, we crept stealthily on, and thanks to the cover managed to get within forty yards or so of the great brutes. Just in front of us and broadside on stood three splendid bulls, one of them with enormous tusks. I whispered to the others that I would take the middle one; Sir Henry covered the one to the left, and Good the bull with the big tusks.

"Now," I whispered.

Boom! boom! boom! went the three heavy rifles, and down went Sir Henry's elephant dead as a hammer, shot right through the heart. Mine fell on to its knees, and I thought he was going to die, but in another moment he was up and off, tearing along straight past me. As he went I gave him the second barrel in the ribs, and this brought him down in good earnest. Hastily slipping in two fresh cartridges, I ran close up to him, and a ball through the brain put an end to the poor brute's struggles. Then I turned to see how Good had fared with the big bull, which I had heard screaming with rage and pain as I gave mine its quietus. On reaching the captain I found him in a great state of excitement. It appeared that on receiving the bullet the bull had turned and come straight for his assailant, who had barely time to get out of his way, and then charged blindly on past him, in the direction of our encampment. Meanwhile the herd had crashed off in wild alarm in the other direction.

For a while we debated whether to go after the wounded bull or follow the herd, and finally decided for the latter alternative, and departed thinking that we had seen the last of those big tusks. I have often wished since that we had. It was easy work to follow the elephants, for they had a trail like a carriage road behind them, crushing down the thick bush in their furious flight as though it were tambouki grass.

But to come up with them was another matter, and we had struggled on under a broiling sun for over two hours before we found them. They were, with the exception of one bull, standing together, and I could see, from their unquiet way and the manner in which they kept lifting their trunks to test the air, that they were on the lookout for mischief. The solitary bull stood fifty yards or so this side of the herd, over which he was evidently keeping sentry, and about sixty yards from us. Thinking that he would see or wind us, and that it would probably start them all off again if we tried to get nearer, especially as the ground was rather open, we all aimed at this bull, and at my whispered word fired. All three shots took effect, and down he went dead. Again the herd started on, but unfortunately for them about a hundred yards farther on was a nullah, or dried water track, with steep banks, a place very much resembling the one the Prince Imperial[1] was killed in in Zululand. Into this the elephants plunged, and when we reached the edge we found them struggling in wild confusion to get up the other bank, and filling the air with their screams, and trumpeting as they pushed one another aside in their selfish panic, just like so many human beings. Now was our opportunity,

---

1 Prince Imperial] during the Zulu war, the son of Napoleon III, Louis Napoleon, the Prince Imperial of France, was killed (June 1, 1879) while accompanying a reconnoitering party of British troops.

and firing away as quick as we could load we killed five of the poor beasts, and no doubt should have bagged the whole herd had they not suddenly given up their attempts to climb the bank and rushed headlong down the nullah. We were too tired to follow them, and perhaps also a little sick of slaughter, eight elephants being a pretty good bag for one day.

So after we had rested a little, and the Kafirs had cut out the hearts of two of the dead elephants for supper, we started homewards, very well pleased with ourselves, having made up our minds to send the bearers on the morrow to chop out the tusks.

Shortly after we had passed the spot where Good had wounded the patriarchal bull we came across a herd of eland, but did not shoot at them, as we had already plenty of meat. They trotted past us, and then stopped behind a little patch of bush about a hundred yards away and wheeled round to look at us. As Good was anxious to get a near view of them, never having seen an eland close, he handed his rifle to Umbopa, and, followed by Khiva, strolled up to the patch of bush. We sat down and waited for him, not sorry of the excuse for a little rest.

The sun was just going down in its reddest glory, and Sir Henry and I were admiring the lovely scene, when suddenly we heard an elephant scream, and saw its huge and charging form with uplifted trunk and tail silhouetted against the great red globe of the sun. Next second we saw something else, and that was Good and Khiva tearing back towards us with the wounded bull (for it was he) charging after them. For a moment we did not dare to fire—though it would have been little use if we had at that distance—for fear of hitting one of them, and the next a dreadful thing happened—Good fell a victim to his passion for civilised dress. Had he consented to discard his trousers and gaiters as we had, and hunt in a flannel shirt and a pair of veldtschoons, it would have been all right, but as it was his trousers cumbered him in that desperate race, and presently, when he was about sixty yards from us, his boot, polished by the dry grass, slipped, and down he went on his face right in front of the elephant.

We gave a gasp, for we knew he must die, and ran as hard as we could towards him. In three seconds it had ended, but not as we thought. Khiva, the Zulu boy, had seen his master fall, and brave lad that he was, had turned and flung his assegai straight into the elephant's face. It stuck in his trunk.

With a scream of pain the brute seized the poor Zulu, hurled him to the earth, and placing his huge foot on to his body about the middle, twined his trunk round his upper part and *tore him in two.*

We rushed up mad with horror, and fired again, and again, and presently the elephant fell upon the fragments of the Zulu.

As for Good, he got up and wrung his hands over the brave man who had given his life to save him, and myself, though an old hand, I felt a lump in my throat. Umbopa stood and contemplated the huge dead elephant and the mangled remains of poor Khiva.

"Ah well," he said presently, "he is dead, but he died like a man."

CHAPTER V.

OUR MARCH INTO THE DESERT.

WE had killed nine elephants, and it took us two days to cut out the tusks and get them home and bury them carefully in the sand under a large tree, which made a conspicuous mark for miles round. It was a wonderfully fine lot of ivory. I never saw a better, averaging as it did between forty and fifty pounds a tusk. The tusks of the great bull that killed poor Khiva scaled one hundred and seventy pounds the pair, as nearly as we could judge.

As for Khiva himself, we buried what remained of him in an ant-bear hole, together with an assegai to protect himself with on his journey to a better world. On the third day we started on, hoping that we might one day return to dig up our buried ivory, and in due course, after a long and wearisome tramp, and many adventures which I have not space to detail, reached Sitanda's Kraal, near the Lukanga River, the real starting-point of our expedition. Very well do I recollect our arrival at that place. To the right was a scattered native settlement with a few stone cattle kraals and some cultivated lands down by the water, where these savages grew their scanty supply of grain, and beyond it great tracts of waving "veldt" covered with tall grass, over which herds of the smaller game were wandering. To the left was the vast desert. This spot appeared to be the outpost of the fertile country, and it would be difficult to say. to what natural causes such an abrupt change in the character of the soil was due. But so it was. Just below our encampment flowed a little stream, on the farther side of which was a stony slope, the same down which I had twenty years before seen poor Silvestre creeping back after his attempt to reach Solomon's Mines, and beyond that slope began the waterless desert covered with a species of karoo shrub.[1] It was evening when we pitched our camp, and the great fiery ball of the sun was sinking into the desert, sending glorious rays of many-coloured light flying over all the vast expanse. Leaving Good to superintend the arrangement of our little camp, I took Sir Henry with me, and we walked to the top of the slope opposite and gazed out across the desert. The air was very clear, and far, far away I could distinguish the faint blue outlines here and there capped with white of the great Suliman Berg.

"There," I said, "there is the wall of Solomon's Mines, but God knows if we shall ever climb it."

"My brother should be there, and if he is, I shall reach him somehow," said Sir Henry, in that tone of quiet confidence which marked the man.

"I hope so," I answered, and turned to go back to the camp, when I saw that we were not alone. Behind us, also gazing earnestly towards the far-off mountains, stood the great Zulu Umbopa.

The Zulu spoke when he saw that I had observed him, but addressed himself to Sir Henry, to whom he had attached himself.

"Is it to that land that thou wouldst journey, Incubu?" (a native word meaning, I believe, an elephant, and the name given to Sir Henry by the Kafirs) he said, pointing towards the mountains with his broad assegai.

I asked him sharply what he meant by addressing his master in that familiar way. It is very well for natives to have a name for one among themselves, but it is not decent that they should call one

---

1   karoo shrub] generic name for various bushes that take the place of grass on the wide
    sandy deserts (the karoo) of South Africa.

by their heathenish appellations to one's face. The man laughed a quiet little laugh which angered me.

"How dost thou know that I am not the equal of the Inkosi I serve?" he said. "He is of a royal house, no doubt; one can see it in his size and in his eye; so, mayhap, am I. At least I am as great a man. Be my mouth, oh Macumazahn, and say my words to the Inkoos Incubu, my master, for I would speak to him and to thee."

I was angry with the man, for I am not accustomed to be talked to in that way by Kafirs, but somehow he impressed me, and besides I was curious to know what he had to say, so I translated, expressing my opinion at the same time that he was an impudent fellow, and that his swagger was outrageous.

"Yes, Umbopa," answered Sir Henry, "I would journey there."

"The desert is wide and there is no water, the mountains are high and covered with snow, and man cannot say what is beyond them behind the place where the sun sets; how shalt thou come thither, Incubu, and wherefore dost thou go?"

I translated again.

"Tell him," answered Sir Henry, "that I go because I believe that a man of my blood, my brother, has gone there before me, and I go to seek him."

"That is so, Incubu; a man I met on the road told me that a white man went out into the desert two years ago towards those mountains with one servant, a hunter. They never came back."

"How do you know it was my brother?" asked Sir Henry.

"Nay, I know not. But the man, when I asked what the white man was like, said that he had thine eyes and a black beard. He said, too, that the name of the hunter with him was Jim, that he was a Bechuana hunter and wore clothes."[1]

"There is no doubt about it," said I; "I knew Jim well."

Sir Henry nodded. "I was sure of it," he said. "If George set his mind upon a thing he generally did it. It was always so from his boyhood. If he meant to cross the Suliman Berg he has crossed it, unless some accident has overtaken him, and we must look for him on the other side."

---

1 Bechuana ... wore clothes] the dominant Matebele "were in the habit of walking about in their birthday garb thereby forcing the modest Bechuana women and children to retire on each appearance of Matebele men" (Plaatje).

Umbopa understood English, though he rarely spoke it.

"It is a far journey, Incubu," he put in, and I translated his remark.

"Yes," answered Sir Henry, "it is far. But there is no journey upon this earth that a man may not make if he sets his heart to it. There is nothing, Umbopa, that he cannot do, there are no mountains he may not climb, there are no deserts he cannot cross, save a mountain and a desert of which you are spared the knowledge, if love leads him and he holds his life in his hand counting it as nothing, ready to keep it or to lose it as Providence may order."

I translated.

"Great words, my father," answered the Zulu (I always called him a Zulu, though he was not really one), "great swelling words fit to fill the mouth of a man. Thou art right, my father Incubu. Listen! what is Life? It is a feather, it is the seed of the grass, blown hither and thither, sometimes multiplying itself and dying in the act, sometimes carried away into the heavens. But if the seed be good and heavy it may perchance travel a little way on the road it wills. It is well to try and journey one's road and to fight with the air. Man must die. At the worst he can but die a little sooner. I will go with thee across the desert and over the mountains, unless perchance I fall to the ground on the way, my father."

He paused awhile, and then went on with one of those strange bursts of rhetorical eloquence which Zulus sometimes indulge in, and which to my mind, full as they are of vain repetitions, show that the race is by no means devoid of poetic instinct and of intellectual power.

"What is life? Tell me, O white men, who are wise, who know the secrets of the world, and the world of stars, and the world that lies above and around the stars; who flash their words from afar without a voice;[1] tell me, white men, the secret of our life— whither it goes and whence it comes!

"Ye cannot answer; ye know not. Listen, I will answer. Out of the dark we came, into the dark we go. Like a storm-driven bird at night we fly out of the Nowhere; for a moment our wings are seen in the light of the fire, and, lo! we are gone again into the

---

1   without a voice] i.e., with a signaling-heliograph, especially effective in the clear desert sunlight.

Nowhere.[1] Life is nothing. Life is all. It is the hand with which we hold off Death. It is the glow-worm that shines in the night-time and is black in the morning; it is the white breath of the oxen in winter; it is the little shadow that runs across the grass and loses itself at sunset."

"You are a strange man," said Sir Henry, when he ceased.

Umbopa laughed. "It seems to me that we are much alike, Incubu. Perhaps *I* seek a brother over the mountains."

I looked at him suspiciously. "What dost thou mean?" I asked; "what dost thou know of the mountains?"

"A little; a very little. There is a strange land there, a land of witchcraft and beautiful things; a land of brave people, and of trees, and streams, and white mountains, and of a great white road. I have heard of it. But what is the good of talking? it grows dark. Those who live to see will see."

Again I looked at him doubtfully. The man knew too much.

"Ye need not fear me, Macumazahn," he said interpreting my look. "I dig no holes for ye to fall in. I make no plots. If ever we cross those mountains behind the sun, I will tell what I know. But Death sits upon them. Be wise and turn back. Go and hunt elephant. I have spoken."

And without another word he lifted his spear in salutation, and returned towards the camp, where shortly afterwards we found him cleaning a gun like any other Kafir.

"That is an odd man," said Sir Henry.

"Yes," answered I, "too odd by half. I don't like his little ways. He knows something, and won't speak out. But I suppose it is no use quarrelling with him. We are in for a curious trip, and a mysterious Zulu won't make much difference one way or another."

Next day we made our arrangements for starting. Of course it was impossible to drag our heavy elephant rifles and other kit with us across the desert, so dismissing our bearers we made an arrangement with an old native who had a kraal close by to take care of them till we returned. It went to my heart to leave such things as those sweet tools to the tender mercies of an old thief, of

---

1 Nowhere] aware of the comparative methodology of ethnographers such as Henry Callaway, Haggard takes this bird-image from a famous passage in the Venerable Bede's *Ecclesiastical History*.

a savage whose greedy eyes I could see gloating over them. But I took some precautions.

First of all I loaded all the rifles, and informed him that if he touched them they would go off. He instantly tried the experiment with my eight bore, and it did go off, and blew a hole right through one of his oxen, which were just then being driven up to the kraal, to say nothing of knocking him head over heels with the recoil. He got up considerably startled, and not at all pleased at the loss of the ox, which he had the impudence to ask me to pay for, and nothing would induce him to touch them again.

"Put the live devils up there in the thatch," he said, "out of the way, or they will kill us all."

Then I told him that if, when we came back, one of those things was missing I would kill him and all his people by witchcraft; and if we died and he tried to steal the things I would come and haunt him and turn his cattle mad and his milk sour till life was a weariness, and make the devils in the guns come out and talk to him in a way he would not like, and generally gave him a good idea of judgment to come. After that he swore he would look after them as though they were his father's spirit. He was a very superstitious old Kafir and a great villain.

Having thus disposed of our superfluous gear we arranged the kit we five—Sir Henry, Good, myself, Umbopa, and the Hottentot Ventvögel—were to take with us on our journey. It was small enough, but do what we would we could not get it down under about forty pounds a man. This is what it consisted of:—

The three express rifles and two hundred rounds of ammunition.

The two Winchester repeating rifles (for Umbopa and Ventvögel), with two hundred rounds of cartridge.

Three "Colt" revolvers and sixty rounds of cartridge.

Five Cochrane's water-bottles, each holding four pints.

Five blankets.

Twenty-five pounds' weight of biltong (sun-dried game flesh).

Ten pounds' weight of best mixed beads for gifts.

A selection of medicine, including an ounce of quinine, and one or two small surgical instruments.

Our knives, a few sundries, such as a compass, matches, a pocket filter, tobacco, a trowel, a bottle of brandy, and the clothes we stood in.

This was our total equipment, a small one indeed for such a venture, but we dared not attempt to carry more. As it was that load was a heavy one per man to travel across the burning desert with, for in such places every additional ounce tells upon one. But try as we would we could not see our way to reducing it. There was nothing but what was absolutely necessary.

With great difficulty, and by the promise of a present of a good hunting knife each, I succeeded in persuading three wretched natives from the village to come with us for the first stage, twenty miles, and to carry each a large gourd holding a gallon of water. My object was to enable us to refill our water-bottles after the first night's march, for we determined to start in the cool of the night. I gave out to these natives that we were going to shoot ostriches, with which the desert abounded. They jabbered and shrugged their shoulders, and said we were mad and should perish of thirst, which I must say seemed very probable; but being desirous of obtaining the knives, which were almost unknown treasures up there, they consented to come, having probably reflected that, after all, our subsequent extinction would be no affair of theirs.

All next day we rested and slept, and at sunset ate a hearty meal of fresh beef washed down with tea, the last, as Good sadly remarked, we were likely to drink for many a long day. Then, having made our final preparations, we lay down and waited for the moon to rise. At last about nine o'clock up she came in all her chastened glory, flooding the wild country with silver light, and throwing a weird sheen on the vast expanse of rolling desert before us, which looked as solemn and quiet and as alien to man as the star-studded firmament above. We rose up, and in a few minutes were ready, and yet we hesitated a little, as human nature is prone to hesitate on the threshold of an irrevocable step. We three white men stood there by ourselves. Umbopa, assegai in hand and the rifle across his shoulders, a few paces ahead of us, looked out fixedly across the desert; the three hired natives, with the gourds of water, and Ventvögel, were gathered in a little knot behind.

"Gentlemen," said Sir Henry, presently, in his low, deep voice, "we are going on about as strange a journey as men can make in this world. It is very doubtful if we can succeed in it. But we are three men who will stand together for good or for evil to the last. And now before we start let us for a moment pray to the Power who shapes the destinies of men, and who ages since has marked out our paths, that it may please Him to direct our steps in accordance with His will."

Taking off his hat he, for the space of a minute or so, covered his face with his hands, and Good and I did likewise.

I do not say that I am a first-rate praying man, few hunters are, and as for Sir Henry I never heard him speak like that before, and only once since, though deep down in his heart I believe be is very religious. Good too is pious, though very apt to swear. Anyhow I do not think I ever, excepting on one single occasion, put in a better prayer in my life than I did during that minute, and somehow I felt the happier for it. Our future was so completely unknown, and I think the unknown and the awful always bring a man nearer to his Maker.

"And now," said Sir Henry, "*trek*."[1]

So we started.

We had nothing to guide ourselves by except the distant mountains and old José da Silvestra's chart, which, considering that it was drawn by a dying and half distraught man on a fragment of linen three centuries ago, was not a very satisfactory sort of thing to work on. Still, such as it was, our sole hope of success depended on it. If we failed in finding that pool of bad water which the old Dom marked as being situated in the middle of the desert, about sixty miles from our starting-point, and as far from the mountains, we must in all probability perish miserably of thirst. And to my mind the chances of our finding it in that great sea of sand and karoo scrub seemed almost infinitesimal. Even supposing da Silvestra had marked it right, what was there to prevent its having been generations ago dried up by the sun, or trampled in by game, or filled with the drifting sand?

On we tramped silently as shades through the night and in the

---

1 "*trek*"] to make a difficult overland journey; one of the most intensely connotative words in South African English because it recalls the Great Trek or migration of the Boers into the Transvaal in the 1830s.

heavy sand. The karoo bushes caught our shins and retarded us, and the sand got into our veldtschoons and Good's shooting boots, so that every few miles we had to stop and empty them; but still the night was fairly cool, though the atmosphere was thick and heavy, giving a sort of creamy feel to the air, and we made fair progress. It was very still and lonely there in the desert, oppressively so indeed. Good felt this, and once began to whistle the "Girl I left behind me,"[1] but the notes sounded lugubrious in that vast place, and he gave it up. Shortly afterwards a little incident occurred which, though it made us jump at the time, gave rise to a laugh. Good, as the holder of the compass, which being a sailor, of course he thoroughly understood, was leading, and we were toiling along in single file behind him, when suddenly we heard the sound of an exclamation, and he vanished. Next second there arose all round us a most extraordinary hubbub, snorts, groans, wild sounds of rushing feet. In the faint light too we could descry dim galloping forms half hidden by wreaths of sand. The natives threw down their loads and prepared to bolt, but remembering that there was nowhere to bolt, cast themselves upon the ground and howled out that it was the devil. As for Sir Henry and myself we stood amazed; nor was our amazement lessened when we perceived the form of Good careering off in the direction of the mountains, apparently mounted on the back of a horse and halloaing like mad. In another second he threw up his arms, and we heard him come to the earth with a thud. Then I saw what had happened; we had stumbled right onto a herd of sleeping quagga, on to the back of one of which Good had actually fallen, and the brute had naturally enough got up and made off with him. Singing out to the others that it was all right I ran towards Good, much afraid lest he should be hurt, but to my great relief found him sitting in the sand, his eye-glass still fixed firmly in his eye, rather shaken and very much startled, but not in any way injured.

After this we travelled on without any further misadventure till after one o'clock, when we called a halt, and having drunk a little water, not much, for water was precious, and rested for half an hour, started on again.

---

1 "Girl I left behind me"] a marching song of the Napoleonic Wars.

On, on we went, till at last the east began to blush like the cheek of a girl. Then there came faint rays of primrose light, that changed presently to golden bars, through which the dawn glided out across the desert. The stars grew pale and paler still till at last they vanished; the golden moon waxed wan, and her mountain ridges stood out clear against her sickly face like the bones on the face of a dying man; then came spear upon spear of glorious light flashing far away across the boundless wilderness, piercing and firing the veils of mist, till the desert was draped in a tremulous golden glow, and it was day.

Still we did not halt, though by this time we should have been glad enough to do so, for we knew that when once the sun was fully up it would be almost impossible for us to travel in it. At length, about six o'clock, we spied a little pile of rocks rising out of the plain, and to this we dragged ourselves. As luck would have it here we found an overhanging slab of rock carpeted beneath with smooth sand, which afforded a most grateful shelter from the heat. Underneath this we crept, and having drank some water each and eaten a bit of biltong, we laid down and were soon sound asleep.

It was three o'clock in the afternoon before we woke, to find our three bearers preparing to return. They had already had enough of the desert, and no number of knives would have tempted them to come a step farther. So we had a hearty drink, and having emptied our water bottles filled them up again from the gourds they had brought with them, and then watched them depart on their twenty miles' tramp home.

At half-past four we also started on. It was lonely and desolate work, for with the exception of a few ostriches there was not a single living creature to be seen on all the vast expanse of sandy plain. It was evidently too dry for game, and with the exception of a deadly-looking cobra or two we saw no reptiles. One insect, however, was abundant, and that was the common or house fly. There they came, "not as single spies, but in battalions," as I think the Old Testament says somewhere.[1] He is an extraordinary animal is the house fly. Go where you will you find him, and so it

---

1 "spies ... battalions"] another Haggard joke (see Stevenson Letter to Haggard, Appendix A); quotation is from *Hamlet* IV.5.79-80.

must always have been. I have seen him enclosed in amber, which must, I was told, have been half a million years old, looking exactly like his descendant of to-day, and I have little doubt but that when the last man lies dying on the earth he will be buzzing round—if that event should happen to occur in summer—watching for an opportunity to settle on his nose.

At sunset we halted, waiting for the moon to rise. At ten she came up beautiful and serene as ever, and with one halt about two o'clock in the morning, we trudged wearily on through the night, till at last the welcome sun put a period to our labours. We drank a little and flung ourselves down, thoroughly tired out, on the sand, and were soon all asleep. There was no need to set a watch, for we had nothing to fear from anybody or anything in that vast untenanted plain. Our only enemies were heat, thirst, and flies, but far rather would I have faced any danger from man or beast than that awful trinity. This time we were not so lucky as to find a sheltering rock to guard us from the glare of the sun, with the result that about seven o'clock we woke up experiencing the exact sensations one would attribute to a beefsteak on a gridiron. We were literally being baked through and through. The burning sun seemed to be sucking our very blood out of us. We sat up and gasped.

"Phew," said I, grabbing at the halo of flies, which buzzed cheerfully round my head. The heat did not affect them.

"My word," said Sir Henry.

"It *is* hot!" said Good.

It was hot, indeed, and there was not a bit of shelter to be had. Look where we would there was no rock or tree, nothing but an unending glare, rendered dazzling by the hot air which danced over the surface of the desert as it does over a red-hot stove.

"What is to be done?" asked Sir Henry; "we can't stand this for long."

We looked at each other blankly.

"I have it," said Good, "we must dig a hole and get in it, and cover ourselves with the karoo bushes."

It did not seem a very promising suggestion, but at least it was better than nothing, so we set to work, and with the trowel we had brought with us and our hands succeeded in about an hour in delving out a patch of ground about ten foot long by twelve wide to the depth of two feet. Then we cut a quantity of low scrub with our hunting knives, and creeping into the hole pulled it over us all, with the exception of Ventvögel, on whom, being a Hottentot, the sun had no particular effect. This gave us some slight shelter from the burning rays of the sun, but the heat in that amateur grave can be better imagined than described. The Black Hole of Calcutta[1] must have been a fool to it; indeed, to this moment I do not know how we lived through the day. There we lay panting, and every now and again moistening our lips from our scanty supply of water. Had we followed our inclinations we should have finished all we had off in the first two hours, but we had to exercise the most rigid care, for if our water failed us we knew that we must quickly perish miserably.

But everything has an end, if only you live long enough to see it, and somehow that miserable day wore on towards evening. About three o'clock in the afternoon we determined that we could stand it no longer. It would be better to die walking than to be slowly killed by heat and thirst in that dreadful hole. So taking each of us a little drink from our fast diminishing supply of water, now heated to about the same temperature as a man's blood, we staggered on.

We had now covered some fifty miles of desert. If my reader will refer to the rough copy and translation of old da Silvestra's map, he will see that the desert is marked as being forty leagues across, and the "pan bad water" is set down as being about in the middle of it. Now forty leagues is one hundred and twenty miles, consequently we ought at the most to be within twelve or fifteen miles of the water if any should really exist.

Through the afternoon we crept slowly and painfully along, scarcely doing more than a mile and a half an hour. At sunset we again rested, waiting for the moon, and after drinking a little managed to get some sleep.

Before we lay down Umbopa pointed out to us a slight and indistinct hillock on the flat surface of the desert about eight miles away. At the distance it looked like an ant-hill, and as I was dropping off to sleep I fell to wondering what it could be.

---

1 Black Hole of Calcutta] a dark cell in which Suraja Dowlah imprisoned 146 British (June 20, 1756), of whom only twenty-three survived until the following morning.

With the moon we started on again, feeling dreadfully exhausted, and suffering tortures from thirst and prickly heat. Nobody who has not felt it can know what we went through. We no longer walked, we staggered, now and again falling from exhaustion, and being obliged to call a halt every hour or so. We had scarcely energy left in us to speak. Up to now Good had chatted and joked, for he was a merry fellow; but now he had not a joke left in him.

At last, about two o'clock, utterly worn out in body and mind, we came to the foot of this queer hill, or sand koppie, which did at first sight resemble a gigantic ant-heap about a hundred feet high, and covering at the base nearly a morgen (two acres) of ground.

Here we halted, and driven by our desperate thirst sucked down our last drops of water. We had but half a pint a head, and we could each have drunk a gallon.

Then we lay down. Just as I was dropping off to sleep I heard Umbopa remark to himself in Zulu—

"If we cannot find water we shall all be dead before the moon rises to-morrow."

I shuddered, hot as it was. The near prospect of such an awful death is not pleasant, but even the thought of it could not keep me from sleeping.

CHAPTER VI.

WATER! WATER!

In two hours time, about four o'clock, I woke up. As soon as the first heavy demand of bodily fatigue had been satisfied, the torturing thirst from which I was suffering asserted itself. I could sleep no more. I had been dreaming that I was bathing in a running stream, with green banks and trees upon them, and I awoke to find myself in that arid wilderness, and to remember that, as Umbopa had said, if we did not find water that day we must certainly perish miserably. No human creature could live long without water in that heat. I sat up and rubbed my grimy face with my dry and horny hands. My lips and eyelids were stuck together, and it was only after some rubbing and with an effort that I was able to open them. It was not far off the dawn, but there was none of the bright feel of dawn in the air, which was thick with a hot murkiness I cannot describe. The others were still sleeping. Presently it began to grow light enough to read, so I drew out a little pocket copy of the "Ingoldsby Legends" I had brought with me, and read the "Jackdaw of Rheims." When I got to where

> "A nice little boy held a golden ewer,
>   Embossed, and filled with water as pure
>   As any that flows between Rheims and Namur,"

I literally smacked my cracked lips, or rather tried to smack them. The mere thought of that pure water made me mad. If the Cardinal had been there with his bell, book, and candle,[1] I would have whipped in and drank his water up, yes, even if he had already filled it with the suds of soap worthy of washing the hands of the Pope, and I knew that the whole concentrated curse of the Catholic Church should fall upon me for so doing. I almost think I must have been a little lightheaded with thirst and weariness and want of food; for I fell to thinking how astonished the Cardinal and his nice little boy and the jackdaw would have looked to see a burnt up, brown-eyed, grizzled-haired little elephant hunter suddenly bound in and put his dirty face into the basin, and swallow every drop of the precious water. The idea amused me so that I laughed or rather cackled aloud, which woke the others up, and they began to rub *their* dirty faces and get *their* gummed-up lips and eyelids apart.

As soon as we were all well awake, we fell to discussing the situation, which was serious enough. Not a drop of water was left. We turned the water-bottles upside down, and licked the tops, but it was a failure, they were as dry as a bone. Good, who had charge of the bottle of brandy, got it out and looked at it longingly; but Sir Henry promptly took it away from him, for to drink raw spirit would only have been to precipitate the end.

---

1 "Namur ... candle] an allusion to R. H. Barham's "The Jackdaw of Rheims," a comic poem of a jackdaw that steals the Cardinal's ring; the punishment of excommunication concluded with the words "Close the book, quench the candle, ring the bell!"

"If we do not find water we shall die," he said.

"If we can trust to the old Don's map there should some about," I said; but nobody seemed to derive much satisfaction from that remark. It was so evident that no great faith could be put in the map. It was now gradually growing light, and as we sat blankly staring at each other, I observed the Hottentot Ventvögel rise and begin to walk about with his eyes on the ground. Presently he stopped short, and uttering a guttural exclamation, pointed to the earth.

"What is it?" we exclaimed; and simultaneously rose and went to where he was standing pointing at the ground.

"Well," I said, "it is pretty fresh Springbok spoor; what of it?"

"Springboks do not go far from water," he answered in Dutch.

"No," I answered, "I forgot; and thank God for it."

This little discovery put new life into us; it is wonderful how, when one is in a desperate position, one catches at the slightest hope, and feels almost happy in it. On a dark night a single star is better than nothing.

Meanwhile Ventvögel was lifting his snub nose, and sniffing the hot air for all the world like an old Impala ram who scents danger. Presently he spoke again.

"I *smell* water," he said.

Then we felt quite jubilant, for we knew what a wonderful instinct these wild-bred men possess.

Just at that moment the sun came up gloriously, and revealed so grand a sight to our astonished eyes that for a moment or two we even forgot our thirst.

For there, not more than forty or fifty miles from us, glittering like silver in the early rays of the morning sun, were Sheba's breasts; and stretching away for hundreds of miles on each side of them was the great Suliman Berg. Now that I, sitting here, attempt to describe the extraordinary grandeur and beauty of that sight language seems to fail me. I am impotent even before its memory. There, straight before us, were two enormous mountains, the like of which are not, I believe, to be seen in Africa, if, indeed, there are any other such in the world, measuring each at least fifteen thousand feet in height, standing not more than a dozen miles apart, connected by a precipitous cliff of rock, and towering up in awful white solemnity straight into the sky. These mountains standing thus, like the pillars of a gigantic gateway, are shaped exactly like a woman's breasts. Their bases swelled gently up from the plain, looking, at that distance, perfectly round and smooth; and on the top of each was a vast round hillock covered with snow, exactly corresponding to the nipple on the female breast. The stretch of cliff which connected them appeared to be some thousand feet in height, and perfectly precipitous, and on each side of them, as far as the eye could reach, extended similar lines of cliff, broken only here and there by flat table-topped mountains, something like the world-famed one at Cape Town; a formation, by the way, very common in Africa.

To describe the grandeur of the whole view is beyond my powers. There was something so inexpressibly solemn and over-powering about those huge volcanoes—for doubtless they are extinct volcanoes—that it fairly took our breath away. For awhile the morning lights played upon the snow and the brown and swelling masses beneath, and then, as though to veil the majestic sight from our curious eyes, strange mists and clouds gathered and increased around them, till presently we could only trace their pure and gigantic outline swelling ghostlike through the fleecy envelope. Indeed, as we afterwards discovered, they were normally wrapped in this curious gauzy mist, which doubtless accounted for one not having made them out more clearly before.

Scarcely had the mountains vanished into cloud-clad privacy before our thirst—literally a burning question—reasserted itself.

It was all very well for Ventvögel to say he smelt water, but look which way we would we could see no signs of it. So far as the eye could reach there was nothing but arid sweltering sand and karoo scrub. We walked round the hillock and gazed about anxiously on the other side, but it was the same story, not a drop of water was to be seen; there was no indication of a pan, a pool, or a spring.

"You are a fool," I said, angrily, to Ventvögel; "there is no water."

But still he lifted his ugly snub nose and sniffed.

"I smell it, Baas" (master), he answered; "it is somewhere in the air."

"Yes," I said, "no doubt it is in the clouds, and about two months hence it will fall and wash our bones."

Sir Henry stroked his yellow beard thoughtfully. "Perhaps it is on the top of the hill," he suggested.

"Rot," said Good; "whoever heard of water being found on the top of a hill!"

"Let us go and look," I put in, and hopelessly enough we scrambled up the sandy sides of the hillock, Umbopa leading. Presently he stopped as though he was petrified.

"Nanzia manzie!" (here is water), he cried with a loud voice.

We rushed up to him, and there, sure enough, in a deep cup or indentation on the very top of the sand koppie was an undoubted pool of water.[1] How it came to be in such a strange place we did not stop to inquire, nor did we hesitate at its black and uninviting appearance. It was water, or a good imitation of it, and that was enough for us. We gave a bound and a rush, and in another second were all down on our stomachs sucking up the uninviting fluid as though it were nectar fit for the gods. Heavens, how we did drink! Then when we had done drinking we tore off our clothes and sat down in it, absorbing the moisture through our parched skins. You, my reader, who have only to turn on a couple of taps and summon "hot" and "cold" from an unseen vasty boiler, can have little idea of the luxury of that muddy wallow in brackish tepid water.

After awhile we arose from it, refreshed indeed, and fell to on our "biltong," of which we had scarcely been able to touch a mouthful for twenty-four hours, and ate our fill. Then we smoked a pipe, and lay down by the side of that blessed pool under the overhanging shadow of the bank, and slept till mid-day.

All that day we rested there by the water, thanking our stars that we had been lucky enough to find it, bad as it was, and not forgetting to render a due share of gratitude to the shade of the long-departed da Silvestra, who had corked it down so accurately on the tail of his shirt. The wonderful thing to us was that it

---

1   pool of water] a koppie (from the Afrikaans, via Dutch "kopje" for "small head"; also called an inselberg or "island-mountain" from the German) is a small but prominent hill often isolated on an otherwise flat South Africa veld or also in the Namib Desert. Sometimes sandy from weathering, it is usually of granite or other igneous rock, or now and then of sandstone. The rock is relatively impermeable and small pools of water concentrate in crevices. These pools can last a long time after the causative rains and though stagnant and saline, they are very important to wildlife.

should have lasted so long, and the only way that I can account for it is by the supposition that it is fed by some spring deep down in the sand.

Having filled both ourselves and our water-bottles as full as possible, in far better spirits we started off again with the moon. That night we covered nearly five-and-twenty miles, but, needless to say, found no more water, though we were lucky enough on the following day to get a little shade behind some ant-heaps. When the sun rose and, for awhile, cleared away the mysterious mists, Suliman's Berg and the two majestic breasts, now only about twenty miles off, seemed to be towering right above us, and looked grander than ever. At the approach of evening we started on again, and, to cut a long story short, by daylight next morning found ourselves upon the lowest slopes of Sheba's left breast, for which we had been steadily steering. By this time our water was again exhausted and we were suffering severely from thirst, nor indeed could we see any chance of relieving it till we reached the snow line far far above us. After resting an hour or two, driven to it by our torturing thirst, we went on again, toiling painfully in the burning heat up the lava slopes, for we found that the huge base of the mountain was composed entirely of lava beds belched out in some far past age.

By eleven o'clock we were utterly exhausted, and were, generally speaking, in a very bad way indeed. The lava clinker, over which we had to make our way, though comparatively smooth compared with some clinker I have heard of, such as that on the Island of Ascension for instance, was yet rough enough to make our feet very sore, and this, together with our other miseries, had pretty well finished us. A few hundred yards above us were some large lumps of lava, and towards these we made with the intention of lying down beneath their shade. We reached them, and to our surprise, so far as we had a capacity for surprise left in us, on a little plateau or ridge close by we saw that the lava was covered with a dense green growth. Evidently soil formed from decomposed lava had rested there, and in due course had become the receptacle of seeds deposited by birds. But we did not take much further interest in the green growth, for one cannot live on grass like

Nebuchadnezzar.[1] That requires a special dispensation of Providence and peculiar digestive organs. So we sat down under the rocks and groaned, and I for one heartily wished that we had never started on this fool's errand. As we were sitting there I saw Umbopa get up and hobble off towards the patch of green, and a few minutes afterwards, to my great astonishment, I perceived that usually uncommonly dignified individual dancing and shouting like a maniac, and waving something green. Off we all scrambled towards him as fast as our wearied limbs would carry us, hoping that he had found water.

"What is it, Umbopa, son of a fool?" I shouted in Zulu.

"It is food and water, Macumazahn," and again he waved the green thing.

Then I saw what he had got. It was a melon. We had hit upon a patch of wild melons, thousands of them, and dead ripe.

"Melons!" I yelled to Good, who was next me; and in another second he had his false teeth fixed in one.

I think we ate about six each before we had done, and, poor fruit as they were, I doubt if I ever thought anything nicer.

But melons are not very satisfying, and when we had satisfied our thirst with their pulpy substance, and set a stock to cool by the simple process of cutting them in two and setting them end on in the hot sun to get cold by evaporation, we began to feel exceedingly hungry. We had still some biltong left, but our stomachs turned from biltong, and besides we had to be very sparing of it, for we could not say when we should get more food. Just at this moment a lucky thing happened. Looking towards the desert I saw a flock of about ten large birds flying straight towards us.

"Skit, Baas, skit!" (shoot, master, shoot), whispered the Hottentot, throwing himself on his face, an example which we all followed.

Then I saw that the birds were a flock of pauw (bustards), and that they would pass within fifty yards of my head. Taking one of the repeating Winchesters I waited till they were nearly over us, and then jumped on to my feet. On seeing me the pauw bunched

<hr>

1   Nebuchadnezzar] an Assyrian king (604-561 BC) who rebuilt Babylon and "was driven from men, and did eat grass as oxen" (Daniel 4:29-33), an allusion to his loss of interest in public affairs.

up together, as I expected they would, and I fired two shots straight into the thick of them, and, as luck would have it, brought one down, a fine fellow, that weighed about twenty pounds. In half an hour we had a fire made of dry melon stalks, and he was toasting over it, and we had such a feed as we had not had for a week. We ate that pauw; nothing was left of him but his bones and his beak, and felt not a little the better afterwards.

That night we again went on with the moon, carrying as many melons as we could with us. As we got higher up we found the air get cooler and cooler, which was a great relief to us, and at dawn, so far as we could judge, were not more than about a dozen miles from the snow line. Here we found more melons, so had no longer any anxiety about water, for we knew that we should soon get plenty of snow. But the ascent had now become very precipitous, and we made but slow progress, not more than a mile an hour. Also that night we ate our last morsel of biltong. As yet, with the exception of the pauw, we had seen no living thing on the mountain, nor had we come across a single spring or stream of water, which struck us as very odd, considering all the snow above us, which must, we thought, melt sometimes. But as we afterwards discovered, owing to some cause,[1] which it is quite beyond my power to explain, all the streams flowed down upon the north side of the mountains.

We now began to grow very anxious about food. We had escaped death by thirst, but it seemed probable that it was only to die of hunger. The events of the next three miserable days are best described by copying the entries made at the time in my note-book.

21st May. —Started 11 a.m., finding the atmosphere quite cold enough to travel by day, carrying some watermelons with us. Struggled on all day, but saw no more melons, having, evidently, passed out of their district. Saw no game of any sort. Halted for the night at sundown, having had no food for many hours. Suffered much during the night from cold.

22nd. —Started at sunrise again, feeling very faint and weak. Only made five miles all day; found some patches of snow, of

---

1 some cause] the high mountain range, intercepting the moist prevailing winds, creates an imbalance of precipitation.

which we ate, but nothing else. Camped at night under the edge of a great plateau. Cold bitter. Drank a little brandy each, and huddled ourselves together, each wrapped up in our blanket to keep ourselves alive. Are now suffering frightfully from starvation and weariness. Thought that Ventvögel would have died during the night.

23rd. — Struggled forward once more as soon as the sun was well up, and had thawed our limbs a little. We are now in a dreadful plight, and I fear that unless we get food this will be our last day's journey. But little brandy left. Good, Sir Henry, and Umbopa bear up wonderfully, but Ventvögel is in a very bad way. Like most Hottentots, he cannot stand cold. Pangs of hunger not so bad, but have a sort of numb feeling about the stomach. Others say the same. We are now on a level with the precipitous chain, or wall of lava, connecting the two breasts, and the view is glorious. Behind us the great glowing desert rolls away to the horizon, and before us lies mile upon mile of smooth hard snow almost level, but swelling gently upwards, out of the centre of which the nipple of the mountain, which appears to be some miles in circumference, rises about four thousand feet into the sky. Not a living thing is to be seen. God help us, I fear our time has come.

And now I will drop the journal, partly because it is not very interesting reading, and partly because what follows requires perhaps rather more accurate telling.

All that day (the 23rd May) we struggled slowly on up the incline of snow, lying down from time to time to rest. A strange, gaunt crew we must have looked, as, laden as we were, we dragged our weary feet over the dazzling plain, glaring round us with hungry eyes. Not that there was much use in glaring, for there was nothing to eat. We did not do more than seven miles that day. Just before sunset we found ourselves right under the nipple of Sheba's left breast, which towered up thousands of feet into the air above us, a vast, smooth hillock of frozen snow. Bad as we felt we could not but appreciate the wonderful scene, made even more wonderful by the flying rays of light from the setting sun, which here and there stained the snow blood red, and crowned the towering mass above us with a diadem of glory.

"I say," gasped Good, presently, "we ought to be somewhere near the cave the old gentleman wrote about."

"Yes," said I, "if there is a cave."

"Come, Quatermain," groaned Sir Henry, "don't talk like that; I have every faith in the Dom; remember the water. We shall find the place soon."

"If we don't find it before dark we are dead men, that is all about it," was my consolatory reply.

For the next ten minutes we trudged on in silence, when suddenly Umbopa, who was marching along beside me, wrapped up in his blanket, and with a leather belt strapped so tight round his stomach to "make his hunger small," as he said, that his waist looked like a girl's, caught me by the arm.

"Look!" he said, pointing towards the springing slope of the nipple.

I followed his glance, and perceived some two hundred yards from us what appeared to be a hole in the snow.

"It is the cave," said Umbopa.

We made the best of our way to the spot, and found sure enough that the hole was the mouth of a cave, no doubt the same as that of which da Silvestra wrote. We were none too soon, for just as we reached shelter the sun went down with startling rapidity, leaving the whole place nearly dark. In these latitudes there is but little twilight. We crept into the cave, which did not appear to be very big, and huddling ourselves together for warmth, swallowed what remained of our brandy — barely a mouthful each — and tried to forget our miseries in sleep. But this the cold was too intense to allow us to do. I am convinced that at that great altitude the thermometer cannot have been less than fourteen or fifteen degrees below freezing point. What this meant to us, enervated as we were by hardship, want of food, and the great heat of the desert, my reader can imagine better than I can describe. Suffice it to say that it was something as near death from exposure as I have ever felt. There we sat hour after hour through the bitter night, feeling the frost wander round and nip us now in the finger, now in the foot, and now in the face. In vain did we huddle up closer and closer; there was no warmth in our miserable starved carcasses. Sometimes one of us would drop into an uneasy slumber for a few minutes, but we could not sleep long, and perhaps it was fortunate, for I doubt if we should ever have woke again. I believe it was only by force of will that we kept ourselves alive at all.

Not very long before dawn I heard the Hottentot Ventvögel, whose teeth had been chattering all night like castanets, give a deep sigh, and then his teeth stopped chattering. I did not think anything of it at the time, concluding that he had gone to sleep. His back was resting against mine, and it seemed to grow colder and colder, till at last it was like ice.

At length the air began to grow grey with light, then swift golden arrows came flashing across the snow, and at last the glorious sun peeped up above the lava wall and looked in upon our half-frozen forms and upon Ventvögel, sitting there amongst us *stone dead*. No wonder his back had felt cold, poor fellow. He had died when I heard him sigh, and was now almost frozen stiff. Shocked beyond measure we dragged ourselves from the corpse (strange the horror we all have of the companionship of a dead body), and left it still sitting there, with its arms clasped round its knees.

By this time the sunlight was pouring its cold rays (for here they were cold) straight in at the mouth of the cave. Suddenly I heard an exclamation of fear from some one, and turned my head down the cave.

And this was what I saw. Sitting, at the end of it, for it was not more than twenty feet long, was another form, of which the head rested on the chest and the long arms hung down. I stared at it, and saw that it too was a *dead man*, and what was more, a white man.

The others saw it too, and the sight proved too much for our shattered nerves. One and all we scrambled out of the cave as fast as our half-frozen limbs would allow.

CHAPTER VII.

SOLOMON'S ROAD.

Outside the cave we halted, feeling rather foolish.

"I am going back," said Sir Henry.

"Why?" asked Good.

"Because it has struck me that — what we saw — may be my brother."

This was a new idea, and we re-entered the cave to put it to the proof. After the bright light outside, our eyes, weak as they were with staring at the snow, could not for awhile pierce the gloom of the cave. Presently however we grew accustomed to the semi-darkness, and advanced on the dead form.

Sir Henry knelt down and peered into its face.

"Thank God," he said, with a sigh of relief, "it is not my brother."

Then I went and looked. The corpse was that of a tall man in middle life with aquiline features, grizzled hair, and a long black moustache. The skin was perfectly yellow, and stretched tightly over the bones. Its clothing, with the exception of what seemed to be the remains of a woollen pair of hose, had been removed, leaving the skeleton-like frame naked. Round the neck hung a yellow ivory crucifix. The corpse was frozen perfectly stiff.

"Who on earth can it be?" said I.

"Can't you guess?" asked Good.

I shook my head.

"Why, the old Dom, José da Silvestra, of course—who else?"

"Impossible," I gasped, "he died three hundred years ago."

"And what is there to prevent his lasting for three thousand years in this atmosphere I should like to know?" asked Good. "If only the air is cold enough flesh and blood will keep as fresh as New Zealand mutton for ever, and Heaven knows it is cold enough here. The sun never gets in here; no animal comes here to tear or destroy. No doubt his slave, of whom he speaks on the map, took off his clothes and left him. He could not have buried him alone. Look here," he went on, stooping down and picking up a queer shaped bone scraped at the end into a sharp point, "here is the 'cleft-bone' that he used to draw the map with."

We gazed astonished for a moment, forgetting our own miseries in this extraordinary and, as it seemed to us, semi-miraculous sight.

"Ay," said Sir Henry, "and here is where he got his ink from," and he pointed to a small wound on the dead man's left arm. "Did ever man see such a thing before?"

There was no longer any doubt about the matter, which I confess for my own part perfectly appalled me. There he sat, the dead man, whose directions, written some ten generations ago, had led us to this spot. There in my own hand was the rude pen with which he had written them, and there round his neck was the crucifix his dying lips had kissed. Gazing at him my imagination could reconstruct the whole scene, the traveller dying of cold and starvation, and yet striving to convey the great secret he had discovered to the world:—the awful loneliness of his death, of which the evidence sat before us. It even seemed to me that I could trace in his strongly marked features a likeness to those of my poor friend Silvestre his descendant, who had died twenty years ago in my arms, but perhaps that was fancy. At any rate, there he sat, a sad memento of the fate that so often overtakes those who would penetrate into the unknown; and there probably he will still sit, crowned with the dread majesty of death, for centuries yet unborn, to startle the eyes of wanderers like ourselves, if any such should ever come again to invade his loneliness. The thing overpowered us, already nearly done to death as we were with cold and hunger.

"Let us go," said Sir Henry, in a low voice; "stay, we will give him a companion," and lifting up the dead body of the Hottentot Ventvögel, he placed it near that of the old Dom. Then he stooped down, and with a jerk broke the rotten string of the crucifix round his neck, for his fingers were too cold to attempt to unfasten it. I believe that he still has it. I took the pen, and it is before me as I write—sometimes I sign my name with it.

Then leaving those two, the proud white man of a past age, and the poor Hottentot, to keep their eternal vigil in the midst of the eternal snows, we crept out of the cave into the welcome sunshine and resumed our path, wondering in our hearts how many hours it would be before we were even as they are.

When we had gone about half a mile we came to the edge of the plateau, for the nipple of the mountain did not rise out of its exact centre, though from the desert side it seemed to do so. What lay below us we could not see, for the landscape was wreathed in billows of morning mist. Presently, however, the higher layers of mist cleared a little, and revealed some five hundred yards beneath us, at the end of a long slope of snow, a patch of green grass, through which a stream was running. Nor was this all. By the stream, basking in the morning sun, stood and lay a group of from ten to fifteen *large antelopes*—at that distance we could not see what they were.

The sight filled us with an unreasoning joy. There was food in plenty if only we could get it. But the question was how to get it. The beasts were fully six hundred yards off, a very long shot, and one not to be depended on when one's life hung on the results.

Rapidly we discussed the advisability of trying to stalk the game, but finally reluctantly dismissed it. To begin with the wind was not favourable, and further, we should be certain to be perceived, however careful we were, against the blinding background of snow, which we should be obliged to traverse.

"Well, we must have a try from where we are," said Sir Henry. "Which shall it be, Quatermain, the repeating rifles or the expresses?"

Here again was a question. The Winchester repeaters—of which we had two, Umbopa carrying poor Ventvögel's as well as his own—were sighted up to a thousand yards, whereas the expresses were only sighted to three hundred and fifty, beyond which distance shooting with them was more or less guess work. On the other land, if they did hit, the express bullets being expanding, were much more likely to bring the game down. It was a knotty point, but I made up my mind that we must risk it and use the expresses.

"Let each of us take the buck opposite to him. Aim well at the point of the shoulder, and high up," said I; "and Umbopa do you give the word, so that we may all fire together."

Then came a pause, each man aiming his level best, as indeed one is likely to do when one knows that life itself depends upon the shot.

"Fire!" said Umbopa, in Zulu, and at almost the same instant the three rifles rang out loudly; three clouds of smoke hung for a moment before us, and a hundred echoes went flying away over the silent snow. Presently the smoke cleared, and revealed—oh, joy!—a great buck lying on its back and kicking furiously in its death agony. We gave a yell of triumph—we were saved, we should not starve. Weak as we were, we rushed down the intervening slope of snow, and in ten minutes from the time of firing the animal's heart and liver were lying smoking before us. But now a new difficulty arose, we had no fuel, and therefore could make no fire to cook them at. We gazed at each other in dismay.

"Starving men must not be fanciful," said Good; "we must eat raw meat."

There was no other way out of the dilemma, and our gnawing hunger made the proposition less distasteful than it would otherwise have been. So we took the heart and liver and buried them for a few minutes in a patch of snow to cool them. Then we washed them in the ice-cold water of the stream, and lastly ate them greedily. It sounds horrible enough, but honestly, I never tasted anything so good as that raw meat. In a quarter of an hour we were changed men. Our life and our vigour came back to us, our feeble pulses grew strong again, and the blood went coursing through our veins. But mindful of the results of over-feeding on starving stomachs, we were careful not to eat too much, stopping whilst we were still hungry.

"Thank God!" said Sir Henry; "that brute has saved our lives. What is it, Quatermain?"

I rose and went to look at the antelope, for I was not certain. It was about the size of a donkey, with large curved horns. I had never seen one like it before, the species was new to me. It was brown, with faint red stripes, and a thick coat. I afterwards discovered that the natives of that wonderful country called the species "Inco." It was very rare, and only found at a great altitude where no other game would live. The animal was fairly shot high up in the shoulder, though whose bullet it was that brought it down we could not, of course, discover. I believe that Good, mindful of his marvellous shot at the giraffe, secretly set it down to his own prowess, and we did not contradict him.

We had been so busy satisfying our starving stomachs that we had hitherto not found time to look about us. But now, having set Umbopa to cut off as much of the best meat as we were likely to be able to carry, we began to inspect our surroundings. The mist had now cleared away, for it was eight o'clock, and the sun had sucked it up, so we were able to take in all the country before us at a glance. I know not how to describe the glorious panorama which unfolded itself to our enraptured gaze. I have never seen anything like it before, nor shall, I suppose, again.

Behind and over us towered Sheba's snowy breasts, and below, some five thousand feet beneath where we stood, lay league on league of the most lovely champaign country. Here were dense patches of lofty forest, there a great river wound its silvery way. To the left stretched a vast expanse of rich undulating veldt or grass land, on which we could just make out countless herds of game or cattle, at that distance we could not tell which. This expanse appeared to be ringed in by a wall of distant mountains. To the right the country was more or less mountainous, that is, solitary hills stood up from its level, with stretches of cultivated lands between, amongst which we could distinctly see groups of dome-shaped huts. The landscape lay before us like a map, in which rivers flashed like silver snakes, and Alp-like peaks crowned with wildly twisted snow wreaths rose in solemn grandeur, whilst over all was the glad sunlight and the wide breath of Nature's happy life.

Two curious things struck us as we gazed. First, that the country before us must lie at least five thousand feet higher than the desert we had crossed, and secondly, that all the rivers flowed from south to north. As we had painful reason to know, there was no water at all on the southern side of the vast range on which we stood, but on the northern side were many streams, most of which appeared to unite with the great river we could trace winding away farther than we could follow it.

We sat down for a while and gazed in silence at this wonderful view. Presently Sir Henry spoke.

"Isn't there something on the map about Solomon's Great Road?" he said.

I nodded, my eyes still looking out over the far country.

"Well, look; there it is!" and he pointed a little to our right.

Good and I looked accordingly, and there, winding away towards the plain, was what appeared to be a wide turnpike road. We had not seen it at first because it, on reaching the plain, turned behind some broken country. We did not say anything, at least not much; we were beginning to lose the sense of wonder. Somehow it did not seem particularly unnatural that we should find a sort of Roman road in this strange land. We accepted the fact, that was all.

"Well," said Good, "it must be quite near us if we cut off to the right. Hadn't we better be making a start?"

This was sound advice, and so soon as we had washed our faces and hands in the stream, we acted on it. For a mile or so we made our way over boulders and across patches of snow, till suddenly, on reaching the top of the little rise, there lay the road at our feet. It was a splendid road cut out of the solid rock, at least fifty feet wide, and apparently well kept; but the odd thing about it was that it seemed to begin there. We walked down and stood on it, but one single hundred paces behind us, in the direction of Sheba's breasts, it vanished, the whole surface of the mountain being strewn with boulders interspersed with patches of snow.

"What do you make of that, Quatermain?" asked Sir Henry.

I shook my head, I could make nothing of it.

"I have it!" said Good; "the road no doubt ran right over the range and across the desert the other side, but the sand of the desert has covered it up, and above us it has been obliterated by some volcanic eruption of molten lava."

This seemed a good suggestion; at any rate, we accepted it, and proceeded down the mountain. It was a very different business travelling along down hill on that magnificent pathway with full stomachs to what it had been travelling up hill over the snow quite starved and almost frozen. Indeed, had it not been for melancholy recollections of poor Ventvögel's sad fate, and of that grim cave where he kept company with the old Don, we should have been positively cheerful, notwithstanding the sense of unknown dangers before us. Every mile we walked the atmosphere grew softer and balmier, and the country before us shone with a yet more luminous beauty. As for the road itself, I never saw such an engineering work, though Sir Henry said that the great road over the St. Gothard[1] in Switzerland was very like it. No difficulty had been too great for the Old World engineer who designed it. At one place we came to a great ravine three hundred feet broad and at least a hundred deep. This vast gulf was actually filled in, apparently with huge blocks of dressed stone, with arches pierced at the bottom for a water-way, over which the road went sublimely on. At another place it was cut in zigzags out of the side of a precipice five hundred feet deep, and in a third it tunnelled right through the base of an intervening ridge a space of thirty yards or more.

Here we noticed that the sides of the tunnel were covered with

---

1   road over the St. Gothard] a carriage road constructed in the early nineteenth century over a 7,000 foot Pass.

quaint sculptures mostly of mailed figures driving in chariots. One, which was exceedingly beautiful, represented a whole battle scene with a convoy of captives being marched off in the distance.

"Well," said Sir Henry, after inspecting this ancient work of art, "it is very well to call this Solomon's Road, but my humble opinion is that the Egyptians have been here before Solomon's people ever set a foot on it. If that isn't Egyptian handiwork, all I have to say is it is very like it."

By midday we had advanced sufficiently far down the mountain to reach the region where wood was to be met with. First we came to scattered bushes which grew more and more frequent, till at last we found the road winding through a vast grove of silver trees similar to those which are to be seen on the slopes of Table Mountain at Cape Town.[1] I had never before met with them in all my wanderings, except at the Cape, and their appearance here astonished me greatly.

"Ah!" said Good, surveying these shining-leaved trees with evident enthusiasm, "here is lots of wood, let us stop and cook some dinner; I have about digested that raw meat."

Nobody objected to this, so leaving the road we made our way to a stream which was babbling away not far off, and soon had a goodly fire of dry boughs blazing. Cutting off some substantial hunks from the flesh of the inco which we had brought with us, we proceeded to toast them on the end of sharp sticks, as one sees the Kafirs do, and ate them with relish. After filling ourselves, we lit our pipes and gave ourselves up to enjoyment, which, compared to the hardships we had recently undergone, seemed almost heavenly.

The brook, of which the banks were clothed with dense masses of a gigantic species of maidenhair fern interspersed with feathery tufts of wild asparagus, babbled away merrily at our side, the soft air murmured through the leaves of the silver trees, doves cooed around, and bright-winged birds flashed like living gems from bough to bough. It was like Paradise.

---

1 silver trees ... Cape Town] Table Mountain, so called because of its level summit, is visible as far as 200 kilometers out to sea and provides Cape Town with a dramatic backdrop; native to its slopes are the shimmering silver trees (*Leucadendron argenteum*, family Proteales), its leaves covered with fine silky hairs that inhibit water loss; not the same as the Transvaal silverleaf with silver-grey, silky leaves.

The magic of the place, combined with the overwhelming sense of dangers left behind, and of the promised land reached at last, seemed to charm us into silence. Sir Henry and Umbopa sat conversing in a mixture of broken English and Kitchin Zulu in a low voice, but earnestly enough, and I lay, with my eyes half shut, upon that fragrant bed of fern and watched them. Presently I missed Good, and looked to see what had become of him. As I did so I observed him sitting by the bank of the stream, in which he had been bathing. He had nothing on but his flannel shirt, and his natural habits of extreme neatness having reasserted themselves, was actively employed in making a most elaborate toilet. He had washed his guttapercha collar, thoroughly shaken out his trousers, coat, and waistcoat, and was now folding them up neatly, till he was ready to put them on, shaking his head sadly as he did so over the numerous rents and tears in them, which had naturally resulted from our frightful journey. Then he took his boots, scrubbed them with a handful of fern, and finally rubbed them over with a piece of fat, which he had carefully saved from the inco meat, till they looked, comparatively speaking, respectable. Having inspected them judiciously through his eye-glass, he put them on and began a fresh operation. From a little bag he carried he produced a pocket comb in which was fixed a tiny looking-glass, and in this he surveyed himself. Apparently he was not satisfied, for he proceeded to do his hair with great care. Then came a pause whilst he again contemplated the effect; still it was not satisfactory. He felt his chin, on which was now the accumulated scrub of a ten days' beard. "Surely," thought I, "he is not going to try and shave." But so it was. Taking the piece of fat with which he had greased his boots he washed it carefully in the stream. Then diving again into the bag he brought out a little pocket razor with a guard to it, such as are sold to people afraid of cutting themselves, or to those about to undertake a sea voyage. Then he vigorously scrubbed his face and chin with the fat and began. But it was evidently a painful process, for he groaned very much over it, and I was convulsed with inward laughter as I watched him struggling with that stubbly beard. It seemed so very odd that a man should take the trouble to shave himself with a piece of fat in such a place and under such circumstances. At last he succeeded in getting the worst of the scrub off the right side of his face and chin, when suddenly I, who was watching, became aware of a flash of light that passed just by his head.

Good sprang up with a profane exclamation (if it had not been a safety razor he would certainly have cut his throat), and so did I, without the exclamation, and this was what I saw. Standing there, not more than twenty paces from where I was, and ten from Good, were a group of men. They were very tall and copper-coloured, and some of them wore great plumes of black feathers and short cloaks of leopard skins; this was all I noticed at the moment. In front of them stood a youth of about seventeen, his hand still raised and his body bent forward in the attitude of a Grecian statue of a spear thrower. Evidently the flash of light had been a weapon, and he had thrown it.

As I looked an old soldier-like looking man stepped forward out of the group, and catching the youth by the arm said something to him. Then they advanced upon us.

Sir Henry, Good, and Umbopa had by this time seized their rifles and lifted them threateningly. The party of natives still came on. It struck me that they could not know what rifles were, or they would not have treated them with such contempt.

"Put down your guns!" I hallooed to the others, seeing that our only chance of safety lay in conciliation. They obeyed, and walking to the front I addressed the elderly man who had checked the youth.

"Greeting," I said, in Zulu, not knowing what language to use. To my surprise I was understood.

"Greeting," answered the man, not, indeed, in the same tongue, but in a dialect so closely allied to it, that neither Umbopa or myself had any difficulty in understanding it. Indeed, as we afterwards found out, the language spoken by this people was an old-fashioned form of the Zulu tongue, bearing about the same relationship to it that the English of Chaucer does to the English of the nineteenth century.

"Whence come ye?" he went on, "what are ye? and why are the faces of three of ye white, and the face of the fourth as the face of our mother's sons?" and he pointed to Umbopa. I looked at Umbopa as he said it, and it flashed across me that he was right.

Umbopa was like the faces of the men before me, so was his great form. But I had not time to reflect on this coincidence.

"We are strangers, and come in peace," I answered, speaking very slow, so that he might understand me, "and this man is our servant."

"Ye lie," he answered, "no strangers can cross the mountains where all things die. But what do your lies matter, if ye are strangers then ye must die, for no strangers may live in the land of the Kukuanas. It is the king's law. Prepare then to die, O strangers!"

I was slightly staggered at this, more especially as I saw the hands of some of the party of men steal down to their sides, where hung on each what looked to me like a large and heavy knife.

"What does that beggar say?" asked Good.

"He says we are going to be scragged," I answered grimly.

"Oh, Lord," groaned Good; and, as was his way when perplexed, put his hand to his false teeth, dragging the top set down and allowing them to fly back to his jaw with a snap. It was a most fortunate move, for next second the dignified crowd of Kukuanas gave a simultaneous yell of horror, and bolted back some yards.

"What's up?" said I.

"It's his teeth," whispered Sir Henry, excitedly. "He moved them. Take them out, Good, take them out!"

He obeyed, slipping the set into the sleeve of his flannel shirt.

In another second curiosity had overcome fear, and the men advanced slowly. Apparently they had now forgotten their amiable intentions of doing for us.

"How is it, O strangers," asked the old man solemnly, "that the teeth of the man (pointing to Good, who had nothing on but a flannel shirt, and had only half finished his shaving) whose body is clothed, and whose legs are bare, who grows hair on one side of his sickly face and not on the other, and who has one shining and transparent eye, and teeth that move of themselves, coming away from the jaws and returning of their own will?"

"Open your mouth," I said to Good, who promptly curled up

his lips and grinned at the old gentleman like an angry dog, revealing to their astonished gaze two thin red lines of gum as utterly innocent of ivories as a new-born elephant. His audience gasped.

"Where are his teeth?" they shouted; "with our eyes we saw them."

Turning his head slowly and with a gesture of ineffable contempt, Good swept his hand across his mouth. Then he grinned again, and lo, there were two rows of lovely teeth.

The young man who had flung the knife threw himself down on the grass and gave vent to a prolonged howl of terror; and as for the old gentleman his knees knocked together with fear.

"I see that ye are spirits," he said, falteringly; "did ever man born of woman have hair on one side of his face and not on the other, or a round and transparent eye, or teeth which moved and melted away and grew again? Pardon us, O my lords."

Here was luck indeed, and, needless to say, I jumped at the chance.

"It is granted," I said, with an imperial smile. "Nay, ye shall know the truth. We come from another world, though we are men such as ye; we come," I went on, "from the biggest star that shines at night."

"Oh! oh!" groaned the chorus of astonished aborigines.

"Yes," I went on, "we do, indeed;" and I again smiled benignly as I uttered that amazing lie. "We come to stay with you a little while, and bless you by our sojourn. Ye will see, O friends, that I have prepared myself by learning your language."

"It is so, it is so," said the chorus.

"Only, my lord," put in the old gentleman, "thou hast learnt it very badly."

I cast an indignant glance at him, and he quailed.

"Now, friends," I continued, "ye might think that after so long a journey we should find it in our hearts to avenge such a reception, mayhap to strike cold in death the impious hand that—that, in short—threw a knife at the head of him whose teeth come and go."

"Spare him, my lords," said the old man in supplication; "he is the king's son, and I am his uncle. If anything befalls him his blood will be required at my hands."

"Yes, that is certainly so," put in the young man with great emphasis.

"You may perhaps doubt our power to avenge," I went on, heedless of this by-play. "Stay, I will show you. Here, you dog and slave (addressing Umbopa in a savage tone), give me the magic tube that speaks;" and I tipped a wink towards my express rifle.

Umbopa rose to the occasion, and with something as nearly resembling a grin as I have ever seen on his dignified face, handed me the rifle.

"It is here, O lord of lords," he said, with a deep obeisance.

Now, just before I asked for the rifle I had perceived a little klipspringer antelope standing on a mass of rock about seventy yards away, and determined to risk a shot at it.

"Ye see that buck," I said, pointing the animal out to the party before me. "Tell me, is it possible for man, born of woman, to kill it from here with a noise?"

"It is not possible, my lord," answered the old man.

"Yet shall I kill it," said I, quietly.

The old man smiled. "That my lord cannot do," he said.

I raised the rifle, and covered the buck. It was a small animal, and one which one might well be excused for missing, but I knew that it would not do to miss.

I drew a deep breath, and slowly pressed on the trigger. The buck stood still as stone.

"Bang! thud!" The buck sprang into the air and fell on the rock dead as a door nail.

A groan of terror burst from the group before us.

"If ye want meat," I remarked coolly, "go fetch that buck."

The old man made a sign, and one of his followers departed, and presently returned bearing the klipspringer. I noticed, with satisfaction, that I had hit it fairly behind the shoulder. They gathered round the poor creature's body, gazing at the bullet hole in consternation.

"Ye see," I said, "I do not speak empty words."

There was no answer.

"If ye yet doubt our power," I went on, "let one of ye go stand upon that rock that I may make him as this buck."

None of them seemed at all inclined to take the hint, till at last the king's son spoke.

"It is well said. Do thou, my uncle, go stand upon the rock. It is but a buck that the magic has killed. Surely it cannot kill a man."

The old gentleman did not take the suggestion in good part. Indeed, he seemed hurt.

"No! no!" he ejaculated, hastily, "my old eyes have seen enough. These are wizards, indeed. Let us bring them to the king. Yet if any should wish a further proof, let *him* stand upon the rock, that the magic tube may speak with him."

There was a most general and hasty expression of dissent.

"Let not good magic be wasted on our poor bodies," said one, "we are satisfied. All the witchcraft of our people cannot show the like of this."

"It is so," remarked the old gentleman, in a tone of intense relief; "without any doubt it is so. Listen, children of the stars, children of the shining eye and the movable teeth, who roar out in thunder and slay from afar. I am Infadoos, son of Kafa, once King of the Kukuana people. This youth is Scragga."

"He nearly scragged me," murmured Good.

"Scragga, son of Twala, the great king—Twala, husband of a thousand wives, chief and lord paramount of the Kukuanas, keeper of the great road, terror of his enemies, student of the Black Arts,[1] leader of an hundred thousand warriors, Twala the One-eyed, the Black, the Terrible."

"So," said I, superciliously, "lead us then to Twala. We do not talk with low people and underlings."

"It is well, my lords, we will lead you, but the way is long. We are hunting three days' journey from the place of the king. But let my lords have patience, and we will lead them."

"It is well," I said, carelessly, "all time is before us, for we do not die. We are ready, lead on. But Infadoos, and thou Scragga, beware! Play us no tricks, make for us no snares, for before your brains of mud have thought of them, we shall know them and avenge them. The light from the transparent eye of him with the bare legs and the half-haired face (Good) shall destroy you, and go through your land: his vanishing teeth shall fix themselves fast in

---

1 Black Arts] practised by wizards who claim to have deaings with the devil and to call up the dead.

you and eat you up, you and your wives and children; the magic tubes shall talk with you loudly, and make you as sieves. Beware!"

This magnificent address did not fail of its effect; indeed, it was hardly needed, so deeply were our friends already impressed with our powers.

The old man made a deep obeisance, and murmured the word "Koom, Koom," which I afterwards discovered was their royal salute, corresponding to the Bayéte of the Zulus, and turning, addressed his followers. These at once proceeded to lay hold of all our goods and chattels, in order to bear them for us, excepting only the guns, which they would on no account touch. They even seized Good's clothes, which were, as the reader may remember, neatly folded up beside him.

He at once made a dive for them, and a loud altercation ensued.

"Let not my lord of the transparent eye and the melting teeth touch them," said the old man. "Surely his slaves shall carry the things."

"But I want to put 'em on!" roared Good, in nervous English.

Umbopa translated.

"Nay, my lord," put in Infadoos, "would my lord cover up his beautiful white legs (although he was so dark Good had a singularly white skin) from the eyes of his servants? Have we offended my lord that he should do such a thing?"

Here I nearly exploded with laughing; and meanwhile, one of the men started on with the garments.

"Damn it!" roared Good, "that black villain has got my trousers."

"Look here, Good," said Sir Henry, "you have appeared in this country in a certain character, and you must live up to it. It will never do for you to put on trousers again. Henceforth you must live in a flannel shirt, a pair of boots, and an eye-glass."

"Yes," I said, "and with whiskers on one side of your face and not on the other. If you change any of these things they will think that we are impostors. I am very sorry for you, but, seriously, you must do it. If once they begin to suspect us, our lives will not he worth a brass farthing."

"Do you really think so?" said Good, gloomily.

"I do, indeed. Your 'beautiful white legs' and your eye-glass are now *the* feature of our party, and as Sir Henry says, you must live up to them. Be thankful that you have got your boots on, and that the air is warm."

Good sighed, and said no more, but it took him a fortnight to get accustomed to his attire.

CHAPTER VIII.

WE ENTER KUKUANALAND.

ALL that afternoon we travelled on along the magnificent road-way, which headed steadily in a north-westerly direction. Infadoos and Scragga walked with us, but their followers marched about one hundred paces ahead.

"Infadoos," I said at length, "who made this road?"

"It was made, my lord, of old time, none know how or when, not even the wise woman Gagool, who has lived for generations. We are not old enough to remember its making. None can make such roads now, but the king lets no grass grow upon it."

"And whose are the writings on the walls of the caves through which we have passed on the road?" I asked, referring to the Egyptian-like sculptures we had seen.

"My lord, the hands that made the road wrote the wonderful writings. We know not who wrote them."

"When did the Kukuana race come into this country?"

"My lord, the race came down here like the breath of a storm ten thousand thousand moons ago, from the great lands which lie there beyond," and he pointed to the north. "They could travel no farther, so say the old voices of our fathers that have come down to us, the children, and so says Gagool, the wise woman, the smeller out of witches, because of the great mountains which ring in the land," and he pointed to the snow-clad peaks. "The country, too, was good, so they settled here and grew strong and pow-erful, and now our numbers are like the sea sand, and when Twala the king calls up his regiments their plumes cover the plain as far as the eye of man can reach."

"And if the land is walled in with mountains, who is there for the regiments to fight with?"

"Nay, my lord, the country is open there," and again he pointed towards the north, "and now and again warriors sweep down upon us in clouds from a land we know not, and we slay them. It is the third part of the life of a man since there was a war. Many thousands died in it, but we destroyed those who came to eat us up. So since then there has been no war."

"Your warriors must grow weary of resting on their spears."

"My lord, there was one war, just after we destroyed the people that came down upon us, but it was a civil war, dog eat dog."

"How was that?"

"My lord, the king, my half-brother, had a brother born at the same birth, and of the same woman. It is not our custom, my lord, to let twins live, the weakest must always die. But the mother of the king hid away the weakest child, which was born the last, for her heart yearned over it, and the child is Twala the king. I am his younger brother born of another wife."

"Well?"

"My lord, Kafa, our father, died when we came to manhood, and my brother Imotu was made king in his place, and for a space reigned and had a son by his favourite wife. When the babe was three years old, just after the great war, during which no man could sow or reap, a famine came upon the land, and the people murmured because of the famine, and looked round like a starved lion for something to rend. Then it was that Gagool, the wise and terrible woman, who does not die, proclaimed to the people, saying, 'The king Imotu is no king.' And at the time Imotu was sick with a wound, and lay in his hut not able to move.

"Then Gagool went into a hut and led out Twala, my half-brother, and the twin brother of the king, whom she had hidden since he was born among the caves and rocks, and stripping the 'moocha' (waist-cloth) off his loins, showed the people of the Kukuanas the mark of the sacred snake coiled round his waist, wherewith the eldest son of the king is marked at birth, and cried out loud, 'Behold, your king whom I have saved for you even to this day!' And the people being mad with hunger, and altogether bereft of reason and the knowledge of truth, cried out, 'The king!

The king!' but I knew that it was not so, for Imotu, my brother, was the elder of the twins, and was the lawful king. And just as the tumult was at its height Imotu the king, though he was very sick, came crawling from his hut holding his wife by the hand, and followed by his little son Ignosi (the lightning).

"'What is this noise?' he asked; 'Why cry ye *The king! The king?'*

"Then Twala, his own brother, born of the same woman and in the same hour, ran to him, and taking him by the hair stabbed him through the heart with his knife. And the people being fickle, and ever ready to worship the rising sun, clapped their hands and cried, '*Twala is king!* Now we know that Twala is king!'"

"And what became of his wife and her son Ignosi? Did Twala kill them too?"

"Nay, my lord. When she saw that her lord was dead, she seized the child with a cry, and ran away. Two days afterwards she came to a kraal very hungry, and none would give her milk or food, now that her lord the king was dead, for all men hate the unfortunate. But at nightfall a little child, a girl, crept out and brought her to eat, and she blessed the child, and went on towards the mountains with her boy before the sun rose again, where she must have perished, for none have seen her since, nor the child Ignosi."

"Then if this child Ignosi had lived, he would be the true king of the Kukuana people?"

"That is so, my lord; the sacred snake is round his middle. If he lives he is the king; but alas! he is long dead."

"See, my lord," and he pointed to a vast collection of huts surrounded with a fence, which was in its turn surrounded by a great ditch, that lay on the plain beneath us. "That is the kraal where the wife of Imotu was last seen with the child Ignosi. It is there that we shall sleep to-night, if, indeed," he added doubtfully, "my lords sleep at all upon this earth."

"When we are among the Kukuanas, my good friend Infadoos, we do as the Kukuanas do," I said, majestically, and I turned round suddenly to address Good, who was tramping along sullenly behind, his mind fully occupied with unsatisfactory attempts to keep his flannel shirt from flapping up in the evening breeze, and to my astonishment butted into Umbopa, who was walking along immediately behind me, and had very evidently been listening with the greatest interest to my conversation with Infadoos. The expression on his face was most curious, and gave the idea of a man who was struggling with partial success to bring something long ago forgotten back into his mind.

All this while we had been pressing on at a good rate down towards the undulating plain beneath. The mountains we had crossed now loomed high above us, and Sheba's breasts were modestly veiled in diaphanous wreaths of mist. As we went on the country grew more and more lovely. The vegetation was luxuriant; without being tropical, the sun was bright and warm, but not burning, and a gracious breeze blew softly along the odorous slopes of the mountains. And, indeed, this new land was little less than an earthly paradise; in beauty, in natural wealth, and in climate I have never seen its like. The Transvaal is a fine country, but it is nothing to Kukuanaland.

So soon as we started, Infadoos had despatched a runner on to warn the people of the kraal, which, by the way, was in his military command, of our arrival. This man had departed at an extraordinary speed, which Infadoos had informed me he would keep up all the way, as running was an exercise much practised among his people.

The result of this message now became apparent. When we got within two miles of the kraal we could see that company after company of men was issuing from its gates and marching towards us.

Sir Henry laid his hand upon my arm, and remarked that it looked as though we were going to meet with a warm reception. Something in his tone attracted Infadoos' attention.

"Let not my lords be afraid," he said hastily, "for in my breast there dwells no guile. This regiment is one under my command, and comes out by my orders to greet you."

I nodded easily, though I was not quite easy in my mind.

About half a mile from the gates of the kraal was a long stretch of rising ground sloping gently upwards from the road, and on this the companies formed up. It was a splendid sight to see them, each company about three hundred strong, charging swiftly up the slope, with flashing spears and waving plumes, and taking their appointed place. By the time we came to the slope twelve such companies, or in all three thousand six hundred men, had passed out and taken up their positions along the road.

Presently we came to the first company, and were able to gaze in astonishment on the most magnificent set of men I have ever seen. They were all men of mature age, mostly veterans of about forty, and not one of them was under six feet in height, whilst many were six feet three or four. They wore upon their heads heavy black plumes of Sakabwla feathers,[1] like those which adorned our guides. Round their waists and also beneath the right knee were bound circlets of white ox tails, and in their left hands were round shields about twenty inches across. These shields were very curious. The framework consisted of an iron plate beaten out thin, over which was stretched milk-white ox hide. The weapons that each man bore were simple, but most effective, consisting of a short and very heavy two-edged spear with a wooden shaft, the blade being about six inches across at the widest part. These spears were not used for throwing, but like the Zulu "bangwan," or stabbing assegai, were for close quarters only, when the wound inflicted by them was terrible. In addition to these bangwans each man also carried three large and heavy knives, each knife weighing about two pounds. One knife was fixed in the ox tail girdle, and the other two at the back of the round shield. These knives, which are called "tollas" by the Kukuanas, take the place of the throwing assegai of the Zulus. A Kukuana warrior can throw them with great accuracy at a distance of fifty yards, and it is their custom on charging to hurl a volley of them at the enemy as they come to close quarters.

Each company stood like a collection of bronze statues till we were opposite to it, when at a signal given by its commanding officer who, distinguished by a leopard skin cloak, stood some paces in front, every spear was raised into the air, and from three hundred throats sprang forth with a sudden roar the royal salute of "*Koom.*" Then when we had passed the company formed up

---

1   Sakabwla feathers] (or Sakaboola, sakabula) from the Zulu *isakabuli*, the long-tailed widow bird (*Diatropura progne*), a species of weaverbird that feeds on grain and weaves nests suspended from reeds.

behind us, and followed us towards the kraal, till at last the whole regiment of the "Greys" (so called from their white shields), the crack corps of the Kukuana people, was marching behind us with a tread that shook the ground.

At length, branching off from Solomon's Great Road, we came to the wide fosse surrounding the kraal, which was at least a mile round, and fenced with a strong palisade of piles formed of the trunks of trees. At the gateway this fosse was spanned by a primitive drawbridge which was let down by the guard to allow us to pass in. The kraal was exceedingly well laid out. Through the centre ran a wide pathway intersected at right angles by other pathways so arranged as to cut the huts into square blocks, each block being the quarters of a company. The huts were dome-shaped, and built, like those of the Zulus, of a framework of wattle, beautifully thatched with grass; but, unlike the Zulu huts, they had doorways through which one could walk. Also they were much larger, and surrounded with a verandah about six feet wide, beautifully paved with powdered lime trodden hard. All along each side of the wide pathway that pierced the kraal were ranged hundreds of women, brought out by curiosity to look at us. These women are, for a native race, exceedingly handsome. They are tall and graceful, and their figures are wonderfully fine. The hair, though short, is rather curly than woolly, the features are frequently aquiline, and the lips are not unpleasantly thick as is the case in most African races. But what struck us most was their exceedingly quiet dignified air. They were as well-bred in their way as the habituées of a fashionable drawing-room, and in this respect differ from Zulu women, and their cousins the Masai who inhabit the district behind Zanzibar. Their curiosity had brought them out to see us, but they allowed no rude expressions of wonder or savage criticism to pass their lips as we trudged wearily in front of them. Not even when old Infadoos with a surreptitious motion of the hand pointed out the crowning wonder of poor Good's "beautiful white legs," did they allow the feeling of intense admiration which evidently mastered their minds to find expression. They fixed their dark eyes upon their snowy loveliness (Good's skin is exceedingly white), and that was all. But this was quite enough for Good, who is modest by nature.

When we got to the centre of the kraal, Infadoos halted at the door of a large hut, which was surrounded at a distance by a circle of smaller ones.

"Enter, sons of the stars," he said, in a magniloquent voice, "and deign to rest awhile in our humble habitations. A little food shall be brought to you, so that ye shall have no need to draw your belts tight from hunger; some honey and some milk, and an ox or two, and a few sheep; not much, my lords, but still a little food."

"It is good," said I, "Infadoos, we are weary with travelling through realms of air; now let us rest."

Accordingly we entered into the hut, which we found amply prepared for our comfort. Couches of tanned skins were spread for us to rest on, and water was placed for us to wash in.

Presently we heard a shouting outside, and stepping to the door, saw a line of damsels bearing milk and roasted mealies, and honey in a pot. Behind these were some youths driving a fat young ox. We received the gifts, and then one of the young men took the knife from his girdle and dexterously cut the ox's throat. In ten minutes it was dead, skinned, and cut up. The best of the meat was then cut off for us, and the rest I, in the name of our party, presented to the warriors round us, who took it off and distributed the "white men's gift."

Umbopa set to work, with the assistance of an extremely prepossessing young woman, to boil our portion in a large earthenware pot over a fire which was built outside the hut, and when it was nearly ready we sent a message to Infadoos, and asked him, and Scragga the king's son, to join us.

Presently they came, and sitting down upon little stools, of which there were several about the hut (for the Kukuanas do not in general squat upon their haunches like the Zulus), helped us to get through our dinner. The old gentleman was most affable and polite, but it struck us that the young one regarded us with suspicion. He had, together with the rest of the party, been overawed by our white appearance and by our magic properties; but it seemed to me that on discovering that we ate, drank, and slept like other mortals, his awe was beginning to wear off and be replaced by a sullen suspicion—which made us feel rather uncomfortable.

In the course of our meal Sir Henry suggested to me that it might be well to try and discover if our hosts knew anything of his brother's fate, or if they had ever seen or heard of him; but, on the whole, I thought that it would be wiser to say nothing of the matter at that time.

After supper we filled our pipes and lit them: a proceeding which filled Infadoos and Scragga with astonishment. The Kukuanas were evidently unacquainted with the divine uses of tobacco-smoke. The herb was grown among them extensively; but, like the Zulus, they only used it for snuff, and quite failed to identify it in its new form.

Presently I asked Infadoos when we were to proceed on our journey, and was delighted to learn that preparations had been made for us to leave on the following morning, messengers having already left to inform Twala the king of our coming. It appeared that Twala was at his principal place, known as Loo, making ready for the great annual feast which was held in the first week of June. At this gathering all the regiments, with the exception of certain detachments left behind for garrison purposes, were brought up and paraded before the king; and the great annual witch-hunt, of which more by-and-by, was held.

We were to start at dawn; and Infadoos, who was to accompany us, expected that we should, unless we were detained by accident or by swollen rivers, reach Loo on the night of the second day.

When they had given us this information our visitors bade us good night; and, having arranged to watch turn and turn about, three of us flung ourselves down and slept the sweet sleep of the weary, whilst the fourth sat up on the look-out for possible treachery.

CHAPTER IX.

TWALA THE KING.

It will not be necessary for me to detail at length the incidents of our journey to Loo. It took two good days' travelling along Solomon's Great Road, which pursued its even course right into the heart of Kukuanaland. Suffice it to say that as we went the country seemed to grow richer and richer, and the kraals, with their wide surrounding belts of cultivation, more and more numerous. They were all built upon the same principles as the first one we had reached, and were guarded by ample garrisons of troops. Indeed, in Kukuanaland, as among the Germans, the Zulus, and the Masai, every able-bodied man is a soldier, so that the whole force of the nation is available for its wars, offensive or defensive. As we travelled along we were overtaken by thousands of warriors hurrying up to Loo to be present at the great annual review and festival, and a grander series of troops I never saw. At sunset on the second day we stopped to rest awhile upon the summit of some heights over which the road ran, and there on a beautiful and fertile plain before us was Loo itself. For a native town it was an enormous place, quite five miles round I should say, with outlying kraals jutting out from it, which served on grand occasions as cantonments for the regiments, and a curious horse-shoe-shaped hill, with which we were destined to become better acquainted, about two miles to the north. It was beautifully situated, and through the centre of the kraal, dividing it into two portions, ran a river, which appeared to be bridged at several places, the same perhaps that we had seen from the slopes of Sheba's Breasts. Sixty or seventy miles away three great snow-capped mountains, placed like the points of a triangle, started up out of the level plain. The conformation of these mountains was unlike that of Sheba's Breasts, being sheer and precipitous, instead of smooth and rounded.

Infadoos saw us looking at them and volunteered a remark—

"The road ends there," he said, pointing to the mountains known among the Kukuanas as the "Three Witches."

"Why does it end?" I asked.

"Who knows?" he answered, with a shrug; "the mountains are full of caves, and there is a great pit between them. It is there that the wise men of old time used to go to get whatever it was they came to this country for, and it is there now that our kings are buried in the Place of Death."

"What was it they came for?" I asked eagerly.

"Nay, I know not. My lords who come from the stars should know," he answered with a quick look. Evidently he knew more than he chose to say.

"Yes," I went on, "you are right, in the stars we know many things. I have heard, for instance, that the wise men of old came to those mountains to get bright stones, pretty playthings, and yellow iron."

"My lord is wise," he answered coldly, "I am but a child and cannot talk with my lord on such things. My lord must speak with Gagool the old, at the king's place, who is wise even as my lord," and he turned away.

As soon as he was gone, I turned to the others and pointed out the mountains. "There are Solomon's diamond mines," I said.

Umbopa was standing with them, apparently plunged in one of the fits of abstraction which were common to him, and caught my words.

"Yes, Macumazahn," he put in, in Zulu, "the diamonds are surely there, and you shall have them since you white men are so fond of toys and money."

"How dost thou know that, Umbopa?" I asked sharply, for I did not like his mysterious ways.

He laughed; "I dreamed it in the night, white men," and then he too turned upon his heel and went.

"Now what," said Sir Henry, "is our black friend at? He knows more than he chooses to say, that is clear. By the way, Quatermain, has he heard anything of—of my brother?"

"Nothing; he has asked every one he has got friendly with, but they all declare no white man has ever been seen in the country before."

"Do you suppose he ever got here at all?" suggested Good; "we have only reached the place by a miracle; is it likely he could have reached it at all without the map?"

"I don't know," said Sir Henry, gloomily, "but somehow I think that I shall find him."

Slowly the sun sank, and then suddenly darkness rushed down on the land like a tangible thing. There was no breathing-space between the day and the night, no soft transformation scene, for in these latitudes twilight does not exist. The change from day to night is as quick and as absolute as the change from life to death. The sun sank and the world was wreathed in shadows. But not for long, for see in the east there is a glow, then a bent edge of silver light, and at last the full bow of the crescent moon peeps above the plain and shoots its gleaming arrows far and wide, filling the earth with a faint refulgence, as the glow of a good man's deeds shines for awhile upon his little world after his sun has set, lighting the faint-hearted travellers who follow on towards a fuller dawn.

We stood and watched the lovely sight, whilst the stars grew pale before this chastened majesty, and felt our hearts lifted up in the presence of a beauty we could not realise, much less describe. Mine has been a rough life, my reader, but there are a few things I am thankful to have lived for, and one of them is to have seen that moon rise over Kukuanaland. Presently our meditations were broken in upon by our polite friend Infadoos.

"If my lords are rested we will journey on to Loo, where a hut is made ready for my lords to-night. The moon is now bright, so that we shall not fall on the way."

We assented, and in an hour's time were at the outskirts of the town, of which the extent, mapped out as it was by thousands of camp fires, appeared absolutely endless. Indeed, Good, who was always fond of a bad joke, christened it "Unlimited Loo."[1] Presently we came to a moat with a drawbridge, where we were met by the rattling of arms and the hoarse challenge of a sentry. Infadoos gave some password that I could not catch, which was met with a salute, and we passed on through the central street of the great grass city. After nearly half an hour's tramp, past endless lines of huts, Infadoos at last halted at the gate of a little

---

1 Loo is a game of cards, not unlike whist, but played both as Limited (five-card Loo with three players) or Unlimited (three-card Loo with as many as seven players).

group of huts which surrounded a small courtyard of powdered limestone, and informed us that these were to be our "poor" quarters.

We entered, and found that a hut had been assigned to each of us. These huts were superior to any which we had yet seen, and in each was a most comfortable bed made of tanned skins spread upon mattresses of aromatic grass. Food too was ready for us, and as soon as we had washed ourselves with water, which stood ready in earthenware jars, some young women of handsome appearance brought us roasted meat and mealie cobs daintily served on wooden platters, and presented it to us with deep obeisances.

We ate and drank, and then the beds having by our request been all moved into one hut, a precaution at which the amiable young ladies smiled, we flung ourselves down to sleep, thoroughly wearied out with our long journey.

When we woke, it was to find that the sun was high in the heavens, and that the female attendants, who did not seem to be troubled by any false shame, were already standing inside the hut, having been ordered to attend and help us to "make ready."

"Make ready, indeed," growled Good, "when one has only a flannel shirt and a pair of boots, that does not take long. I wish you would ask them for my trousers."

I asked accordingly, but was informed that these sacred relics had already been taken to the king, who would see us in the forenoon.

Having, somewhat to their astonishment and disappointment, requested the young ladies to step outside, we proceeded to make the best toilet that the circumstances admitted of. Good even went the length of again shaving the right side of his face; the left, on which now appeared a very fair crop of whiskers, we impressed upon him he must on no account touch. As for ourselves, we were contented with a good wash and combing our hair. Sir Henry's yellow locks were now almost down to his shoulders, and he looked more like an ancient Dane than ever, while my grizzled scrub was fully an inch long, instead of half an inch, which in a general way I considered my maximum length.

By the time that we had eaten our breakfasts, and smoked a pipe, a message was brought to us by no less a personage than

Infadoos himself that Twala, the king, was ready to see us, if we would be pleased to come.

We remarked in reply that we should prefer to wait till the sun was a little higher, we were yet weary with our journey, &c. &c. It is always well, when dealing with uncivilised people, not to be in too great a hurry. They are apt to mistake politeness for awe or servility. So, although we were quite as anxious to see Twala as Twala could be to see us, we sat down and waited for an hour, employing the interval in preparing such presents as our slender stock of goods permitted—namely, the Winchester rifle which had been used by poor Ventvögel, and some beads. The rifle and ammunition we determined to present to his Royal Highness, and the beads were for his wives and courtiers. We had already given a few to Infadoos and Scragga, and found that they were delighted with them, never having seen anything like them before. At length we declared that we were ready, and guided by Infadoos, started off to the levée, Umbopa carrying the rifle and beads.

After walking a few hundred yards, we came to an enclosure, something like that which surrounded the huts that had been allotted to us, only fifty times as big. It could not have been less than six or seven acres in extent. All round the outside fence was a row of huts, which were the habitations of the king's wives. Exactly opposite the gateway, on the further side of the open space, was a very large hut, which stood by itself, in which his Majesty resided. All the rest was open ground; that is to say, it would have been open had it not been filled by company after company of warriors, who were mustered there to the number of seven or eight thousand. These men stood still as statues as we advanced through them, and it would be impossible to give an idea of the grandeur of the spectacle which they presented, in their waving plumes, their glancing spears, and iron-backed ox-hide shields.

The space in front of the large hut was empty, but before it were placed several stools. On three of these, at a sign from Infadoos, we seated ourselves, Umbopa standing behind us. As for Infadoos, he took up a position by the door of the hut. So we waited for ten minutes or more in the midst of a dead silence, but conscious that we were the object of the concentrated gaze of some eight thousand pairs of eyes. It was a somewhat trying ordeal, but we carried it off as best we could. At length the door of the hut opened, and a gigantic figure, with a splendid tiger-skin karross flung over its shoulders, stepped out, followed by the boy Scragga, and what appeared to us to be a withered-up monkey, wrapped in a fur cloak. The figure seated itself upon a stool, Scragga took his stand behind it, and the withered-up monkey crept on all fours into the shade of the hut and squatted down.

Still there was silence.

Then the gigantic figure slipped off the karross and stood up before us, a truly alarming spectacle. It was that of an enormous man with the most entirely repulsive countenance we had ever beheld. The lips were as thick as a negro's, the nose was flat, it had but one gleaming black eye (for the other was represented by a hollow in the face), and its whole expression was cruel and sensual to a degree. From the large head rose a magnificent plume of white ostrich feathers, the body was clad in a shirt of shining chain armour, whilst round the waist and right knee was the usual garnish of white ox-tails. In the right hand was a huge spear. Round the neck was a thick torque of gold, and bound on to the forehead was a single and enormous uncut diamond.

Still there was silence; but not for long. Presently the figure, whom we rightly guessed to be the king, raised the great spear in its hand. Instantly eight thousand spears were raised in answer, and from eight thousand throats rang out the royal salute of "*Koom*." Three times this was repeated, and each time the earth shook with the noise, that can only be compared to the deepest notes of thunder.

"Be humble, O people," piped out a thin voice which seemed to come from the monkey in the shade, "it is the king."

"*It is the king*," boomed out eight thousand throats, in answer. "*Be humble, O people, it is the king.*"

Then there was silence again—dead silence. Presently, however, it was broken. A soldier on our left dropped his shield, which fell with a clatter on the limestone flooring.

Twala turned his one cold eye in the direction of the noise.

"Come hither, thou," he said, in a voice of thunder.

A fine young man stepped out of the ranks, and stood before him.

"It was thy shield that fell, thou awkward dog. Wilt thou make me a reproach in the eyes of strangers from the stars? What hast thou to say?"

And then we saw the poor fellow turn pale under his dusky skin.

"It was by chance, O calf of the black cow," he murmured.

"Then it is a chance for which thou must pay. Thou hast made me foolish; prepare for death."

"I am the king's ox," was the low answer.

"Scragga," roared the king, "let me see how thou canst use thy spear. Kill me this awkward dog."

Scragga stepped forward with an ill-favoured grin, and lifted his spear. The poor victim covered his eyes with his hand and stood still. As for us, we were petrified with horror.

"Once, twice," he waved the spear and then struck, ah God! right home—the spear stood out a foot behind the soldier's back. He flung up his hands and dropped dead. From the multitude around rose something like a murmur, it rolled round and round, and died away. The tragedy was finished; there lay the corpse, and we had not yet realised that it had been enacted. Sir Henry sprang up and swore a great oath, then, overpowered by the sense of silence, sat down again.

"The thrust was a good one," said the king; "take him away."

Four men stepped out of the ranks, and lifting the body of the murdered man, carried it away.

"Cover up the blood-stains, cover them up," piped out the thin voice from the monkey-like figure; "the king's word is spoken, the king's doom is done."

Thereupon a girl came forward from behind the hut, bearing a jar filled with powdered lime, which she scattered over the red mark, blotting it from sight.

Sir Henry meanwhile was boiling with rage at what had happened; indeed, it was with difficulty that we could keep him still.

"Sit down, for heaven's sake," I whispered; "our lives depend on it."

He yielded and remained quiet.

Twala sat still until the traces of the tragedy had been removed, then he addressed us.

"White people," he said, "who come hither, whence I know not, and why I know not, greeting."

"Greeting Twala, King of the Kukuanas," I answered.

"White people, whence come ye, and what seek ye?"

"We come from the stars, ask us not how. We come to see this land."

"Ye come from far to see a little thing. And that man with ye," pointing to Umbopa, "does he too come from the stars?"

"Even so; there are people of thy colour in the heavens above; but ask not of matters too high for thee, Twala, the king."

"Ye speak with a loud voice, people of the stars," Twala answered, in a tone which I scarcely liked. "Remember that the stars are far off, and ye are here. How if I make ye as him whom they bear away?"

I laughed out loud, though there was little laughter in my heart.

"O king," I said, "be careful, walk warily over hot stones, lest thou shouldst burn thy feet; hold the spear by the handle, lest thou shouldst cut thy hands. Touch but one hair of our heads, and destruction shall come upon thee. What, have not these," pointing to Infadoos and Scragga (who, young villain that he was, was employed in cleaning the blood of the soldier off his spear), "told thee what manner of men we are? Hast thou ever seen the like of us?" and I pointed to Good, feeling quite sure that he had never seen anybody before who looked in the least like *him* as he then appeared.

"It is true, I have not," said the king.

"Have they not told thee how we strike with death from afar?" I went on.

"They have told me, but I believe them not. Let me see you kill. Kill me a man among those who stand yonder"—and he pointed to the opposite side of the kraal—"and I will believe."

"Nay," I answered; "we shed no blood of man except in just punishment; but if thou wilt see, bid thy servants drive in an ox through the kraal gates, and before he has run twenty paces I will strike him dead."

"Nay," laughed the king, "kill me a man, and I will believe."

"Good, O king, so be it," I answered, coolly; "do thou walk across the open space, and before thy feet reach the gate thou shall be dead; or if thou wilt not, send thy son Scragga" (whom at that moment it would have given me much pleasure to shoot).

On hearing this suggestion Scragga gave a sort of howl, and bolted into the hut.

Twala frowned majestically; the suggestion did not please him.

"Let a young ox be driven in," he said.

Two men at once departed, running swiftly.

"Now, Sir Henry," said I, "do you shoot. I want to show this ruffian that I am not the only magician of the party."

Sir Henry accordingly took the "express," and made ready.

"I hope I shall make a good shot," he groaned.

"You must," I answered. "If you miss with the first barrel, let him have the second. Sight for 150 yards, and wait till the beast turns broadside on."

Then came a pause, till presently we caught sight of an ox running straight for the kraal gate. It came on through the gate, and then, catching sight of the vast concourse of people, stopped stupidly, turned round, and bellowed.

"Now's your time," I whispered.

Up went the rifle.

Bang! thud! and the ox was kicking on his back, shot in the ribs. The semi-hollow bullet had done its work well, and a sigh of astonishment went up from the assembled thousands.

I turned coolly round—

"Have I lied, O king?"

"Nay, white man, it is a truth," was the somewhat awed answer.

"Listen, Twala," I went on. "Thou hast seen. Now know we come in peace, not in war. See here" (and I held up the Winchester repeater); "here is a hollow staff that shall enable you to kill even as we kill, only this charm I lay upon it, thou shalt kill no man with it. If thou liftest it against a man, it shall kill thee. Stay, I will show thee. Bid a man step forty paces and place the shaft of a spear in the ground so that the flat blade looks towards us."

In a few seconds it was done.

"Now, see, I will break the spear."

Taking a careful sight I fired. The bullet struck the flat of the spear, and broke the blade into fragments.

Again the sigh of astonishment went up.

"Now, Twala" (handing him the rifle), "this magic tube we give to thee, and by-and-by I will show thee how to use it; but beware how thou usest the magic of the stars against a man of earth," and I handed him the rifle. He took it very gingerly, and laid it down at his feet. As he did so I observed the wizened monkey-like figure creeping up from the shadow of the hut. It crept on all fours, but when it reached the place where the king sat, it rose upon its feet, and throwing the furry covering off its face, revealed a most extraordinary and weird countenance. It was (apparently) that of a woman of great age, so shrunken that in size it was no larger than that of a year-old child, and was made up of a collection of deep yellow wrinkles. Set in the wrinkles was a sunken slit, that represented the mouth, beneath which the chin curved outwards to a point. There was no nose to speak of; indeed, the whole countenance might have been taken for that of a sun-dried corpse had it not been for a pair of large black eyes, still full of fire and intelligence, which gleamed and played under the snow-white eyebrows, and the projecting parchment-coloured skull, like jewels in a charnel-house. As for the skull itself, it was perfectly bare, and yellow in hue, while its wrinkled scalp moved and contracted like the hood of a cobra.

The figure to whom this fearful countenance, which caused a shiver of fear to pass through us as we gazed on it, belonged, stood still for a moment, and then suddenly projected a skinny claw armed with nails nearly an inch long, and laid it on the shoulder of Twala, the king, and began to speak in a thin, piercing voice—

"Listen, O king! Listen, O people! Listen, O mountains and plains and rivers, home of the Kukuana race! Listen, O skies and sun, O rain and storm and mist! Listen, all things that live and must die! Listen, all dead things that must live again—again to die! Listen, the spirit of life is in me, and I prophesy. I prophesy! I prophesy!"

The words died away in a faint wail, and terror seemed to seize upon the hearts of all who heard them, including ourselves. The old woman was very terrible.

"*Blood! blood! blood!* rivers of blood; blood everywhere. I see it, I smell it, I taste it—it is salt; it runs red upon the ground, it rains down from the skies.

"*Footsteps! footsteps! footsteps!* the tread of the white man coming from afar. It shakes the earth; the earth trembles before her master.

"Blood is good, the red blood is bright; there is no smell like the smell of new-shed blood. The lions shall lap it and roar, the vultures shall wash their wings in it, and shriek in joy.

"I am old! I am old! I have seen much blood; ha, ha! but I shall see more ere I die, and be merry. How old am I, think ye? Your fathers knew me, and *their* fathers knew me, and *their* fathers' fathers. I have seen the white man, and know his desires. I am old, but the mountains are older than I. Who made the great road, tell me? Who wrote in pictures on the rocks, tell me? Who reared up the three silent ones yonder, who gaze across the pit, tell me?" (And she pointed towards the three precipitous mountains we had noticed on the previous night.)

"Ye know not, but I know. It was a white people who were before ye are, who shall be when ye are not, who shall eat ye up, and destroy ye. *Yea! yea! yea!*

"And what came they for, the white ones, the terrible ones, the skilled in magic and all learning, the strong, the unswerving? What is that bright stone upon thy forehead, O king? Whose hands made the iron garments upon thy breast, O king? Ye know not, but I know. I the old one, I the wise one, I the Isanusi!" (witch doctress.)

Then she turned her bald vulture-head towards us.

"What seek ye, white men of the stars—ah, yes, of the stars? Do ye seek a lost one? Ye shall not find him here. He is not here. Never for ages upon ages has a white foot pressed this land; never but once, and he left it but to die. Ye come for bright stones; I know it—I know it; ye shall find them when the blood is dry; but shall ye return whence ye came, or shall ye stop with me? Ha! ha! ha!

"And thou, thou with the dark skin and the proud bearing" (pointing her skinny finger at Umbopa), "who art *thou*, and what seekest *thou*? Not stones that shine, not yellow metal that gleams, that thou leavest to 'white men from the stars.' Methinks I know thee; methinks I can smell the smell of the blood in thy veins. Strip off the girdle——"

Here the features of this extraordinary creature became convulsed, and she fell to the ground foaming in an epileptic fit, and was carried off into the hut.

The king rose up trembling, and waved his hand. Instantly the regiments began to file off, and in ten minutes, save for ourselves, the king, and a few attendants, the great space was left clear.

"White people," he said, "it passes in my mind to kill ye. Gagool has spoken strange words. What say ye?"

I laughed. "Be careful, O king, we are not easy to slay. Thou hast seen the fate of the ox; wouldst thou be as the ox?"

The king frowned. "It is not well to threaten a king."

"We threaten not, we speak what is true. Try to kill us, O king, and learn."

The great man put his hand to his forehead.

"Go in peace," he said, at length. "To-night is the great dance. Ye shall see it. Fear not that I shall set a snare for ye. To-morrow I shall think."

"It is well, O king," I answered, unconcernedly, and then, accompanied by Infadoos, we rose, and went back to our kraal.

CHAPTER X.

THE WITCH-HUNT.

On reaching our hut, I motioned to Infadoos to enter with us.

"Now, Infadoos," I said, "we would speak with thee."

"Let my lords say on."

"It seems to us, Infadoos, that Twala, the king, is a cruel man."

"It is so, my lords. Alas! the land cries out with his cruelties. To-night ye will see. It is the great witch-hunt,[1] and many will be smelt out as wizards and slain. No man's life is safe. If the king covets a man's cattle, or a man's life, or if he fears a man that he should excite a rebellion against him, then Gagool, whom ye saw, or some of the witch-finding women whom she has taught, will smell that man out as a wizard, and he will be killed. Many will die before the moon grows pale to-night. It is ever so. Perhaps I

---

1 witch-hunt] see Haggard, "A Zulu War-Dance," Appendix B; also Fred Fynney, *Zululand and the Zulus*, Appendix C.

too shall be killed. As yet I have been spared, because I am skilled in war, and beloved by the soldiers; but I know not how long I shall live. The land groans at the cruelties of Twala, the king; it is wearied of him and his red ways."

"Then why is it, Infadoos, that the people do not cast him down?"

"Nay, my lords, he is the king, and if he were killed Scragga would reign in his place, and the heart of Scragga is blacker than the heart of Twala, his father. If Scragga were king the yoke upon our neck would be heavier than the yoke of Twala. If Imotu had never been slain, or if Ignosi, his son, had lived, it had been otherwise; but they are both dead."

"How know you that Ignosi is dead?" said a voice behind us. We looked round with astonishment to see who spoke. It was Umbopa.

"What meanest thou, boy?" asked Infadoos; "who told thee to speak?"

"Listen, Infadoos," was the answer, "and I will tell thee a story. Years ago the King Imotu was killed in this country, and his wife fled with the boy Ignosi. Is it not so?"

"It is so."

"It was said that the woman and the boy died upon the mountains. Is it not so?"

"It is even so."

"Well, it came to pass that the mother and the boy Ignosi did not die. They crossed the mountains, and were led by a tribe of wandering desert men across the sands beyond, till at last they came to water and grass and trees again."

"How knowest thou that?"

"Listen. They travelled on and on, many months' journey, till they reached a land where a people called the Amazulu,[1] who too are of the Kukuana stock, live by war, and with them they tarried many years, till at length the mother died. Then the son, Ignosi, again became a wanderer, and went on into a land of wonders, where white people live, and for many more years learned the wisdom of the white people."

---

1   Amazulu] "Ama" is the plural prefix and "Zulu" signifies High or the Heavens; hence the Amazulu are "people of the sky."

"It is a pretty story," said Infadoos, incredulously.

"For many years he lived there working as a servant and a soldier, but holding in his heart all that his mother had told him of his own place, and casting about in his mind to find how he might get back there to see his own people and his father's house before he died. For many years he lived and waited, and at last the time came, as it ever comes to him who can wait for it, and he met some white men who would seek this unknown land, and joined himself to them. The white men started and journeyed on and on, seeking for one who is lost. They crossed the burning desert, they crossed the snow-clad mountains, and reached the land of the Kukuanas, and there they met thee, oh Infadoos."

"Surely thou art mad to talk thus," said the astonished old soldier.

"Thou thinkest so; see, I will show thee, oh my uncle.

"*I am Ignosi, rightful king of the Kukuanas!*"

Then with a single movement he slipped off the "moocha" or girdle round his middle, and stood naked before us.

"Look," he said; "what is this?" and he pointed to the mark of a great snake tattooed in blue round his middle, its tail disappearing in its open mouth just above where the thighs are set into the body.

Infadoos looked, his eyes starting nearly out of his head, and then fell upon his knees.

"*Koom! Koom!*" he ejaculated; "it is my brother's son; it is the king."

"Did I not tell thee so, my uncle? Rise; I am not yet the king, but with thy help, and with the help of these brave white men, who are my friends, I shall be. But the old woman Gagool was right, the land shall run with blood first, and hers shall run with it, for she killed my father with her words, and drove my mother forth. And now, Infadoos, choose thou. Wilt thou put thy hands between my hands and be my man? Wilt thou share the dangers that lie before me, and help me to overthrow this tyrant and murderer, or wilt thou not? Choose thou."

The old man put his hand to his head and thought. Then he rose, and advancing to where Umbopa, or rather Ignosi, stood, knelt before him and took his hand.

"Ignosi, rightful king of the Kukuanas, I put my hand between thy hands, and am thy man till death. When thou wast a babe I dandled thee upon my knee, now shall my old arm strike for thee and freedom."

"It is well, Infadoos; if I conquer, thou shalt be the greatest man in the kingdom after the king. If I fail, thou canst only die, and death is not far off for thee. Rise, my uncle."

"And ye, white men, will ye help me? What have I to offer ye! The white stones, if I conquer and can find them, ye shall have as many as ye can carry hence. Will that suffice ye?"

I translated this remark.

"Tell him," answered Sir Henry, "that he mistakes an Englishman. Wealth is good, and if it comes in our way we will take it; but a gentleman does not sell himself for wealth. But, speaking for myself, I say this. I have always liked Umbopa, and so far as lies in me will stand by him in this business. It will be very pleasant to me to try and square matters with that cruel devil, Twala. What do you say, Good, and you, Quatermain?"

"Well," said Good, to adopt the language of hyperbole, in which all these people seem to indulge, "you can tell him that a row is surely good, and warms the cockles of the heart, and that so far as I am concerned I'm his boy. My only stipulation is, that he allows me to wear trousers."

I translated these answers.

"It is well, my friends," said Ignosi, late Umbopa; "and what say you, Macumazahn, art thou too with me, old hunter, cleverer than a wounded buffalo?"

I thought awhile and scratched my head.

"Umbopa, or Ignosi," I said, "I don't like revolutions. I am a man of peace, and a bit of a coward" (here Umbopa smiled), "but, on the other hand, I stick to my friends, Ignosi. You have stuck to us and played the part of a man, and I will stick to you. But mind you I am a trader, and have to make my living, so I accept your offer about those diamonds in case we should ever be in a position to avail ourselves of it. Another thing: we came, as you know, to look for Incubu's (Sir Henry's) lost brother. You must help us to find him."

"That will I do," answered Ignosi. "Stay, Infadoos, by the sign of the snake round my middle, tell me the truth. Has any white man to thy knowledge set his foot within the land?"

"None, oh Ignosi."

"If any white man had been seen or heard of, wouldst thou have known it?"

"I should certainly have known."

"Thou hearest, Incubu," said Ignosi to Sir Henry, "he has not been here."

"Well, well," said Sir Henry, with a sigh; "there it is; I suppose he never got here. Poor fellow, poor fellow! So it has all been for nothing. God's will be done."

"Now for business," I put in, anxious to escape from a painful subject. "It is very well to be a king by right divine, Ignosi, but how dost thou purpose to become a king indeed?"

"Nay, I know not. Infadoos, hast thou a plan?"

"Ignosi, son of the lightning," answered his uncle, "to-night is the great dance and witch-hunt. Many will be smelt out and perish, and in the hearts of many others there will be grief and anguish and anger against the King Twala. When the dance is over, then will I speak to some of the great chiefs, who in turn, if I can win them over, shall speak to their regiments. I shall speak to the chiefs softly at first, and bring them to see that thou art indeed the king, and I think that by to-morrow's light thou shalt have twenty thousand spears at thy command. And now must I go and think, and hear, and make ready. After the dance is done I will, if I am yet alive, and we are all alive, meet thee here, and we will talk. At the best there will be war."

At this moment our conference was interrupted by the cry that messengers had come from the king. Advancing to the door of the hut we ordered that they should be admitted, and presently three men entered, each bearing a shining shirt of chain armour, and a magnificent battle-axe.

"The gifts of my lord the king to the white men from the stars!" exclaimed a herald who came with them.

"We thank the king," I answered; "withdraw."

The men went, and we examined the armour with great interest. It was the most beautiful chain work we had ever seen. A whole coat fell together so closely that it formed a mass of links scarcely too big to be covered with both hands.

"Do you make these things in this country, Infadoos?" I asked; "they are very beautiful."

"Nay, my lord, they come down to us from our forefathers. We know not who made them, and there are but few left. None but those of royal blood may wear them. They are magic coats through which no spear can pass. He who wears them is well-nigh safe in the battle. The king is well pleased or much afraid, or he would not have sent them. Wear them to-night, my lords."

The rest of the day we spent quietly resting and talking over the situation, which was sufficiently exciting. At last the sun went down, the thousand watch-fires glowed out, and through the darkness we heard the tramp of many feet and the clashing of hundreds of spears, as the regiments passed to their appointed places to be ready for the great dance. About ten the full moon came up in splendour, and as we stood watching her ascent Infadoos arrived, clad in full war toggery, and accompanied by a guard of twenty men to escort us to the dance. We had already, as he recommended, donned the shirts of chain armour which the king had sent us, putting them on under our ordinary clothing, and finding to our surprise that they were neither very heavy nor uncomfortable. These steel shirts, which had evidently been made for men of a very large stature, hung somewhat loosely upon Good and myself, but Sir Henry's fitted his magnificent frame like a glove. Then strapping our revolvers round our waists, and taking the battle-axes which the king had sent with the armour in our hands, we started.

On arriving at the great kraal, where we had that morning been interviewed by the king, we found that it was closely packed with some twenty thousand men arranged in regiments round it. The regiments were in turn divided into companies, and between each company was a little path to allow free passage to the witch-finders to pass up and down. Anything more imposing than the sight that was presented by this vast and orderly concourse of armed men it is impossible for one to conceive. There they stood perfectly silent, and the moonlight poured its light upon the forest of their raised spears, upon their majestic forms, waving plumes, and the harmonious shading of their various-coloured shields. Wherever we looked was line upon line of set faces surmounted by range upon range of glittering spears.

"Surely," I said to Infadoos, "the whole army is here?"

"Nay, Macumazahn," he answered, "but a third part of it. One third part is present at this dance each year, another third part is mustered outside in case there should be trouble when the killing begins, ten thousand more garrison the outposts round Loo, and the rest watch at the kraals in the country. Thou seest it is a very great people."

"They are very silent," said Good; and indeed the intense stillness among such a vast concourse of living men was almost overpowering.

"What says Bougwan?" asked Infadoos.

I translated.

"Those over whom the shadow of Death is hovering are silent," he answered, grimly.

"Will many be killed?"

"Very many."

"It seems," I said to the others, "that we are going to assist at a gladiatorial show arranged regardless of expense."

Sir Henry shivered, and Good said that he wished that we could get out of it.

"Tell me," I asked Infadoos, "are we in danger?"

"I know not, my lords, I trust not; but do not seem afraid. If ye live through the night all may go well. The soldiers murmur against the king."

All this while we had been advancing steadily towards the centre of the open space, in the midst of which were placed some stools. As we proceeded we perceived another small party coming from the direction of the royal hut.

"It is the king, Twala, and Scragga his son, and Gagool the old, and see, with them are those who slay," and he pointed to a little group of about a dozen gigantic and savage-looking men, armed with spears in one hand and heavy kerries in the other.

The king seated himself upon the centre stool, Gagool crouched at his feet, and the others stood behind.

"Greeting, white lords," he cried, as we came up; "be seated, waste not the precious time—the night is all too short for the deeds that must be done. Ye come in a good hour, and shall see a glorious show. Look round, white lords; look round," and he rolled his one wicked eye from regiment to regiment. "Can the stars show ye such a sight as this? See how they shake in their wickedness, all those who have evil in their hearts and fear the judgment of 'heaven above.'"

"*Begin! begin!*" cried out Gagool in her thin piercing voice; "the hyænas are hungry, they howl for food. *Begin! begin!*" Then for a moment there was intense stillness, made horrible by a presage of what was to come.

The king lifted his spear, and suddenly twenty thousand feet were raised, as though they belonged to one man, and brought down with a stamp upon the earth. This was repeated three times, causing the solid ground to shake and tremble. Then from a far point of the circle a solitary voice began a wailing song, of which the refrain ran something as follows:—

"*What is the lot of man born of woman?*"

Back came the answer rolling out from every throat in that vast company—

"*Death!*"

Gradually, however, the song was taken up by company after company, till the whole armed multitude were singing it, and I could no longer follow the words, except in so far as they appeared to represent various phases of human passions, fears, and joys. Now it seemed to be a love song, now a majestic swelling war chant, and last of all a death-dirge ending suddenly in one heartbreaking wail that went echoing and rolling away in a volume of blood-curdling sound. Again the silence fell upon the place, and again it was broken by the king lifting up his hand. Instantly there was a pattering of feet, and from out of the masses of the warriors strange and awful figures came running towards us. As they drew near we saw that they were those of women, most of them aged, for their white hair, ornamented with small bladders taken from fish, streamed out behind them. Their faces were painted in stripes of white and yellow; down their backs hung snake-skins, and round their waists rattled circlets of human bones, while each held in her shrivelled hand a small forked wand. In all there were ten of them. When they arrived in front of us they halted, and one of them pointing with her wand towards the crouching figure of Gagool, cried out—

"Mother, old mother, we are here."

"*Good! good! good!*" piped out that aged iniquity. "Are your eyes keen, Isanusis (witch doctresses), ye seers in dark places?"

"Mother, they are keen."

"*Good! good! good!* Are your ears open, Isanusis, ye who hear words that come not from the tongue?"

"Mother, they are open."

"*Good! good! good!* Are your senses awake, Isanusis—can ye smell blood, can ye purge the land of the wicked ones who compass evil against the king and against their neighbours? Are ye ready to do the justice of 'Heaven above,' ye whom I have taught, who have eaten of the bread of my wisdom and drunk of the water of my magic?"

"Mother, we can."

"Then go! Tarry not, ye vultures; see the slayers," pointing to the ominous group of executioners behind; "make sharp their spears; the white men from afar are hungry to see. *Go.*"

With a wild yell the weird party broke away in every direction, like fragments from a shell, and the dry bones round their waists rattling as they ran, made direct for various points of the dense human circle. We could not watch them all, so fixed our eyes upon the Isanusi nearest us. When she came within a few paces of the warriors, she halted and began to dance wildly, turning round and round with an almost incredible rapidity, and shrieking out sentences such as "I smell him, the evil-doer!" "He is near, he who poisoned his mother!" "I hear the thoughts of him who thought evil of the king!"

Quicker and quicker she danced, till she lashed herself into such a frenzy of excitement that the foam flew in flecks from her gnashing jaws, her eyes seemed to start from her head, and her flesh to quiver visibly. Suddenly she stopped dead, and stiffened all over, like a pointer dog when he scents game, and then with outstretched wand began to creep stealthily towards the soldiers before her. It seemed to us that as she came their stoicism gave way, and that they shrank from her. As for ourselves, we followed her movements with a horrible fascination. Presently, still creeping and crouching like a dog, she was before them. Then she stopped and pointed, and then again crept on a pace or two.

Suddenly the end came. With a shriek she sprang in and touched a tall warrior with the forked wand. Instantly two of his comrades, those standing immediately next to him, seized the doomed man, each by one arm, and advanced with him towards the king.

He did not resist, but we saw that he dragged his limbs as though they were paralysed, and his fingers, from which the spear had fallen, were limp as those of a man newly dead.

As he came, two of the villainous executioners stepped forward to meet him. Presently they met, and the executioners turned round towards the king as though for orders.

"*Kill!*" said the king.

"*Kill!*" squeaked Gagool.

"*Kill!*" re-echoed Scragga, with a hollow chuckle.

Almost before the words were uttered, the horrible deed was done. One man had driven his spear into the victim's heart, and to make assurance doubly sure, the other had dashed out his brains with his great club.

"*One,*" counted Twala the king, just like a black Madame Defarge,[1] as Good said, and the body was dragged a few paces away and stretched out.

Hardly was this done, before another poor wretch was brought up, like an ox to the slaughter. This time we could see, from the leopard-skin cloak, that the man was a person of rank. Again the awful syllables were spoken, and the victim fell dead.

"*Two,*" counted the king.

And so the deadly game went on, till some hundred bodies were stretched in rows behind us. I have heard of the gladiatorial shows of the Cæsars, and of the Spanish bull-fights, but I take the liberty of doubting if they were either of them half as horrible as this Kukuana witch hunt. Gladiatorial shows and Spanish bull-

---

1 Mme. Defarge] in Dickens's *A Tale of Two Cities* (1859), she was a bloodthirsty woman of the Parisian proletariat who knitted the names of those to be guillotined and called their numbers.

fights, at any rate, contributed to the public amusement, which certainly was not the case here. The most confirmed sensation-monger would fight shy of sensation if he knew that it was well on the cards that he would, in his own proper person, be the subject of the next "event."

Once we rose and tried to remonstrate, but were sternly repressed by Twala.

"Let the law take its course, white men. These dogs are magicians and evil-doers; it is well that they should die," was the only answer vouchsafed to us.

About midnight there was a pause. The witch-finders gathered themselves together, apparently exhausted with their bloody work, and we thought that the whole performance was done with. But it was not so, for presently, to our surprise, the old woman, Gagool, rose from her crouching position, and supporting herself with a stick, staggered off into the open space. It was an extraordinary sight to see this frightful vulture-headed old creature, bent nearly double with extreme age, gather strength by degrees till at last she rushed about almost as actively as her ill-omened pupils. To and fro she ran, chanting to herself, till suddenly she made a dash at a tall man standing in front of one of the regiments, and touched him. As she did so, a sort of groan went up from the regiment, which he evidently commanded. But all the same, two of its members seized him and brought him up for execution. We afterwards learned that he was a man of great wealth and importance, being, indeed, a cousin of the king's.

He was slain, and the king counted one hundred and three. Then Gagool again sprang to and fro, gradually drawing nearer and nearer to ourselves.

"Hang me if I don't believe she is going to try her games on us," ejaculated Good in horror.

"Nonsense!" said Sir Henry.

As for myself, as I saw that old fiend dancing nearer and nearer, my heart positively sank into my boots. I glanced behind us at the long rows of corpses, and shivered.

Nearer and nearer waltzed Gagool, looking for all the world like an animated crooked stick, her horrid eyes gleaming and glowing with a most unholy lustre.

Nearer she came, and nearer yet, every pair of eyes in that vast assemblage watching her movements with intense anxiety. At last she stood still and pointed.

"Which is it to be?" asked Sir Henry to himself.

In a moment all doubts were set at rest, for the old woman had rushed in and touched Umbopa, alias Ignosi, on the shoulder.

"I smell him out," she shrieked. "Kill him, kill him, he is full of evil; kill him, the stranger, before blood flows for him. Slay him, O king."

There was a pause, which I instantly took advantage of.

"O King," I called out, rising from my seat, "this man is the servant of thy guests, he is their dog; whosoever sheds the blood of our dog sheds our blood. By the sacred law of hospitality I claim protection for him."

"Gagool, mother of the witch doctors, has smelt him out; he must die, white men," was the sullen answer.

"Nay, he shall not die," I replied; "he who tries to touch him shall die indeed."

"Seize him!" roared Twala to the executioners, who stood around red to the eyes with the blood of their victims.

They advanced towards us, and then hesitated. As for Ignosi, he raised his spear, and raised it as though determined to sell his life dearly.

"Stand back, ye dogs," I shouted, "if ye would see to-morrow's light. Touch one hair of his head and your king dies," and I covered Twala with my revolver. Sir Henry and Good also drew their pistols, Sir Henry pointing his at the leading executioner, who was advancing to carry out the sentence, and Good taking a deliberate aim at Gagool.

Twala winced perceptibly, as my barrel came in a line with his broad chest.

"Well," I said, "what is it to be, Twala?"

Then he spoke.

"Put away your magic tubes," he said; "ye have adjured me in the name of hospitality, and for that reason, but not from fear of what ye can do, I spare him. Go in peace."

"It is well," I answered, unconcernedly; "we are weary of slaughter, and would sleep. Is the dance ended?"

"It is ended," Twala answered, sulkily. "Let these dogs," pointing to the long rows of corpses, "be flung out to the hyænas and the vultures," and he lifted his spear.

Instantly the regiments began in perfect silence to defile off through the kraal gateway, a fatigue party only remaining behind to drag away the corpses of those who had been sacrificed.

Then we too rose, and making our salaam to his majesty, which he hardly deigned to acknowledge, departed to our kraal.

"Well," said Sir Henry, as we sat down, having first lit a lamp of the sort used by the Kukuanas, of which the wick is made of the fibre of a species of palm leaf, and the oil of clarified hippopotamus fat, "well, I feel uncommonly inclined to be sick."

"If I had any doubts about helping Umbopa to rebel against that infernal blackguard," put in Good, "they are gone now. It was as much as I could do to sit still while that slaughter was going on. I tried to keep my eyes shut, but they would open just at the wrong time. I wonder where Infadoos is. Umbopa, my friend, you ought to be grateful to us; your skin came near to having an air-hole made in it."

"I am grateful, Bougwan," was Umbopa's answer, when I had translated, "and I shall not forget. As for Infadoos, he will be here by-and-by. We must wait."

So we lit our pipes and waited.

CHAPTER XI.

WE GIVE A SIGN.

For a long while—two hours, I should think—we sat there in silence, for we were too overwhelmed by the recollection of the horrors we had seen to talk. At last, just as we were thinking of turning in—for already there were faint streaks of light in the eastern sky—we heard the sound of steps. Then came the challenge of the sentry, who was posted at the kraal gate, which was apparently answered, though not in an audible tone, for the steps came on; and in another second Infadoos had entered the hut, followed by some half-dozen stately looking chiefs.

"My lords," he said, "I have come according to my word. My lords and Ignosi, rightful King of the Kukuanas, I have brought with me these men," pointing to the row of chiefs, "who are great men among us, having each one of them the command of three thousand soldiers, who live but to do their bidding, under the king's. I have told them of what I have seen, and what my ears have heard. Now let them also see the sacred snake around thee, and hear thy story, Ignosi, that they may say whether or no they will make cause with thee against Twala, the king."

For answer, Ignosi again stripped off his girdle, and exhibited the snake tattooed around him. Each chief in turn drew near and examined it by the dim light of the lamp, and without saying a word passed on to the other side.

Then Ignosi resumed his moocha, and addressing them, repeated the history he had detailed in the morning.

"Now ye have heard, chiefs," said Infadoos, when he had done, "what say ye; will ye stand by this man and help him to his father's throne, or will ye not? The land cries out against Twala, and the blood of the people flows like the waters in spring. Ye have seen to-night. Two other chiefs there were with whom I had it in my mind to speak, and where are they now? The hyænas howl over their corpses. Soon will ye be as they are if ye strike not. Choose then, my brothers."

The eldest of the six men, a short, thick-set warrior with white hair, stepped forward a pace and answered—

"Thy words are true, Infadoos; the land cries out. My own brother is among those who died to-night; but this is a great matter, and the thing is hard to believe. How know we that if we lift our spears it may not be for an impostor? It is a great matter, I say, and none may see the end of it. For of this be sure, blood will flow in rivers before the deed is done; many will still cleave to the king, for men worship the sun that still shines bright in the heavens, and not that which has not risen. These white men from the stars, their magic is great, and Ignosi is under the cover of their wing. If he be indeed the rightful king, let them give us a sign, and let the people have a sign, that all may see. So shall men cleave to us, knowing that the white man's magic is with them."

"Ye have the sign of the snake," I answered.

"My lord, it is not enough. The snake may have been placed there since the man's birth. Show us a sign. We will not move without a sign."

The others gave a decided assent, and I turned in perplexity to Sir Henry and Good, and explained the situation.

"I think I have it," said Good, exultingly; "ask them to give us a moment to think."

I did so, and the chiefs withdrew. As soon as they were gone, Good went to the little box in which his medicines were, unlocked it, and took out a note-book, in the front of which was an almanack. "Now, look here, you fellows, isn't to-morrow the fourth of June?"

We had kept a careful note of the days, so were able to answer that it was.

"Very good; then here we have it—'4 June, total eclipse of the sun[1] commences at 11:15 Greenwich time, visible in these Islands —*Africa, &c.*' There's a sign for you. Tell them that you will darken the sun to-morrow."

The idea was a splendid one; indeed, the only fear about it was a fear lest Good's almanack might be incorrect. If we made a false prophecy on such a subject, our prestige would be gone for ever, and so would Ignosi's chance of the throne of the Kukuanas.

"Suppose the almanack is wrong," suggested Sir Henry to Good, who was busily employed is working out something on the fly-leaf of the book.

"I don't see any reason to suppose anything of the sort," was his answer. "Eclipses always come up to time; at least, that is my experience of them, and it especially states that it will be visible in Africa. I have worked out the reckonings as well as I can, without knowing our exact position; and I make out that the eclipse should begin here about one o'clock to-morrow, and last till half-past two. For half an hour or more there should be total darkness."

"Well," said Sir Henry, "I suppose we had better risk it."

---

1   eclipse of the sun] HRH changed "sun" to "moon" in 1887, at the "37th thousand" printing, because the time and the location—seen both in "these Islands" (meaning the British Isles) and in Africa—were impossiblities; the moon eclipse in subsequent copies is "visible in Teneriffe, *Africa*, &c."

I acquiesced, though doubtfully, for eclipses are queer cattle to deal with, and sent Umbopa to summon the chiefs back. Presently they came, and I addressed them thus—

"Great men of the Kukuanas, and thou, Infadoos, listen. We are not fond of showing our powers, since to do so is to interfere with the course of nature, and plunge the world into fear and confusion; but as this matter is a great one, and as we are angered against the king because of the slaughter we have seen, and because of the act of the Isanusi Gagool, who would have put our friend Ignosi to death, we have determined to do so, and to give such a sign as all men may see. Come hither," and I led them to the door of the hut and pointed to the fiery ball of the rising sun; "what see ye there?"

"We see the rising sun," answered the spokesman of the party.

"It is so. Now tell me, can any mortal man put out that sun, so that night comes down on the land at mid-day?"

The chief laughed a little. "No, my lord, that no man can do. The sun is stronger than man who looks on him."

"Ye say so. Yet I tell you that this day, one hour after mid-day, will we put out that sun for a space of an hour, and darkness shall cover the earth, and it shall be for a sign that we are indeed men of honour, and that Ignosi is indeed King of the Kukuanas. If we do this thing, will it satisfy ye?"

"Yea, my lords," answered the old chief with a smile, which was reflected on the faces of his companions; "*if* ye do this thing we will be satisfied indeed."

"It shall be done; we three, Incubu the Elephant, Bougwan the clear-eyed, and Macumazahn, who watches in the night, have said it, and it shall be done. Dost thou hear, Infadoos?"

"I hear, my lord, but it is a wonderful thing that ye promise, to put out the sun, the father of all things, who shines for ever."

"Yet shall we do it, Infadoos."

"It is well, my lords. To-day, a little after mid-day, will Twala send for my lords to witness the girls dance, and one hour after the dance begins shall the girl whom Twala thinks the fairest be killed by Scragga, the king's son, as a sacrifice to the silent stone ones, who sit and keep watch by the mountains yonder," and he pointed to the three strange-looking peaks where Solomon's road was supposed to end. "Then let my lords darken the sun, and save the maiden's life, and the people will indeed believe."

"Ay," said the old chief, still smiling a little, "the people will believe indeed."

"Two miles from Loo," went on Infadoos, "there is a hill curved like the new moon, a stronghold, where my regiment, and three other regiments which these men command, are stationed. This morning we will make a plan whereby other regiments, two or three, may be moved there also. Then if my lords can indeed darken the sun, in the darkness I will take my lords by the hand and lead them out of Loo to this place, where they shall be safe, and thence can we make war upon Twala, the king."

"It is good," said I. "Now leave us to sleep awhile and make ready our magic."

Infadoos rose, and, having saluted us, departed with the chiefs.

"My friends," said Ignosi, as soon as they were gone, "can ye indeed do this wonderful thing, or were ye speaking empty words to the men?"

"We believe that we can do it, Umbopa—Ignosi, I mean."

"It is strange," he answered, "and had ye not been Englishmen I would not have believed it; but English 'gentlemen' tell no lies. If we live through the matter, be sure I will repay ye!"

"Ignosi," said Sir Henry, "promise me one thing."

"I will promise, Incubu, my friend, even before I hear it," answered the big man with a smile. "What is it?"

"This: that if you ever come to be king of this people you will do away with the smelling out of witches such as we have seen last night; and that the killing of men without trial shall not take place in the land."

Ignosi thought for a moment, after I had translated this, and then answered—

"The ways of black people are not as the ways of white men, Incubu, nor do we hold life so high as ye. Yet will I promise it. If it be in my power to hold them back, the witch-finders shall hunt no more, nor shall any man die the death without judgment."

"That's a bargain, then," said Sir Henry; "and now let us get a little rest."

Thoroughly wearied out, we were soon sound asleep, and slept till Ignosi woke us about eleven o'clock. Then we got up, washed, and ate a hearty breakfast, not knowing when we should get any more food. After that we went outside the hut and stared at the sun, which we were distressed to observe presented a remarkably healthy appearance, without a sign of an eclipse anywhere about it.

"I hope it will come off," said Sir Henry, doubtfully. "False prophets often find themselves in painful positions."

"If it does not, it will soon be up with us," I answered, mournfully; "for so sure as we are living men, some of those chiefs will tell the whole story to the king, and then there will be another sort of eclipse, and one that we shall not like."

Returning to the hut we dressed ourselves, putting on the mail shirts which the king had sent us as before. Scarcely had we done so when a messenger came from Twala to bid us to the great annual "dance of girls" which was about to be celebrated.

Taking our rifles and ammunition with us so as to have them handy in case we had to fly, as suggested by Infadoos, we started boldly enough, though with inward fear and trembling. The great space in front of the king's kraal presented a very different appearance from what it had done on the previous evening. In the place of the grim ranks of serried warriors were company after company of Kukuana girls, not overdressed, so far as clothing went, but each crowned with a wreath of flowers, and holding a palm leaf in one hand and a tall white lily (the arum) in the other. In the centre of the open space sat Twala, the king, with old Gagool at his feet, attended by Infadoos, the boy Scragga, and about a dozen guards. There were also present about a score of chiefs, amongst whom I recognised most of our friends of the night before.

Twala greeted us with much apparent cordiality, though I saw him fix his one eye viciously on Umbopa.

"Welcome, white men from the stars," he said; "this is a different sight from what your eyes gazed on by the light of last night's moon, but it is not so good a sight. Girls are pleasant, and were it not for such as these" (and he pointed round him) "we should none of us be here to-day; but men are better. Kisses and the tender words of women are sweet, but the sound of the clashing of men's spears, and the smell of men's blood, are sweeter far!

Would ye have wives from among our people, white men? If so, choose the fairest here, and ye shall have them, as many as ye will," and he paused for an answer.

As the prospect did not seem to be without attractions to Good, who was, like most sailors, of a susceptible nature, I, being elderly and wise, and foreseeing the endless complications that anything of the sort would involve (for women bring trouble as surely as the night follows the day), put in a hasty answer—

"Thanks, O king, but we white men wed only with white women like ourselves. Your maidens are fair, but they are not for us!"

The king laughed. "It is well. In our land there is a proverb which says, 'Woman's eyes are always bright, whatever the colour,' and another which says, 'Love her who is present, for be sure she who is absent is false to thee;' but perhaps these things are not so in the stars. In a land where men are white all things are possible. So be it, white men; the girls will not go begging! Welcome again; and welcome, too, thou black one; if Gagool here had had her way thou wouldst have been stiff and cold now. It is lucky that thou, too, camest from the stars; ha! ha!"

"I can kill thee before thou killest me, O king," was Ignosi's calm answer, "and thou shalt be stiff before my limbs cease to bend."

Twala started. "Thou speakest boldly, boy," he replied, angrily; "presume not too far."

"He may well be bold in whose lips are truth. The truth is a sharp spear which flies home and fails not. It is a message from 'the stars,' O king!"

Twala scowled, and his one eye gleamed fiercely, but he said nothing more.

"Let the dance begin," he cried, and next second the flower-crowned girls sprang forward in companies, singing a sweet song and waving the delicate palms and white flowers. On they danced, now whirling round and round, now meeting in mimic warfare, swaying, eddying here and there, coming forward, falling back in an ordered confusion delightful to witness. At last they paused, and a beautiful young woman sprang out of the ranks and began to pirouette in front of us with a grace and vigour which would have put most ballet girls to shame. At length she fell back exhausted, and another took her place, then another and another, but none of them, either in grace, skill, or personal attractions, came up to the first.

At length the king lifted his hand. "Which think ye the fairest, white men?" he asked.

"The first," said I, unthinkingly. Next second I regretted it, for I remembered that Infadoos had said that the fairest woman was offered as a sacrifice.

"Then is my mind as your minds, and my eyes as your eyes. She is the fairest; and a sorry thing it is for her, for she must die!"

"*Ay, must die!*" piped out Gagool, casting a glance from her quick eyes in the direction of the poor girl, who, as yet ignorant of the awful fate in store for her, was standing some twenty yards off in front of a company of girls, engaged in nervously picking a flower from her wreath to pieces, petal by petal.

"'Why, O king?" said I, restraining my indignation with difficulty; "the girl has danced well and pleased us; she is fair, too; it would be hard to reward her with death."

Twala laughed as he answered—

"It is our custom, and the figures who sit in stone yonder" (and he pointed towards the three distant peaks) "must have their due. Did I fail to put the fairest girl to death to-day misfortune would fall upon me and my house. Thus runs the prophecy of my people: 'If the king offer not a sacrifice of a fair girl on the day of the dance of maidens to the old ones who sit and watch on the mountains, then shall he fall and his house.' Look ye, white men, my brother who reigned before me offered not the sacrifice, because of the tears of the woman, and he fell, and his house, and I reign in his stead. It is finished; she must die!" Then turning to the guards—"Bring her hither; Scragga, make sharp thy spear."

Two of the men stepped forward, and as they did so, the girl, for the first time realising her impending fate, screamed aloud and turned to fly. But the strong hands caught her fast, and brought her, struggling and weeping, up before us.

"What is thy name, girl?" piped Gagool. "What! wilt thou not answer; shall the king's son do his work at once?"

At this hint Scragga, looking more evil than ever, advanced a step and lifted his great spear, and as he did so I saw Good's hand creep to his revolver. The poor girl caught the glint of the cold steel through her tears, and it sobered her anguish. She ceased struggling, but merely clasped her hands convulsively, and stood shuddering from head to foot.

"See," cried Scragga in high glee, "she shrinks from the sight of my little plaything even before she has tasted it," and he tapped the broad blade of the spear.

"If ever I get the chance, you shall pay for that, you young hound!" I heard Good mutter beneath his breath.

"Now that thou art quiet, give us thy name, my dear. Come, speak up, and fear not," said Gagool in mockery.

"Oh, mother," answered the girl in trembling accents, "my name is Foulata, of the house of Suko. Oh, mother, why must I die? I have done no wrong!"

"Be comforted," went on the old woman, in her hateful tone of mockery. "Thou must die indeed, as a sacrifice to the old ones who sit yonder" (and she pointed to the peaks); "but it is better to sleep in the night than to toil in the day-time; it is better to die than to live, and thou shalt die by the royal hand of the king's own son."

The girl Foulata wrung her hands in anguish, and cried out aloud: "Oh, cruel; and I so young! What have I done that I should never again see the sun rise out of the night, or the stars come following on his track in the evening: that I should no more gather the flowers when the dew is heavy, or listen to the laughing of the waters! Woe is me, that I shall never see my father's hut again, nor feel my mother's kiss, nor tend the kid that is sick! Woe is me, that no lover shall put his arm around me and look into my eyes, nor shall men children be born of me! Oh, cruel, cruel!" and again she wrung her hands and turned her tear-stained, flower-crowned face to Heaven, looking so lovely in her despair—for she was indeed a beautiful woman—that it would assuredly have melted the hearts of any one less cruel than the three fiends before us. Prince Arthur's appeal to the ruffians who came to blind him was not more touching than this savage girl's.[1]

---

1 Prince Arthur] See Shakespeare's *King John*, 4.1.90–125.

But it did not move Gagool or Gagool's master, though I saw signs of pity among the guard behind, and on the faces of the chiefs; and as for Good, he gave a sort of snort of indignation, and made a motion as though to go to her. With all a woman's quickness, the doomed girl interpreted what was passing in his mind, and with a sudden movement flung herself before him, and clasped his "beautiful white legs" with her hands.

"Oh, white father from the stars!" she cried, "throw over me the mantle of thy protection; let me creep into the shadow of thy strength, that I may be saved. Oh, keep me from these cruel men and from the mercies of Gagool!"

"All right, my hearty, I'll look after you," sang out Good, in nervous Saxon. "Come, get up, there's a good girl," and he stooped and caught her hand.

Twala turned and motioned to his son, who advanced with his spear lifted.

"Now's your time," whispered Sir Henry to me; "what are you waiting for?"

"I am waiting for the eclipse," I answered; "I have had my eye on the sun for the last half-hour, and I never saw it look healthier."

"Well, you must risk it now, or the girl will be killed. Twala is losing patience."

Recognising the force of the argument, having cast one more despairing look at the bright face of the sun, for never did the most ardent astronomer with a theory to prove await a celestial event with such anxiety, I stepped with all the dignity I could command between the prostrate girl and the advancing spear of Scragga.

"King," I said, "this shall not be; we will not tolerate such a thing; let the girl go in safety."

Twala rose from his seat in his wrath and astonishment, and from the chiefs and serried ranks of girls, who had slowly closed up upon us in anticipation of the tragedy, came a murmur of amazement.

"*Shall not be*, thou white dog, who yaps at the lion in his cave, *shall not be!* art thou mad? Be careful lest this chicken's fate overtakes thee, and those with thee. How canst thou prevent it? Who art thou that thou standest between me and my will? Withdraw, I say. Scragga, kill her. Ho, guards! seize these men."

At his cry armed men came running swiftly from behind the hut, where they had evidently been placed beforehand.

Sir Henry, Good, and Umbopa ranged themselves alongside of me, and lifted their rifles.

"Stop!" I shouted boldly, though at the moment my heart was in my boots. "Stop! we, the white men from the stars, say that it shall not be. Come but one pace nearer, and we will put out the sun and plunge the land in darkness. Ye shall taste of our magic."

My threat produced an effect; the men halted, and Scragga stood still before us, his spear lifted.

"Hear him! hear him!" piped Gagool; "hear the liar who says he will put out the sun like a lamp. Let him do it, and the girl shall be spared. Yes, let him do it, or die with the girl, he and those with him."

I glanced up at the sun, and to my intense joy and relief saw that we had made no mistake. On the edge of its brilliant surface was a faint rim of shadow.

I lifted my hand solemnly towards the sky, an example which Sir Henry and Good followed, and quoted a line or two of the "Ingoldsby Legends" at it in the most impressive tones I could command. Sir Henry followed suit with a verse out of the Old Testament, whilst Good addressed the King of Day in a volume of the most classical bad language that he could think of.

Slowly the dark rim crept on over the blazing surface, and as it did so I heard a deep gasp of fear rise from the multitude around.

"Look, O king! look, Gagool! Look, chiefs and people and women, and see if the white men from the stars keep their word, or if they be but empty liars!"

"The sun grows dark before your eyes; soon there will be night—ay, night in the noontime. Ye have asked for a sign; it is given to ye. Grow dark, O sun! withdraw thy light, thou bright one; bring the proud heart to the dust, and eat up the world with shadows."

A groan of terror rose from the onlookers. Some stood

petrified with fear, others threw themselves upon their knees, and cried out. As for the king, he sat still and turned pale beneath his dusky skin. Only Gagool kept her courage.

"It will pass," she cried; "I have seen the like before; no man can put out the sun; lose not heart; sit still—the shadow will pass."

"Wait, and ye shall see," I replied, hopping with excitement.

"Keep it up, Good, I can't remember any more poetry. Curse away, there's a good fellow."

Good responded nobly to the tax upon his inventive faculties. Never before had I the faintest conception of the breadth and depth and height of a naval officer's objurgatory powers. For ten minutes he went on without stopping, and he scarcely ever repeated himself.

Meanwhile the dark ring crept on. Strange and unholy shadows encroached upon the sunlight, an ominous quiet filled the place, the birds chirped out frightened notes, and then were still; only the cocks began to crow.

On, yet on, crept the ring of darkness; it was now more than half over the reddening orb. The air grew thick and dusky. On, yet on, till we could scarcely see the fierce faces of the group before us. No sound rose now from the spectators, and Good stopped swearing.

"The sun is dying—the wizards have killed the sun," yelled out the boy Scragga at last. "We shall all die in the dark," and animated by fear or fury, or both, he lifted his spear, and drove it with all his force at Sir Henry's broad chest. But he had forgotten the mail shirts that the king had given us, and which we wore beneath our clothing. The steel rebounded harmless, and before he could repeat the blow Sir Henry had snatched the spear from his hand, and sent it straight through him. He dropped dead.

At the sight, and driven mad with fear at the gathering gloom, the companies of girls broke up in wild confusion, and ran screeching for the gateways. Nor did the panic stop there. The king himself, followed by the guards, some of the chiefs, and Gagool, who hobbled away after them with marvellous alacrity, fled for the huts, so that in another minute or so ourselves, the would-be victim, Foulata, Infadoos, and some of the chiefs, who had interviewed us on the previous night, were left alone upon the scene with the dead body of Scragga.

"Now, chiefs," I said, "we have given you the sign. If ye are satisfied, let us fly swiftly to the place ye spoke of. The charm cannot now be stopped. It will work for an hour. Let us take advantage of the darkness."

"Come," said Infadoos, turning to go, an example which was followed by the awed chiefs, ourselves, and the girl Foulata, whom Good took by the hand.

Before we reached the gate of the kraal the sun went out altogether.

Holding each other by the hand we stumbled on through the darkness.

CHAPTER XII.

BEFORE THE BATTLE.

LUCKILY for us, Infadoos and the chiefs knew all the pathways of the great town perfectly, so that notwithstanding the intense gloom we made fair progress.

For an hour or more we journeyed on, till at length the eclipse began to pass, and that edge of the sun which had disappeared the first, became again visible. In another five minutes there was sufficient light to see our whereabouts, and we then discovered that we were clear of the town of Loo, and approaching a large flat-topped hill, measuring some two miles in circumference. This hill, which was of a formation very common in Southern Africa, was not very high; indeed, its greatest elevation was not more than 200 feet, but it was shaped like a horse-shoe, and its sides were rather precipitous, and strewn with boulders. On the grass table-land at the top was ample camping ground, which had been utilised as a military cantonment of no mean strength. Its ordinary garrison was one regiment of three thousand men, but as we toiled up the steep side of the hill in the returning daylight, we perceived that there were many more warriors than that upon it.

Reaching the table-land at last, we found crowds of men huddled together in the utmost consternation at the natural phenomenon which they were witnessing. Passing through these without a word, we gained a hut in the centre of the ground, where we were astonished to find two men waiting, laden with our few goods and chattels, which of course we had been obliged to leave behind in our hasty flight.

"I sent for them," explained Infadoos; "also for these," and he lifted up Good's long-lost trousers.

With an exclamation of rapturous delight Good sprang at them, and instantly proceeded to put them on.

"Surely my lord will not hide his beautiful white legs!" exclaimed Infadoos, regretfully.

But Good persisted, and once only did the Kukuana people get the chance of seeing his beautiful legs again. Good is a very modest man. Henceforward they had to satisfy their æsthetic longings with his one whisker, his transparent eye, and his movable teeth.

Still gazing with fond remembrance at Good's trousers, Infadoos next informed us that he had summoned the regiments to explain to them fully the rebellion which was decided on by the chiefs, and to introduce to them the rightful heir to the throne, Ignosi.

In half an hour the troops, in all nearly twenty thousand men, constituting the flower of the Kukuana army, were mustered on a large open space, to which we proceeded. The men were drawn up in three sides of a dense square, and presented a magnificent spectacle. We took our station on the open side of the square, and were speedily surrounded by all the principal chiefs and officers.

These, after silence had been proclaimed, Infadoos proceeded to address. He narrated to them in vigorous and graceful language—for like most Kukuanas of high rank, he was a born orator—the history of Ignosi's father, how he had been basely murdered by Twala, the king, and his wife and child driven out to starve. Then he pointed out how the land suffered and groaned under Twala's cruel rule, instancing the proceedings of the previous night, when, under pretence of their being evildoers, many of the noblest in the land had been hauled forth and cruelly done to death. Next he went on to say that the white lords from the stars, looking down on the land, had perceived its trouble, and determined, at great personal inconvenience, to alleviate its lot; how they had accordingly taken the real king of the country, Ignosi, who was languishing in exile, by the hand, and led him over the mountains; how they had seen the wickedness of Twala's doings, and for a sign to the wavering, and to save the life of the girl Foulata, had actually, by the exercise of their high magic, put out the sun, and slain the young fiend Scragga; and how they were prepared to stand by them, and assist them to overthrow Twala, and set up the rightful king, Ignosi, in his place.

He finished his discourse amidst a murmur of approbation, and then Ignosi stepped forward, and began to speak. Having reiterated all that Infadoos his uncle had said, he concluded a powerful speech in these words: —

"O chiefs, captains, soldiers, and people, ye have heard my words. Now must ye make choice between me and him who sits upon my throne, the uncle who killed his brother, and hunted his brother's child forth to die in the cold and the night. That I am indeed the king these" — pointing to the chiefs — "can tell ye, for they have seen the snake about my middle. If I were not the king, would these white men be on my side, with all their magic? Tremble, chiefs, captains, soldiers, and people! Is not the darkness they have brought upon the land to confound Twala, and cover our flight, yet before your eyes?"

"It is," answered the soldiers.

"I am the king; I say to ye, I am the king," went on Ignosi, drawing up his great stature to its full, and lifting his broad-bladed battle-axe above his head. "If there be any man among ye who says that it is not so, let him stand forth, and I will fight him now, and his blood shall be a red token that I tell ye true. Let him stand forth, I say;" and he shook the great axe till it flashed in the sunlight.

As nobody seemed inclined to respond to this heroic version of "Dilly, Dilly, come and be killed,"[1] our late henchman proceeded with his address.

"I am indeed the king, and if ye do stand by my side in the battle, if I win the day ye shall go with me to victory and honour.

---

1 dilly ... killed] from a comic nursery rhyme, "Dilly, Dilly"; a dilly is a farmyard duck or anyone silly enough to go to slaughter.

I will give ye oxen and wives, and ye shall take place of all the regiments; and if ye fall I will fall with ye.

"And, behold, this promise do I give ye, that when I sit upon the seat of my fathers, bloodshed shall cease in the land. No longer shall ye cry for justice to find slaughter, no longer shall the witch-finder hunt ye out so that ye be slain without a cause. No man shall die save he who offendeth against the laws. The 'eating up' of your kraals shall cease; each shall sleep secure in his own hut and fear not, and justice shall walk blind throughout the land. Have ye chosen, chiefs, captains, soldiers, and people?"

"We have chosen, O king," came back the answer.

"It is well. Turn your heads and see how Twala's messengers go forth from the great town, east and west, and north and south, to gather a mighty army to slay me and ye, and these my friends and my protectors. To-morrow, or perchance the next day, will he come with all who are faithful to him. Then shall I see the man who is indeed my man, the man who fears not to die for his cause; and I tell ye he shall not be forgotten in the time of spoil. I have spoken, O chiefs, captains, soldiers, and people. Now go to your huts and make you ready for war."

There was a pause, and then one of the chiefs lifted his hand, and out rolled the royal salute, "Koom." It was a sign that the regiments accepted Ignosi as their king. Then they marched off in battalions.

Half an hour afterwards we held a council of war, at which all the commanders of regiments were present. It was evident to us that before very long we should be attacked in overwhelming force. Indeed, from our point of vantage on the hill we could see troops mustering, and messengers going forth from Loo in every direction, doubtless to summon regiments to the king's assistance. We had on our side about twenty thousand men, composed of seven of the best regiments in the country. Twala had, so Infadoos and the chiefs calculated, at least thirty to thirty-five thousand on whom he could rely at present assembled in Loo, and they thought that by midday on the morrow he would be able to gather another five thousand or more to his aid. It was, of course, possible that some of his troops would desert and come over to us, but it was not a contingency that could be reckoned on.

Meanwhile, it was clear that active preparations were being made to subdue us. Already strong bodies of armed men were patrolling round and round the foot of the hill, and there were other signs of a coming attack.

Infadoos and the chiefs, however, were of opinion that no attack would take place that night, which would be devoted to preparation and to the removal by every possible means of the moral effect produced upon the minds of the soldiery by the supposed magical darkening of the sun. The attack would be on the morrow, they said, and they proved to be right.

Meanwhile, we set to work to strengthen the position as much as possible. Nearly the entire force was turned out, and in the two hours which yet remained to sundown wonders were done. The paths up the hill, which was rather a sanitarium than a fortress, being used generally as the camping place of regiments suffering from recent service in unhealthy portions of the country, were carefully blocked with masses of stones, and every other possible approach was made as impregnable as time would allow. Piles of boulders were collected at various spots to be rolled down upon an advancing enemy, stations were appointed to the different regiments, and every other preparation which our joint ingenuity could suggest was taken.

Just before sundown we perceived a small company of men advancing towards us from the direction of Loo, one of whom bore a palm leaf in his hand as a sign that he came as a herald.

As he came, Ignosi, Infadoos, one or two chiefs, and ourselves, went down to the foot of the mountain to meet him. He was a gallant-looking fellow, with the regulation leopard-skin cloak.

"Greeting!" he cried, as he came near; "the king's greeting to those who make unholy war against the king; the lion's greeting to the jackals who snarl around his heels."

"Speak," I said.

"These are the king's words. Surrender to the king's mercy ere a worse thing befall ye. Already the shoulder has been torn from the black bull, and the king drives him bleeding about the camp."*

---

* This cruel custom is not confined to the Kukuanas, but is by no means uncommon amongst African tribes on the occasion of the outbreak of war or any other important public event. — A.Q.

"What are Twala's terms?" I asked for curiosity.

"His terms are merciful, worthy of a great king. These are the words of Twala, the one-eyed, the mighty, the husband of a thousand wives, lord of the Kukuanas, keeper of the great road (Solomon's Road), beloved of the strange ones who sit in silence at the mountains yonder (the three Witches), calf of the black cow, elephant whose tread shakes the earth, terror of the evildoer, ostrich whose feet devour the desert, huge one, black one, wise one, king from generation to generation! these are the words of Twala: 'I will have mercy and be satisfied with a little blood. One in every ten shall die, the rest shall go free; but the white man Incubu, who slew Scragga, my son, and the black man, his servant, who pretends to my throne, and Infadoos, my brother, who brews rebellion against me, these shall die by torture as an offering to the silent ones.' Such are the merciful words of Twala."

After consulting with the others a little, I answered him in a loud voice, so that the soldiers might hear, thus—

"Go back, thou dog, to Twala, who sent thee, and say that we, Ignosi, veritable king of the Kukuanas, Incubu, Bougwan, and Macumazahn, the wise white ones from the stars, who make dark the sun, Infadoos, of the royal house, and the chiefs, captains, and people here gathered, make answer and say, 'That we will not surrender; that before the sun has twice gone down Twala's corpse shall stiffen at Twala's gate, and Ignosi, whose father Twala slew, shall reign in his stead.' Now go, ere we whip thee away, and beware how ye lift a hand against such as we."

The herald laughed loud. "Ye frighten not men with such swelling words," he cried out. "Show yourselves as bold to-morrow, O ye who darken the sun. Be bold, fight, and be merry, before the crows pick your bones till they are whiter than your faces. Farewell; perhaps we may meet in the fight; wait for me, I pray, white men." And with this shaft of sarcasm he retired, and almost immediately the sun sank.

That night was a busy one for us, for as far as was possible by the moonlight all preparations for the morrow's fight were continued. Messengers were constantly coming and going from the place where we sat in council. At last, about an hour after midnight, everything that could be done was done, and the camp, save for the occasional challenge of a sentry, sank into sleep. Sir Henry and I, accompanied by Ignosi and one of the chiefs, descended the hill and made the round of the outposts. As we went, suddenly, from all sorts of unexpected places, spears gleamed out in the moonlight, only to vanish again as we uttered the password. It was clear to us that none were sleeping at their posts. Then we returned, picking our way through thousands of sleeping warriors, many of whom were taking their last earthly rest.

The moonlight flickered along their spears, and played upon their features and made them ghastly; the chilly night wind tossed their tall and hearse-like plumes. There they lay in wild confusion, with arms outstretched and twisted limbs; their stern, stalwart forms looking weird and unhuman in the moonlight.

"How many of these do you suppose will be alive at this time to-morrow?" asked Sir Henry.

I shook my head and looked again at the sleeping men, and to my tired and yet excited imagination it seemed as though death had already touched them. My mind's eye singled out those who were sealed to slaughter, and there rushed in upon my heart a great sense of the mystery of human life, and an overwhelming sorrow at its futility and sadness. To-night these thousands slept their healthy sleep, to-morrow they, and many others with them, ourselves perhaps among them, would be stiffening in the cold; their wives would be widows, their children fatherless, and their place know them no more for ever. Only the old moon would shine serenely on, the night wind would stir the grasses, and the wide earth would take its happy rest, even as it did æons before these were, and will do æons after they have been forgotten.

Yet man dies not whilst the world, at once his mother and his monument, remains. His name is forgotten, indeed, but the breath he breathed yet stirs the pine-tops on the mountains, the sound of the words he spoke yet echoes on through space; the thoughts his brain gave birth to we have inherited to-day; his passions are our cause of life; the joys and sorrows that he felt are our familiar friends — the end from which he fled aghast will surely overtake us also!

Truly the universe is full of ghosts, not sheeted churchyard spectres, but the inextinguishable and immortal elements of life, which, having once been, can never *die*, though they blend and change and change again for ever.

All sorts of reflections of this sort passed through my mind—for as I get older I regret to say that a detestable habit of thinking seems to be getting a hold of me—while I stood and stared at those grim yet fantastic lines of warriors sleeping, as their saying goes, "upon their spears."

"Curtis," I said to Sir Henry, "I am in a condition of pitiable funk."

Sir Henry stroked his yellow beard and laughed, as he answered—

"I've heard you make that sort of remark before, Quatermain."

"Well, I mean it now. Do you know, I very much doubt if one of us will be alive to-morrow night. We shall be attacked in over-whelming force, and it is exceedingly doubtful if we can hold this place."

"We'll give a good account of some of them, at any rate. Look here, Quatermain, the business is a nasty one, and one with which, properly speaking, we ought not to be mixed up, but we are in for it, so we must make the best of it. Speaking personally, I had rather be killed fighting than any other way, and now that there seems little chance of my finding my poor brother, it makes the idea easier to me. But fortune favours the brave, and we may succeed. Anyway, the slaughter will be awful, and as we have a reputation to keep up, we shall have to be in the thick of it."

Sir Henry made this last remark in a mournful voice, but there was a gleam in his eye which belied it. I have a sort of idea that Sir Henry Curtis actually likes fighting.

After this we went and slept for a couple of hours.

Just about dawn we were awakened by Infadoos, who came to say that great activity was to be observed in Loo, and that parties of the king's skirmishers were driving in our outposts.

We got up and dressed ourselves for the fray, each putting on our chain-armour shirt, for which at the present juncture we felt exceedingly thankful. Sir Henry went the whole length about the matter, and dressed himself like a native warrior. "When you are in Kukuanaland, do as the Kukuanas do," he remarked, as he drew the shining steel over his broad shoulders, which it fitted like a glove. Nor did he stop there. At his request, Infadoos had provided him with a complete set of war uniform. Round his throat he fastened the leopard-skin cloak of a commanding officer, on his brows he bound the plume of black ostrich feathers, worn only by generals of high rank, and round his centre a magnificent moocha of white ox-tails. A pair of sandals, a leglet of goats' hair, a heavy battle-axe, with a rhinoceros-horn handle, a round iron shield, covered with white ox-hide, and the regulation number of tollas, or throwing knives, made up his equipment, to which, however, he added his revolver. The dress was, no doubt, a savage one, but I am bound to say I never saw a finer sight than Sir Henry Curtis presented in this guise. It showed off his magnificent physique to the greatest advantage, and when Ignosi arrived presently, arrayed in similar costume, I thought to myself that I never before saw two such splendid men. As for Good and myself, the chain armour did not suit us nearly so well. To begin with, Good insisted upon keeping on his trousers, and a stout, short gentleman with an eye-glass, and one half of his face shaved, arrayed in a mail shirt carefully tucked into a very seedy pair of corduroys, looks more striking than imposing. As for myself, my chain shirt being too big for me, I put it on over all my clothes, which caused it to bulge out in a somewhat ungainly fashion. I discarded my trouser, however, determined to go into battle with bare legs, in order to be the lighter, in case it became necessary to retire quickly, retaining only my veldtschoons. This, a spear, a shield, which I did not know how to use, a couple of tollas, a revolver, and a huge plume, which I pinned into the top of my shooting hat, in order to give a bloodthirsty finish to my appearance, completed my modest equipment. In addition to all these articles, of course we had our rifles, but as ammunition was scarce, and they would be useless in case of a charge, we had arranged to have them carried behind us by bearers.

As soon as we had equipped ourselves, we hastily swallowed some food, and then started out to see how things were progressing. At one point in the table-land of the mountain there was a little koppie of brown stone, which served for the double purpose of headquarters and a conning tower. Here we found Infadoos surrounded by his own regiment, the Greys, which was undoubtedly the finest in the Kukuana army, and the same which we had first seen at the outlying kraal. This regiment, now three thousand five hundred strong, was being held in reserve, and the men were lying down on the grass in companies, and watching the king's forces creep out of Loo in long ant-like columns. There seemed to be no end to those columns—three in all, and each numbering at least eleven or twelve thousand men.

As soon as they were clear of the town, they formed up. Then one body marched off to the right, one to the left, and the third came slowly on towards us.

"Ah," said Infadoos, "they are going to attack us on three sides at once."

This was rather serious news, for as our position on the top of the mountain, which was at least a mile and a half in circumference, was an extended one, it was important to us to concentrate our comparatively small defending force as much as possible. But as it was impossible for us to dictate in what way we should be attacked, we had to make the best of it, and accordingly sent orders to the various regiments to prepare to receive the separate onslaughts.

CHAPTER XIII.

THE ATTACK.

SLOWLY, and without the slightest appearance of haste or excitement, the three columns crept on. When within about five hundred yards of us, the main or centre column halted at the root of a tongue of open plain which ran up into the hill, to enable the other two to circumvent our position, which was shaped more or less in the form of a horse-shoe, the two points being towards the town of Loo, their object being, no doubt, that the threefold assault should be delivered simultaneously.

"Oh, for a gatling!"[1] groaned Good, as he contemplated the

---

1   a gatling] an early form of machine gun, recently invented in America by R.J. Gatling, with a large number of revolving barrels.

serried phalanxes beneath us. "I would clear the plain in twenty minutes."

"We have not got one, so it is no use yearning for it; but suppose, you try a shot, Quatermain. See how near you can go to that tall fellow who appears to be in command. Two to one you miss him, and an even sovereign, to be honestly paid if ever we get out of this, that you don't drop the ball within ten yards."

This piqued me, so, loading the express with solid ball, I waited till my friend walked some ten yards out from his force, in order to get a better view of our position, accompanied only by an orderly, and then, lying down and resting the express upon a rock, I covered him. The rifle, like all expresses, was only sighted to three hundred and fifty yards, so to allow for the drop in trajectory I took him half-way down the neck, which ought, I calculated, to find him in the chest. He stood quite still and gave me every opportunity, but whether it was the excitement or the wind, or the fact of the man being a long shot, I don't know, but this was what happened. Getting dead on, as I thought, a fine sight, I pressed, and when the puff of smoke had cleared away, I, to my disgust, saw my man standing unharmed, whilst his orderly, who was at least three paces to the left, was stretched upon the ground, apparently dead. Turning swiftly, the officer I had aimed at began to run towards his force, in evident alarm.

"Bravo, Quatermain!" sang out Good; "you've frightened him."

This made me very angry, for if possible to avoid it, I hate to miss in public. When one can only do one thing well, one likes to keep up one's reputation in that thing. Moved quite out of myself at my failure, I did a rash thing. Rapidly covering the general as he ran, I let drive with the second barrel. The poor man threw up his arms, and fell forward on to his face. This time I had made no mistake; and—I say it as a proof of how little we think of others when our own pride or reputation are in question—I was brute enough to feel delighted at the sight.

The regiments who had seen the feat cheered wildly at this exhibition of the white man's magic, which they took as an omen of success, while the force to which the general had belonged— which, indeed, as we afterwards ascertained, he had commanded—began to fall back in confusion. Sir Henry and Good now took up their rifles, and began to fire, the latter industriously "browning"[1] the dense mass before him with a Winchester repeater, and I also had another shot or two, with the result that so far as we could judge we put some eight or ten men *hors de combat*[2] before they got out of range.

Just as we stopped firing there came an ominous roar from our far right, then a similar roar from out left. The two other divisions were engaging us.

At the sound, the mass of men before us opened out a little, and came on towards the hill up the spit of bare grass-land at a slow trot, singing a deep-throated song as they advanced. We kept up a steady fire from our rifles as they came, Ignosi joining in occasionally, and accounted for several men, but of course produced no more effect upon that mighty rush of armed humanity than he who throws pebbles does on the advancing wave.

On they came, with a shout and the clashing of spears; now they were driving in the outposts we had placed among the rocks at the foot of the hill. After that the advance was a little slower, for though as yet we had offered no serious opposition, the attacking force had to come up hill, and came slowly to save their breath. Our first line of defence was about half-way up the side, our second fifty yards further back, while our third occupied the edge of the plain.

On they came, shouting their war-cry, "*Twala! Twala! Chielé! Chielé!*" (Twala! Twala! Smite! Smite!). "*Ignosi! Ignosi! Chielé! Chielé!*" answered our people. They were quite close now, and the tollas, or throwing knives, began to flash backwards and forwards, and now with an awful yell the battle closed in.

To and fro swayed the mass of struggling warriors, men falling thick as leaves in an autumn wind; but before long the superior weight of the attacking force began to tell, and our first line of defence was slowly pressed back, till it merged into the second. Here the struggle was very fierce, but again our people were driven back and up, till at length, within twenty minutes of the commencement of the fight, our third line came into action.

---

1 "browning"] shooting indiscriminately, possibly from Robert Brown's discovery earlier in the century of the rapid oscillatory motion of small particles in liquid.

2 *hors de combat*] (French) out of the fight; disabled.

But by this time the assailants were much exhausted, and had besides lost many men killed and wounded, and to break through that third impenetrable hedge of spears proved beyond their powers. For awhile the dense mass of struggling warriors swung backwards and forwards in the fierce ebb and flow of battle, and the issue was doubtful. Sir Henry watched the desperate struggle with a kindling eye, and then without a word he rushed off, followed by Good, and flung himself into the hottest of the fray. As for myself, I stopped where I was.

The soldiers caught sight of his tall form as he plunged into the battle, and there rose a cry of—

"*Nanzia Incubu!*" (Here is the Elephant!) "*Chielé! Chielé!*"

From that moment the issue was no longer in doubt. Inch by inch, fighting with desperate gallantry, the attacking force was pressed back down the hillside, till at last it retreated upon its reserves in something like confusion. At that moment, too, a messenger arrived to say that the left attack had been repulsed; and I was just beginning to congratulate myself that the affair was over for the present, when, to our horror, we perceived our men who had been engaged in the right defence being driven towards us across the plain, followed by swarms of the enemy, who had evidently succeeded at this point.

Ignosi, who was standing by me, took in the situation at a glance, and issued a rapid order. Instantly the reserve regiment round us (the Greys) extended itself.

Again Ignosi gave a word of command, which was taken up and repeated by the captains, and in another second, to my intense disgust, I found myself involved in a furious onslaught upon the advancing foe. Getting as much as I could behind Ignosi's huge frame, I made the best of a bad job, and toddled along to be killed, as though I liked it. In a minute or two — the time seemed all too short to me — we were plunging through the flying groups of our men, who at once began to re-form behind us, and then I am sure I do not know what happened. All I can remember is a dreadful rolling noise of the meeting of shields, and the sudden apparition of a huge ruffian, whose eyes seemed literally to be starting out of his head, making straight at me with a bloody spear. But — I say it with pride — I rose to the occasion. It was an occasion before which most people would have collapsed once and for all. Seeing that if I stood where I was I must be done for, I, as the horrid apparition came, flung myself down in front of him so cleverly, that, being unable to stop himself, he took a header right over my prostrate form. Before be could rise again, I had risen and settled the matter from behind with my revolver.

Shortly after this, somebody knocked me down, and I remember no more of the charge.

When I came to, I found myself back at the koppie, with Good bending over me with some water in a gourd.

"How do you feel, old fellow?" he asked, anxiously.

I got up and shook myself before answering.

"Pretty well, thank you," I answered.

"Thank Heaven! when I saw them carry you in I felt quite sick; I thought you were done for."

"Not this time, my boy. I fancy I only got a rap on the head, which knocked me out of time. How has it ended?"

"They are repulsed at every point for the time. The loss is dreadfully heavy; we have lost quite two thousand killed and wounded, and they must have lost three. Look, there's a sight!" and he pointed to long lines of men advancing by fours. In the centre of, and being borne by each group of four, was a kind of hide tray, of which a Kukuana force always carried a quantity, with a loop for a handle at each corner. On these trays—and their number seemed endless—lay wounded men, who as they arrived were hastily examined by the medicine men, of whom ten were attached to each regiment. If the wound was not of a fatal character, the sufferer was taken away and attended to as carefully as circumstances would allow. But if, on the other hand, the wounded man's condition was hopeless, what followed was very dreadful, though doubtless it was the truest mercy. One of the doctors, under pretence of carrying out an examination, swiftly opened an artery with a sharp knife, and in a minute or two the sufferer expired painlessly. There were many cases that day in which this was done. In fact, it was done in most cases when the wound was in the body, for the gash made by the entry of the enormously broad spears used by the Kukuanas generally rendered recovery hopeless. In most cases the poor sufferers were already unconscious, and in others the fatal "nick" of the artery was done so swiftly and painlessly that they did not seem to notice it. Still it was a ghastly sight, and one from which we were glad to escape; indeed, I never remember one which affected me more than seeing those gallant soldiers thus put out of pain by the red-handed medicine men, except, indeed, on an occasion when, after an attack, I saw a force of Swazis burying their hopelessly wounded *alive*.

Hurrying from this dreadful scene to the further side of the koppie, we found Sir Henry (who still held a bloody battle-axe in his hand), Ignosi, Infadoos, and one or two of the chiefs in deep consultation.

"Thank heavens, here you are, Quatermain! I can't quite make out what Ignosi wants to do. It seems that, though we have beaten off the attack, Twala is now receiving large reinforcements, and is showing a disposition to invest us, with a view of starving us out."

"That's awkward."

"Yes; especially as Infadoos says that the water supply has given out."

"My lord, that is so," said Infadoos; "the spring cannot supply the wants of so great a multitude, and is failing rapidly. Before night we shall all be thirsty. Listen, Macumazahn. Thou art wise, and hast doubtless seen many wars in the lands from whence thou camest—that is if, indeed, they make wars in the stars. Now tell us, what shall we do? Twala has brought up many fresh men to take the place of those who have fallen. But Twala has learnt a lesson; the hawk did not think to find the heron ready; but our beak has pierced his breast; he will not strike at us again. We too are wounded, and he will wait for us to die; he will wind himself round us like a snake round a buck, and fight the fight of 'sit down.'"

"I hear you," I said.

"So, Macumazahn, thou seest we have no water here, and but a little food, and we must choose between these three things—to languish like a starving lion in his den, or to strive to break away towards the north, or"—and here he rose and pointed towards the dense mass of our foes—"to launch ourselves straight at

Twala's throat. Incubu, the great warrior—for to-day he fought like a buffalo in a net, and Twala's soldiers went down before his axe like corn before the hail; with these eyes I saw it—Incubu says 'Charge;' but the Elephant is ever prone to charge. Now what says Macumazahn, the wily old fox, who has seen much, and loves to bite his enemy from behind? The last word is in Ignosi the king, for it is a king's right to speak of war; but let us hear thy voice, O Macumazahn, who watchest by night, and the voice too of him of the transparent eye."

"What sayest thou, Ignosi?" I asked.

"Nay, my father," answered our quondam servant, who now, clad as he was in the full panoply of savage war, looked every inch a warrior king, "do thou speak, and let me, who am but a child in wisdom beside thee, hearken to thy words."

Thus abjured, I, after taking hasty counsel with Good and Sir Henry, delivered my opinion briefly to the effect that, being trapped, our best chance, especially in view of the failure of our water supply, was to initiate an attack upon Twala's forces, and then I recommended that the attack should be delivered at once, "before our wounds grew stiff," and also before the sight of Twala's overpowering force caused the hearts of our soldiers "to wax small like fat before a fire." Otherwise, I pointed out, some of the captains might change their minds, and, making peace with Twala, desert to him, or even betray us into his hands.

This expression of opinion seemed, on the whole, to be favourably received; indeed, among the Kukuanas my utterances met with a respect which has never been accorded to them before or since. But the real decision as to our course lay with Ignosi, who, since he had been recognised as rightful king, could exercise the almost unbounded rights of sovereignty, including, of course, the final decision on matters of generalship, and it was to him that all eyes were now turned.

At length, after a pause, during which he appeared to be thinking deeply, he spoke:—

"Incubu, Macumazahn, and Bougwan, brave white men, and my friends; Infadoos, my uncle, and chiefs; my heart is fixed. I will strike at Twala this day, and set my fortunes on the blow, ay, and my life; my life and your lives also. Listen: thus will I strike. Ye see how the hill curves round like the half-moon, and how the plain runs like a green tongue towards us within the curve?"

"We see," I answered.

"Good; it is now mid-day, and the men eat and rest after the toil of battle. When the sun has turned and travelled a little way towards the dark, let thy regiment, my uncle, advance with one other down to the green tongue. And it shall be that when Twala sees it he shall hurl his force at it to crush it. But the spot is narrow, and the regiments can come against thee one at a time only; so shall they be destroyed one by one, and the eyes of all Twala's army shall be fixed upon a struggle the like of which has not been seen by living man. And with thee my uncle shall go Incubu my friend; that when Twala sees his battle-axe flashing in the first rank of the 'Greys' his heart may grow faint. And I will come with the second regiment, that which follows thee, so that if ye are destroyed, as it may happen, there may yet be a king left to fight for; and with me shall come Macumazahn the wise."

"It is well, O king," said Infadoos, apparently contemplating the certainty of the complete annihilation of his regiment with perfect calmness. Truly these Kukuanas are a wonderful people. Death has no terrors for them when it is incurred in the course of duty.

"And whilst the eyes of the multitude of Twala's regiments are thus fixed upon the fight," went on Ignosi, "behold, one-third of the men who are left alive to us (*i.e.*, about 6,000) shall creep along the right horn of the hill and fall upon the left flank of Twala's force, and one-third shall creep along the left horn and fall upon Twala's right flank. And when I see that the horns are ready to toss Twala, then will I, with the men who are left to me, charge home in Twala's face, and if fortune goes with us the day will be ours, and before Night drives her horses from the mountains to the mountains we shall sit in peace at Loo. And now let us eat and make ready; and, Infadoos, do thou prepare, that the plan be carried out; and stay, let my white father Bougwan go with the right horn, that his shining eye may give courage to the men."

The arrangements for attack thus briefly indicated were set in motion with a rapidity that spoke well for the perfection of the Kukuana military system. Within little more than an hour rations had been served out to the men and devoured, the three divisions were formed, the plan of attack explained to the leaders, and the whole force, with the exception of a guard left with the wounded, now numbering about 18,000 men in all, was ready to be put in motion.

Presently Good came up and shook bands with Sir Henry and myself.

"Good-bye, you fellows," he said, "I am off with the right wing according to orders; and so I have come to shake hands in case we should not meet again, you know," he added, significantly.

We shook hands in silence, and not without the exhibition of as much emotion as Englishmen are wont to show.

"It is a queer business," said Sir Henry, his deep voice shaking a little, "and I confess I never expect to see to-morrow's sun. As far as I can make out, the Greys, with whom I am to go, are to fight until they are wiped out in order to enable the wings to slip round unawares and outflank Twala. Well, so be it; at any rate, it will be a man's death! Good-bye, old fellow. God bless you! I hope you will pull through and live to collar the diamonds; but if you do, take my advice and don't have anything more to do with pretenders!"[1]

In another second Good had wrung us both by the hand and gone; and then Infadoos came up and led off Sir Henry to his place in the forefront of the Greys, whilst, with many misgivings, I departed with Ignosi to my station in the second attacking regiment.

CHAPTER XIV.

THE LAST STAND OF THE GREYS.

In a few more minutes the regiments destined to carry out the flanking movements had tramped off in silence, keeping carefully under the lee of the rising ground in order to conceal the movement from the keen eyes of Twala's scouts.

---

1 pretender] a claimant of a throne who is an heir of a deposed dynasty.

Half an hour or more was allowed to elapse between the setting out of the horns or wings of the army before any movement was made by the Greys and the supporting regiment, known as the Buffaloes, which formed its chest, and which were destined to bear the brunt of the battle.

Both of these regiments were almost perfectly fresh, and of full strength, the Greys having been in reserve in the morning, and having lost but a small number of men in sweeping back that part of the attack which had proved successful in breaking the line of defence, on the occasion when I charged with them and got knocked silly for my pains. As for the Buffaloes, they had formed the third line of defence on the left, and as the attacking force at that point had not succeeded in breaking through the second, had scarcely come into action at all.

Infadoos, who was a wary old general, and knew the absolute importance of keeping up the spirits of his men on the eve of such a desperate encounter, employed the pause in addressing his own regiment, the Greys, in poetical language: in explaining to them the honour that they were receiving in being put thus in the forefront of the battle, and in having the great white warrior from the stars to fight with them in their ranks, and in promising large rewards of cattle and promotions to all who survived in the event of Ignosi's arms being successful.

I looked down the long lines of waving black plumes and stern faces beneath them, and sighed to think that within one short hour most, if not all, of those magnificent veteran warriors, not a man of whom was under forty years of age, would be laid dead or dying in the dust. It could not be otherwise; they were being condemned, with that wise recklessness of human life that marks the great general, and often saves his forces and attains his ends, to certain slaughter, in order to give the cause and the remainder of the army a chance of success. They were foredoomed to die, and they knew it. It was to be their task to engage regiment after regiment of Twala's army on the narrow strip of green beneath us, till they were exterminated, or till the wings found a favourable opportunity for their onslaught. And yet they never hesitated, nor could I detect a sign of fear upon the face of a single warrior. There they were—going to certain death, about to quit the blessed light of day for ever, and yet able to contemplate their doom without a tremor. I could not even at that moment help contrasting their state of mind with my own, which was far from comfortable, and breathing a sigh of envy and admiration. Never before had I seen such an absolute devotion to the idea of duty, and such a complete indifference to its bitter fruits.

"Behold your king!" ended old Infadoos, pointing to Ignosi; "go fight and fall for him, as is the duty of brave men, and cursed and shameful forever be the name of him who shrinks from death for his king, or who turns his back to his enemy. Behold your king! chiefs, captains, and soldiers; now do your homage to the sacred snake, and then follow on, that Incubu and I may show ye the road to the heart of Twala's forces."

There was a moment's pause, then suddenly there rose from the serried phalanxes before us a murmur, like the distant whisper of the sea, caused by the gentle tapping of the handles of six thousand spears against their holders' shields. Slowly it swelled, till its growing volume deepened and widened into a roar of rolling noise, that echoed like thunder against the mountains, and filled the air with heavy waves of sound. Then it decreased and slowly died away into nothing, and suddenly out crashed the royal salute.

Ignosi, I thought to myself, might well be a proud man that day, for no Roman emperor ever had such a salutation from gladiators "about to die."[1]

Ignosi acknowledged this magnificent act of homage by lifting his battle-axe, and then the Greys filed off in a triple-line formation, each line containing about one thousand fighting men, exclusive of officers. When the last line had gone some five hundred yards, Ignosi put himself at the head of the Buffaloes, which regiment was drawn up in a similar three-line formation, and gave the word to march, and off we went, I, needless to say, uttering the most heartfelt prayers that I might come out of that job with a whole skin. Many a queer position have I found myself in, but never before in one quite so unpleasant as the present, or one in which my chance of coming off safe was so small.

By the time that we reached the edge of the plateau the Greys

---

1 "about to die"] *morituri te salutamus*: we (who are) about to die salute you.

were already half-way down the slope ending in the tongue of grass-land that ran up into the bend of the mountain, something as the frog of a horse's foot runs into the shoe. The excitement in Twala's camp on the plain beyond was very great, and regiment after regiment were starting forward at a long swinging trot in order to reach the root of the tongue of land before the attacking force could emerge into the plain of Loo.

This tongue of land, which was some three hundred yards in depth, was even at its root or widest part not more than three hundred and fifty paces across, while at its tip it scarcely measured ninety. The Greys, who, in passing down the side of the hill and on to the tip of the tongue, had formed in column, on reaching the spot where it broadened out again reassumed their triple-line formation, and halted dead.

Then we—that is, the Buffaloes—moved down the tip of the tongue and took our stand in reserve, about one hundred yards behind the last line of the Greys, and on slightly higher ground. Meanwhile we had leisure to observe Twala's entire force, which had evidently been reinforced since the morning attack, and could not now, notwithstanding their losses, number less than forty thousand, moving swiftly up towards us. But as they drew near the root of the tongue they hesitated, having discovered that only one regiment could advance into the gorge at a time, and that there, some seventy yards from the mouth of it, unassailable except in front, on account of the high walls of boulder-strewn ground on either side, stood the famous regiment of Greys, the pride and glory of the Kukuana army, ready to hold the way against their forces as the three Romans once held the bridge[1] against thousands. They hesitated, and finally stopped their advance; there was no eagerness to cross spears with those three lines of grim warriors who stood so firm and ready. Presently, however, a tall general, with the customary head-dress of nodding ostrich plumes, came running up, attended by a group of chiefs and orderlies, being, I thought, none other than Twala himself, and gave an order, and the first regiment raised a shout, and charged up towards the Greys, who remained perfectly still and

---

1   Romans ... bridge] the story from Livy of "how Horatius kept the bridge" against the
    Tuscan bands is told in Thomas Babington Macaulay's *Lays of Ancient Rome* (1842).

silent till the attacking troops were within forty yards, and a volley of tollas, or throwing knives, came rattling among their ranks.

Then suddenly, with a bound and a roar, they sprang forward with uplifted spears, and the two regiments met in deadly strife. Next second, the roll of the meeting shields came to our ears like the sound of thunder, and the whole plain seemed to be alive with flashes of light reflected from the stabbing spears. To and fro swung the heaving mass of struggling, stabbing humanity, but not for long. Suddenly the attacking lines seemed to grow thinner, and then with a slow, long heave the Greys passed over them, just as a great wave heaves up and passes over a sunken ridge. It was done; that regiment was completely destroyed, but the Greys had but two lines left now; a third of their number were dead.

Closing up shoulder to shoulder once more, they halted in silence and awaited attack; and I was rejoiced to catch sight of Sir Henry's yellow beard as he moved to and fro, arranging the ranks. So he was yet alive!

Meanwhile we moved up on to the ground of the encounter, which was cumbered by about four thousand prostrate human beings, dead, dying, and wounded, and literally stained red with blood. Ignosi issued an order, which was rapidly passed down the ranks, to the effect that none of the enemies' wounded were to be killed, and so far as we could see this order was scrupulously carried out. It would have been a shocking sight, if we had had time to think of it.

But now a second regiment, distinguished by white plumes, kilts, and shields, was moving up to the attack of the two thousand remaining Greys, who stood waiting in the same ominous silence as before, till the foe was within forty yards or so, when they hurled themselves with irresistible force upon them. Again there came the awful roll of the meeting shields, and as we watched, the grim tragedy repeated itself. But this time the issue was left longer in doubt; indeed, it seemed for awhile almost impossible that the Greys should again prevail. The attacking regiment, which was one formed of young men, fought with the utmost fury, and at first seemed by sheer weight to be driving the veterans back. The slaughter was something awful, hundreds falling every minute; and from among the shouts of the warriors and the groans of the dying, set to the clashing music of meeting spears, came a continuous hissing undertone of "*S'gee, s'gee,*" the note of triumph of each victor as he passed his spear through and through the body of his fallen foe.

But perfect discipline and steady and unchanging valour can do wonders, and one veteran soldier is worth two young ones, as soon became apparent in the present case. For just as we thought that it was all up with the Greys, and were preparing to take their place so soon as they made room by being destroyed, I heard Sir Henry's deep voice ringing out above the din, and caught a glimpse of his circling battle-axe as he waved it high above his plumes. Then came a change; the Greys ceased to give; they stood still as a rock, against which the furious waves of spearmen broke again and again, only to recoil. Presently they began to move again — forward this time; as they had no firearms, there was no smoke, so we could see it all. Another minute and the onslaught grew fainter.

"Ah, they are *men* indeed; they will conquer again," called out Ignosi, who was grinding his teeth with excitement at my side. "See, it is done!"

Suddenly, like puffs of smoke from the month of a cannon, the attacking regiment broke away in flying groups, their white head-dresses streaming behind them in the wind, and left their opponents victors, indeed, but, alas! no more a regiment. Of the gallant triple line, which, forty minutes before, had gone into action three thousand strong, there remained at most, some six hundred blood-bespattered men; the rest were under foot. And yet they cheered and waved their spears in triumph, and then, instead of falling back upon us as we expected, they ran forward, for a hundred yards or so, after the flying groups of foemen, took possession of a gently rising knoll of ground, and, resuming the old triple formation, formed a threefold ring around it. And then, thanks be to God, standing on the top of the mound for a minute, I saw Sir Henry, apparently unharmed, and with him our old friend Infadoos. Then Twala's regiments rolled down upon the doomed band, and once more the battle closed in.

As those who read this history will probably long ago have gathered, I am, to be honest, a bit of a coward, and certainly in no way given to fighting, though, somehow, it has often been my lot to get into unpleasant positions, and to be obliged to shed man's blood. But I have always hated it, and kept my own blood as undiminished in quantity as possible, sometimes by a judicious use of my heels. At this moment, however, for the first time in my life, I felt my bosom burn with martial ardour. Warlike fragments from the "Ingoldsby Legends," together with numbers of sanguinary verses from the Old Testament, sprang up in my brain like mushrooms in the dark; my blood, which hitherto had been half-frozen with horror, went beating through my veins, and there came upon me a savage desire to kill and spare not. I glanced round at the serried ranks of warriors behind us, and somehow, all in an instant, began to wonder if my face looked like theirs. There they stood, their heads craned forward over their shields, the hands twitching, the lips apart, the fierce features instinct with the hungry lust of battle, and in the eyes a look like the glare of a bloodhound when he sights his quarry.

Only Ignosi's heart seemed, to judge from his comparative self-possession, to all appearance, to beat as calmly as ever beneath his leopard-skin cloak, though even *he* still kept on grinding his teeth. I could stand it no longer.

"Are we to stand here till we put out roots, Umbopa—Ignosi, I mean—while Twala swallows our brothers yonder?" I asked.

"Nay, Macumazahn," was the answer; "see, now is the ripe moment: let us pluck it."

As he spoke, a fresh regiment rushed past the ring upon the little mound, and wheeling round, attacked it from the hither side.

Then, lifting his battle-axe, Ignosi gave the signal to advance, and, raising the Kukuana battle-cry, the Buffaloes charged home with a rush like the rush of the sea.

What followed immediately on this it is out of my power to tell. All I can remember is a wild yet ordered rushing, that seemed to shake the ground; a sudden change of front and forming up on the part of the regiment against which the charge was directed; then an awful shock, a dull roar of voices, and a continuous flashing of spears, seen through a red mist of blood.

When my mind cleared I found myself standing inside the remnant of the Greys near the top of the mound, and just behind no less a person than Sir Henry himself. How I got there I had, at the moment, no idea, but Sir Henry afterwards told me that I was borne up by the first furious charge of the Buffaloes almost to his feet, and then left, as they in turn were pressed back. Thereon he dashed out of the circle and dragged me into it.

As for the fight that followed, who can describe it? Again and again the multitudes surged up against our momentarily lessening circle, and again and again we beat them back.

> "The stubborn spearmen still made good
> The dark impenetrable wood;
> Each stepping where his comrade stood
> The instant that he fell,"[1]

as I think the "Ingoldsby Legends" beautifully puts it.

It was a splendid thing to see those brave battalions come on time after time over the barriers of their dead, sometimes holding corpses before them to receive our spear thrusts, only to leave their own corpses to swell the rising piles. It was a gallant sight to see that sturdy old warrior, Infadoos, as cool as though he were on parade, shouting out orders, taunts, and even jests, to keep up the spirit of his few remaining men, and then, as each charge rolled up, stepping forward to wherever the fighting was thickest, to bear his share in repelling it. And yet more gallant was the vision of Sir Henry, whose ostrich plumes had been shorn off by a spear stroke, so that his long yellow hair streamed out in the breeze behind him. There he stood, the great Dane, for he was nothing else, his hands, his axe, and his armour, all red with blood, and none could live before his stroke. Time after time I saw it come sweeping down, as some great warrior ventured to give him battle, and as he struck be shouted, "*O-hoy! O-hoy!*" like his Bersekir[2] forefathers, and the blow went crashing through shield and spear, through head-dress, hair, and skull, till at last none would of their own will come near the great white "tagati" (wizard), who killed and failed not.

---

1 spearmen ... fell] from Sir Walter Scott, *Marmion*, 6.34; see R.L. Stevenson, Letter to Haggard, Appendix A.

2 Bersekir] in Norse legend an invulnerable warrior who fought with a frenzy known as the "berserker rage."

But suddenly there rose a cry of "*Twala, y' Twala*," and out of the press sprang forward none other than the gigantic one-eyed king himself, also armed with battle-axe and shield, and clad in chain armour.

"Where art thou, Incubu, thou white man, who slew Scragga, my son—see if thou canst kill me!" he shouted, and at the same time hurled a tolla straight at Sir Henry, who, fortunately, saw it coming, and caught it on his shield, which it transfixed, remaining wedged in the iron plate behind the hide.

Then, with a cry, Twala, sprang forward straight at him, and with his battle-axe struck him such a blow upon the shield, that the mere force and shock of it brought Sir Henry, strong man as he was, down upon his knees.

But at the time the matter went no further, for at that instant there rose from the regiments pressing round us something like a shout of dismay, and on looking up I saw the cause.

To the right and to the left the plain was alive with the plumes of charging warriors. The outflanking squadrons had come to our relief. The time could not have been better chosen. All Twala's army had, as Ignosi had predicted would be the case, fixed their attention on the bloody struggle which was raging round the remnant of the Greys and the Buffaloes, who were now carrying on a battle of their own at a little distance, which two regiments had formed the chest of our army. It was not until the horns were about to close upon them that they had dreamed of their approach. And now, before they could even assume a proper formation for defence, the outflanking Impis leapt, like greyhounds, on their flanks.

In five minutes the fate of the battle was decided. Taken on both flanks, and dismayed by the awful slaughter inflicted upon them by the Greys and Buffaloes, Twala's regiments broke into flight, and soon the whole plain between us and Loo was scattered with groups of flying soldiers, making good their retreat. As for the forces that had so recently surrounded us and the Buffaloes, they melted away as though by magic, and presently we were left standing there like a rock from which the sea has retreated. But what a sight it was! Around us the dead and dying lay in heaped-up masses, and of the gallant Greys there remained alive but ninety-five men. More than 2,900 had fallen in this one regiment, most of them never to rise again.

"Men," said Infadoos, calmly, as between the intervals of binding up a wound in his arm he surveyed what remained to him of his corps, "ye have kept up the reputation of your regiment, and this day's fighting will be spoken of by your children's children." Then he turned round and shook Sir Henry Curtis by the hand. "Thou art a great man, Incubu," he said, simply; "I have lived a long life among warriors, and known many a brave one, yet have I never seen a man like thee."

At this moment the Buffaloes began to march past our position on the road to Loo, and as they did so a message was brought to us from Ignosi requesting Infadoos, Sir Henry, and myself to join him. Accordingly, orders having been issued to the remaining ninety men of the Greys to employ themselves in collecting the wounded, we joined Ignosi, who informed us that he was pressing on to Loo to complete the victory by capturing Twala, if that should be possible. Before we had gone far we suddenly discovered the figure of Good sitting on an ant-heap about one hundred paces from us. Close beside him was the body of a Kukuana.

"He must be wounded," said Sir Henry, anxiously. As he made the remark, an untoward thing happened. The dead body of the Kukuana soldier, or rather what had appeared to be his dead body, suddenly sprang up, knocked Good head over heels off the ant-heap, and began to spear him. We rushed forward in terror, and as we drew near we saw the brawny warrior making dig after dig at the prostrate Good, who at each prod jerked all his limbs into the air. Seeing us coming, the Kukuana gave one final most vicious dig, and with a shout of "Take that, wizard," bolted off. Good did not move, and we concluded that our poor comrade was done for. Sadly we came towards him, and were indeed astonished to find him pale and faint indeed, but with a serene smile upon his face, and his eye-glass still fixed in his eye.

"Capital armour this," he murmured, on catching sight of our faces bending over him. "How sold he must have been," and then he fainted. On examination we discovered that he had been seriously wounded in the leg by a tolla in the course of the pursuit, but that the chain armour had prevented his last assailant's spear from doing anything more than bruise him badly. It was a merciful escape. As nothing could be done for him at the moment, he was placed on one of the wicker shields used for the wounded, and carried along with us.

On arriving before the nearest gate of Loo, we found one of our regiments watching it in obedience to orders received from Ignosi. The remaining regiments were in the same way watching the other exits to the town. The officer in command of this regiment coming up, saluted Ignosi as king, and informed him that Twala's army had taken refuge in the town, whither Twala himself had also escaped, but that he thought that they were thoroughly demoralised, and would surrender. Thereupon Ignosi, after taking counsel with us, sent forward heralds to each gate ordering the defenders to open, and promising on his royal word life and forgiveness to every soldier who laid down his arms. The message was not without its effect. Presently, amid the shouts and cheers of the Buffaloes, the bridge was dropped across the fosse, and the gates upon the further side flung open.

Taking due precautions against treachery, we marched on into the town. All along the roadways stood dejected warriors, their heads drooping, and their shields and spears at their feet, who, as Ignosi passed, saluted him as king. On we marched, straight to Twala's kraal. When we reached the great space, where a day or two previously we had seen the review and the witch hunt, we found it deserted. No, not quite deserted, for there, on the further side, in front of his hut, sat Twala himself, with but one attendant — Gagool.

It was a melancholy sight to see him seated there, his battle-axe and shield by his side, his chin upon his mailed breast, with but one old crone for companion, and notwithstanding his cruelties and misdeeds, a pang of compassion shot through me as I saw him thus "fallen from his high estate."[1] Not a soldier of all his armies, not a courtier out of the hundreds who had cringed round him, not even a solitary wife, remained to share his fate or halve the bitterness of his fall. Poor savage! he was learning the lesson that Fate teaches to most who live long enough, that the eyes of

---

1 "fallen ... estate"] from John Dryden's "Alexander's Feast" (stz.4), but also an echo of John Milton's *Samson Agonistes*, lines 169-170.

mankind are blind to the discredited, and that he who is defence-less and fallen finds few friends and little mercy. Nor, indeed, in this case did he deserve any.

Filing through the kraal gate, we marched straight across the open space to where the ex-king sat. When within about fifty yards the regiment was halted, and accompanied only by a small guard we advanced towards him, Gagool reviling us bitterly as we came. As we drew near, Twala, for the first time, lifted up his plumed head, and fixed his one eye, which seemed to flash with suppressed fury almost as brightly as the great diamond bound round his forehead, upon his successful rival—Ignosi.

"Hail, O king!" he said, with bitter mockery; "thou who hast eaten of my bread, and now by the aid of the white man's magic hast seduced my regiments and defeated mine army, hail! what fate hast thou for me, O king?"

"The fate thou gavest to my father, whose throne thou hast sat on these many years!" was the stern answer.

"It is well. I will show thee how to die, that thou mayest remember it against thine own time. See, the sun sinks in blood," and he pointed with his red battle-axe towards the fiery orb now going down; "it is well that my sun should sink with it. And now, O king! I am ready to die, but I crave the boon of the Kukuana royal house* to die fighting. Thou canst not refuse it, or even those cowards who fled to-day will hold thee shamed."

"It is granted. Choose—with whom wilt thou fight? Myself I cannot fight with thee, for the king fights not except in war."

Twala's sombre eye ran up and down our ranks, and I felt, as for a moment it rested on myself, that the position had developed a new horror. What if he chose to begin by fighting *me*? What chance should I have against a desperate savage six feet five high, and broad in proportion? I might as well commit suicide at once. Hastily I made up my mind to decline the combat, even if I were hooted out of Kukuanaland as a consequence. It is, I think, better to be hooted than to be quartered with a battle-axe.

---

* It is a law amongst the Kukuanas that no man of the royal blood can be put to death unless by his own consent, which is, however, never refused. He is allowed to choose a succession of antagonists, to be approved by the king, with whom he fights, till one of them kills him.

Presently he spoke.

"Incubu, what sayest thou, shall we end what we began to-day, or shall I call thee coward, white—even to the liver?"

"Nay," interposed Ignosi, hastily; "thou shalt not fight with Incubu."

"Not if he is afraid," said Twala.

Unfortunately Sir Henry understood this remark, and the blood flamed up into his cheeks.

"I will fight him," he said; "he shall see if I am afraid."

"For God's sake," I entreated, "don't risk your life against that of a desperate man. Anybody who saw you to-day will know that you are not a coward."

"I will fight him," was the sullen answer. "No living man shall call me a coward. I am ready now!" and he stepped forward and lifted his axe.

I wrung my hands over this absurd piece of Quixotism; but if he was determined on fighting, of course I could not stop him.

"Fight not, my white brother," said Ignosi, laying his hand affectionately on Sir Henry's arm; "thou hast fought enough, and if aught befell thee at his hands it would cut my heart in twain."

"I will fight, Ignosi," was Sir Henry's answer.

"It is well, Incubu; thou art a brave man. It will be a good fight. Behold, Twala, the Elephant is ready for thee."

The ex-king laughed savagely, and stepped forward and faced Curtis. For a moment they stood thus, and the setting sun caught their stalwart frames and clothed them both in fire. They were a well-matched pair.

Then they began to circle round each other, their battle-axes raised.

Suddenly Sir Henry sprang forward and struck a fearful blow at Twala, who stepped to one side. So heavy was the stroke that the striker half overbalanced himself, a circumstance of which his antagonist took a prompt advantage. Circling his heavy battle-axe round his head, he brought it down with tremendous force. My heart jumped into my mouth; I thought that the affair was already finished. But no; with a quick upward movement of the left arm Sir Henry interposed his shield between himself and the axe, with the result that its outer edge was shorn clean off, the axe falling on his left shoulder, but not heavily enough to do any serious damage. In another second Sir Henry got in another blow, which was also received by Twala upon his shield. Then followed blow upon blow, which were, in turn, either received upon the shield or avoided. The excitement grew intense; the regiment which was watching the encounter forgot its discipline, and, drawing near, shouted and groaned at every stroke. Just at this time, too, Good, who had been laid upon the ground by me, recovered from his faint, and, sitting up, perceived what was going on. In an instant he was up, and, catching hold of my arm, hopped about from place to place on one leg dragging me after him, yelling out encouragements to Sir Henry —

"Go it, old fellow!" he hallooed. "That was a good one! Give it him amidships," and so on.

Presently Sir Henry, having caught a fresh stroke upon his shield, hit out with all his force. The stroke cut through Twala's shield and through the tough chain armour behind it, gashing him in the shoulder. With a yell of pain and fury Twala returned the stroke with interest, and, such was his strength, shore right through the rhinoceros' horn handle of his antagonist's battle-axe, strengthened as it was with bands of steel, wounding Curtis in the face.

A cry of dismay rose from the Buffaloes as our hero's broad axe-head fell to the ground; and Twala, again raising his weapon, flew at him with a shout. I shut my eyes. When I opened them again, it was to see Sir Henry's shield lying on the ground, and Sir Henry himself with his great arms twined round Twala's middle. To and fro they swung, hugging each other like bears, straining with all their mighty muscles for dear life, and dearer honour. With a supreme effort Twala swung the Englishman clean off his feet, and down they came together, rolling over and over on the lime paving, Twala striking out at Curtis' head with the battle-axe, and Sir Henry trying to drive the tolla he had drawn from his belt through Twala's armour.

It was a mighty struggle, and an awful thing to see.

"Get his axe!" yelled Good; and perhaps our champion heard him.

At any rate, dropping the tolla, he made a grab at the axe,

which was fastened to Twala's wrist by a strip of buffalo hide, and still rolling over and over, they fought for it like wild cats, drawing their breath in heavy gasps. Suddenly the hide string burst, and then, with a great effort, Sir Henry freed himself, the weapon remaining in his grasp. Another second and he was up upon his feet, the red blood streaming from the wound in his face, and so was Twala. Drawing the heavy tolla from his belt, he staggered straight at Curtis and struck him upon the breast. The blow came home true and strong, but whoever it was made that chain armour understood his art, for it withstood the steel. Again Twala struck out with a savage yell, and again the heavy knife rebounded, and Sir Henry went staggering back. Once more Twala came on, and as he came our great Englishman gathered himself together, and, swinging the heavy axe round his head, hit at him with all his force. There was a shriek of excitement from a thousand throats, and, behold! Twala's head seemed to spring from his shoulders, and then fell and came rolling and bounding along the ground towards Ignosi, stopping just at his feet. For a second the corpse stood upright, the blood spouting in fountains from the severed arteries; then with a dull crash it fell to the earth, and the gold torque from the neck went rolling away across the pavement. As it did so Sir Henry, overpowered by faintness and loss of blood, fell heavily across it.

In a second he was lifted up, and eager hands were pouring water on his face. Another minute, and the great grey eyes opened wide.

He was not dead.

Then I, just as the sun sank, stepping to where Twala's head lay in the dust, unloosed the diamond from the dead brows, and handed it to Ignosi.

"Take it," I said, "lawful King of the Kukuanas."

Ignosi bound the diadem upon his brows, and then advancing, placed his foot upon the broad chest of his headless foe and broke out into a chant, or rather a pæan of victory, so beautiful, and yet so utterly savage, that I despair of being able to give an adequate idea of it. I once heard a scholar with a fine voice read aloud from the Greek poet Homer, and I remember that the sound of the rolling lines seemed to make my blood stand still. Ignosi's chant, uttered as it was in a language as beautiful and sonorous as the old

Greek, produced exactly the same effect on me, although I was exhausted with toil and many emotions.

"Now," he began, *"now is our rebellion swallowed up in victory, and our evil-doing justified by strength.*

"In the morning the oppressors rose up and shook themselves; they bound on their plumes and made them ready for war.

"They rose up and grasped their spears: the soldiers called to the captains, 'Come, lead us'—and the captains cried to the king, 'Direct thou the battle.'

"They rose up in their pride, twenty thousand men, and yet a twenty thousand.

"Their plumes covered the earth, as the plumes of a bird cover her nest; they shook their spears and shouted, yea, they hurled their spears into the sunlight; they lusted for the battle and were glad.

"They came up against me; their strong ones came running swiftly to crush me; they cried, 'Ha! ha! he is as one already dead.'

"Then breathed I on them, and my breath was as the breath of a storm, and lo! they were not.

"My lightnings pierced them; I licked up their strength with the lightning of my spears; I shook them to the earth with the thunder of my shouting.

"They broke—they scattered—they were gone as the mists of the morning.

"They are food for the crows and the foxes, and the place of battle is fat with their blood.

"Where are the mighty ones who rose up in the morning?

"Where are the proud ones who tossed their plumes and cried, 'He is as one already dead?'

"They bow their heads, but not in sleep; they are stretched out, but not in sleep.

"They are forgotten; they have gone into the blackness, and shall not return; yea, others shall lead away their wives, and their children shall remember them no more.

"And I—I! the king—like an eagle have I found my eyrie.

"Behold! far have I wandered in the night time, yet have I returned to my little ones at the daybreak.

"Creep ye under the shadow of my wings, O people, and I will comfort ye, and ye shall not be dismayed.

"Now is the good time, the time of spoil.

"Mine are the cattle in the valleys, the virgins in the kraals are mine also.

"The winter is overpast, the summer is at hand.

"Now shall Evil cover up her face, and Prosperity shall bloom in the land like a lily.

"Rejoice, rejoice, my people! let all the land rejoice in that the tyranny is trodden down, in that I am the king."

He paused, and out of the gathering gloom there came back the deep reply —

"Thou art the king."

Thus it was that my prophecy to the herald came true, and within the forty-eight hours Twala's headless corpse was stiffening at Twala's gate.

CHAPTER XV.

GOOD FALLS SICK.

AFTER the fight was ended, Sir Henry and Good were carried into Twala's hut, where I joined them. They were both utterly exhausted by exertion and loss of blood, and, indeed, my own condition was little better. I am very wiry, and can stand more fatigue than most men, probably on account of my light weight and long training; but that night I was fairly done up, and, as is always the case with me when exhausted, that old wound the lion gave me began to pain me. Also my head was aching violently from the blow I had received in the morning, when I was knocked senseless. Altogether, a more miserable trio than we were that evening it would have been difficult to discover; and our only comfort lay in the reflection that we were exceedingly fortunate to be there to feel miserable, instead of being stretched dead upon the plain, as so many thousands of brave men were that night, who had risen well and strong in the morning. Somehow, with the assistance of the beautiful Foulata, who, since we had been the means of saving her life, had constituted herself our handmaiden, and especially Good's, we managed to get off the chain shirts, which had certainly saved the lives of two of us that day, when we found that the flesh underneath was terribly bruised, for though the steel links had prevented the weapons from entering, they had not prevented them from bruising. Both Sir Henry and Good were a mass of bruises, and I was by no means free. As a remedy Foulata brought us some pounded green leaves, with an aromatic odour, which, when applied as a plaster, gave us considerable relief. But though the bruises were painful, they did not give us such anxiety as Sir Henry's and Good's wounds. Good had a hole right through the fleshy part of his "beautiful white leg," from which he had lost a great deal of blood; and Sir Henry had a deep cut over the jaw, inflicted by Twala's battle-axe. Luckily Good was a very decent surgeon, and as soon as his small box of medicines was forthcoming, he, having thoroughly cleansed the wounds, managed to stitch up first Sir Henry's and then his own pretty satisfactorily, considering the imperfect light given by the primitive Kukuana lamp in the hut. Afterwards he plentifully smeared the wounds with some antiseptic ointment, of which there was a pot in the little box, and we covered them with the remains of a pocket-handkerchief which we possessed.

Meanwhile Foulata had prepared us some strong broth, for we were too weary to eat. This we swallowed, and then threw ourselves down on the piles of magnificent karosses, or fur rugs, which were scattered about the dead king's great hut. By a very strange instance of the irony of fate, it was on Twala's own couch, and wrapped in Twala's own particular kaross, that Sir Henry, the man who had slain him, slept that night.

I say slept; but after that day's work sleep was indeed difficult. To begin with, in very truth the air was full

> "Of farewells to the dying
> And mournings for the dead."[1]

From every direction came the sound of the wailing of women whose husbands, sons, and brothers had perished in the fight. No wonder that they wailed, for over twenty thousand men, or nearly a third of the Kukuana army, had been destroyed in that awful struggle. It was heart-rending to lie and listen to their cries for

1 "Of farewells to the dying ..."] Henry Wadsworth Longfellow, "Resignation," stz. 2.

those who would never return; and it made one realise the full horror of the work done that day to further man's ambition. Towards midnight, however, the ceaseless crying of the women grew less frequent, till at length the silence was only broken at intervals of a few minutes by a long, piercing howl that came from a hut in our immediate rear, and which I afterwards discovered proceeded from Gagool wailing for the dead king Twala.

After that I got a little fitful sleep, only to wake from time to time with a start, thinking that I was once more an actor in the terrible events of the last twenty-four hours. Now I seemed to see that warrior, whom my hand had sent to his last account, charging at me on the mountain-top; now I was once more in that glorious ring of Greys, which made its immortal stand against all Twala's regiments, upon the little mound; and now again I saw Twala's plumed and gory head roll past my feet with gnashing teeth and glaring eye. At last, somehow or other, the night passed away; but when dawn broke I found that my companions had slept no better than myself. Good, indeed, was in a high fever, and very soon afterwards began to grow light-headed, and also, to my alarm, to spit blood, the result, no doubt, of some internal injury inflicted by the desperate efforts made by the Kukuana warrior on the previous day to get his big spear through the chain armour. Sir Henry, however, seemed pretty fresh, notwithstanding his wound on the face, which made eating difficult and laughter an impossibility, though he was so sore and stiff that he could scarcely stir.

About eight o'clock we had a visit from Infadoos, who seemed but little the worse—tough old warrior that he was—for his exertions on the previous day, though he informed us he had been up all night. He was delighted to see us, though much grieved at Good's condition, and shook hands cordially; but I noticed that he addressed Sir Henry with a kind of reverence, as though he were something more than man; and indeed, as we afterwards found out, the great Englishman was looked on throughout Kukuanaland as a supernatural being. No man, the soldiers said, could have fought as he fought, or could, at the end of a day of such toil and bloodshed, have slain Twala, who, in addition to being the king, was supposed to be the strongest warrior in Kukuanaland, in single combat, sheering through his bull-neck at a stroke. Indeed, that stroke became proverbial in

Kukuanaland, and any extraordinary blow or feat of strength was thenceforth known as "Incubu's blow."

Infadoos told us also that all Twala's regiments had submitted to Ignosi, and that like submissions were beginning to arrive from chiefs in the country. Twala's death at the hands of Sir Henry had put an end to all further chance of disturbance; for Scragga had been his only son, and there was no rival claimant left alive.

I remarked that Ignosi had swum to the throne through blood. The old chief shrugged his shoulders. "Yes," he answered; "but the Kukuana people can only be kept cool by letting the blood flow sometimes. Many were killed indeed, but the women were left, and others would soon grow up to take the places of the fallen. After this the land would be quiet for a while."

Afterwards, in the course of the morning, we had a short visit from Ignosi, on whose brows the royal diadem was now bound. As I contemplated him advancing with kingly dignity, an obsequious guard following his steps, I could not help recalling to my mind the tall Zulu who had presented himself to us at Durban some few months back, asking to be taken into our service, and reflecting on the strange revolutions of the wheel of fortune.

"Hail, O king!" I said, rising.

"Yes, Macumazahn. King at last, by the grace of your three right hands," was the ready answer.

All was, he said, going on well; and he hoped to arrange a great feast in two weeks' time, in order to show himself to the people.

I asked him what he had settled to do with Gagool.

"She is the evil genius of the land," he answered, "and I shall kill her, and all the witch-doctors with her! She has lived so long that none can remember when she was not old, and always she it is who has trained the witch-hunters, and made the land evil in the sight of the heavens above."

"Yet she knows much," I replied; "it is easier to destroy knowledge, Ignosi, than to gather it."

"It is so," he said, thoughtfully. "She, and she only, knows the secret of the 'Three Witches' yonder, whither the great road runs, where the kings are buried, and the silent ones sit."

"Yes, and the diamonds are. Forget not thy, promise, Ignosi; thou must lead us to the mines, even if thou hast to spare Gagool alive to show the way."

"I will not forget, Macumazahn, and I will think on what thou sayest."

After Ignosi's visit I went to see Good, and found him quite delirious. The fever from his wound seemed to have taken a firm hold of his system, and to be complicated by an internal injury. For four or five days his condition was most critical; indeed, I firmly believe that had it not been for Foulata's indefatigable nursing he must have died.

Women are women, all the world over, whatever their colour. Yet somehow it seemed curious to watch this dusky beauty bending night and day over the fevered man's couch, and performing all the merciful errands of a sick-room swiftly, gently, and with as fine an instinct as a trained hospital nurse. For the first night or two I tried to help her, and so did Sir Henry so soon as his stiffness allowed him to move, but she bore our interference with impatience, and finally insisted upon our leaving him to her, saying that our movements made him restless, which I think was true. Day and night she watched him and tended him, giving him his only medicine, a native cooling drink made of milk, in which was infused the juice of the bulb of a species of tulip, and keeping the flies from settling on him. I can see the whole picture now as it appeared night after night by the light of our primitive lamp, Good tossing to and fro, his features emaciated, his eyes shining large and luminous, and jabbering nonsense by the yard; and seated on the ground by his side, her back resting against the wall of the hut, the soft-eyed, shapely Kukuana beauty, her whole face, weary as it was, animated by a look of infinite compassion—or was it something more than compassion?

For two days we thought that he must die, and crept about with heavy hearts. Only Foulata would not believe it.

"He will live," she said.

For three hundred yards or more around Twala's chief hut, where the sufferer lay, there was silence; for by the king's order all who lived in the habitations behind it had, except Sir Henry and myself, been removed, lest any noise should come to the sick man's ears. One night, it was the fifth of his illness, as was my habit, I went across to see how he was getting on before turning in for a few hours.

I entered the hut carefully. The lamp placed upon the floor showed the figure of Good, tossing no more, but lying quite still.

So it had come at last! and in the bitterness of my heart I gave something like a sob.

"Hush—h—h!" came from the patch of dark shadow behind Good's head.

Then, creeping closer, I saw that he was not dead, but sleeping soundly, with Foulata's taper fingers clasped tightly in his poor white hand. The crisis had passed, and he would live. He slept like that for eighteen hours; and I scarcely like to say it, for fear I should not be believed, but during the entire period did that devoted girl sit by him, fearing that if she moved and drew away her hand it would wake him. What she must have suffered from cramp, stiffness, and weariness, to say nothing of want of food, nobody will ever know; but it is a fact that, when at last he woke, she had to be carried away—her limbs were so stiff that she could not move them.

After the turn had once been taken, Good's recovery was rapid and complete. It was not till he was nearly well that Sir Henry told him of all he owed to Foulata; and when he came to the story of how she sat by his side for eighteen hours, fearing lest by moving she should wake him, the honest sailor's eyes filled with tears. He turned and went straight to the hut where Foulata was preparing the mid-day meal (we were back in our old quarters now), taking me with him to interpret in case he could not make his meaning clear to her, though I am bound to say that she understood him marvellously as a rule, considering how extremely limited was his foreign vocabulary.

"Tell her," said Good, "that I owe her my life, and that I will never forget her kindness."

I interpreted, and under her dark skin she actually seemed to blush.

Turning to him with one of those swift and graceful motions that in her always reminded me of the flight of a wild bird, she answered softly, glancing at him with her large brown eyes—

"Nay, my lord; my lord forgets! Did he not save *my* life, and am I not my lord's handmaiden?"

It will be observed that the young lady appeared to have

entirely forgotten the share which Sir Henry and myself had had in her preservation from Twala's clutches. But that is the way of women! I remember my dear wife was just the same. I retired from that little interview sad at heart. I did not like Miss Foulata's soft glances, for I knew the fatal amorous propensities of sailors in general, and Good in particular.

There are two things in the world, as I have found it, which cannot be prevented: you cannot keep a Zulu from fighting, or a sailor from falling in love upon the slightest provocation!

It was a few days after this last occurrence that Ignosi held his great "indaba" (council), and was formally recognised as king by the "indunas" (head men) of Kukuanaland. The spectacle was a most imposing one, including, as it did, a grand review of troops. On this day the remaining fragment of the Greys were formally paraded, and in the face of the army thanked for their splendid conduct in the great battle. To each man the king made a large present of cattle, promoting them one and all to the rank of officers in the new corps of Greys which was in process of formation. An order was also promulgated throughout the length and breadth of Kukuanaland that, whilst we honoured the country by our presence, we three were to be greeted with the royal salute, to be treated with the same ceremony and respect that was by custom accorded to the king, and the power of life and death[1] was publicly conferred upon us. Ignosi, too, in the presence of his people, reaffirmed the promises that he had made, to the effect that no man's blood should be shed without trial, and that witch-hunting should cease in the land.

When the ceremony was over, we waited upon Ignosi, and informed him that we were now anxious to investigate the mystery of the mines to which Solomon's Road ran, asking him if he had discovered anything about them.

"My friends," he answered, "this I have discovered. It is there that the three great figures sit, who here are called the 'Silent Ones,' and to whom Twala would have offered the girl, Foulata, as a sacrifice. It is there, too, in a great cave deep in the mountain, that the kings of the land are buried; there shall ye find Twala's

---

1 power of life and death] identical to the privileges of an Old English lord, designated by the terms *in-* and *ūtfangentheóf*.

body, sitting with those who went before him. There, too, is a great pit, which, at some time, long-dead men dug out, mayhap for the stones ye speak of, such as I have heard men in Natal speak of at Kimberley. There, too, in the Place of Death is a secret chamber, known to none but the king and Gagool. But Twala, who knew it, is dead, and I know it not, nor know I what is in it. But there is a legend in the land that once, many generations gone, a white man crossed the mountains, and was led by a woman to the secret chamber and shown the wealth, but before he could take it she betrayed him, and he was driven by the king of the day back to the mountains, and since then no man has entered the chamber."

"The story is surely true, Ignosi, for on the mountains we found the white man," I said.

"Yes, we found him. And now I have promised ye that if ye can find that chamber, and the stones are there—"

"The stone upon thy forehead proves that they are there," I put in, pointing to the great diamond I had taken from Twala's dead brows.

"Mayhap; if they are there," he said, "ye shall have as many as ye can take hence—if, indeed, ye would leave me, my brothers."

"First we must find the chamber," said I.

"There is but one who can show it to thee—Gagool."

"And if she will not?"

"Then she must die," said Ignosi, sternly. "I have saved her alive but for this. Stay, she shall choose," and calling to a messenger he ordered Gagool to be brought.

In a few minutes she came, hurried along by two guards, whom she was cursing as she walked.

"Leave her," said the king to the guards.

As soon as their support was withdrawn, the withered old bundle, for she looked more like a bundle than anything else, sank into a heap on to the floor, out of which her two bright wicked eyes gleamed like a snake's.

"What will ye with me, Ignosi?" she piped. "Ye dare not touch me. If ye touch me I will blast ye as ye sit. Beware of my magic."

"Thy magic could not save Twala, old she-wolf, and it cannot hurt me," was the answer. "Listen: I will this of thee, that thou reveal where is the chamber where are the shining stones."

"Ha! ha!" she piped, "none know but I, and I will never tell thee. The white devils shall go hence empty-handed."

"Thou wilt tell me. I will make thee tell me."

"How, O king? Thou art great, but can thy power wring the truth from a woman?"

"It is difficult, yet will I do it."

"How, O king?"

"Nay, thus; if thou tellest not thou shalt slowly die."

"Die!" she shrieked, in terror and fury; "ye dare not touch me—man, ye know not who I am. How old think ye am I? I knew your fathers, and your fathers' fathers' fathers. When the country was young I was here, when the country grows old I shall still be here. I cannot die unless I be killed by chance, for none dare slay me."

"Yet will I slay thee. See, Gagool, mother of evil, thou art so old thou canst no longer love thy life. What can life be to such a hag as thee, who hast no shape, nor form, nor hair, nor teeth— hast naught, save wickedness and evil eyes? It will be mercy to slay thee, Gagool."

"Thou fool," shrieked the old fiend, "thou accursed fool, thinkest thou that life is sweet only to the young? It is not so, and naught thou knowest of the heart of man to think it. To the young, indeed, death is sometimes welcome, for the young can feel. They love and suffer, and it wrings them to see their beloved pass to the land of shadows. But the old feel not, they love not, and, *ha! ha!* they laugh to see another go out into the dark; *ha! ha!* they laugh to see the evil that is done under the sun. All they love is life, the warm, warm sun, and the sweet, sweet air. They are afraid of the cold, afraid of the cold and the dark, *ha! ha! ha!*" and the old hag writhed in ghastly merriment on the ground.

"Cease thine evil talk and answer me," said Ignosi, angrily. "Wilt thou show the place where the stones are, or wilt thou not? If thou wilt not thou diest, even now," and he seized a spear and held it over her.

"I will not show it; thou darest not kill me, darest not. He who slays me will be accursed for ever."

Slowly Ignosi brought down the spear till it pricked the prostrate heap of rags.

With a wild yell she sprang to her feet, and then again fell and rolled upon the floor.

"Nay, I will show it. Only let me live, let me sit in the sun and have a bit of meat to suck, and I will show thee."

"It is well. I thought I should find a way to reason with thee. To-morrow shalt thou go with Infadoos and my white brothers to the place, and beware how thou failest, for if thou showest it not, then shalt thou slowly die. I have spoken."

"I will not fail, Ignosi. I always keep my word: *ha! ha! ha!* Once a woman showed the place to a white man before, and behold evil befell him," and here her wicked eyes glinted. "Her name was Gagool too. Perchance I was that woman."

"Thou liest," I said, "that was ten generations gone."

"Mayhap, mayhap; when one lives long one forgets. Perhaps it was my mother's mother who told me, surely her name was Gagool also. But mark, ye will find in the place where the bright playthings are, a bag of hide full of stones. The man filled that bag, but he never took it away. Evil befell him, I say, evil befell him! Perhaps it was my mother's mother who told me. It will be a merry journey — we can see the bodies of those who died in the battle as we go. Their eyes will be gone by now, and their ribs will be hollow. *Ha! ha! ha!*"

CHAPTER XVI.

THE PLACE OF DEATH.

It was already dark on the third day after the scene described in the previous chapter, when we camped in some huts at the foot of the "Three Witches," as the triangle of mountains were called to which Solomon's great road ran. Our party consisted of our three selves and Foulata, who waited on us — especially on Good — Infadoos, Gagool, who was borne along in a litter, inside which she could be heard muttering and cursing all day long, and a party of guards and attendants. The mountains, or rather the three peaks of the mountains, for the whole mass evidently consisted of a solitary upheaval, were, as I have said, in the form of a triangle, of which the base was towards us, one peak being on our right, one on our left, and one straight in front of us. Never shall I forget the sight afforded by those three towering peaks in the early sunlight of the following morning. High, high above us, up into the blue air, soared their twisted snow-wreaths. Beneath the snow the peaks were purple with heaths, and so were the wild moors that ran up the slopes towards them. Straight before us the white ribbon of Solomon's great road stretched away uphill to the foot of the centre peak, about five miles from us, and there stopped. It was its terminus.

I had better leave the feelings of intense excitement with which we set out on our march that morning to the imagination of those who read this history. At last we were drawing near to the wonderful mines that had been the cause of the miserable death of the old Portuguese Dom, three centuries ago, of my poor friend, his ill-starred descendant, and also, as we feared, of George Curtis, Sir Henry's brother. Were we destined, after all that we had gone through, to fare any better? Evil befell them, as that old fiend Gagool said, would it also befall us? Somehow, as we were marching up that last stretch of beautiful road, I could not help feeling a little superstitious about the matter, and so I think did Good and Sir Henry.

For an hour and a half or more we tramped on up the heather-fringed road, going so fast in our excitement that the bearers with Gagool's hammock could scarcely keep pace with us, and its occupant piped out to us to stop.

"Go more slowly, white men," she said, projecting her hideous shrivelled countenance between the curtains, and fixing her gleaming eyes upon us; "why will ye run to meet the evil that shall befall ye, ye seekers after treasure?" and she laughed that horrible laugh which always sent a cold shiver down my back, and which for a while quite took the enthusiasm out of us.

However, on we went, till we saw before us, and between ourselves and the peak, a vast circular hole with sloping sides, three hundred feet or more in depth, and quite half a mile round.[1]

"Can't you guess what this is?" I said to Sir Henry and Good,

---

1 half a mile round] see Trollope, *South Africa* (1878), II: 173.

who were staring in astonishment down into the awful pit before us.

They shook their heads.

"Then it is clear that you have never seen the diamond mines at Kimberley. You may depend on it that this is Solomon's Diamond Mine; look there," I said, pointing to the stiff blue clay which was yet to be seen among the grass and bushes which clothed the sides of the pit, "the formation is the same. I'll be bound that if we went down there we should find 'pipes' of soapy brecciated rock. Look, too," and I pointed to a series of worn flat slabs of rock which were placed on a gentle slope below the level of a watercourse which had in some past age been cut out of the solid rock; "if those are not tables once used to wash the 'stuff,' I'm a Dutchman."

At the edge of this vast hole, which was the pit marked on the old Don's map, the great road branched into two and circumvented it. In many places this circumventing road was built entirely of vast blocks of stone, apparently with the object of supporting the edges of the pit and preventing falls of reef. Along this road we pressed, driven by curiosity to see what the three towering objects were which we could discern from the hither side of the great hole. As we got nearer we perceived that they were colossi of some sort or another, and rightly conjectured that these were the three "Silent Ones" that were held in such awe by the Kukuana people. But it was not until we got quite close that we recognised the full majesty of these "Silent Ones."

There upon huge pedestals of dark rock, sculptured in unknown characters, twenty paces between each, and looking down the road which crossed some sixty miles of plain to Loo, were three colossal seated forms—two males and one female— each measuring about twenty feet from the crown of the head to the pedestal.

The female form, which was nude, was of great though severe beauty, but unfortunately the features were injured by centuries of exposure to the weather. Rising from each side of her head were the points of a crescent. The two male colossi were, on the contrary, draped, and presented a terrifying cast of features, especially the one to our right, which had the face of a devil. That to our left was serene in countenance, but the calm upon it was dreadful. It was the calm of inhuman cruelty, the cruelty, Sir Henry remarked, that the ancients attributed to beings potent for good, who could yet watch the sufferings of humanity, if not with rejoicing, at least without suffering themselves. The three formed a most awe-inspiring trinity, as they sat there in their solitude and gazed out across the plain for ever. Contemplating these "Silent Ones," as the Kukuanas called them, an intense curiosity again seized us to know whose were the hands that had shaped them, who was it that had dug the pit and made the road. Whilst I was gazing and wondering, it suddenly occurred to me (being familiar with the Old Testament) that Solomon went astray after strange gods,[1] the names of three of whom I remembered — "Ashtoreth the goddess of the Zidonians, Chemosh the god of the Moabites, and Milcom the god of the children of Ammon" — and I suggested to my companions that the three figures before us might represent these false divinities.

"Hum," said Sir Henry, who was a scholar, having taken a high degree in classics at college, "there may be something in that; Ashtoreth of the Hebrews was the Astarte of the Phœnicians, who were the great traders of Solomon's time. Astarte, who afterwards was the Aphrodite of the Greeks, was represented with horns like the half-moon, and there on the brow of the female figure are distinct horns. Perhaps these colossi were designed by some Phœnician official who managed the mines. Who can say?"

Before we had finished examining these extraordinary relics of remote antiquity, Infadoos came up, and, having saluted the "Silent Ones" by lifting his spear, asked us if we intended entering the "Place of Death" at once, or if we would wait till after we had taken food at mid-day. If we were ready to go at once, Gagool had announced her willingness to guide us. As it was not more than eleven o'clock, we — driven to it by a burning curiosity — announced our intention of proceeding instantly, and I suggested that, in case we should be detained in the cave, we should take some food with us. Accordingly Gagool's litter was brought up, and that lady herself assisted out of it; and meanwhile Foulata, at

---

1   after strange gods] see Editor's Introduction; also the *Kebra Nagast*, Appendix D.

my request, stored some "biltong," or dried game-flesh, together with a couple of gourds of water in a reed basket. Straight in front of us, at a distance of some fifty paces from the backs of the colossi, rose a sheer wall of rock, eighty feet or more in height, that gradually sloped up till it formed the base of the lofty snow-wreathed peak, which soared up into the air three thousand feet above us. As soon as she was clear of her hammock, Gagool cast one evil grin upon us, and then, leaning on a stick, hobbled off towards the sheer face of the rock. We followed her till we came to a narrow portal solidly arched, that looked like the opening of a gallery of a mine.

Here Gagool was waiting for us, still with that evil grin upon her horrid face.

"Now, white men from the stars," she piped; "great warriors, Incubu, Bougwan, and Macumazahn the wise, are ye ready? Behold, I am here to do the bidding of my lord the king, and to show ye the store of bright stones."

"We are ready," I said.

"Good! good! Make strong your hearts to bear what ye shall see. Comest thou too, Infadoos, who didst betray thy master?"

Infadoos frowned as he answered—

"Nay, I come not, it is not for me to enter there. But thou, Gagool, curb thy tongue, and beware how thou dealest with my lords. At thy hands will I require them, and if a hair of them be hurt, Gagool, be'st thou fifty times a witch, thou shalt die. Hearest thou?"

"I hear, Infadoos; I know thee, thou didst ever love big words; when thou wast a babe I remember thou didst threaten thine own mother. That was but the other day. But fear not, fear not, I live but to do the bidding of the king. I have done the bidding of many kings, Infadoos, till in the end they did mine. *Ha! ha!* I go to look upon their faces once more, and Twala's too! Come on, come on, here is the lamp," and she drew a great gourd full of oil, and fitted with a rush wick, from under her fur cloak.

"Art thou coming Foulata?" asked Good in his villainous kitchen Kukuana, in which he had been improving himself under that young lady's tuition.

"I fear, my lord," the girl answered, timidly.

"Then give me the basket."

"Nay, my lord, whither thou goest, there will I go also."

"The deuce you will!" thought I to myself; "that will be rather awkward if ever we get out of this."

Without further ado Gagool plunged into the passage, which was wide enough to admit of two walking abreast, and quite dark, we following her voice as she piped to us to come on, in some fear and trembling, which was not allayed by the sound of a sudden rush of wings.

"Hullo! what's that?" halloed Good; "somebody hit me in the face."

"Bats," said I; "on you go."

When we had, so far as we could judge, gone some fifty paces, we perceived that the passage was growing faintly light. Another minute, and we stood in the most wonderful place that the eyes of living man ever lit on.

Let the reader picture to himself the hall of the vastest cathedral he ever stood in, windowless indeed, but dimly lighted from above (presumably by shafts connected with the outer air and driven in the roof, which arched away a hundred feet above our head), and he will get some idea of the size of the enormous cave[1] in which we stood, with the difference that this cathedral designed of nature was loftier and wider than any built by man. But its stupendous size was the least of the wonders of the place, for running in rows adown its length were gigantic pillars of what looked like ice, but were, in reality, huge stalactites. It is impossible for me to convey any idea of the overpowering beauty and grandeur of these pillars of white spar, some of which were not less than twenty feet in diameter at the base, and sprang up in lofty and yet delicate beauty sheer to the distant roof. Others again were in process of formation. On the rock floor there was in these cases what looked, Sir Henry said, exactly like a broken column in an old Grecian temple, whilst high above, depending

---

1   enormous cave] HRH visited a cave at Wonderfontein in 1877 full of "moist and glistening stalactite formations.... The dripping water from above, charged with lime, had formed numerous pillars ... [including] a very thick pillar resembling a pulpit" (Kotzé in Higgins, *Haggard*).

from the roof, the point of a huge icicle could be dimly seen. And even as we gazed we could hear the process going on, for presently with a tiny splash a drop of water would fall from the far-off icicle on to the column below. On some columns the drops only fell once in two or three minutes, and in these cases it would form an interesting calculation to discover how long, at that rate of dripping, it would take to form a pillar, say eighty feet high by ten in diameter. That the process was, in at least one instance, incalculably slow, the following instance will suffice to show. Cut on one of these pillars we discovered a rude likeness of a mummy, by the head of which sat what appeared to be one of the Egyptian gods, doubtless the handiwork of some old-world labourer in the mine. This work of art was executed at about the natural height at which an idle fellow, be he Phœnician workman or British cad, is in the habit of trying to immortalise himself at the expense of nature's masterpieces, namely, about five feet from the ground; yet at the time that we saw it, which *must* have been nearly three thousand years after the date of the execution of the drawing, the column was only eight feet high, and was still in process of formation, which gives a rate of growth of a foot to a thousand years, or an inch and a fraction to a century. This we knew because, as we were standing by it, was heard a drop of water fall.

Sometimes the stalactites took strange forms, presumably where the dropping of the water had not always been on the same spot. Thus, one huge mass, which must have weighed a hundred tons or so, was in the form of a pulpit, beautifully fretted over outside with what looked like lace. Others resembled strange beasts, and on the sides of the cave were fan-like ivory tracings, such as the frost leaves upon a pane.

Out of the vast main aisle, there opened here and there smaller caves, exactly, Sir Henry said, as chapels open out of great cathedrals. Some were large, but one or two—and this is a wonderful instance of how nature carries out her handiwork by the same unvarying laws, utterly irrespective of size—were tiny. One little nook, for instance, was no larger than an unusually big doll's house, and yet it might have been the model of the whole place, for the water dropped, the tiny icicles hung, and the spar columns were forming in just the same way.

We had not, however, as much time to examine this beautiful place as thoroughly as we should have liked to do, for unfortunately Gagool seemed to be indifferent to stalactites, and only anxious to get her business over. This annoyed me the more, as I was particularly anxious to discover, if possible, by what system the light was admitted into the place, and whether it was by the hand of man or of nature that this was done, also if it had been used in any way in ancient times, as seemed probable. However, we consoled ourselves with the idea that we would examine it thoroughly on our return, and followed on after our uncanny guide.

On she led us, straight to the top of the vast and silent cave, where we found another doorway, not arched as the first was, but square at the top, something like the doorways of Egyptian temples.

"Are ye prepared to enter the Place of Death?" asked Gagool, evidently with a view to making us feel uncomfortable.

"Lead on, Macduff,"[1] said Good, solemnly, trying to look as though he was not at all alarmed, as indeed did we all except Foulata, who caught Good by the arm for protection.

"This is getting rather ghastly," said Sir Henry, peeping into the dark doorway. "Come on, Quatermain—*seniores priores.*[2] Don't keep the old lady waiting!" and he politely made way for me to lead the van, for which I inwardly did not bless him.

Tap, tap, went old Gagool's stick down the passage, as she trotted along, chuckling hideously; and still overcome by some unaccountable presentiment of evil, I hung back.

"Come, get on, old fellow," said Good, "or we shall lose our fair guide."

Thus adjured, I started down the passage, and after about twenty paces found myself in a gloomy apartment some forty feet long by thirty broad, and thirty high, which in some past age had evidently been hollowed, by hand-labour, out of the mountain. This apartment was not nearly so well lighted as the vast stalactite antecave, and at the first glance all I could make out was a massive stone table running its length, with a colossal white figure at its

---

1   "Lead on, Macduff"] a misquotation of *Macbeth* 5.8:33.

2   *seniores priores*] (Latin) elders first.

head, and life-sized white figures all round it. Next I made out a brown thing, seated on the table in the centre, and in another moment my eyes grew accustomed to the light, and I saw what all these things were, and I was tailing out of it as hard as my legs would carry me. I am not a nervous man, in a general way, and very little troubled with superstitions, of which I have lived to see the folly; but I am free to own that that sight quite upset me, and had it not been that Sir Henry caught me by the collar and held me, I do honestly believe that in another five minutes I should have been outside that stalactite cave, and that the promise of all the diamonds in Kimberley would not have induced me to enter it again. But he held me tight, so I stopped because I could not help myself. But next second his eyes got accustomed to the light, too, and he let go of me, and began to mop the perspiration off his forehead. As for Good he swore feebly, and Foulata threw her arms round his neck and shrieked.

Only Gagool chuckled loud and long.

It *was* a ghastly sight. There at the end of the long stone table, holding in his skeleton fingers a great white spear, sat *Death* himself, shaped in the form of a colossal human skeleton, fifteen feet or more in height. High above his head he held the spear, as though in the act to strike; one bony hand rested on the stone table before him, in the position a man assumes on rising from his seat, whilst his frame was bent forward so that the vertebrae of the neck and the grinning, gleaming skull projected towards us, and fixed its hollow eye-places upon us, the jaws a little open, as though it were about to speak.

"Great heavens!" said I, faintly, at last, "what can it be?"

"And what are *those things?*" said Good, pointing to the white company round the table.

"And what on earth is *that thing?*" said Sir Henry, pointing to the brown creature seated on the table.

"Hee! hee! hee!" laughed Gagool. "To those who enter the Hall of the Dead, evil comes. Hee! hee! hee! ha! ha!"

"Come, Incubu, brave in battle, come and see him thou slewest;" and the old creature caught his coat in her skinny fingers, and led him away towards the table. We followed.

Presently she stopped and pointed at the brown object seated on the table. Sir Henry looked, and started back with an exclamation; and no wonder, for there seated, quite naked, on the table, the head which Sir Henry's battle-axe had shorn from the body resting on its knees, was the gaunt corpse of Twala, last king of the Kukuanas. Yes, there, the head perched upon the knees, it sat in all its ugliness, the vertebrae projecting a full inch above the level of the shrunken flesh of the neck, for all the world like a black double of Hamilton Tighe.* Over the whole surface of the corpse there was gathered a thin, glassy film, which made its appearance yet more appalling, and for which we were, at the moment, quite unable to account, till we presently observed that from the roof of the chamber the water fell steadily, *drip! drop! drip!* on to the neck of the corpse, from whence it ran down over the entire surface, and finally escaped into the rock through a tiny hole in the table. Then I guessed what it was — *Twala's body was being transformed into a stalactite.*

A look at the white forms seated on the stone bench that ran around that ghastly board confirmed this view. They were human forms indeed, or rather had been human forms; now they were *stalactites.* This was the way in which the Kukuana people had from time immemorial preserved their royal dead. They petrified them. What the exact system was, if there was any, beyond placing them for a long period of years under the drip, I never discovered, but there they sat, iced over and preserved for ever by the silicious fluid. Anything more awe-inspiring than the spectacle of this long line of departed royalties, wrapped in a shroud of ice-like spar, through which the features could be dimly made out (there were twenty-seven of them, the last being Ignosi's father), and seated round that inhospitable board, with Death himself for a host, it is impossible to imagine. That the practice of thus preserving their kings must have been an ancient one is evident from the number, which, allowing for an average reign of fifteen years, would, supposing that every king who reigned was placed here — an

---

* "Now haste ye, my handmaidens, haste and see
How he sits there and glowers with his head on his knee."[1]

---

1 Hamilton Tighe] R.H. Barham, *Ingoldsby Legends*, "Legend of Hamilton Tighe," lines 53-54.

improbable thing, as some are sure to have perished in battle far from home—fix the date of its commencement at four and a quarter centuries back. But the colossal Death, who sits at the head of the board, is far older than that, and unless I am much mistaken, owes his origin to the same artist who designed the three colossi. He was hewn out of a single stalactite, and, looked at as a work of art, was most admirably conceived and executed. Good, who understood anatomy, declared that so far as he could see the anatomical design of the skeleton was perfect down to the smallest bones.

My own idea is, that this terrific object was a freak of fancy on the part of some old-world sculptor, and that its presence had suggested to the Kukuanas the idea of placing their royal dead under its awful presidency. Or perhaps it was placed there to frighten away any marauders who might have designs upon the treasure chamber beyond. I cannot say. All I can do is to describe it as it is, and the reader must form his own conclusion.

Such, at any rate, was the White Death, and such were the White Dead!

CHAPTER XVII.

SOLOMON'S TREASURE CHAMBER.

While we had been engaged in getting over our fright, and in examining the grisly wonders of the place, Gagool had been differently occupied. Somehow or other—for she was marvellously active when she chose—she had scrambled on to the great table, and made her way to where our departed friend Twala was placed, under the drip, to see, suggested Good, how be was "pickling," or for some dark purpose of her own. Then she came hobbling back, stopping now and again to address a remark (the tenor of which I could not catch) to one or other of the shrouded forms, just as you or I might greet an old acquaintance. Having gone through this mysterious and horrible ceremony, she squatted herself down on the table immediately under the White Death, and began, so far as I could make out, to offer up prayers to it. The spectacle of this wicked old creature pouring out supplications (evil ones, no doubt) to the arch enemy of mankind, was so uncanny that it caused us to hasten our inspection.

"Now, Gagool," said I, in a low voice—somehow one did not dare to speak above a whisper in that place—"lead us to the chamber."

The old creature promptly scrambled down off the table.

"My lords are not afraid?" she said, leering up into my face.

"Lead on."

"Good, my lords;" and she hobbled round to the back of the great Death. "Here is the chamber; let my lords light the lamp, and enter," and she placed the gourd full of oil upon the floor, and leaned herself against the side of the cave. I took out a match, of which we still had a few in a box, and lit the rush wick, and then looked for the doorway, but there was nothing before us but the solid rock. Gagool grinned. "The way is there, my lords."

"Do not jest with us," I said, sternly.

"I jest not, my lords. See!" and she pointed at the rock.

As she did so, on holding up the lamp we perceived that a mass of stone was slowly rising from the floor and vanishing into the rock above, where doubtless there was a cavity prepared to receive it. The mass was of the width of a good-sized door, about ten feet high and not less than five feet thick. It must have weighed at least twenty or thirty tons, and was clearly moved upon some simple balance principle, probably the same as that upon which the opening and shutting of an ordinary modern window is arranged. How the principle was set in motion, of course none of us saw; Gagool was careful to avoid that; but I have little doubt that there was some very simple lever, which was moved ever so little by pressure on a secret spot, thereby throwing additional weight on to the hidden counterbalances, and causing the whole huge mass to be lifted from the ground. Very slowly and gently the great stone raised itself, till at last it had vanished altogether, and a dark hole presented itself to us in the place which it had filled.

Our excitement was so intense, as we saw the way to Solomon's treasure chamber at last thrown open, that I for one began to tremble and shake. Would it prove a hoax after all, I wondered, or was old Da Silvestra right? and were there vast hoards of wealth stored in that dark place, hoards which would make us the richest men in the whole world? We should know in a minute or two.

"Enter, white men from the stars," said Gagool, advancing into the doorway; "but first hear your servant, Gagaoola the old. The bright stones that ye will see were dug out of the pit over which the Silent Ones are set, and stored here, I know not by whom. But once has this place been entered since the time that those who stored the stones departed in haste, leaving them behind. The report of the treasure went down among the people who lived in the country from age to age, but none knew where the chamber was, nor the secret of the door. But it happened that a white man reached this country from over the mountain, perchance he too came 'from the stars,' and was well received of the king of the day. He it is who sits yonder," and she pointed to the fifth king at the table of the dead. "And it came to pass that he and a woman of the country who was with him came to this place, and that by chance the woman learnt the secret of the door—a thousand years might ye search, but ye should never find it. Then the white man entered with the woman, and found the stones, and filled with stones the skin of a small goat, which the woman had with her to hold food. And as he was going from the chamber he took up one more stone, a large one, and held it in his hand." Here she paused.

"Well," I asked, breathless with interest as we all were, "what happened to Da Silvestra?"

The old hag started at the mention of the name.

"How knowest thou the dead man's name?" she asked, sharply; and then, without waiting for an answer, went on—

"None know what happened; but it came about that the white man was frightened, for he flung down the goat-skin, with the stones, and fled out with only the one stone in his hand, and that the king took, and it is the stone that thou, Macumazahn, didst take from Twala's brows."

"Have none entered here since?" I asked, peering again down the dark passage.

"None, my lords. Only the secret of the door hath been kept, and every king hath opened it, though he hath not entered. There is a saying, that those who enter there will die within a moon, even as the white man died in the cave upon the mountain, where ye found him, Macumazahn. *Ha! ha!* mine are true words."

Our eyes met as she said it, and I turned sick and cold. How did the old hag know all these things?

"Enter, my lords. If I speak truth the goat-skin with the stones will lie upon the floor; and if there is truth as to whether it is death to enter here, that will ye learn afterwards. Ha! ha! ha!" And she hobbled through the doorway, bearing the light with her; but I confess that once more I hesitated about following.

"Oh, confound it all!" said Good, "here goes. I am not going to be frightened by that old devil;" and followed by Foulata, who, however, evidently did not at all like the job, for she was shivering with fear, he plunged into the passage after Gagool—an example which we quickly followed.

A few yards down the passage, in the narrow way hewn out of the living rock, Gagool had paused, and was waiting for us.

"See, my lords," she said, holding the light before her, "those who stored the treasure here fled in haste, and bethought them to guard against any who should find the secret of the door, but had not the time," and she pointed to large square blocks of stone, which had, to the height of two courses (about two feet three), been placed across the passage with a view to walling it up. Along the side of the passage were similar blocks ready for use, and, most curious of all, a heap of mortar and a couple of trowels, which, so far as we had time to examine them, appeared to be of a similar shape and make to those used by workmen to this day.

Here Foulata, who had throughout been in a state of great fear and agitation, said that she felt faint and could go no farther, but would wait there. Accordingly we set her down on the unfinished wall, placing the basket of provisions by her side, and left her to recover.

Following the passage for about fifteen paces farther, we suddenly came to an elaborately painted wooden door. It was standing wide open. Whoever was last there had either not had the time, or had forgotten, to shut it.

Across the threshold lay a skin bag, formed of a goat-skin, that appeared to be full of pebbles.

"Hee! hee! white men," sniggered Gagool, as the light from the lamp fell upon it. "What did I tell ye, that the white man who came here fled in haste, and dropped the woman's bag—behold it!"

Good stooped down and lifted it. It was heavy and jingled.

"By Jove! I believe it's full of diamonds," he said, in an awed whisper; and, indeed, the idea of a small goat-skin full of diamonds is enough to awe anybody.

"Go on," said Sir Henry, impatiently. "Here, old lady, give me the lamp," and taking it from Gagool's hand, he stepped through the doorway and held it high above his head.

We pressed in after him, forgetful, for the moment, of the bag of diamonds, and found ourselves in Solomon's treasure chamber.

At first, all that the somewhat faint light given by the lamp revealed was a room hewn out of the living rock, and apparently not more than ten feet square. Next there came into sight, stored one on the other as high as the roof, a splendid collection of elephant-tusks. How many of them there were we did not know, for of course we could not see how far they went back, but there could not have been less than the ends of four or five hundred tusks of the first quality visible to our eyes. There, alone, was enough ivory before us to make a man wealthy for life. Perhaps, I thought, it was from this very store that Solomon drew his material for his "great throne of ivory,"[1] of which there was not the like made in any kingdom.

On the opposite side of the chamber were about a score of wooden boxes, something like Martini-Henry ammunition boxes, only rather larger, and painted red.

"There are the diamonds," cried I; "bring the light."

Sir Henry did so, holding it close to the top box, of which the lid, rendered rotten by time even in that dry place, appeared to have been smashed in, probably by Da Silvestra himself. Pushing my hand through the hole in the lid I drew it out full, not of diamonds, but of gold pieces, of a shape that none of us had seen before, and with what looked like Hebrew characters stamped upon them.

"Ah!" I said, replacing the coin, "we shan't go back empty-

---

1   "great throne of ivory"] I Kings 10:18.

handed, anyhow. There must be a couple of thousand pieces in each box, and there are eighteen boxes. I suppose it was the money to pay the workmen and merchants."

"Well," put in Good, "I think that is the lot; I don't see any diamonds, unless the old Portuguese put them all into this bag."

"Let my lords look yonder where it is darkest, if they would find the stones," said Gagool, interpreting our looks. "There my lords will find a nook, and three stone chests in the nook, two sealed and one open."

Before interpreting this to Sir Henry, who had the light, I could not resist asking how she knew these things, if no one had entered the place since the white man, generations ago.

"Ah, Macumazahn, who watchest by night," was the mocking answer, "ye who live in the stars, do ye not know that some have eyes that can see through rock?"

"Look in that corner, Curtis," I said, indicating the spot Gagool had pointed out.

"Hullo, you fellows," he said, "here's a recess. Great heavens! look here."

We hurried up to where he was standing in a nook, something like a small bow window. Against the wall of this recess were placed three stone chests, each about two feet square. Two were fitted with stone lids, the lid of the third rested against the side of the chest, which was open.

"*Look!*" he repeated, hoarsely, holding the lamp over the open chest. We looked, and for a moment could make nothing out, on account of a silvery sheen that dazzled us. When our eyes got used to it, we saw that the chest was three-parts full of uncut diamonds, most of them of considerable size. Stooping, I picked some up. Yes, there was no mistake about it, there was the unmistakable soapy feel about them.

I fairly gasped as I dropped them.

"We are the richest men in the whole world," I said. "Monte Christo[1] is a fool to us."

"We shall flood the market with diamonds," said Good.

"Got to get them there first," suggested Sir Henry.

---

1   Monte Christo] Edmond Dantès deciphers directions to a buried treasure in *Le Comte de Monte-Cristo* (1844) by Alexandre Dumas.

And we stood with pale faces and stared at each other, with the lantern in the middle, and the glimmering gems below, as though we were conspirators about to commit a crime, instead of being, as we thought, the three most fortunate men on earth.

"Hee! hee! hee!" went old Gagool behind us, as she flitted about like a vampire bat. "There are the bright stones that ye love, white men, as many as ye will; take them, run them through your fingers, *eat* of them, hee! hee! *drink* of them, ha! ha!"

There was something so ridiculous at that moment to my mind in the idea of eating and drinking diamonds, that I began to laugh outrageously, an example which the others followed, without knowing why. There we stood and shrieked with laughter over the gems which were ours, which had been found for *us* thousands of years ago by the patient delvers in the great hole yonder, and stored for *us* by Solomon's long-dead overseer, whose name, perchance, was written in the characters stamped on the faded wax that yet adhered to the lids of the chest. Solomon never got them, nor David, nor Da Silvestra, nor anybody else. *We* had got them; there before us were millions of pounds' worth of diamonds, and thousands of pounds' worth of gold and ivory, only waiting to be taken away.

Suddenly the fit passed off, and we stopped laughing.

"Open the other chests, white men," croaked Gagool, "there are surely more therein. Take your fill, white lords!"

Thus adjured, we set to work to pull up the stone lids on the other two, first — not without a feeling of sacrilege — breaking the seals that fastened them.

Hoorah! they were full too, full to the brim; at least, the second one was; no wretched Da Silvestra had been filling goat-skins out of that. As for the third chest, it was only about a fourth full, but the stones were all picked ones; none less than twenty carats, and some of them as large as pigeon-eggs. Some of these biggest ones, however, we could see by holding them up to the light, were a little yellow, "off coloured," as they call it at Kimberley.

What we did *not* see, however, was the look of fearful malevolence that old Gagool favoured us with as she crept, crept like a snake, out of the treasure chamber and down the passage towards the massive door of solid rock.

Hark! Cry upon cry comes ringing up the vaulted path. It is Foulata's voice!

"*Oh, Bougwan! help! help! the rock falls!*"

"Leave go, girl! Then——"

"*Help! help! she has stabbed me!*"

By now we are running down the passage, and this is what the light from the lamp falls on. The door of rock is slowly closing down; it is not three feet from the floor. Near it struggle Foulata and Gagool. The red blood of the former runs to her knee, but still the brave girl holds the old witch, who fights like a wild cat. Ah! she is free! Foulata falls, and Gagool throws herself on the ground, to twist herself like a snake through the crack of the closing stone. She is under—ah, God! too late! too late! The stone nips her, and she yells in agony. Down, down, it comes, all the thirty tons of it, slowly pressing her old body against the rock below. Shriek upon shriek, such as we never heard, then a long sickening *crunch*, and the door was shut just as we, rushing down the passage, hurled ourselves against it.

It was all done in four seconds.

Then we turned to Foulata. The poor girl was stabbed in the body, and could not, I saw, live long.

"Ah! Bougwan, I die!" gasped the beautiful creature. "She crept out—Gagool; I did not see her, I was faint—and the door began to fall; then she came back, and was looking up the path—and I saw her come in through the slowly falling door, and caught her and held her, and she stabbed me, and *I die*, Bougwan."

"Poor girl! poor girl!" Good cried; and then, as he could do nothing else, he fell to kissing her.

"Bougwan," she said, after a pause, "is Macumazahn there? it grows so dark, I cannot see."

"Here I am, Foulata."

"Macumazahn, be my tongue for a moment, I pray thee, for Bougwan cannot understand me, and before I go into the darkness—I would speak a word."

"Say on, Foulata, I will render it."

"Say to my lord, Bougwan, that—I love him, and that I am glad to die because I know that he cannot cumber his life with such as me, for the sun cannot mate with the darkness, nor the white with the black.

"Say that at times I have felt as though there were a bird in my bosom, which would one day fly hence and sing elsewhere. Even now, though I cannot lift my hand, and my brain grows cold, I do not feel as though my heart were dying; it is so full of love that could live a thousand years, and yet be young. Say that if I live again, mayhap I shall see him in the stars, and that—I will search them all, though perchance I should there still be black and he would—still he white. Say—nay, Macumazahn, say no more, save that I love—Oh, hold me closer, Bougwan, I cannot feel thine arms—*oh! oh!*"

"She is dead—she is dead!" said Good, rising in grief, the tears running down his honest face.

"You need not let that trouble you, old fellow," said Sir Henry.

"Eh!" said Good; "what do you mean?"

"I mean that you will soon be in a position to join her. *Man, don't you see that we are buried alive?*"

Until Sir Henry uttered these words, I do not think the full horror of what had happened had come home to us, preoccupied as we were with the sight of poor Foulata's end. But now we understood. The ponderous mass of rock had closed, probably for ever, for the only brain which knew its secret was crushed to powder beneath it. This was a door that none could hope to force with anything short of dynamite in large quantities. And we were the wrong side of it!

For a few minutes we stood horrified there over the corpse of Foulata. All the manhood seemed to have gone out of us. The first shock of this idea of the slow and miserable end that awaited us was overpowering. We saw it all now; that fiend Gagool had planned this snare for us from the first. It would have been just the jest that her evil mind would have rejoiced in, the idea of the three white men, whom, for some reason of her own, she had always hated, slowly perishing of thirst and hunger in the company of the treasure they had coveted. I saw the point of that sneer of hers about eating and drinking the diamonds now. Perhaps somebody had tried to serve the poor old Don in the same way, when he abandoned the skin full of jewels.

"This will never do," said Sir Henry, hoarsely; "the lamp will soon go out. Let us see if we can't find the spring that works the rock."

We sprang forward with desperate energy, and standing in a bloody ooze, began to feel up and down the door and the sides of the passage. But no knob or spring could we discover.

"Depend on it," I said, "it does not work from the inside; if it did Gagool would not have risked trying to crawl underneath the stone. It was the knowledge of this that made her try to escape at all hazards, curse her."

"At all events," said Sir Henry, with a hard little laugh, "retribution was swift; hers was almost as awful an end as ours is likely to be. We can do nothing with the door; let us go back to the treasure room." We turned and went, and as we did so I perceived by the unfinished wall across the passage the basket of food which poor Foulata had carried. I took it up, and brought it with me back to that accursed treasure chamber that was to be our grave. Then we went back and reverently bore in Foulata's corpse, laying it on the floor by the boxes of coin.

Next we seated ourselves, leaning our backs against the three stone chests of priceless treasures.

"Let us divide the food," said Sir Henry, "so as to make it last as long as possible." Accordingly we did so. It would, we reckoned, make four infinitesimally small meals for each of us, enough, say, to support life for a couple of days. Besides the "biltong," or dried game-flesh, there were two gourds of water, each holding about a quart.

"Now," said Sir Henry, "let us eat and drink, for to-morrow we die."

We each ate a small portion of the "biltong," and drank a sip of water. We had, needless to say, but little appetite, though we were sadly in need of food, and felt better after swallowing it. Then we got up and made a systematic examination of the walls of our prison-house, in the faint hope of finding some means of exit, sounding them and the floor carefully.

There was none. It was not probable that there would be one to a treasure chamber.

The lamp began to burn dim. The fat was nearly exhausted.

"Quatermain," said Sir Henry, "what is the time—your watch goes?"

I drew it out, and looked at it. It was six o'clock; we had entered the cave at eleven.

"Infadoos will miss us," I suggested. "If we do not return to-night, he will search for us in the morning, Curtis."

"He may search in vain. He does not know the secret of the door, not even where it is. No living person knew it yesterday, except Gagool. To-day no one knows it. Even if he found the door he could not break it down. All the Kukuana army could not break through five feet of living rock. My friends, I see nothing for it but to bow ourselves to the will of the Almighty. The search for treasure has brought many to a bad end; we shall go to swell their number."

The lamp grew dimmer yet.

Presently it flared up and showed the whole scene in strong relief, the great mass of white tusks, the boxes full of gold, the corpse of poor Foulata stretched before them, the goat-skin full of treasure, the dim glimmer of the diamonds, and the wild, wan faces of us three white men seated there awaiting death by starvation.

Suddenly it sank, and expired.

CHAPTER XVIII.

WE ABANDON HOPE.

I CAN give no adequate description of the horrors of the night which followed. Mercifully they were to some extent mitigated by sleep, for even in such a position as ours, wearied nature will sometimes assert itself. But I, at any rate, found it impossible to sleep much. Putting aside the terrifying thought of our impending doom—for the bravest man on earth might well quail from such a fate as awaited us, and I never had any great pretensions to be brave—the *silence* itself was too great to allow of it. Reader, you may have lain awake at night and thought the silence oppressive, but I say with confidence that you can have no idea what a vivid tangible thing perfect silence really is. On the surface of the earth there is always some sound or motion, and though it may in itself be imperceptible, yet does it deaden the sharp edge of absolute silence. But here there was none. We were buried in the bowels of a huge snow-clad peak. Thousands of feet above us the fresh air rushed over the white snow, but no sound of it reached us. We were separated by a long tunnel and five feet of rock even from the awful chamber of the dead; and the dead make no noise. The crashing of all the artillery of earth and heaven could not have come to our ears in our living tomb. We were cut off from all echoes of the world—we were as already dead.

And then the irony of the situation forced itself upon me. There around us lay treasures enough to pay off a moderate national debt, or to build a fleet of ironclads, and yet we would gladly have bartered them all for the faintest chance of escape. Soon, doubtless, we should be glad to exchange them for a bit of food or a cup of water, and, after that, even for the privilege of a speedy close to our sufferings. Truly wealth, which men spend all their lives in acquiring, is a valueless thing at the last.

And so the night wore on.

"Good," said Sir Henry's voice at last, and it sounded awful in the intense stillness, "how many matches have you in the box?"

"Eight, Curtis."

"Strike one, and let us see the time."

He did so, and in contrast to the dense darkness the flame nearly blinded us. It was five o'clock by my watch. The beautiful dawn was now blushing on the snow-wreaths far over our heads, and the breeze would be stirring the night mists in the hollows.

"We had better eat something and keep up our strength," said I.

"What is the good of eating?" answered Good; "the sooner we die and get it over the better."

"While there is life there is hope," said Sir Henry.

Accordingly we ate and sipped some water, and another period of time passed, when somebody suggested that it might be as well to get as near to the door as possible and halloa, on the faint chance of somebody catching a sound outside. Accordingly Good, who, from long practice at sea, has a fine piercing note, groped his way down the passage and began, and I must say he made a most diabolical noise. I never heard such yells; but it might have been a mosquito buzzing for all the effect it produced.

After a while he gave it up, and came back very thirsty, and had to have some water. After that we gave up yelling, as it encroached on the supply of water.

So we all sat down once more against our chests of useless diamonds in that dreadful inaction, which was one of the hardest circumstances of our fate; and I am bound to say that, for my part, I gave way in despair. Laying my head against Sir Henry's broad shoulder I burst into tears; and I think I heard Good gulping away on the other side, and swearing hoarsely at himself for doing so.

Ah, how good and brave that great man was! Had we been two frightened children, and he our nurse, he could not have treated us more tenderly. Forgetting his own share of miseries, he did all he could to soothe our broken nerves, telling stories of men who had been in somewhat similar circumstances, and miraculously escaped; and when these failed to cheer us, pointing out how, after all, it was only anticipating an end that must come to us all, that it would soon be over, and that death from exhaustion was a merciful one (which is not true). Then, in a diffident sort of a way, as I had once before heard him do, he suggested that we should throw ourselves on the mercy of a higher Power, which for my part I did with great vigour.

His is a beautiful character, very quiet, but very strong.

And so somehow the day went as the night had gone (if, indeed, one can use the terms where all was densest night), and when I lit a match to see the time it was seven o'clock.

Once more we ate and drank, and as we did so an idea occurred to me.

"How is it," said I, "that the air in this place keeps fresh? It is thick and heavy, but it is perfectly fresh."

"Great heavens!" said Good, starting up, "I never thought of that. It can't come through the stone door, for it is air-tight, if ever a door was. It must come from somewhere. If there were no current of air in the place we should have been stifled when we first came in. Let us have a look."

It was wonderful what a change this mere spark of hope wrought in us. In a moment we were all three groping about the place on our hands and knees, feeling for the slightest indication of a draught. Presently my ardour received a check. I put my hand on something cold. It was poor Foulata's dead face.

For an hour or more we went on feeling about, till at last Sir Henry and I gave it up in despair, having got considerably hurt by constantly knocking our heads against tusks, chests, and the sides of the chamber. But Good still persevered, saying, with an approach to cheerfulness, that it was better than doing nothing.

"I say, you fellows," he said, presently, in a constrained sort of voice, "come here."

Needless to say we scrambled over towards him quick enough.

"Quatermain, put your hand here where mine is. Now, do you feel anything?"

"I *think* I feel air coming up."

"Now listen." He rose and stamped upon the place, and a flame of hope shot up in our hearts. *It rang hollow.*

With trembling hands I lit a match. I had only three left, and we saw that we were in the angle of the far corner of the chamber, a fact that accounted for our not having noticed the hollow ring of the place during our former exhaustive examination. As the match burnt we scrutinised the spot. There was a join in the solid rock floor, and, great heavens! there, let in level with the rock, was a stone ring. We said no word, we were too excited, and our hearts beat too wildly with hope to allow us to speak. Good had a knife, at the back of which was one of those hooks that are made to extract stones from horses' hoofs. He opened it, and scratched away at the ring with it. Finally he got it under, and levered away gently for fear of breaking the hook. The ring began to move. Being of stone, it had not got set fast in all the centuries it had lain there, as would have been the case had it been of iron. Presently it was upright. Then he got his hands into it and tugged with all his force, but nothing budged.

"Let me try," I said, impatiently, for the situation of the stone, right in the angle of the corner, was such that it was impossible for two to pull at once. I got hold and strained away, but with no results.

Then Sir Henry tried and failed.

Taking the hook again, Good scratched all round the crack where we felt the air coming up.

"Now, Curtis," he said, "tackle on, and put your back into it;

you are as strong as two. Stop," and he took off a stout black silk handkerchief, which, true to his habits of neatness, he still wore, and ran it through the ring. "Quatermain, get Curtis round the middle and pull for dear life when I give the word. *Now*."

Sir Henry put out all his enormous strength, and Good and I did the same, with such power as nature had given us.

"Heave! heave! it's giving," gasped Sir Henry; and I heard the muscles of his great back cracking. Suddenly there came a parting sound, then a rush of air, and we were all on our backs on the floor with a great flag-stone on the top of us. Sir Henry's strength had done it, and never did muscular power stand a man in better stead.

"Light a match Quatermain," he said, as soon as we had picked ourselves up and got one breath; "carefully, now."

I did so, and there before us was, God be praised! the *first step of a stone stair.*

"Now what is to be done?" asked Good.

"Follow the stair, of course, and trust to Providence."

"Stop!" said Sir Henry; "Quatermain, get the bit of biltong and the water that is left; we may want them."

I went creeping back to our place by the chests for that purpose, and as I was coming away an idea struck me. We had not thought much of the diamonds for the last twenty-four hours or so; indeed, the idea of diamonds was nauseous, seeing what they had entailed upon us; but, thought I, I may as well pocket a few in case we ever should get out of this ghastly hole. So I just stuck my fist into the first chest and filled all the available pockets of my old shooting coat,[1] topping up — this was a happy thought — with a couple of handfuls of big ones out of the third chest.

"I say, you fellows," I sung out, "won't you take some diamonds with you? I've filled my pockets."

"Oh! hang the diamonds!" said Sir Henry. I hope that I may never see another."

As for Good, he made no answer. He was, I think, taking a last farewell of all that was left of the poor girl who loved him so well. And, curious as it may seem to you, my reader, sitting at home at

---

1   shooting coat] a coat of canvas or other tough material with large pockets, worn by hunters.

ease and reflecting on the vast, indeed the immeasurable, wealth which we were thus abandoning, I can assure you that if you had passed some twenty-eight hours with next to nothing to eat and drink in that place, you would not have cared to cumber yourself with diamonds whilst plunging down into the unknown bowels of the earth, in the wild hope of escape from an agonising death. If it had not, from the habits of a lifetime, become a sort of second nature with me never to leave anything worth having behind, if there was the slightest chance of my being able to carry it away, I am sure I should not have bothered to fill my pockets.

"Come on, Quatermain," said Sir Henry, who was already standing on the first step of the stone stair. "Steady, I will go first."

"Mind where you put your feet; there may be some awful hole underneath," said I.

"Much more likely to be another room," said Sir Henry, as he slowly descended, counting the steps as he went.

When he got to "fifteen" he stopped. "Here's the bottom," he said. "Thank goodness! I think it's a passage. Come on down."

Good descended next, and I followed last, and on reaching the bottom lit one of the two remaining matches. By its light we could just see that we were standing in a narrow tunnel, which ran right and left at right angles to the staircase we had descended. Before we could make out any more, the match burnt my fingers and went out. Then arose the delicate question of which way to turn. Of course, it was impossible to know what the tunnel was or where it ran to, and yet to turn one way might lead us to safety, and the other to destruction. We were utterly perplexed, till suddenly it struck Good that when I had lit the match the draught of the passage blew the flame to the left.

"Let us go against the draught," he said; "air draws inwards, not outwards."

We took this suggestion, and feeling along the wall with the hand, whilst trying the ground before us at every step, we departed from that accursed treasure chamber on our terrible quest. If ever it should be entered again by living man, which I do not think it will be, he will find a token of our presence in the open chests of jewels, the empty lamp, and the white bones of poor Foulata.

When we had groped our way for about a quarter of an hour along the passage, it suddenly took a sharp turn, or else was bisected by another, which we followed, only in course of time to be led into a third. And so it went on for some hours. We seemed to be in a stone labyrinth which led nowhere. What all these passages are, of course I cannot say, but we thought that they must be the ancient workings of a mine, of which the various shafts travelled hither and thither as the ore led them. This is the only way in which we could account for such a multitude of passages.

At length we halted, thoroughly worn out with fatigue, and with that hope deferred which maketh the heart sick,[1] and ate up our poor remaining piece of biltong, and drank our last sup of water, for our throats were like lime-kilns. It seemed to us that we had escaped Death in the darkness of the chamber only to meet him in the darkness of the tunnels.

As we stood, once more utterly depressed, I thought I caught a sound, to which I called the attention of the others. It was very faint and very far off, but it *was* a sound, a faint, murmuring sound, for the others heard it too, and no words can describe the blessedness of it after all those hours of utter, awful stillness.

"By heaven! it's running water," said Good. "Come on."

Off we started again in the direction from which the faint murmur seemed to come, groping our way as before along the rocky walls. As we went it got more and more audible, till at last it seemed quite loud in the quiet. On, yet on; now we could distinctly make out the unmistakable swirl of rushing water. And yet how could there be running water in the bowels of the earth? Now we were quite near to it, and Good, who was leading, swore that he could smell it.

"Go gently, Good," said Sir Henry, "we must be close." *Splash!* and a cry from Good.

He had fallen in.

"Good! Good! where are you?" we shouted, in terrified distress. To our intense relief, an answer came back in a choky voice.

"All right; I've got hold of a rock. Strike a light to show me where you are."

Hastily I lit the last remaining match. Its faint gleam discovered

---

1 hope ... sick] Proverbs 13:12.

to us a dark mass of water running at our feet. How wide it was we could not see, but there, some way out, was the dark form of our companion hanging on to a projecting rock.

"Stand clear to catch me," sung out Good. "I must swim for it."

Then we heard a splash, and a great struggle. Another minute and he had grabbed at and caught Sir Henry's outstretched hand, and we had pulled him up high and dry into the tunnel.

"My word!" he said, between his gaps, "that was touch and go. If I hadn't caught that rock, and known how to swim, I should have been done. It runs like a mill-race, and I could feel no bottom."

It was clear that this would not do; so after Good had rested a little, and we had drunk our fill from the water of the subterranean river, which was sweet and fresh, and washed our faces, which sadly needed it, as well as we could, we started from the banks of this African Styx,[1] and began to retrace our steps along the tunnel, Good dripping unpleasantly in front of us. At length we came to another tunnel leading to our right.

"We may as well take it," said Sir Henry, wearily; "all roads are alike here; we can only go on till we drop."

Slowly, for a long, long while we stumbled, utterly weary, along this new tunnel, Sir Henry leading now.

Suddenly he stopped, and we bumped up against him.

"Look!" he whispered, "is my brain going, or is that light?"

We stared with all our eyes, and there, yes, there, far ahead of us, was a faint glimmering spot, no larger than a cottage window pane. It was so faint that I doubt if any eyes, except those which, like ours, had for days seen nothing but blackness, could have perceived it at all.

With a sort of gasp of hope we pushed on. In five minutes there was no longer any doubt: it *was* a patch of faint light. A minute more and a breath of real live air was fanning us. On we struggled. All at once the tunnel narrowed. Sir Henry went on his knees. Smaller yet it grew, till it was only the size of a large fox's

---

1 Styx] the river that flowed through the Underworld, across which Charon ferried the spirits of the dead.

earth[1]—it was *earth* now, mind you; the rock had ceased. A squeeze, a struggle, and Sir Henry was out, and so was Good, and so was I; and there above us were the blessed stars, and in our nostrils was the sweet air; then suddenly something gave, and we were all rolling over and over and over through grass and bushes, and soft, wet soil.

I caught at something and stopped. Sitting up I hallooed lustily. An answering shout came from just below, where Sir Henry's wild career had been stopped by some level ground. I scrambled to him, and found him unhurt, though breathless. Then we looked for Good. A little way off we found him too, jammed in a forked root. He was a good deal knocked about, but soon came to.

We sat down together there on the grass, and the revulsion of feeling was so great, that I really think we cried for joy. We had escaped from that awful dungeon, that was so near to becoming our grave. Surely some merciful Power must have guided our footsteps to the jackal hole at the termination of the tunnel, (for that is what it must have been). And see, there on the mountains, the dawn we had never thought to look upon again was blushing rosy red.

Presently the grey light stole down the slopes, and we saw that we were at the bottom, or rather, nearly at the bottom, of the vast pit in front of the entrance to the cave. Now we could make out the dim forms of the three colossi who sat upon its verge. Doubtless those awful passages, along which we had wandered the livelong night, had originally been, in some way, connected with the great diamond mine. As for the subterranean river in the bowels of the mountain, Heaven only knows what it was, or whence it flows, or whither it goes. I for one have no anxiety to trace its course.

Lighter it grew, and lighter yet. We could see each other now, and such a spectacle as we presented I have never set eyes on before or since. Gaunt-cheeked, hollow-eyed wretches, smeared all over with dust and mud, bruised, bleeding, the long fear of imminent death yet written on our countenances, we were,

---

1 fox's earth] the hole of a fox, a burrowing animal.

indeed, a sight to frighten the daylight. And yet it is a solemn fact that Good's eye-glass was still fixed in Good's eye. I doubt whether he had ever taken it out at all. Neither the darkness, nor the plunge in the subterranean river, nor the roll down the slope, had been able to separate Good and his eye-glass.

Presently we rose, fearing that our limbs would stiffen if we stopped there longer, and commenced with slow and painful steps to struggle up the sloping sides of the great pit. For an hour or more we toiled steadfastly up the blue clay, dragging ourselves on by the help of the roots and grasses with which it was clothed.

At last it was done, and we stood on the great road, on the side of the pit opposite to the colossi.

By the side of the road, a hundred yards off, a fire was burning in front of some huts, and round the fire were figures. We made towards them, supporting one another, and halting every few paces. Presently, one of the figures rose, saw us, and fell on to the ground, crying out for fear.

"Infadoos, Infadoos! it is us, thy friends."

We rose; he ran to us, staring wildly, and still shaking with fear.

"Oh, my lords, my lords, it is indeed you come back from the dead! — come back from the dead!"

And the old warrior flung himself down before us, and clasped Sir Henry's knees, and wept aloud for joy.

CHAPTER XIX.

IGNOSI'S FAREWELL.

TEN days from that eventful morning found us once more in our old quarters at Loo; and, strange to say, but little the worse for our terrible experience, except that my stubbly hair came out of that cave about three shades greyer than it went in, and that Good never was quite the same after Foulata's death, which seemed to move him very greatly. I am bound to say that, looking at the thing from the point of view of an oldish man of the world, I consider her removal was a fortunate occurrence, since, otherwise, complications would have been sure to ensue. The poor creature was no ordinary native girl, but a person of great, I had almost said stately, beauty, and of considerable refinement of mind. But no amount of beauty or refinement could have made an entanglement between Good and herself a desirable occurrence; for, as she herself put it, "Can the sun mate with the darkness, or the white with the black?"

I need hardly state that we never again penetrated into Solomon's treasure chamber. After we had recovered from our fatigues, a process which took us forty-eight hours, we descended into the great pit in the hope of finding the hole by which we had crept out of the mountain, but with no success. To begin with, rain had fallen, and obliterated our spoor; and what is more, the sides of the vast pit were full of ant-bear[1] and other holes. It was impossible to say to which of these we owed our salvation. We also, on the day before we started back to Loo, made a further examination of the wonders of the stalactite cave, and, drawn by a kind of restless feeling, even penetrated once more into the Chamber of the Dead; and, passing beneath the spear of the white Death, gazed, with sensations which it would be quite impossible for me to describe, at the mass of rock which had shut us off from escape, thinking, the while, of the priceless treasures beyond, of the mysterious old hag whose flattened fragments lay crushed beneath it, and of the fair girl of whose tomb it was the portal. I say gazed at the "rock," for examine as we would, we could find no traces of the join of the sliding door; nor, indeed, could we hit upon the secret, now utterly lost, that worked it, though we tried for an hour or more. It was certainly a marvellous bit of mechanism, characteristic in its massive and yet inscrutable simplicity, of the age which produced it; and I doubt if the world has such another to show.

At last we gave it up in disgust; though, if the mass had suddenly risen before our eyes, I doubt if we should have screwed up courage to step over Gagool's mangled remains, and once more enter the treasure chamber, even in the sure and certain hope of unlimited diamonds. And yet I could have cried at the idea of leaving all that treasure, the biggest treasure probably that has ever

---

1 ant-bear] aardvark.

in the world's history been accumulated in one spot. But there was no help for it. Only dynamite could force its way through five feet of solid rock. And so we left it. Perhaps, in some remote unborn century, a more fortunate explorer may hit upon the "Open Sesame," and flood the world with gems. But, myself, I doubt it. Somehow, I seem to feel that the millions of pounds' worth of gems that lie in the three stone coffers will never shine round the neck of an earthly beauty. They and Foulata's bones will keep cold company till the end of all things.

With a sigh of disappointment we made our way back, and next day started for Loo. And yet it was really very ungrateful of us to be disappointed; for, as the reader will remember, I had, by a lucky thought, taken the precaution to fill the pockets of my old shooting coat with gems before we left our prison-house. A good many of these fell out in the course of our roll down the side of the pit, including most of the big ones, which I had crammed in on the top. But, comparatively speaking, an enormous quantity still remained, including eighteen large stones ranging from about one hundred to thirty carats in weight. My old shooting coat still held enough treasure to make us all, if not millionaires, at least exceedingly wealthy men, and yet to keep enough stones each to make the three finest sets of gems in Europe. So we had not done so badly.

On arriving at Loo, we were most cordially received by Ignosi, whom we found well, and busily engaged in consolidating his power, and reorganising the regiments which had suffered most in the great struggle with Twala.

He listened with breathless interest to our wonderful story; but when we told him of old Gagool's frightful end, he grew thoughtful.

"Come hither," he called, to a very old Induna (councillor), who was sitting with others in a circle round the king, but out of ear-shot. The old man rose, approached, saluted, and seated himself.

"Thou art old," said Ignosi.

"Ay, my lord the king!"

"Tell me, when thou wast little, didst thou know Gagaoola the witch doctress?"

"Ay, my lord the king!"

"How was she then—young, like thee?"

"Not so, my lord the king! She was even as now; old and dried, very ugly, and full of wickedness."

"She is no more; she is dead."

"So, O king! then is a curse taken from the land."

"Go!"

"*Koom!* I go, black puppy, who tore out the old dog's throat. *Koom!*"

"Ye see, my brothers," said Ignosi, "this was a strange woman, and I rejoice that she is dead. She would have let ye die in the dark place, and mayhap afterwards she had found a way to slay me as she found a way to slay my father, and set up Twala, whom her heart loved, in his place. Now go on with the tale; surely there never was the like!"

After I had narrated all the story of our escape, I, as we had agreed between ourselves that I should, took the opportunity to address Ignosi as to our departure from Kukuanaland.

"And now, Ignosi, the time has come for us to bid thee farewell, and start to seek once more our own land. Behold, Ignosi, with us thou camest a servant, and now we leave thee a mighty king. If thou art grateful to us, remember to do even as thou didst promise: to rule justly, to respect the law, and to put none to death without a cause. So shalt thou prosper. To-morrow, at break of day, Ignosi, wilt thou give us an escort who shall lead us across the mountains? Is it not so, O king?"

Ignosi covered his face with his hands for a while before answering.

"My heart is sore," he said at last; "your words split my heart in twain. What have I done to ye, Incubu, Macumazahn, and Bougwan, that ye should leave me desolate? Ye who stood by me in rebellion and in battle, will ye leave me in the day of peace and victory? What will ye—wives? Choose from out the land! A place to live in? Behold, the land is yours as far as ye can see. The white man's houses? Ye shall teach my people how to build them. Cattle for beef and milk? Every married man shall bring ye an ox or a cow. Wild game to hunt? Does not the elephant walk through my forests, and the river-horse sleep in the reeds? Would ye make war? My Impis (regiments) wait your word. If there is anything more that I can give, that will I give ye."

"Nay, Ignosi, we want not these things," I answered; "we would seek our own place."

"Now do I perceive," said Ignosi, bitterly, and with flashing eyes, "that it is the bright stones that ye love more than me, your friend. Ye have the stones; now would ye go to Natal and across the moving black water and sell them, and be rich, as it is the desire of a white man's heart to be. Cursed for your sake be the stones, and cursed he who seeks them. Death shall it be to him who sets foot in the place of Death to seek them. I have spoken, white men; ye can go."

I laid my hand upon his arm. "Ignosi," I said, "tell us, when thou didst wander in Zululand, and among the white men in Natal, did not thine heart turn to the land thy mother told thee of, thy native land, where thou didst see the light, and play when thou wast little, the land where thy place was?"

"It was even so, Macumazahn."

"Then thus does our heart turn to our land and to our own place."

Then came a pause. When Ignosi broke it, it was in a different voice.

"I do perceive that thy words are, now as ever, wise and full of reason, Macumazahn; that which flies in the air loves not to run along the ground; the white man loves not to live on the level of the black. Well, ye must go, and leave my heart sore, because ye will be as dead to me, since from where ye will be no tidings can come to me.

"But listen, and let all the white men know my words. No other white man shall cross the mountains, even if any may live to come so far. I will see no traders with their guns and rum. My people shall fight with the spear, and drink water, like their forefathers before them. I will have no praying-men to put fear of death into men's hearts, to stir them up against the king, and make a path for the white men who follow to run on. If a white man comes to my gates I will send him back; if a hundred come, I will push them back; if an army comes, I will make war on them with all my strength, and they shall not prevail against me. None shall ever come for the shining stones; no, not an army, for if they come I will send a regiment and fill up the pit, and break down the white columns in the caves and fill them with rocks, so that none can come even to that door of which ye speak, and whereof the way to move it is lost. But for ye three, Incubu, Macumazahn, and Bougwan, the path is always open; for behold, ye are dearer to me than aught that breathes.

"And ye would go. Infadoos, my uncle, and my Induna, shall take thee by the hand and guide thee, with a regiment. There is, as I have learnt, another way across the mountains that he shall show ye. Farewell, my brothers, brave white men. See me no more, for I have no heart to bear it. Behold, I make a decree, and it shall be published from the mountains to the mountains, your names, Incubu, Macumazahn, and Bougwan, shall be as the names of dead kings, and he who speaks them shall die.* So shall your memory, be preserved in the land for ever.

"Go now, ere my eyes rain tears like a woman's. At times when ye look back down the path of life, or when ye are old and gather yourselves together to crouch before the fire, because the sun has no more heat, ye will think of how we stood shoulder to shoulder in that great battle that thy wise words planned, Macumazahn, of how thou wast the point of that horn that galled Twala's flank, Bougwan; whilst thou stoodst in the ring of the Greys, Incubu, and men went down before thine axe like corn before a sickle; ay, and of how thou didst break the wild bull's (Twala's) strength, and bring his pride to dust. Fare ye well for ever, Incubu, Macumazahn, and Bougwan, my lords and my friends."

He rose, looked earnestly at us for a few seconds, and then threw the corner of his kaross over his head, so as to cover his face from us.

We went in silence.

Next day at dawn we left Loo, escorted by our old friend Infadoos, who was heart-broken at our departure, and the regiment of Buffaloes. Early as the hour was, all the main street of the

---

* This extraordinary and negative way of showing intense respect is by no means unknown among African people, and the result is that if, as is usual, the name in question has a significance, the meaning has to be expressed by an idiom or another word. In this way a memory is preserved for generations, or until the new word supplants the old one.

town was lined with multitudes of people, who gave us the royal salute as we passed at the head of the regiment, while the women blessed us as having rid the land of Twala, throwing flowers before us as we went. It really was very affecting, and not the sort of thing one is accustomed to meet with from natives.

One very ludicrous incident occurred, however, which I rather welcomed, as it gave us something to laugh at.

Just before we got to the confines of the town, a pretty young girl, with some beautiful lilies in her hand, came running forward and presented them to Good (somehow they all seemed to like Good; I think his eye-glass and solitary whisker gave him a fictitious value), and then said she had a boon to ask.

"Speak on."

"Let my lord show his servant his beautiful white legs, that his servant may look on them, and remember them all her days, and tell of them to her children; his servant has travelled four days' journey to see them, for the fame of them has gone throughout the land."

"I'll be hanged if I do!" said Good, excitedly.

"Come, come, my dear fellow," said Sir Henry, "you can't refuse to oblige a lady."

"I won't," said Good, obstinately; "it is positively indecent."

However, in the end he consented to draw up his trousers to the knee, amidst notes of rapturous admiration from all the women present, especially the gratified young lady, and in this guise he had to walk till we got clear of the town.

Good's legs will, I fear, never be so greatly admired again. Of his melting teeth, and even of his "transparent eye," they wearied more or less, but of his legs, never.

As we travelled, Infadoos told us that there was another pass over the mountains to the north of the one followed by Solomon's great road, or rather that there was a place where it was possible to climb down the wall of cliff that separated Kukuanaland from the desert, and was broken by the towering shapes of Sheba's Breasts. It appeared, too, that rather more than two years previously a party of Kukuana hunters had descended this path into the desert in search of ostriches, whose plumes were much prized among them for war head-dresses, and that in the course of their hunt they had been led far from the mountains, and were much troubled by thirst. Seeing, however, trees on the horizon, they made towards them, and discovered a large and fertile oasis of some miles in extent, and plentifully watered. It was by way of this oasis that he suggested that we should return, and the idea seemed to us a good one, as it appeared that we should escape the rigours of the mountain pass, and as some of the hunters were in attendance to guide us to the oasis, from which, they stated, they could perceive more fertile spots far away in the desert.*

Travelling easily, on the night of the fourth day's journey we found ourselves once more on the crest of the mountains that separate Kukuanaland from the desert, which rolled away in sandy billows at our feet, and about twenty-five miles to the north of Sheba's Breasts.

At dawn on the following day, we were led to the commencement of a precipitous descent, by which we were to descend the precipice, and gain the desert two thousand and more feet below.

Here we bade farewell to that true friend and sturdy old warrior, Infadoos, who solemnly wished all good upon us, and nearly wept with grief. "Never, my lords," he said, "shall mine old eyes see the like of ye again. Ah! the way that Incubu cut his men down in the battle! Ah! for the sight of that stroke with which he swept off my brother Twala's head! It was beautiful—beautiful! I may never hope to see such another, except perchance in happy dreams."

We were very sorry to part from him; indeed, Good was so moved that he gave him as a souvenir—what do you think?—an

---

* It often puzzled all of us to understand how it was possible that Ignosi's mother, bearing the child with her, should have survived the dangers of the journey across the mountains and the desert, dangers which so nearly proved fatal to ourselves. It has since occurred to me, and I give the idea to the reader for what it is worth, that she must have taken this second route, and wandered out like Hagar[1] into the desert. If she did so, there is no longer anything inexplicable about the story, since she may well, as Ignosi himself related, have been picked up by some ostrich hunters before she or the child were exhausted, and led by them to the oasis, and thence by stages to the fertile country, and so on by slow degrees southwards to Zululand. —A. Q.

---

1 Hagar] Genesis 21:14-21.

eye-glass. (Afterwards we discovered that it was a spare one.) Infadoos was delighted, foreseeing that the possession of such an article would enormously increase his prestige, and after several vain attempts actually succeeded in screwing it into his own eye. Anything more incongruous than the old warrior looked with an eye-glass I never saw. Eye-glasses don't go well with leopard-skin cloaks and black ostrich plumes.

Then, having seen that our guides were well laden with water and provisions, and having received a thundering farewell salute from the Buffaloes, we wrung the old warrior's hand, and began our downward climb. A very arduous business it proved to be, but somehow that evening we found ourselves at the bottom without accident.

"Do you know," said Sir Henry that night, as we sat by our fire and gazed up at the beetling cliffs above us, "I think that there are worse places than Kukuanaland in the world, and that I have spent unhappier times than the last month or two, though I have never spent such queer ones. Eh! you fellows?"

"I almost wish I were back," said Good, with a sigh.

As for myself, I reflected that all's well that ends well; but in the course of a long life of shaves, I never had such shaves as those I had recently experienced. The thought of that battle still makes me feel cold all over, and as for our experience in the treasure chamber——!

Next morning we started on a toilsome march across the desert, having with us a good supply of water carried by our five guides, and camped that night in the open, starting again at dawn on the morrow.

By mid-day of the third day's journey we could see the trees of the oasis of which the guides spoke, and by an hour before sundown we were once more walking upon grass and listening to the sound of running water.

CHAPTER XX.

FOUND.

AND now I come to perhaps the strangest thing that happened to us in all that strange business, and one which shows how wonderfully things are brought about.

I was walking quietly along, some way in front of the other two, down the banks of the stream, which ran from the oasis till it was swallowed up in the hungry desert sands, when suddenly I stopped and rubbed my eyes, as well I might. There, not twenty yards in front, placed in a charming situation, under the shade of a species of fig tree, and facing to the stream, was a cosy hut, built more or less on the Kafir principle of grass and withes, only with a full-length door instead of a bee-hole.

"What the dickens," said I to myself, "can a hut be doing here!" Even as I said it, the door of the hut opened, and there limped out of it *a white man* clothed in skins, and with an enormous black beard. I thought that I must have got a touch of the sun. It was impossible. No hunter ever came to such a place as this. Certainly no hunter would ever settle in it. I stared and stared, and so did the other man, and just at that juncture Sir Henry and Good came up.

"Look here, you fellows," I said, "is that a white man, or am I mad?"

Sir Henry looked, and Good looked, and then all of a sudden the lame white man with the black beard gave a great cry, and came hobbling towards us. When he got close, he fell down in a sort of faint.

With a spring Sir Henry was by his side.

"Great Powers!" he cried, "*it is my brother George!*"

At the sound of the disturbance, another figure, also clad in skins, emerged from the hut, with a gun in his hand, and came running towards us. On seeing me he too gave a cry.

"Macumazahn," he halloed, "don't you know me, Baas? I'm Jim the hunter. I lost the note you gave me to give to the Baas, and we have been here nearly two years." And the fellow fell at my feet, and rolled over and over, weeping for joy.

"You careless scoundrel!" I said; "you ought to be well hided."

Meanwhile the man with the black beard had recovered and got up, and he and Sir Henry were pump-handling away at each other, apparently without a word to say. But whatever they had quarrelled about in the past (I suspect it was a lady, though I never asked), it was evidently forgotten now.

"My dear old fellow," burst out Sir Henry at last, "I thought that you were dead. I have been over Solomon's Mountains to find you, and now I come across you perched in the desert, like an old Aasvögel (vulture)."

"I tried to go over Solomon's Mountains nearly two years ago," was the answer, spoken in the hesitating voice of a man who has had little recent opportunity of using his tongue, "but when I got here, a boulder fell on my leg and crushed it, and I have been able to go neither forward nor back."

Then I came up. "How do you do, Mr. Neville?" I said; "do you remember me?"

"Why," he said, "isn't it Quatermain, eh, and Good too? Hold on a minute, you fellows, I am getting dizzy again. It is all so very strange, and, when a man has ceased to hope, so very happy."

That evening, over the camp fire, George Curtis told us his story, which, in its way, was almost as eventful as our own, and amounted shortly to this. A little short of two years before, he had started from Sitanda's Kraal, to try and reach the mountains. As for the note I had sent him by Jim, that worthy had lost it, and he had never heard of it till to-day. But, acting upon information he had received from the natives, he made, not for Sheba's Breasts, but for the ladder-like descent of the mountains down which we had just come, which was clearly a better route than that marked out in old Dom Silvestra's plan. In the desert he and Jim suffered great hardships, but finally they reached this oasis, where a terrible accident befell George Curtis. On the day of their arrival, he was sitting by the stream, and Jim was extracting the honey from the nest of a stingless bee, which is to be found in the desert, on the top of the bank immediately above him. In so doing he loosed a great boulder of rock, which fell upon George Curtis' right leg, crushing it frightfully. From that day he had been so dreadfully lame, that he had found it impossible to go either forward or back, and had preferred to take the chances of dying on the oasis to the certainty of perishing in the desert.

As for food, however, they had got on pretty well, for they had a good supply of ammunition, and the oasis was frequented, especially at night, by large quantities of game, which came thither for water. These they shot, or trapped in pitfalls, using their flesh for food, and, after their clothes wore out, their hides for covering.

"And so," he ended, "we have lived for nearly two years, like a second Robinson Crusoe and his man Friday, hoping against hope that some natives might come here and help us away, but none have come. Only last night we settled that Jim should leave me, and try to reach Sitanda's Kraal and get assistance. He was to go tomorrow, but I had little hope of ever seeing him back again. And now *you*, of all people in the world, *you*, who I fancied had long ago forgotten all about me, and were living comfortably in old England, turn up in a promiscuous way and find me where you least expected. It is the most wonderful thing I ever heard of, and the most merciful too."

Then Sir Henry set to work and told him the main facts of our adventures, sitting till late into the night to do it.

"By Jove!" he said, when I showed him some of the diamonds; "well, at least you have got something for your pains, besides my worthless self."

Sir Henry laughed. "They belong to Quatermain and Good. It was part of the bargain that they should share any spoils there might be."

This remark set me thinking, and having spoken to Good I told Sir Henry that it was our unanimous wish that he should take a third share of the diamonds, or if he would not, that his share should be handed to his brother, who had suffered even more than ourselves on the chance of getting them. Finally, we prevailed upon him to consent to this arrangement, but George Curtis did not know of it till some time afterwards.

*   *   *   *   *

And here, at this point, I think I shall end this history. Our journey across the desert back to Sitanda's Kraal was most arduous, especially as we had to support George Curtis, whose right leg was very weak indeed, and continually throwing out splinters of bone; but we did accomplish it somehow, and to give its details would only be to reproduce much of what happened to us on the former occasion.

Six months from the date of our re-arrival at Sitanda's, where we found our guns and other goods quite safe, though the old scoundrel in charge was much disgusted at our surviving to claim them, saw us all once more safe and sound at my little place on the Berea, near Durban, where I am now writing, and whence I bid farewell to all who have accompanied me throughout the strangest trip I ever made in the course of a long and varied experience.

Just as I had written the last word, a Kafir came up my avenue of orange trees, with a letter in a cleft stick, which he had brought from the post. It turned out to be from Sir Henry, and as it speaks for itself I give it in full.

"Brayley Hall, Yorkshire.

"My Dear Quatermain,—

"I sent you a line a few mails back to say that the three of us, George, Good, and myself, fetched up all right in England. We got off the boat at Southampton, and went up to town. You should have seen what a swell Good turned out the very next day, beautifully shaved, frock coat fitting like a glove, brand new eye-glass, &c. &c. I went and walked in the park with him, where I met some people I know, and at once told them the story of his 'beautiful white legs.'

"He is furious, especially as some ill-natured person has printed it in a society paper.

"To come to business, Good and I took the diamonds to Streeter's to be valued, as we arranged, and I am really afraid to tell you what they put them at, it seems so enormous. They say that of course it is more or less guess-work, as such stones have never to their knowledge been put on the market in anything like such quantities. It appears that they are (with the exception of one or two of the largest) of the finest water, and equal in every way to the best Brazilian stones. I asked them if they would buy them, but they said that it was beyond their power to do so, and recommended us to sell by degrees, for fear we should flood the market. They offer, however, a hundred and eighty thousand for a small portion of them.

"You must come home, Quatermain, and see about these things, especially if you insist upon making the magnificent present of the third share, which does *not* belong to me, to my brother George. As for Good, he is *no good*. His time is too much occupied in shaving, and other matters connected with the vain adorning of the body. But I think he is still down on his luck about Foulata. He told me that since he had been home he hadn't seen a woman to touch her, either as regards her figure or the sweetness of her expression.

"I want you to come home, my dear old comrade, and buy a place near here. You have done your day's work, and have lots of money now, and there is a place for sale quite close which would suit you admirably. Do come; the sooner the better; you can finish writing the story of our adventures on board ship. We have refused to tell the story till it is written by you, for fear that we shall not be believed. If you start on receipt of this, you will reach here by Christmas, and I book you to stay with me for that. Good is coming, and George, and so, by the way, is your boy Harry (there's a bribe for you). I have had him down for a week's shooting, and like him. He is a cool young hand; he shot me in the leg, cut out the pellets, and then remarked upon the advantage of having a medical student in every shooting party.

"Good-bye, old boy; I can't say any more, but I know that you will come, if it is only to oblige

"Your sincere friend,

"Henry Curtis.

"P.S. — The tusks of the great bull that killed poor Khiva have now been put up in the hall here, over the pair of buffalo horns you gave me, and look magnificent; and the axe with which I chopped off Twala's head is stuck up over my writing table. I wish we could have managed to bring away the coats of chain armour.

"H.C."

To-day is Tuesday. There is a steamer going on Friday, and I really think I must take Curtis at his word, and sail by her for England, if it is only to see my boy Harry and see about the printing of this history, which is a task I do not like to trust to anybody else.

THE END.

Appendix A: Victorian Critical Reaction

1. Andrew Lang, "King Solomon's Mines," *The Saturday Review* (October 10, 1885)

Like *Treasure Island*, *King Solomon's Mines* deals with the quest for hidden wealth. But in the latter volume it is not the gold of buccaneers which is sought, in the last century, by a crew of pirates ... [but] nothing less than the diamond mines whence the Sidonian galleons[1] brought King Solomon his jewels. The scene is the centre of Southern Africa, Kukuanaland, a region unexplored. The time is the present day, and the seekers are Allan Quatermain, an old elephant-hunter, in whose mouth the narrative is put, Sir Henry Curtis, an Englishman in quest of a lost brother, Captain Good, his friend, and Umbopa, a mysterious Zulu recruit who is not all a Zulu.... Curtis is a man with a giant's strength, and a hero, withal, of the noblest daring and equanimity. Good, his friend, adds the comic element, and, if we had a fault to find with this enthralling tale, it is that Mr. Haggard gives us too good measure of comedy.... We have only praise for the very remarkable and uncommon powers of invention and gift of "vision" which Mr. Haggard displays. He is not one of the hack book-makers for boys who describe adventures they never tasted in lands which they only know from geography books. He is intimately acquainted with the wild borders of Zululand, Bechuana, and the Transvaal,[2] and he has a most sympathetic knowledge of the Zulu. The Kukuanas of the tale are, in fact, Zulus, long isolated, wholly ignorant of European ways, and better organized, on the whole, than the tribesmen of Chaka and Mpanda[3]....

The scene ... of "Solomon's Road," a vast raised causeway, winding off into the dim recesses of Kukuanaland ... is justified by the "wide waggon road, cut out of the solid rock," with "stacks of gold quartz piled up ready for crushing," which have been discovered in the Lydenburg district of the Transvaal. No mature archæological opinion has been given, as far as we know, about these extraordinary remains of South African civilization. Mr. Haggard does not mention, in this connexion, a Bushman tradition reported by Mr. Orpen. That traveller made the

---

1 Sidon was the chief city of ancient Phoenicia, famous for its commercial sailing-ships.
2 On the political map of the time, these largely tribal territories, not at all or only thinly colonized, lay north and north-west of Natal Colony.
3 Chaka was the founder of the Zulu dynasty; Mpanda was his son and successor. See Haggard's "A Zulu War-Dance" (Appendix B).

acquaintance of Qing, a Bushman who "had never seen a white man before except fighting." Now Qing, among the myths and traditions of his people, related that the Bushmen had once been able to make roads "and stone things which went over rivers." There is here no collusion, and who shall be sure that Bushman tradition does not retain a true memory of a civilization from which it fell in some immemorial past?

Haggard is so correct in his descriptive touches and pictures of African life, that one is constantly tempted into discussion too grave for the task in hand…. [T]here is a splendid savage battle-piece, on the lines of the combat between the two brigades of Mpanda's army, near the Tugela, some forty years ago.[1] All through the battle-piece, "The Last Stand of the Greys," Mr. Haggard, like Scott at Flodden, "never stoops his wing."[2] The slaying is Homeric. Naturally the white men, with Umbopa, win, and then we have a duel, as good as the greater combat, between Sir Henry and Twala, the gigantic one-eyed king. Twala is slain. Umbopa is accepted as king, and he makes Gagool, the impish witch-finder, guide the Englishmen to Solomon's Mines. But, first, they must look on the White Death and the White Dead, a scene of high and even poetical imagination, of which we shall not spoil the interest by an explanation or analysis. What chanced in the awful treasure cave, what was the last dread trump in the hand of the undefeated Gagool, how Good's lover, the Kukuana Pocahontas, fared (for this amount of "feminine interest" Mr. Haggard offers), and the conclusion of the whole matter, we leave the reader to discover….

In this narrative Mr. Haggard seems, as the French say, to have "found himself." He has added a new book to a scanty list, the list of good, manly, and stirring fictions of pure adventure. The sentiment of his regular novels, *Dawn* and *The Witch's Head*, is absent, of course, but perhaps, at least in the former of these, sentiment was unduly to the fore. No one can call Allan Quatermain sentimental. And, to tell the truth, we would give many novels, say eight hundred (that is about the yearly harvest), for such a book as *King Solomon's Mines*.

---

1 The Tugela River forms the boarder between Natal and Zululand. The battle was between the sons of Mpanda (Umpande) for succession to the chiefdom. See Appendix B: Haggard, "Anecdote."

2 Flodden Field in Northumberland, England, was the scene of a famous battle of 1513 between the English and the Scots. Sir Walter Scott's *Marmion* (1808) told the tale in six cantos.

2. R.L. Stevenson, Letter to H.Rider Haggard (October 1885), *The Letters of Robert Louis Stevenson* (1995)

Dear Sir, Some kind hand has sent me your tale of *Solomon's Mines*; I know not who did this good thing to me; so I send my gratitude to head-quarters and the fountainhead. You should be more careful; you do quite well enough to take more trouble, and some parts of your book are infinitely beneath you. But I find there flashes of a fine weird imagination and a fine poetic use and command of the savage way of talking: things which both thrilled me. The reflections of your hero before the battle are singularly fine; the King's song of victory a very noble imitation. But how, in the name of literature, could you mistake some lines from Scott's *Marmion*—ay, and some of the best—for the slack-sided, clerical-cob effusions of the Rev. Ingoldsby? Barham is very good, but Walter Scott is vastly better.[1] I am, dear sir, Your obliged reader, Robert Louis Stevenson.

3. Anonymous, "King Solomon's Mines," *The Spectator* (London: November 7, 1885)

Mr. Haggard's invention ... enables him to invest the central incident of his story with a certain weird originality which takes away all idea from the reader that he has been reading the same things before. It was a happy thought, in the first place, to make the treasure King Solomon's. There is a name to conjure with as well in the West as in the East; and though we do not remember that diamonds figure in the Scripture catalogue of that potentate's wealth, we are ready to believe that his treasury was rich beyond the dreams of avarice. It may even be said that the Scriptural associations of the name give a certain verisimilitude to the story.... But there is more than this. It is an absolute stroke of genius when, in the ice-cavern, the discoverers find frozen into permanence the actual form of the old Portuguese adventurer of three hundred years before, and can even trace—so unchanged is the figure—the very wound in his arm from which he drew the blood wherewith he was to trace the map that was to guide some more fortunate adventurer. We felt when we reached that point that we were in the hands of a story-teller of

---

1 Richard Barham composed the *Ingoldsby Legends* (1840), a collection of humorous poems. Haggard says he replied pointing out that RLS "had overlooked the fact that Allan Quatermain's habit of attributing sundry quotations to the Old Testament and the Ingoldsby Legends, the only books with which he was familiar, was a literary joke."

no common powers; nor did the rest of the narrative, so skilfully and so high is the interest piled up, at all disappoint our expectations. The descriptions of battles do not easily admit of striking variations; yet no one will hesitate to allow this merit to the great fight between King Twala and King Ignosi, with the forlorn hope of the Greys, who go into battle two thousand strong and come out with sixty, and the truly Homeric duel between King Twala and Sir Henry Curtis. It reeks, perhaps, a little too much of blood, but it is as effective a piece of writing as we have seen for a long time. The final scene in the cave, too, is very thrilling, the apparent hopelessness of the situation and the final escape being equally well managed.

Besides incident, two other elements are almost essential in a tale of this kind,— sentiment and humour. Of sentiment there is little; but that little is good and cleverly contrived. That the susceptible sailor, Captain John Good, should fall in love with his pretty Kukuana nurse, Foulata, was, of course, inevitable; and we should have been even disappointed by any other result; but the situation is a difficult one, and the incident by which the white lover is extricated from it is as ingenious as it is pathetic. If the sailor supplies the sentiment of the story, he also supplies the humour.... Scarcely two persons can be found to agree about what is humorous; but to our mind, Captain John Good is a real "figure of fun," though he is also something more, and plays an important part in the story. Sometimes Mr. Haggard is, we think, a little too audacious, as when he makes Ignosi burst out into almost the same language as that with which the priest of the Saxon gods answered the invitation of Paullinus: — "Like a storm-driven bird at night we fly out of the nowhere; for a moment our wings are seen in the light," &c.[1]

4. Anonymous, "*King Solomon's Mines,*" *The Literary World* (Boston: January 23, 1886)

This is a bloody and ghastly story of the improbable in Central Africa. An old parchment is found locating a mysterious cave in an inaccessible group of mountains beyond an impassable desert, which cave is said to have been the source of King Solomon's wealth, and to be still full of diamonds and gold. Of course a party must be organized to find the treasure, and off go the seekers, almost dying of heat and thirst in the desert on the way. On reaching the reputed mines, they fall into the hands of a savage king, his witches, and his warriors, and are treated to all

---

1   Quoted in Chapter 5 of *KSM*; see note 1, p. 83.

sorts of horrors. The book reeks with brutality and suffering, and is enough to make the reader as haggard as its author.

5. G.M.Hopkins, Letter to Bridges (October 28, 1886), *The Letters of Gerard Manley Hopkins to Robert Bridges* (1935)

I have not read *Treasure Island*. When I do, as I hope to, I will bear your criticisms in mind. (By the bye, I am sorry those poor boys lost the book.... However give 'em Rider Haggard's *King Solomon's Mines*. They certainly will enjoy it; anyone would and the author is not a highflier.)

6. Samuel M. Clark, "Mr. Haggard's Romances," *The Dial* (Chicago: May 1887)

A ... critic notes that in "King Solomon's Mines" the crescent moon in full bow rises over Kukuanaland from the east a little after sunset; the next evening it has suddenly become full; and the following day after it has become full it totally eclipses the sun. The critic justly doubts whether even in Kukuanaland moon and sun should play such hocus-pocus arts with astronomy. And even the least exacting reader will be more than once annoyed by the crudeness of many of Mr. Haggard's sentences. But it takes more and greater faults than these to damn a writer if his work is vital and strong....

He has shown the old distinction between the novel and the romance. In the former the imagination pictures what is: in the latter it invents what is not. The novel dealing with the actual but slightly transposed has come in these latter days to an almost unmixed realism. In the degree it has become realistic we are all outgrowing romance. While we are all in this mood Mr. Haggard surprises us with romances as fantastic as those that Cervantes caricatured to immortal death.[1] He chose his line with deliberation. Here is a scene from one of his first stories: "'Well, Ernest,' she said, 'what are you thinking about? You are as dull as—as the dullest thing in the world, whatever that may be. What is the dullest thing in the world?' 'I don't know,' he answered, awakening; 'yes I think I do: an American novel.' 'Yes, that is a good definition. You are as dull as an American novel.'" And in the outset of "King Solomon's Mines" Allan Quatermain promises: "This history won't be dull, whatever else it may be." Thus Mr. Haggard has entered the lists against the dulness of

---

1   Clark alludes to Cervantes' *Don Quixote* and to the Don's insane fantasies. The leading exponent of American realism at this time was the novelist, William Dean Howells.

the American fashion in novels, and resolute to keep you awake as one of his prime purposes....

He has overdone his romance time and again. Gagool was so evidently made to scare you, that she fails to do it because she is an absurd stage devil made for the occasion. The battle between the loyal and insurgent parts of King Twala's army misses the satire of Gulliver or Don Quixote, if that is what was intended, and is farcical. Many of the devices made to get your wonder are too stagey.... Every chapter of his writings has something crude and defective. Yet over and above these, he is a great story-writer. He has freshened and quickened literature by showing in a distinctive and original way that the stories are not all told. He has shown that the alternative of the vapid commonplace of realism is not what Mr. Ruskin[1] calls foul fiction—a morbid introspection of evil passions on their way from the slums to the morgue[2]—but that romanticism, using a clean imagination, appealing to the faculty of wonder, is for most men and women the supreme and perpetually attractive form and matter of story-telling.

7. Anonymous, "Editorial," *The Book Buyer* (New York: August 1887)

It speaks well for the interest felt in the subject that the discussion of the tendency of American fiction has continued well into the summer.... Meanwhile the public buy thousands of copies of Mr. Haggard's story. This simple fact is a stronger argument than could be framed in a dozen pages against the theory of the Commonplace School that romance is a thing of the past—something that died, and deserved to die, with the author of "Ivanhoe."[3] Put this argument to the out-and-out realist, and he would perhaps reply that the popularity of Mr. Haggard's stories showed the wide (and, of course, regrettable) prevalence of a morbid and unhealthy taste for the sensational and absurdly improbable. The truth remains, however, that these widely-impossible tales find multitudes of eager readers, and that, too, among intelligent people, so far as one's observation goes. The significant thing, then, is, not that these tales of adventure deserve high rank, or, in fact, any rank at all, as literature, but that, despite the realistic tendencies of the time, of which one hears so much, the love of romance, with its heroes and heroines, its incidents, its

---

1   John Ruskin (1819-1900), English essayist and art critic. See Appendix C, Ruskin, "Lectures on Art."

2   That is, literary Naturalism (See Appendix B, "About Fiction").

3   Sir Walter Scott's novel (1819), a romance of history and adventure in the Middle Ages; a book for boys.

sentiment and its humor—that is, with its imaginative and idealistic treatment of humanity—still exerts a powerful influence in determining the choice of the buyers of books.

8. Crummell, A., "The Culture of the Horrible: Mr. Haggard's Stories," *The Church Quarterly Review* (London: January 1888)

One incident follows another so quickly as to keep the story from flagging, and the writer's acquaintance with African scenery and manners, and with the details of hunting larger game, gives reality and vigour to his pages.... There is very little delineation of character, and the author relies for his effects upon the skill, such as it is, with which he can interweave horrors into his narrative. We have them in every conceivable form. Indiscriminate and individual slaughter, whole corpses and dismembered limbs, skulls and bones, duels and suicide, torture and treachery, witchcraft and madness—all are available material for Mr. Haggard's purpose. He presents us with all the minutiae of the shambles and all the imagery of the charnel-house, and when the frightful scenes of suffering and slaughter have been duly exhausted in action, we have a distorted repetition of them in the actor's dreams. That the narrative at times trembles on the verge of sensuality, that the writer's humour does not disclaim the broadest farce, that his well-bred Englishmen can hardly be acquitted of vulgarity, and that sceptical theories should be gratuitously scattered broadcast in his pages, are subsidiary but serious blemishes in what may be designated as the culture of the horrible..... His elaborate detail is too often only tawdry ornament. His raptures are so insincere and unreal as to suggest the uncomfortable suspicion that he is laughing at his readers. He knows not, or he utterly disregards, the sanctities with which mankind deems it fitting to shroud the secrets of the tomb and the solemn presence chamber of death.... What imaginable purpose save that of making our minds familiar with all that is repulsive can be served by the sickening description of the witch-hunt with its infernal cold-blooded murders, or by the elaborate conceit of the Hall of Death, in which a colossal skeleton figure presided at the board, around which are gathered the grinning and petrified corpses of the royal house of Kukuana? The sight of a filthy hag, pouring out a stream of foul abuse, is not one over which we would willingly let our children linger.

9. Anonymous, "The Fall of Fiction," *Fortnightly Review* (September 1, 1888)

Speaking broadly, there are three means by which this writer produces his characteristic effects; and as these means are one and all eminently devoid of any such subtlety and complexity as might make the definition of them difficult, they can be specified and described with no less adequacy than ease. Firstly, there is the element of the physically revolting, as in circumstantial narratives of massacre, cruelty, and bloody death. Secondly, there is the element of the fantastic, preternatural, and generally marvellous. Thirdly, there is that odd and simple but infinitely variable expedient which may be described, metaphorically, as digging a hole in order that somebody may be helped out of it, ... with an inevitableness which we foresee from the first, and which therefore considerably lessens our interest in the problem of rescue, extricating the sufferer in the crowning moment of crisis and supreme suspense....

In *King Solomon's Mines* we have of course to wade through much minutely circumstantial slaughter of men, women, and elephants before we are rewarded with a vision of the fabulous Ophir....[1] It is not that we grudge Mr. Haggard his undeserved success, but that we grudge the comparative neglect of meritorious fiction which the rage for meretricious fiction implies. We believe Mr. Haggard's own inmost literary conscience will ratify our pronouncement. He is a clever man, well able to take the measure of his own charlatanry — very likely the last person in the world to mistake his own charlatanry for genius. He is a clever man, for to gauge public taste is not done by a sort of fluke, but argues very considerable if not always scrupulous talents; and he has accurately gauged the taste of a section of the reading public, which the triumph of his experiment proves to be a large section. But that taste — the taste for such an ill-compounded *mélange* of the sham-real and the sham-romantic — is a deplorable symptom.... When we have abundance of exquisite grapes in our vineyards, is it not almost incredible that persons who pretend to some connoisseurship should be content to besot themselves with a thick, raw concoction, destitute of fragrance, destitute of sparkle, destitute of everything but the power to induce a crude inebriety of mind and a morbid state of the intellectual peptics?[2]

---

1   The lost African city of Solomon. See Appendix D, Bible; also Walmsley, *Zulu Land*.
2   indigestion.

10. Margaret Oliphant, "Success in Fiction," *Forum* (May 1889)

[It is not surprising that] the general reader should have gone back with a spring of evident relief to records of wild adventure, fighting, and bloodshed. This is a sort of natural recoil from fare too ethereal for human nature's daily food.... And now the fine workmanship, say of Mr. Henry James, who carries that art to perfection ... naturally gives the fascinated yet unsatisfied reader an appetite for the downright effects of Mr. Rider Haggard. While the American Hamlet of the day wavers and hesitates, the Zulu's straightforward rules of action are delightful to the less sophisticated intelligence.... This is quite enough to account for the sudden surging of the ancient legend of adventure and movement, amidst a society which has had its fill of philosophy, of democracy, of criticism, and all the analytical processes.

Appendix B: Haggard on Africa and Romance

1. From H. Rider Haggard, "Notes on *King Solomon's Mines*" (1906), in Lilias Haggard, *The Cloak That I Left* (1951)

When I was a lad in Africa I met many men, the pioneers of settlement and exploration—those who had first become acquainted with some of the great savage races of the interior.... [T]he country which is now Rhodesia ... must have become engrained in my mind that it had once been occupied by an ancient people. How I came to conclude that this people was Phoenician I have no idea. Nor to the best of my memory did I hear of the great ruins of Zimbabwe, or that an ancient civilization had carried on a vast gold mining enterprise in the part of Africa where it stands.... All of these ... were the fruit of imagination, conceived I suppose from chance words spoken long ago that lay dormant in the mind.... But of the Matabele,[1] who, in the tale, are named Kukuanas, I did know something. Indeed I went near to knowing too much, for when, in 1877 my friends Captain Patterson and Mr. J. Sergeant were sent by Sir Bartle Frere[2] on an embassy to their king, Lobengula,[3] I asked leave to go with them. It was refused as I could not be spared from the office. Had I gone my fate would have been theirs, for Lobengula murdered them both, and my two servants whom I had lent them. These two, Khiva, the bastard Zulu, and Ventvogel, the Hottentot,[4] I have tried to preserve in *King Solomon's Mines*, for they were such men as I have described.

2. "Anecdote" (*circa* 1876) from *The Days of My Life* (1923).[5]

I heard many a story of savage Africa from Sir Theophilus [Shepstone] himself, from [Melmoth] Osborn and from [Fred] Fynney[6].... Osborn

---

1 Or, today, Ndebele; natives of Zulu descent living in Zimbabwe and the Transvaal.
2 Sir Henry Bartle Edward Frere (1815-84), a British administrator and Governor of the Cape Colony.
3 Lobengula (1836-94) succeeded his father Moselekatze in 1868 as King of the Matebele.
4 An indigenous tribe that occupied the Cape Colony region when it was first settled by the Dutch; now called the Khoi.
5 See Appendix C: Fynney, *Zululand*
6 Sir Theophilus Shepstone (1817-93) was Natal's Secretary for Native Affairs; Sir Melmoth Osborn (1833-99) served as the Colonial Secretary of the Transvaal; Fred Fynney was a Natal Border Agent and Inspector of Native Schools.

actually saw the battle of the Tugela, which took place between the rival princes Cetewayo and Umbelazi in 1856.[1] With the temerity of a young man he swam his horse across the river and hid himself in a wooded kopje[2] in the middle of the battlefield. He saw Umbelazi's host driven back and the veteran regiment, nearly three thousand strong, that Panda had sent to aid his favourite son, move up to its support. He described to me the frightful fray that followed. Cetewayo sent out a regiment against it. They met, and he said that the roll of the shields as they came together was like to that of deepest thunder. Then the Greys passed over Cetewayo's regiment as a wave passes over a sunken ridge of rock, and left it dead. Another regiment came against them and the scene repeated itself, only more slowly, for many of the veterans were down. Now the six hundred of them who remained formed themselves in a ring upon the hillock and fought on till they were buried beneath the heaps of the slain...

It is wonderful that Osborn should have escaped with his life. This he did by hiding close and tying his coat over his horse's head to prevent it from neighing. When darkness fell he rode back to the Tugela and swam its corpse-crowded waters.

3. "A Zulu War-Dance," the *Gentleman's Magazine* (1877)

[This was Haggard's first published work and is reproduced here *in toto* because it illuminates Haggard's early political ideas and, together with "About Fiction" (the next entry), is the best source of authorial commentary pertaining to *King Solomon's Mines*.]

In all that world-wide empire which the spirit of English colonisation has conquered from out of the realms of the distant and unknown, and added year by year to the English dominions, it is doubtful whether there be any one spot of corresponding area, presenting so many large questions—social and political—as the colony of Natal. Wrested some thirty years ago from the patriarchal Boers, and peopled by a few scattered scores of adventurous emigrants, Natal has with hard toil gained for itself a precarious foothold hardly yet to be called an existence. Known chiefly to the outside world as the sudden birthplace of those tremendous polemical missiles which battered so fiercely, some few years ago, against

---

1   See Appendix A: Lang, "KSM," note 1, p. 246. Cetewayo (or Ketshewayo) (died 1884), son of Panda, defeated his brother Umbelazi to become King of the Zulus.

2   This is the Dutch spelling of "koppie," a small hillock on the veldt.

the walls of the English Church,[1] it is now attracting attention to the shape and proportion of that unsolved riddle of the future, the Native Question.[2] In those former days of rude and hand-to-mouth legislation, when the certain evil of the day had to be met and dealt with before the possible evil of the morrow, the seeds of great political trouble were planted in the young colony, seeds whose fruit is fast ripening before our eyes.

When the strong aggressive hand of England has grasped some fresh portion of the earth's surface, there is yet a spirit of justice in her heart and head which prompts the question, among the first of such demands, as to how best and most fairly to deal by the natives of the newly-acquired land. In earlier times, when steam was not, and telegraphs and special correspondents were equally unknown agencies for getting at the truth of things, this question was more easily answered across a width of dividing ocean or continent. Then distant action might be prompt and sharp on emergency, and no one would be the wiser. But of late years, owing to these results of civilisation, harsh measures have, by the mere pressure of public opinion, and without consideration of their necessity in the eyes of the colonists, been set aside as impracticable and inhuman. In the case of Natal, most of the early questions of possession and right were settled, sword in hand, by the pioneer Dutch, who, after a space of terrible warfare, drove back the Zulus over the Tugela, and finally took possession of the land. But they did not hold it long. The same hateful invading Englishman, with his new ideas and his higher forms of civilisation, who had caused them to quit the "Old Colony," the land of their birth, came and drove them, *vi et armis*,[3] from the land of their adoption. And it was not long before these same English became lords of this red African soil, from the coast up to the Drakensberg.[4] Still there were difficulties; for although the new-comers might be lords of the soil, there remained yet a remnant, and a very troublesome remnant, of its original and natural masters: shattered fragments of the Zulu power in Natal, men who had once swept over the country in the army of Chaka the Terrible, Chaka of the Short Spear, but who had remained behind in the fair new land, when Chaka's raids had been checked by the white man and his deadly weapons. Remnants, too, of conquered aboriginal tribes, who

---

1 J. W. Colenso (1814-83), English bishop of Natal; not only did he tolerate polygamy among native converts but questions from his Zulu parishioners led him to question scriptural inerrancy.

2 Colonial rule created the problem of native land ownership and their political rights; see Editor's Introduction and Plaatje's novel *Mhudi*.

3 (Latin) by force and arms; by main force.

4 A range of mountains separating the settled coastal region of Natal from the interior.

had found even Chaka's rule easier than that of their own chieftains, swelled the amount to a total of some 100,000 souls.

One of the first acts of the English Government when it took up the reins was to allot to each of these constituent fragments a large portion of land. This might perhaps have been short-sighted legislation, but it arose from the necessity of the moment. According to even the then received ideas of colonisation and its duties, it was hardly possible — danger apart — to drive all the natives over the frontier, so they were allowed to stay and share the rights and privileges of British subjects. But the evil did not stop there. Ere long some political refugees, defeated in battle, fled before the avenging hand of the conqueror, and craved place and protection from the Government of Natal. It was granted; and the principle once established, body after body of men poured in: for, in stepping over the boundary line, they left the regions of ruin and terrible death, and entered those of peace, security, and plenty.

Thus it is that the native population of Natal, fed from within and without, has in thirty years more than quadrupled its numbers. Secluded from the outside world in his location, the native has lived in peace and watched his cattle grow upon a thousand hills. His wealth has become great and his wives many. He no longer dreads swift "death by order of the king," or by word of the witch-doctor. No "impi," or native regiment, can now sweep down on him and "eat him up," that is, carry off his cattle, put his kraal to the flames, and himself, his people, his wives, and children to the assegai.[1] For the first time in the story of the great Kafir[2] race, he can, when he rises in the morning, be sure that he will not sleep that night, stiff, in a bloody grave. He has tasted the blessings of peace and security, and what is the consequence? He has increased and multiplied until his numbers are as grains of sand on the sea-shore. Overlapping the borders of his location, he squats on private lands, he advances like a great tidal wave, he cries aloud for room, more room. This is the trouble which stares us in the face, looming larger and more distinct year by year; the great ever-growing problem which thoughtful men fear must one day find a sudden and violent solution. Thus it comes to pass that there hangs low on the horizon of South Africa the dark cloud of the Native Question. How and when it will burst no man can pretend to say, but some time and in some way burst it must, unless means of dispersing it can be found.

There is now at work among the Kafir population the same motive power which has raised in turn all white nations, and, having built them

---

1 A short or long iron-bladed spear.
2 A member of the Xhosa or affiliated tribes.

up to a certain height has then set to work to sap them until they have fallen—the power of civilisation. Hand in hand the missionary and the trader have penetrated the locations. The efforts of the teacher have met with but a partial success. "A Christian may be a good man in his way, but he is a Zulu spoiled," said Cetywayo, King of the Zulus, when arguing the question of Christianity with the Secretary for Native Affairs;[1] and such is, not altogether wrongly, the general feelings of the natives. With the traders it has been different. Some have dealt honestly—and more, it is to be feared, dishonestly—not only with those with whom they have had dealings, but with their fellow-subjects and their Government. It is these men chiefly who have, in defiance of the law, supplied the natives with those two great modern elements of danger and destruction, the gin-bottle and the rifle. The first is as yet injurious only to the recipients, but it will surely re-act on those who have taught them its use; the danger of possessing the rifle may come home to us any day and at any moment.

Civilisation, it would seem, when applied to black races, produces effects diametrically opposite to those we are accustomed to observe in white nations: it debases before it can elevate; and as regards the Kafirs it is doubtful, and remains to be proved, whether it has much power to elevate them at all. Take the average Zulu warrior, and it will be found that, in his natural state, his vices are largely counterbalanced by his good qualities. In times of peace he is a simple, pastoral man, leading a good-humoured easy life with his wives and his cattle, perfectly indolent and perfectly happy. He is a kind husband and a kinder father, he never disowns his poor relations, his hospitality is extended alike to white and black, he is open in his dealings and faithful to his word, and his honesty is a proverb in the land. True, if war breaks out and the thirst for slaughter comes upon him, he turns into a different man. When the fierce savage spirit is once aroused, blood alone will cool it. But even then he has virtues. If he is cruel, he is brave in the battle; if he is reckless of the lives of others, he regards not his own; and when death comes, he meets it without fear, and goes to the spirits of his fathers boldly, as a warrior should. And now reverse the picture, and see him in the dawning light of that civilisation which by intellect and by nature he is some five centuries behind. See him, ignoring its hidden virtues, eagerly seize and graft its most prominent vices on to his own besetting sins. Behold him by degrees adding cunning to his cruelty, avarice to his love of possession, replacing his bravery by coarse bombast and insolence, and his truth by lies. Behold him inflaming all his passions with the maddening drink

---

[1] Sir T. Shepstone.

of the white man, and then follow him through many degrees of degradation until he falls into crime and ends in a gaol. Such are, in only too many instances, the consequences of this partial civilisation, and they are not even counterbalanced, except in individual cases, by the attempt to learn the truths of a creed which he cannot, does not, pretend to understand. And if this be the result in the comparatively few individuals who have been brought under these influences, it may be fair to argue that it will differ only in degree, not in kind, when the same influences are brought to bear on the same material in corresponding proportions. Whatever may or may not be the effects of our partial civilisation when imperfectly and spasmodically applied to the vast native population of South Africa, one thing must, in course of time, result from it. The old customs, the old forms, the old feelings, must each in turn die away. The outer expression of these will die first, and it will not be long before the very memory of them will fade out of the barbaric heart. The rifle must replace, and, indeed, actually has replaced, the assegai and the shield, and portions of the cast-off uniforms of all the armies of Europe are to be seen where until lately the bronze-like form of the Kafir warrior went naked as on the day he was born. But so long as native customs and ceremonies still linger in some of the more distant locations, so long will they exercise a certain attraction for dwellers amid tamer scenes. It is therefore from a belief in the magnetism of contrast that the highly-civilised reader is invited to come to where he can still meet the barbarian face to face and witness that wild ceremony, half jest, half grim earnest — a Zulu war-dance.

It was the good fortune of the writer of this paper to find himself, early in the past year, travelling through the up-country districts of Natal, in the company of certain high officials of the English Government. The journey dragged slowly enough by waggon, and some monotonous weeks had passed before we pitched our camp, one drizzling gusty night, on a high plateau surrounded by still loftier hills. A wild and dismal place it looked in the growing dusk of an autumn evening, nor was it more suggestively cheerful when we rode away from it next morning in the sunshine, leaving the waggons to follow slowly. Our faces were set towards a great mountain, towering high above its fellows, called Pagadi's Kop[1] — Pagadi being a powerful chief who had fled from the Zulus in the early days of the colony, and had ever since dwelt loyally and peacefully here in this wild place, beneath the protection of the Crown. Messengers had been duly sent to inform him that he was to receive the honour of a visit, for your true savage never likes to be taken by surprise.

---

1   Hill of Pagadi, who was chief of the Amocuna, a Zulu tribe.

Other swift-footed runners had come back with the present of a goat, and the respectful answer, so Oriental in its phraseology, that "Pagadi was old, he was infirm, yet he would arise and come to greet his lords." Every mile or so of our slow progress a fresh messenger would spring up before us suddenly, as though he had started out of the earth at our feet, and prefixing his greeting with the royal salute, given with up-raised right arm, 'Bayēte, Bayētē!'—a salutation only accorded to Zulu royalty, to the Governors of the different provinces, and to Sir T.Shepstone, the Secretary for Native Affairs—he would deliver his message or his news and fall into the rear. Presently came one saying, "Pagadi is very old and weak; Pagadi is weary; let his lords forgive him if he meet them not this day. To-morrow, when the sun is high, he will come to their place of encampment and greet his lords and hold festival before them. But let his lords, the white lords of all the land from the Great Mountains to the Black Water, go on up to his kraal, and let them take the biggest hut and drink of the strongest beer. There his son, the chief that is to be, and all his wives, shall greet them; let his lords be honoured by Pagadi, through them." An acknowledgement was sent, and we still rode on, beginning the ascent of the formidable stronghold, on the flat top of which was placed the chief's kraal. A hard and stiff climb it was, up a bridle path with far more resemblance to a staircase than a road. But if the road was bad, the scenery and the vegetation were wild and beautiful in the extreme. Now we came to a deep "kloof" or cleft in the steep mountain side, at the bottom of which, half hidden by the masses of ferns and rich rank greenery, trickled a little stream; now to an open space of rough ground, covered only with huge, weather-washed boulders. A little further on lay a Kafir mealie-garden,[1] where the tall green stalks were fairly bent to the ground by the weight of the corn-laden heads, and beyond that, again, a park-like slope of grassy veldt. And ever, when we looked behind us, the vast undulating plain over which we had come, stretched away in its mysterious sunlit silence, till it blended at length with the soft blue horizon.

At last, after much hard and steady climbing, we reached the top and stood upon a perfectly level space ten or twelve acres in extent, exactly in the centre of which was placed the chief's kraal. Before we dismounted we rode to the extreme western edge of the plateau, to look at one of the most perfectly lovely views it is possible to imagine. It was like coming face to face with great primeval Nature, not Nature as we civilised people know her, smiling in corn-fields, waving in well-ordered woods, but Nature as she was on the morrow of the Creation. There, to our left,

---

1   A garden of Indian corn (maize), a staple food of South Africa.

cold and grey and grand, rose the great peak, flinging its dark shadow far beyond its base. Two thousand feet and more beneath us lay the valley of the Mooi river, with the broad tranquil stream flashing silver through its midst. Over against us rose another range of towering hills, with sudden openings in their blue depths through which could be seen the splendid distances of a champaign country. Immediately at our feet, and seeming to girdle the great gaunt peak, lay a deep valley, through which the Little Bushman's River forced its shining way. All around rose the great bush-clad hills, so green, so bright in the glorious streaming sunlight, and yet so awfully devoid of life, so solemnly silent. It was indeed a sight never to be forgotten, this wide panoramic out-look, with its towering hills, its smiling valleys, its flashing streams, its all-pervading sunlight, and its deep sad silence. But it was not always so lifeless and so still. Some few years ago those hills, those plains, those rivers were teeming each with their various creatures. But a short time since, and standing here at eventide, the traveller could have seen herds of elephants cooling themselves yonder after their day's travel, whilst the black-headed white-tusked sea-cow[1] rose and plunged in the pool below. That bush-clad hill was the favourite haunt of droves of buffaloes and elands, and on that plain swarmed thousands upon thousands of springbok and of quagga, of hartebeest and of oribi.[2] All alien life must cease before the white man, and so these wild denizens of forest, stream, and plain have passed away never to return.

Turning at length from the contemplation of a scene so new and so surprising, we entered the stockade of the kraal. These kraals consist of a stout outer palisade, and then, at some distance from the first, a second enclosure, between which the cattle are driven at night, or in case of danger. At the outer entrance we were met by the chief's eldest son, a finely-built man, who greeted us with much respect and conducted us through rows of huts to the dwelling-places of the chief's family, fenced off from the rest by a hedge of Tambouki grass.[3] In the centre of these stood Pagadi's hut, which was larger and more finely woven and thatched than the rest. It is impossible to describe these huts better than by saying that they resemble enormous straw beehives of the old-fashioned pattern. In front of the hut were grouped a dozen or so of women clad in that airiest of costumes, a string of beads. They were Pagadi's wives, and ranged from the first shrivelled-up wife of his youth to the plump young damsel bought last month. The spokeswoman of the party, however, was

---

1 The hippopotamus, so called by the Dutch in the early days.
2 Three types of antelope and the now-extinct zebra-striped quagga, a wild ass.
3 A tall grass used for thatching.

not one of the wives, but a daughter of Pagadi's, a handsome girl, tall, and splendidly formed, with a finely-cut face. This prepossessing young lady entreated her lords to enter, which they did, in a very unlordly way, on their hands and knees. So soon as the eye became accustomed to the cool darkness of the hut, it was sufficiently interesting to notice the rude attempts at comfort with which it was set forth. The flooring, of a mixture of clay and cow-dung, looked exactly like black marble, so smooth and polished had it been made, and on its shining, level surface couches of buckskin and gay blankets were spread in an orderly fashion. Some little three-legged wooden sleeping-pillows and a few cooking-pots made up its sole furniture besides. In one corner rested a bundle of assegais and war-shields, and opposite the door were ranged several large calabashes full of "twala" or native beer. The chief's son and all the women followed us into the hut. The ladies sat themselves down demurely in a double row opposite to us, but the young chieftain crouched in a distant corner apart and played with his assegais. We partook of the beer and exchanged compliments, almost Oriental in their dignified courtesy, in the soft and liquid Zulu language, but not for long, for we had still far to ride. The stars were shining in southern glory before we reached the place of our night's encampment, and supper and bed were even more than usually welcome. There is a pleasure in the canvas-sheltered meal, in the after-pipe and evening talk of the things of the day that has been and those of the day to come, here, amid these wild surroundings, which is unfelt and unknown in scenes of greater comfort and higher civilisation. There is a sense of freshness and freedom in the wind-swept waggon-bed that is not to be exchanged for the softest couch in the most luxurious chamber. And when at length the morning comes, sweet in the scent of flowers, and glad in the voice of birds, it finds us ready to greet it, not hiding it from us with canopy and blind, as is the way of cities.

The scene of the coming spectacle of this bright new day lies spread before us, and certainly no spot could have been better chosen for dramatic effect. In front of the waggons is a large, flat, open space, backed by bold rising ground with jutting crags and dotted clumps of luxuriant vegetation. All around spreads the dense thorn-bush, allowing but of one way of approach, from the left. During the morning we could hear snatches of distant chants growing louder and louder as time wore on, and could catch glimpses of wild figures threading the thorns, warriors hastening to the meeting-place. All through the past night the farmers for miles around had been aroused by the loud insistent cries of the chief's messengers as they flitted far and wide, stopping but a moment wherever one of their tribe sojourned, and bidding him come, and bring plume and shield, for Pagadi had need of him. This day, we may be sure, the herds are left untended, the mealie-heads ungathered, for the herdsmen and the reapers have come hither to answer to the summons of their chief. Little reck they whether it be for festival or war; he needs them and has called them, and that is enough. Higher and higher rose the fitful distant chant, but no one could be seen. Suddenly there stood before us a creature, a woman, who, save for the colour of her skin, might have been the original of any one of Macbeth's "weird sisters."[1] Little, withered, and bent nearly double by age, her activity was yet past comprehension. Clad in a strange jumble of snake-skins, feathers, furs, and bones, a forked wand in her outstretched hand, she rushed to and fro before the little group of white men. Her eyes gleamed like those of a hawk through her matted hair, and the genuineness of her frantic excitement was evident by the quivering flesh and working face, and the wild, spasmodic words she spoke. The spirit at least of her rapid utterances may thus be rendered: —

"Ou, ou, ou, ai, ai, ai. Oh, ye warriors that shall dance before the great ones of the earth, come! Oh, ye dyers of spears, ye plumed suckers of blood, come! I, the Isanusi, I, the witch-finder, I, the wise woman, I, the seer of strange sights, I, the reader of dark thoughts, call ye! Come, ye fierce ones; come, ye brave ones, come, and do honour to the white lords! Ah, I hear ye! Ah, I smell ye! Ah, I see ye; ye come, ye come!"

Hardly had her invocation trailed off into the "Ou, ou, ou, ai, ai, ai," with which it had opened, when there rushed over the edge of the hill, hard by, another figure scarcely less wild, but not so repulsive in appearance. This last was a finely-built warrior arrayed in the full panoply of savage war. With his right hand he grasped his spears, and on his left hung his large black ox-hide shield, lined on its inner side with spare assegais. From the "man's" ring round his head arose a single tall grey plume, robbed from the Kafir crane.[2] His broad shoulders were bare, and beneath the arm-pits was fastened a short garment of strips of skin, intermixed with ox-tails of different colours. From his waist hung a rude kilt made chiefly of goat's hair, whilst round the calf of the right leg was fixed a short fringe of black ox-tails. As he stood before us with lifted weapon and outstretched shield, his plume bending to the breeze, and his savage aspect made more savage still by the graceful, statuesque pose, the dilated eye and warlike mould of the set features, as he stood there, an emblem and a type of the times and the things which are passing away, his feet

---

1   *Macbeth* 1:3.32.
2   As a prefix for a plant or animal name, "kaffir-" indicates that it is wild or indigenous; possibly this is the "crowned crane" (*Balearica regulorum*).

resting on ground which he held on sufferance, and his hands grasping weapons impotent as a child's toy against those of the white man,—he who was the rightful lord of all,—what reflections did he not induce, what a moral did he not teach!

The warrior left us little time, however, for either reflections or deductions, for, striking his shield with his assegai, he rapidly poured forth this salutation: —

"Bayēte, Bayēte,[1] O chief from the olden times, O lords and chief of chiefs! Pagadi, the son of Masingorano, the great chief, the leader of brave ones, the son of Ulubako, greets you. Pagadi is humble before you; he comes with warrior and with shield, but he comes to lay them at your feet. O father of chiefs, son of the great Queen over the water, is it permitted that Pagad' approach you? Ou, I see it is, your face is pleasant; Bayēte, Bayēte!"

He ends, and, saluting again, springs forward, and, flying hither and thither, chants the praises of his chief. "Pagadi," he says, "Pagad', chief and father of the Amocuna, is coming. Pagad', the brave in battle, the wise in council, the slayer of warriors; Pagad' who slew the tiger[2] in the night time; Pagadi, the rich in cattle, the husband of many wives, the father of many children. Pagad' is coming, but not alone; he comes surrounded with his children, his warriors. He comes like a king at the head of his brave children. Pagad''s soldiers are coming; his soldiers who know well how to fight; his soldiers and his captains who make the hearts of brave men to sink down; his shakers of spears; his quaffers of blood. Pagad' and his soldiers are coming; tremble all ye, ou, ou, ou!"

As the last words die on his lips the air is filled with a deep, murmuring sound like distant thunder; it swells and rolls, and finally passes away to give place to the sound of the rushing of many feet. Over the brow of the hill dashes a compact body of warriors running swiftly in lines of four with their captain at their head, all clad in the same wild garb as the herald. Each bears a snow-white shield carried on the slant, and above each warrior's head rises a grey heron's plume. These are the advance-guard, formed of the "greys" or veteran troops. As they come into full view the shields heave and fall, and then from every throat out bursts the war-song of the Zulus. Passing us swiftly, they take up their position in a double line on our right, and stand there solemnly chanting all the while. Another rush of feet, and another company flits over the hill towards us,

---

1 The royal greeting of the Zulus ("Hail, O Majesty"); originally for the paramount chief, later also for high-ranking guests.
2 Leopards are called tigers (from the Dutch) in South African English; there are no true tigers in South Africa.

but they bear coal-black shields, and the drooping plumes are black as night; they fall into position next the first comers, and take up the chant. Now they come faster and faster, but all through the same gap in the bush. The red shields, the dun shields, the mottled shields, the yellow shields, follow each other in quick but regular succession, till at length there stands before us a body of some 500 men, presenting, in their savage dress, their various shields and flashing spears, as wild a spectacle as it is possible to conceive.

But it is not our eyes only that are astonished, for from each of those five hundred throats there swells a chant never to be forgotten. From company to company it passes, that wild, characteristic song, so touching in its simple grandeur, so expressive in its deep, pathetic volume. The white men who listened had heard the song of choirs ringing down resounding aisles, they had been thrilled by the roll of oratorios pealing in melody, beautiful and complex, through the grandest of man's theatres, but never till now had they heard music of voices so weird, so soft and yet so savage, so simple and yet so all-expressive of the fiercest passions known to the human heart. Hark! now it dies; lower and lower it sinks, it grows faint, despairing: "Why does he not come, our chief, our lord? why does he not welcome his singers? Ah! see, they come, the heralds of our lord! our chief is coming to cheer his praisers, our chief is coming to lead his warriors." Again it rises and swells louder and louder, a song of victory and triumph. It rolls against the mountains, it beats against the ground: "He is coming, he is here, attended by his chosen. Now shall we go forth to slay; now shall we taste of the battle." Higher yet and higher, till at length the chief, Pagadi, swathed in war-garments of splendid furs, preceded by runners and accompanied by picked warriors, creeps slowly up. He is old and tottering, and of an unwieldy bulk. Two attendants support him, whilst a third bears his shield, and a fourth (oh bathos!) a cane-bottomed chair. One moment the old man stands and surveys his warriors and listens to the familiar war-cry. As he stands, his face is lit with the light of battle, the light of remembered days. The tottering figure straightens itself, the feeble hand becomes strong once more. With a shout, the old man shakes off his supporters and grasps his shield, and then, forgetting his years and his weakness, he rushes to his chieftain's place in the midst of his men. And as he comes the chant grows yet louder, the time yet faster, till it rises, and rings, and rolls, no longer a chant, but a war-cry, a pæan of power. Pagadi stops and raises his hand, and the place is filled with a silence that may be felt. But not for long. The next moment five hundred shields are tossed aloft, five hundred spears flash in the sunshine, and with a sudden roar, forth springs the royal salute, "Bayētē!"

The chief draws back and gives directions to his *indunas*, his thinkers, his wise ones, men distinguished from their fellows by the absence of shield and plume; the *indunas* pass on the orders to the captains, and at once the so-called dance begins. First they manœuvre a little in absolute silence, and changing their position with wonderful precision and rapidity; but as their blood warms there comes a sound as of the hissing of ten thousand snakes, and they charge and charge again. A pause, and the company of "greys" on our right, throwing itself into open order, flits past us like so many vultures to precipitate itself with a wild, whistling cry on an opposing body which rushed to meet it. They join issue, they grapple; on them swoops another company, then another and another, until nothing is to be distinguished except a mass of wild faces heaving; of changing forms rolling and writhing, twisting and turning, and, to all appearance, killing and being killed, whilst the whole air is pervaded with a shrill, savage sibillation. It is not always the same cry; now it is the snorting of a troop of buffaloes, now the shriek of the eagle as he seizes his prey, anon the terrible cry of the "night-prowler," the lion, and now—more thrilling than all—the piercing wail of a woman. But whatever the cry, the cadence rises and falls in perfect time and unanimity; no two mix with one another so as to mar the effect of each.

Again the combatants draw back and pause, and then, forth from the ranks springs a chosen warrior, and hurls himself on an imaginary foe. He darts hither and thither with wild activity, he bounds five feet into the air like a panther, he twists through the grass like a snake, and, finally, making a tremendous effort, he seems to slay his airy opponent, and sinks exhausted to the ground. The onlookers mark their approval or disapproval of the dancer's feats by the rising and falling of the strange whistling noise, which, without the slightest apparent movement of face or lip, issues from each mouth. Warrior after warrior comes forth in turn from the ranks and does battle with his invisible foe, and receives his meed of applause. The last warrior to spring forward with a wild yell is the future chief, Pagadi's son and successor, our friend of yesterday. He stands, with his shield in one hand and his lifted battle-axe—borne by him alone—in the other, looking proudly around, and rattling his lion-claw necklets, whilst from every side bursts forth a storm of sibillating applause, not from the soldiers only, but from the old men, women and children. Through all his fierce pantomimic dance, it continues, and when he has ended it redoubles, then dies away, but only to burst out again and again, with unquenchable enthusiasm.

In order, probably, to give the warriors a brief breathing space, another song is now set up, and it is marvellous the accuracy and knowledge of melody with which the parts are sung, like a glee or catch, the time being kept by a conductor, who rushes from rank to rank beating time with a wand. Yet it is hardly like chanting, rather like a weird, sobbing melody, with tones in it which range from the deepest bass to the shrillest treble. It ends in a long sigh, and then follows a scene, a tumult, a mêlée, which hardly admits of a description in words. The warriors engage in mimic combat, once more they charge, retreat, conquer, and are defeated, all in turns. In front of them, exciting them to new exertions, with word and gesture, undulate in a graceful dance of their own the "intombas,"[1] the young beauties of the tribe, with green branches in their hands, and all their store of savage finery glittering on their shapely limbs. Some of these maidens are really handsome, and round them again dance the children, armed with mimic spears and shields. Wild as seems the confusion, through it all, even in the moments of highest excitement, some sort of rough order is maintained; more, it would seem, by mutual sounds than by word of command or sense of discipline.

Even a Zulu warrior must, sooner or later, grow weary, and at length the signal is given for the dance to end. The companies are drawn up in order again, and receive the praise and thanks of those in whose honour they had been called together. To these compliments they reply in a novel and imposing fashion. At a given signal each man begins to softly tap his ox-hide shield with the handle of his spear, producing a sound somewhat resembling the murmur of the distant sea. By slow degrees it grows louder and louder, till at length it rolls and re-echoes from the hills like thunder, and comes to its conclusion with a fierce, quick rattle. This is the royal war-salute of the Zulus, and is but rarely to be heard. One more sonorous salute with voice and hand, and then the warriors disappear as they came, dropping swiftly and silently over the brow of the hill in companies. In a few moments no sign or vestige of dance or dancers remained, save, before our eyes, the well-trodden ground, a few lingering girls laden with large calabashes of beer, and in our ears some distant dying snatches of chants. The singers were on their joyful way to slay and devour the oxen provided as a stimulus and reward for them by their chief's liberality.

When the last dusky figure had topped the rising ground over which the homeward path lay, and had stood out for an instant against the flaming background of the westering sun, and then dropped, as it were, back into its native darkness beyond those gates of fire, the old chief drew near. He had divested himself of his heavy war-dress, and sat down amicably amongst us.

---

1   Zulu word (Nguni languages) for "nubile" — virgins of marriageable age. Cf. Foulata in *KSM*.

"Ah," he said, taking the hand of Sir Theophilus Shepstone, and addressing him by his native name, "Ah! t'Sompseu, t'Sompseu, the seasons are many since first I held this your hand. Then we two were young, and life lay bright before us, and now you have grown great, and are growing grey, and I have grown very old! I have eaten the corn of my time, till only the cob is left for me to suck, and, *ow*, it is bitter. But it is well that I should grasp this your hand once more, oh, holder of the Spirit of Chaka,[1] before I sit down and sleep with my fathers. *Ow*, I am glad."

Imposing as was this old-time war-dance, it is not difficult to imagine the heights to which its savage grandeur must swell when it is held—as is the custom at each new year—at the kraal of Cetywayo, King of the Zulus. Then 30,000 warriors take part in it, and a tragic interest is added to the fierce spectacle by the slaughter of many men. It is, in fact, a great political opportunity for getting rid of the "irreconcilable" element from council and field. Then, in the moment of wildest enthusiasm, the witch-finder darts forward and lightly touches with a switch some doomed man, sitting, it may be, quietly among the spectators, or capering with his fellow soldiers. Instantly he is led away, and his place knows him no more.[2]

Throughout the whole performance there was one remarkable and genuine feature, the strong personal attachment of each member of the tribe to its chief—not only to the fine old chief, Pagadi, their leader in former years, but to the head and leader of the years to come.

It must be remembered that this system of chieftainship and its attendant law is, to all the social bearings of South African native life, what the tree is to its branches; it has grown through long, long ages amid a people slow to forget old traditions, and equally slow to receive new ideas; dependent on it are all the native's customs, all his keen ideas of right and justice; in it lies embodied his history of the past, and from it springs his hope for the future. Surely even the most uncompromising of those marching under the banner of civilisation must hesitate before they condemn this deep-rooted system to instant uprootal. The various influences of the white man have eaten into the native system as rust into iron, and their action will never cease till all be destroyed. The bulwarks of barbarism, its minor customs and minor laws, are gone, or exist only in name; but its two great principles, polygamy and chieftainship, yet flour-

---

1 The reader must bear in mind that the Zulu warrior is buried sitting and in full war-dress. Chaka, or T'Shaka, was the founder of the Zulu power, and his spirit is supposed to have passed into the white chief. [Haggard's note]
2 Cf. Appendix C: Fynney, *Zululand*; Gagool in *KSM*.

ish and are strong. Time will undo his work and find for these also a place among forgotten things. And it is the undoubted duty of us English, who absorb peoples and territories in the high name of civilisation, to be true to our principles and our aim, and aid the great destroyer by any and every safe and justifiable means. But between the legitimate means and the rash, miscalculating uprootal of customs and principles, which are not the less venerable and good in their way because they do not accord with our own present ideas, there is a great gulf fixed. Such an uprootal might precipitate an outburst of the very evils it aims at destroying.

What the ultimate effect of our policy will be, when the leaven has leavened the whole, when the floodgates are lifted, and this vast native population (which, contrary to all ordinary precedent, does *not* melt away before the sun of the white man's power) is let loose in its indolent thousands, unrestrained, save by the bonds of civilised law, who can presume to say? But this is not for present consideration. Subject to due precautions, the path of progress must of necessity be followed, and the results of such following left in the balancing hands of Fate and the future.

4. From "About Fiction," *Contemporary Review* (1887)

[This essay is the best authorial commentary on the aesthetics of *KSM*.]

In the face of this constant and ever-growing demand at home and abroad writers of romance must often find themselves questioning their inner consciousness as to what style of art it is best for them to adopt, not only with the view of pleasing their readers, but in the interests of art itself. There are several schools from which they may choose. For instance, there is that followed by the American novelists. These gentlemen, as we know, declare that there are no stories left to be told, and certainly, if it may be said without disrespect to a clever and laborious body of writers, their works go far towards supporting the statement. They have developed a new style of romance. Their heroines are things of silk and cambric, who soliloquize and dissect their petty feelings, and elaborately review the feeble promptings which serve them for passions. Their men — well, they are emasculated specimens of an overwrought age, and, with culture on their lips, and emptiness in their hearts, they dangle round the heroines till their three-volumed[1] fate is accomplished. About their work is an atmosphere like that of the boudoir of a luxurious

---

1   Victorian first editions were often published in deluxe three-volume formats.

woman, faint and delicate, and suggesting the essence of white rose. How different is all this to the swiftness, and strength, and directness of the great English writers of the past. Why,

> "The surge and thunder of the Odyssey"[1]

is not more widely separated from the tinkling of modern society verses, than the laboured nothingness of this new American school of fiction from the giant life and vigour of Swift and Fielding, and Thackeray and Hawthorne.[2] Perhaps, however, it is the art of the future, in which case we may hazard a shrewd guess that the literature of past ages will be more largely studied in days to come than it is at present.

Then, to go from Pole to Pole, there is the Naturalistic school, of which Zola is the high priest. Here things are all the other way. Here the chosen function of the writer is to

> "Paint the mortal shame of nature with the living hues of art."[3]

Here are no silks and satins to impede our vision of the flesh and blood beneath, and here the scent is patchouli.[4] Lewd, and bold, and bare, living for lust and lusting for this life and its good things, and naught beyond, the heroines of realism dance, with Bacchanalian revellings, across the astonished stage of literature. Whatever there is brutal in humanity — and God knows that there is plenty — whatever there is that is carnal and filthy, is here brought into prominence, and thrust before the reader's eyes. But what becomes of the things that are pure and high — of the great aspirations and the lofty hopes and longings, which *do*, after all, play their part in our human economy, and which it is surely the duty of a writer to call attention to and nourish according to his gifts? ...

In England, to come to the third great school of fiction, we have as yet little or nothing of all this. Here, on the other hand, we are at the mercy of the Young Person, and a dreadful nuisance most of us find her. The present writer is bound to admit that, speaking personally and with humility, he thinks it a little hard that all fiction should be judged by the

---

1   Andrew Lang, "The Odyssey" in *The Odyssey of Homer* (London: Macmillan, 1881).

2   See Henry James' "The Art of Fiction" (1884) and R.L. Stevenson's reply, "A Humble Remonstrance" (1884), quoted in Katz, *Haggard*.

3   Tennyson, "Locksley Hall Sixty Years After," line 139; Émile Zola (1840–1902), founder of the French school of naturalism, analyzed the brutal and degrading forces beyond man's control with minute objectivity.

4   An essence from an East Indian mint herb, a cheap (ergo, tawdry) perfume of the brothel.

test as to whether or no it is suitable reading for a girl of sixteen. There are plenty of people who write books for little girls in the schoolroom; let the little girls read them, and leave the works written for men and women to their elders. It may strike the reader as inconsistent, after the remarks made above, that a plea should now be advanced for greater freedom in English literary art. But French naturalism is one thing, and the unreal, namby-pamby nonsense with which the market is flooded here is quite another. Surely there is a middle path!

Surely, what is wanted in English fiction is a higher ideal and more freedom to work it out. It is impossible, or, if not impossible, it requires the very highest genius, such as, perhaps, no writers possess to-day, to build up a really first-class work without the necessary materials in their due proportion. As it is, in this country, while crime may be used to any extent, passion in its fiercer and deeper forms is scarcely available, unless it is made to receive some conventional sanction. For instance, the right of dealing with bigamy is by custom conceded to the writer of romance, because in cases of bigamy vice has received the conventional sanction of marriage. True, the marriage is a mock one, but such as it is, it provides the necessary cloak. But let him beware how he deals with the same subject when the sinner of the piece has not added a sham or a bigamous marriage to his evil doings, for the book will in this case be certainly called immoral. English life is surrounded by conventionalism, and English fiction has come to reflect the conventionalism, not the life, and has in consequence, with some notable exceptions, got into a very poor way, both as regards art and interest.

If this moderate and proper freedom is denied to imaginative literature alone among the arts (for, though Mr. Horsley[1] does not approve of it, sculptors may still model from the naked), it seems probable that the usual results will follow. There will be a great reaction, the Young Person will vanish into space and be no more seen, and Naturalism in all its horror will take its root among us. At present it is only in the French tongue that people read about the inner mysteries of life in brothels, or follow the interesting study of the passions of senile and worn-out debauchees. By-and-by, if liberty is denied, they will read them in the English. Art in the purity of its idealized truth should resemble some perfect Grecian statue. It should be cold but naked, and looking thereon men should be led to think of naught but beauty. Here, however, we attire Art in every sort of dress, some of them suggestive enough in their own way, but for the most part in a pinafore. The difference between literary Art, as the

---

1   John Callcott Horsley (1817-1903), designer of the first Christmas card, derided as J. C(lothes) Horsley because he denounced paintings of nudes.

present writer submits it ought to be, and the Naturalistic Art of France is the difference between the Venus of Milo and an obscene photograph taken from the life. It seems probable that the English-speaking people will in course of time have to choose between the two.

But however this is — and the writer only submits an opinion — one thing remains clear, fiction à l'Anglaise[1] becomes, from the author's point of view, day by day more difficult to deal with satisfactorily under its present conditions. This age is not a romantic age. Doubtless under the surface human nature is the same to-day as it was in the time of Rameses.[2] Probably, too, the respective volumes of vice and virtue are, taking the altered circumstances into consideration, much as they were then or at any other time. But neither our good nor our evil doing is of an heroic nature, and it is things heroic and their kin and not petty things that best lend themselves to the purposes of the novelist, for by their aid he produces his strongest effects. Besides, if by chance there is a good thing on the market it is snapped up by a hundred eager newspapers, who tell the story, whatever it may be, and turn it inside out, and draw morals from it till the public loathes its sight and sound. Genius, of course, can always find materials wherewith to weave its glowing web. But these remarks, it is scarcely necessary to explain, are not made from that point of view, for only genius can talk of genius with authority, but rather from the humbler standing-ground of the ordinary conscientious labourer in the field of letters, who, loving his art for her own sake, yet earns a living by following her, and is anxious to continue to do so with credit to himself. Let genius, if genius there be, come forward and speak on its own behalf! But if the reader is inclined to doubt the proposition that novel writing is becoming every day more difficult and less interesting, let him consult his own mind, and see how many novels proper among the hundreds that have been published within the last five years, and which deal in any way with every day contemporary life, have excited his profound interest. The present writer can at the moment recall but two — one was called "My Trivial Life and Misfortunes," by an unknown author, and the other, "The Story of a South African Farm," by Ralph Iron.[3] But then

---

1   "after the British fashion"

2   Name of 12 kings of Egypt, the most famous was Rameses II (reigned 1292-1225 BC).

3   See Editor's Introduction. What drew Haggard to Schreiner's narrative of everyday life, aside from its parallel to his own experience of African ostrich farming, was her allegorically-imbued style; that is, her partiality for the presentation of character through mythic or symbolic patterns and her visionary intensity of an ideal love that is lost or never found. Haggard comments in *Private Diaries*, 210-11, on the occasion of Schreiner's death. Norman Etherington, *Rider Haggard* (Boston: Twayne, 1984), 21-22, 25-26, notes other correlations with Schreiner. Schreiner herself seems to have been unreceptive to Haggard's narrative style — in her Preface to her novel (second edition), she con-

neither of these books if examined into would be found to be a novel such as the ordinary writer produces once or twice a year. Both of them are written from within, and not from without; both convey the impression of being the outward and visible result of inward personal suffering on the part of the writer, for in each the key-note is a note of pain. Differing widely from the ordinary run of manufactured books, they owe their chief interest to a certain atmosphere of spiritual intensity, which could not in all probability be even approximately reproduced. Another recent work of the same powerful class, though of more painful detail, is called "Mrs. Keith's Crime."[1] It is, however, almost impossible to conceive their respective authors producing a second "Trivial Life and Misfortunes" or a further edition of the crimes of Mrs. Keith. These books were written from the heart. Next time their authors write it will probably be from the head and not from the heart, and they must then come down to the use of the dusty materials which are common to us all. There is indeed a refuge for the less ambitious among us, and it lies in the paths and calm retreats of pure imagination. Here we may weave our humble tale, and point our harmless moral without being mercilessly bound down to the prose of a somewhat dreary age. Here we may even—if we feel that our wings are strong enough to bear us in that thin air—cross the bounds of the known, and, hanging between earth and heaven, gaze with curious eyes into the great profound beyond. There are still subjects that may be handled *there* if the man can be found bold enough to handle them. And, although some there be who consider this a lower walk in the realms of fiction, and who would probably scorn to become a "mere writer of romances," it may be urged in defence of the school that many of the most lasting triumphs of literary art belong to the producers of purely romantic fiction, witness the "Arabian Nights," "Gulliver's Travels," "The Pilgrim's Progress," "Robinson Crusoe," and other immortal works. If the present writer may be allowed to hazard an opinion, it is that, when Naturalism has had its day, when Mr. Howells[2] ceases to charm, and the Society novel is utterly played out, the kindly race of men in their latter as in their earlier developments will still take pleasure in those works of fancy which appeal, not to a class, or a nation, or even to an age, but to all time and humanity at large.

temptuously dismissed "wild adventure" and "hair-breadth escapes" as works of "imagination, untrammelled by contact with any fact." *My Trivial Life and Misfortune* (not "misfortunes") was by "a plain woman" (Edinburgh: W. Blackwood, 1883; new ed. 1888); presumably the "misfortune" is "spinsterhood."

1   W.K. Clifford, *Mrs. Keith's Crime: a Record* (1885).
2   William Dean Howells (1837-1920), American novelist of social realism; his finest novel is *The Rise of Silas Lapham* (1885).

Appendix C: Historical Documents: Natives and Imperialists in South Africa

1. Fred Fynney, from *Zululand and the Zulus* (1880)

[As chief interpreter on Shepstone's staff—and at the time of this writing "Inspector of Native Schools, Natal (Late Border Agent)"—Fynney is frequently alluded to in Haggard's *Days of My Life* (1:56, 74-76; 2:20). Though this entry—from a scarce and nearly unknown publication— begins with a wildly incorrect conjecture on Zulu origins, Fynney like Haggard is trying to understand local customs in terms of comparative anthropology; his description of a Zulu witch dance makes it evident that Haggard almost without exaggeration drew Gagool's "smelling-out" from historical fact.]

I am inclined to think that our natives, as represented in the Zulus, must have had at one time an intimate connection with the Jewish nation, as many of their customs are decidedly similar to those practiced by the latter people—to whom they may have possibly been in bondage in the far past.

Take, for instance, their Feast of the First Fruits and their offerings at the same. When the first crops are ripe not a head of the maize, not an ear of native corn, can be touched until the head of the nation has *yety-wama'd* (or prepared himself by certain rites to partake of the same); then follows the *Umkosi*, or annual gathering of the nation at headquarters, when a jubilee ceremony is performed; maidens take portions of the first fruits to the different rivers as an offering. After that, and only then, can the fruits of the field be partaken of.

There is another custom of the maidens proceeding to the hills annually, to mourn or wail, which reminds one forcibly of Jephtha's daughter.[1]

There is the custom of *Ukungena* (taking the deceased brother's wife); also their laws of uncleanness and many other things, which ... in conjunction with what I shall have to say with reference to their belief, will possibly lead you to think with me, that the Zulus must have known something of the Israelites and the laws by which they were guided....

$$\star \quad \star \quad \star \quad \star \quad \star$$

---

1 Judges 11:40.

There are among the natives a class known as the *Izanusi* or *Abangoma*, who profess to have direct intercourse with the spirit-world, and to practice divination. Their influence is invoked in the "smelling-out" or finding out of the *abatakati*.[1] In Natal, they have been forbidden to practice their dark arts, but they do so secretly, all the same, and cause a deal of mischief; for though no one, within the boundaries of this colony, dare openly accuse another of witchcraft, still there are many heart-burnings and much bitter feeling caused by their hints and inuendoes.

In Zululand, where these *abangoma* are unrestrained, the influence they exercise is something awful, for during the last sixty years they have been the means of causing the death of hundreds of thousands of innocent creatures, through their minor "smellings out" and the more fearful *Ingomboco*—which means, within the circle, or surrounded. When I refer to the minor "smellings out," I mean that of individuals; but the *Ingomboco* is a tribal affair, which I can, perhaps, best explain by relating an incident that happened within my own knowledge in the year 1856. During that year, I went to Zululand, accompanied by a staff of carriers, for the purpose of hunting and trading. We formed a large party, and it was therefore necessary, in looking out for a resting place at night, to secure the most commodious kraals along our line of travel. After a weary day's march, on one occasion, I noticed a large kraal some two miles ahead, in a beautiful valley, which seemed to give promise of rest to our weary bodies, and furnish the necessary food for the party; we therefore decided upon staying there for the night. On arriving at the gate, however, we discovered that the kraal was unoccupied, and there was altogether an uninviting weirdness about the place which the glorious rays of a setting sun could not dispel; so, with one accord, we decided to move onward, late though it was. I had noticed crowds of vultures in the valley below the kraal, and altogether the appearances of the place were an enigma to me. We had not gone far down the valley before we came upon another kraal, of much larger dimensions than that just quitted, and which, I soon found out, belonged to Nobeta, a cousin of Umpande,[2] who was then king. As in courtesy bound, I reported myself to the chief, with the intention of at once passing on, as I had heard that Nobeta was not one of the most amiable magnates of Zululand. The old chief, however, would not hear of my going past him, and he gave instructions that quarters were to be prepared for us.... I mentioned incidentally that it was by mere chance that we had got that far, as we had purposed staying at a kraal farther back, only we had found it deserted. The old reptile there-

---

1   Wizards or witches; the singular is *umtakati*.
2   Umpanda (or Panda) (died 1872). Brother of Dingaan, he led a party of Zulus across the Tugela to Natal to receive aid from the Boers and become Zulu King (1840).

upon callously observed, "Oh, yes; I wiped them all out two days ago. They were all *abatakatis*; they killed my mother, or assisted in doing so; but there are more *abatakatis* to be smelt out yet."

We were treated most hospitably the night we stayed at Nobeta's kraal, and next morning, on my proceeding to bid the chief good-bye, I was surprised to find that he would not hear of my going just then. He wanted my presence at his kraal that morning, he said, as they had a great piece of business on, and I must see how he punished evil-doers. I pleaded the urgent necessity of our getting forward on our journey, but all to no purpose, so we made a virtue of necessity and remained with the chief, as requested.

I noticed, about 10 o'clock that morning, that batches of natives began to arrive outside the kraal, from all directions. They came with sullen, downcast looks, and observed an ominous silence; each enveloped in a blanket, and carrying only a short stick. After some little time a bevy of girls came out of the kraal, and began a sort of chant, to the music of which they kept time by clapping their hands; young men, armed with knob kerries,[1] next came upon the scene; and last of all, five of the fearful *abangoma* advanced toward where the sable throng was seated. The appearance of these fearful creatures, enveloped as they were in everything which tended to make them hideous, in the shape of snake skins and portions of reptiles and other animals, would baffle description. Reluctant observer of such a scene as I was, they inspired me with a feeling of awe and disgust, for I then realized what their presence foreboded. Each carried in his left hand a bundle of small assegais and shield, whilst in the right hand was the tail of a gnu,—their gaunt forms according well with their panther-like actions. The young warriors drew round the terror-stricken lines of defenceless natives. The chant was struck up, and the smelling out began. Victim after victim was revealed by the aid of the spirits as an *umtakati*, upon which, the *umgoma*, bounding over each, switched him with the Gnu's tail; this was the signal for his being seized upon the spot and dragged away, as food for the ever-ready vultures and wolves. No sooner were the different victims disposed of, than a band of warriors were dispatched to the several kraals to continue the work of destruction, and seize the cattle. I do not know the number of those killed, but I believe there were seventeen, all kraal owners, together with their families, which constituted a total, in one day, that makes one's very heart revolt at the thought of it.

Whilst compelled to sit by Nobeta in the kraal, I observed a lot of vultures settled on a tree above our heads, and I was so disgusted with the old fellow's mercilessness, that I indiscreetly remarked that he had not

---

1 Ironwood fighting club with ceremonial significance.

yet satisfied his friends the vultures, asking if he could not find another *umtakati*. He flew into a fearful rage, charged me with ingratitude, and bade me begone. I obeyed at once.

2. John Ruskin, from *Lectures on Art* (1873)

[Ruskin, one of the most influential professors at Oxford, "describes the present passage as 'the most pregnant and essential' of all his teaching" (Cook and Wedderburn). It is a quintessential statement of British imperialism. Compare Jomo Kenyatta's Gikuyu tale in *Facing Mount Kenya* (London: Secker and Warburg, 1938), 47-52, on this practice of "seizing every piece of fruitful waste ground."]

There is a destiny now possible to us—the highest ever set before a nation to be accepted or refused. We are still undegenerate in race; a race mingled of the best northern blood. We are not yet dissolute in temper, but still have the firmness to govern, and the grace to obey. We have been taught a religion of pure mercy, which we must either now betray, or learn to defend by fulfilling. And we are rich in an inheritance of honour, bequeathed to us through a thousand years of noble history, which it should be our daily thirst to increase with splendid avarice, so that Englishmen, if it be a sin to covet honour, should be the most offending souls alive....

And this is what she [England] must either do, or perish: she must found colonies as fast and as far as she is able, formed of her most energetic and worthiest men;—seizing every piece of fruitful waste ground she can set her foot on, and there teaching these her colonists that their chief virtue is to be fidelity to their country, and that their first aim is to be to advance the power of England by land and sea: and that, though they live on a distant plot of ground, they are no more to consider themselves therefore disfranchised from their native land, than the sailors of her fleets do, because they float on distant waves. So that literally, these colonies must be fastened fleets; and every man of them must be under authority of captains and officers, whose better command is to be over fields and streets instead of ships of the line; and England, in these her motionless navies (or, in the true and mightiest sense, motionless *churches*, ruled by pilots on the Galilean lake[1] of all the world), is to "expect every man to do his duty";[2] recognizing that duty is indeed possible no less in peace than war; and that if we can get men, for little pay, to cast them-

---

1   The Sea of Galilee frequented by Christ and his disciples; therefore, the Christian world.
2   "Nelson's signal at Trafalgar" (Cook and Wedderburn).

selves against cannon-mouths for love of England,[1] we may find men also who will plough and sow for her, who will behave kindly and right-eously for her, who will bring up their children to love her, and who will gladden themselves in the brightness of her glory, more than in all the light of tropic skies.

But that they may be able to do this, she must make her own majesty stainless; she must give them thoughts of their home of which they can be proud. The England who is to be mistress of half the earth, cannot remain herself a heap of cinders, trampled by contending and miserable crowds; she must yet again become the England she was once, and in all beautiful ways,—more: so happy, so secluded, and so pure, that in her sky—polluted by no unholy clouds—she may be able to spell rightly of every star that heaven doth show; and in her fields, ordered and wide and fair, of every herb that sips the dew; and under the green avenues of her enchanted garden, a sacred Circe, true Daughter of the Sun,[2] she must guide the human arts, and gather the divine knowledge, of distant nations, transformed from savageness to manhood, and redeemed from despairing into peace.

3. Cecil Rhodes, from "Rhodes' 'Confession of Faith'" (1877) in Flint, *Rhodes*

[Rhodes became the greatest nineteenth-century political figure in Africa, after whom—once he had machine-gunned resisting natives—the territory of Rhodesia was named. Even without Rhodes' explicit acknowledgement of his indebtedness to Ruskin's lecture (preceding extract), one can see the influence given his choice of words here: "it is our duty to seize every opportunity of acquiring more territory." This essay was written as a young man of twenty-three just before he left for Africa.]

I contend that we are the finest race in the world and that the more of the world we inhabit the better it is for the human race. Just fancy those parts that are at present inhabited by the most despicable specimens of human beings, what an alteration there would be if they were brought under Anglo-Saxon influence; look again at the extra employment a new country added to our dominions gives. I contend that every acre added to our territory means, in the future, birth to some more of the English race who otherwise would not be brought into existence. Added

---

1   Ruskin is thinking of Tennyson's "Charge of the Light Brigade."
2   That is, not the malign enchantress (cf. Milton, *Comus*, 50–53) but goddess of enlight-enment.

to this, the absorption of the greater portion of the world under our rule simply means the end of all wars....

The idea gleaming and dancing before one's eyes like a will-of-the-wisp at last frames itself into a plan. Why should we not form a secret Society with but one object, the furtherance of the British Empire and the bringing of the whole uncivilised world under British rule, for the recovery of the United States, for the making the Anglo-Saxon race but one Empire? What a dream; but yet it is probable, it is possible.... We learn from having lost to cling to what we possess. We know the size of the world, we know the total extent. Africa is still lying ready for us; it is our duty to take it. It is our duty to seize every opportunity of acquiring more territory; and we should keep this one idea steadily before our eyes, that more territory simply means more of the Anglo-Saxon race, more of the best, the most human, most honourable race the world possesses.

4. Cecil Rhodes, from *Speeches* (1881-1900) in "Vindex," *Rhodes*

[These parliamentary comments on denying natives the right to vote (the "Glen Grey Act") mark the end of military pacification and "the beginning of the era of making South Africa 'a white man's country' in which the African himself would be reduced to 'a muscular machine' to valorize South Africa's mineral wealth from the bowels of the earth" (Bernard Magubane).]

I prefer to call a spade a spade.... Do you believe that the native population of this country should vote or not? Do not let us humbug ourselves.... Let us boldly say: In the past we have made mistakes about native representation. Let us boldly say: We intend now to change all that.... All that I say is, that we have to govern the natives as a subject race. I do not go so far as the honourable member for Victoria West, who would not give the black man a vote.[1] All I say is, that you must govern natives living under communal tenure as a subject race.... Behind you there is a huge mass of barbarism, and you say, "We are going to be lords of this people, and keep them in a subject position"; and you say, "They should not have the franchise, because we don't want them on an equality with us." By the last census there are 1,250,000 natives in the Colony, and 250,000 Europeans. Under the present franchise, if they were to exercise it, the natives would have a majority of votes.... On account

---

1 Rhodes would allow a native to vote if he met preposterous property and educational qualifications — ownership of a quality house, recipient of a substantial salary, and attainment of basic (English) literacy.

of an extreme philanthropic sympathy, there are those who wish to endow the native at once with the privileges it has taken the European eighteen hundred years to acquire.... Does this House think it is right that men in a state of pure barbarism should have the franchise and vote? The natives do not want it.... We are to be lords over them. These are my politics on native affairs, and these are the politics of South Africa. Treat the natives as a subject people as long as they continue in a state of barbarism and communal tenure; be the lords over them, and let them be a subject race, and keep the liquor from them.... We must adopt a system of despotism, such as works so well in India, in our relations with the barbarians of South Africa.... I know exactly what I am after. I have got my interest in this country, I have my mining speculations, I have my interest in its future, and coupled with all this, I am a member of the House....

There is, I think, a general feeling that the natives are a distinct source of trouble and loss to the country. Now, I take a different view.... In fact, I think the natives should be a source of great assistance to most of us. At any rate, if the whites maintain their position as the supreme race, the day may come when we shall all be thankful that we have the natives with us in their proper position.... As I have stated once before in this House, the natives have had in the past an interesting employment for their minds in going to war and in consulting in their councils as to war. But by our wise government we have taken away all that employment from them. We have given them no share in the government—and I think rightly, too—and no interest in the local development of their country.... We want to get hold of these young men and make them go out to work, and the only way to do this is to compel them to pay a certain labour tax. But we must prepare these people for the change. Every black man cannot have three acres and a cow, or four morgen and a commonage right.[1] We have to face the question and it must be brought home to them that in the future nine-tenths of them will have to spend their lives in daily labour, in physical work, in manual labour.... Now, I say the natives are children. They are just emerging from barbarism. They have human minds, and I would like them to devote themselves wholly to the local matters that surround them and appeal to them.

5. Olive Schreiner, from *Trooper Peter Halket of Mashonaland* (1897)

[Schreiner as a young woman was half in love with Rhodes; but in her polemical novella she attacks his greed and cruelty by describing scenes that actually occurred and imagining how a British trooper (not so much

---

1 That is, a right to community land; a "morgen" is a Dutch and South African unit of land slightly more than two acres.

evil as a gullible tool of imperialism) would describe Rhodes with unconscious irony.]

Now as he looked into the crackling blaze, it seemed to be one of the fires they had made to burn the natives' grain by, and they were throwing in all they could not carry away: then, he seemed to see his mother's fat ducks waddling down the little path with the green grass on each side. Then, he seemed to see his huts where he lived with the prospectors, and the native women who used to live with him; and he wondered where the women were. Then — he saw the skull of an old Mashona blown off at the top, the hands still moving. He heard the loud cry of the native women and children as they turned the maxims[1] on to the kraal; and then he heard the dynamite explode that blew up a cave. Then again he was working a maxim gun, but it seemed to him it was more like the reaping machine he used to work in England, and that what was going down before it was not yellow corn, but black men's heads; and he thought when he looked back they lay behind him in rows, like the corn in sheaves....

"Have you seen Cecil Rhodes?"

"Yes, I have seen him," said the stranger.

"Now *he's* death on niggers," said Peter Halket, warming his hands by the fire; "they say when he was Prime Minister down in the Colony he tried to pass a law that would give masters and mistresses the right to have their servants flogged whenever they did anything they didn't like; but the other Englishmen wouldn't let him pass it. But *here* he can do what he likes. That's the reason some fellows don't want him to be sent away. They say, 'If we get the British Government here, they'll be giving the niggers land to live on; and let them have the vote, and get civilised and educated, and all that sort of thing; but Cecil Rhodes, he'll keep their noses to the grindstone.' *I prefer land to niggers*, he says. They say he's going to parcel them out, and make them work on our lands whether they like it or not — just as good as having slaves, you know: and you haven't the bother of looking after them when they're old. Now, there I'm with Rhodes; I think it's an awfully good move. We don't come out here to work; it's all very well in England; but we've come here to make money, and how are we to make it, unless you get niggers to work for you, or start a syndicate?[2] He's death on niggers, is

---

1   Named after its inventor, Sir Hiram Maxim, it was the biggest early machine gun consisting of a cluster of revolving barrels; here it embodies raw domination, the power of destruction, imperialism's parodic harvest.

2   syndicate] a cartel of absentee investors; Schreiner felt they abdicated personal responsibility for the economic crimes perpetrated on their behalf.

Rhodes!" said Peter, meditating; "they say if we had the British Government here and you were thrashing a nigger and something happened,
there'd be an investigation, and all that sort of thing. But, with Cecil, it's
all right, you can do what you like with the niggers, provided you don't
get *him* into trouble."

6. Olive Schreiner, from *Thoughts on South Africa* (1890–92; collected and republished 1923)

[The way in which colonial viewpoints struggle with idealism, prejudice
with tolerance, marks these "thoughts" on the troubled racial diversity in
South Africa as forged in the same crucible as Haggard's very different
Anglo-Africanism. But on the dangers of racial mixing, Haggard's
Quatermain and Schreiner seem very much agreed.]

One of my earliest memories is of walking up and down on the rocks
behind the little Mission House[1] in which I was born and making
believe that I was Queen Victoria and that all the world belonged to me.
That being the case, I ordered all the black people in South Africa to be
collected and put into the desert of Sahara, and a wall built across Africa
shutting it off; I then ordained that any black person returning south of
that line should have his head cut off. I did not wish to make slaves of
them, but I wished to put them where I need never see them, because I
considered them ugly. I do not remember planning that Dutch South
Africans should be put across the wall, but my objection to them was
only a little less....

It has been ascertained by those who have profoundly studied the
matter, that where two varieties of the same domestic animal ... which
have for generations bred perfectly true, are crossed, that in certain cases
the progeny resulting from this cross resembles not so much either of its
parent forms, but *reverts in colour, shape, and other characteristics, to that original parent stock from which both varieties have descended....* If, now, we apply
the same law of inheritance to human creatures, and suppose that two
wholly distinct human varieties cross, and take, for example, the Zulu
and the Englishman—both of which varieties breed perfectly true, the
Englishman always producing a white European and the Zulu a black
Bantu; both races being characterized by the strongest social feeling, and
both being remarkable for their bravery; if we leave this law of reversion
out of consideration, the natural supposition would then be, that the
offspring of such a cross, while in colour and other matters they repre-

---

1 Schreiner's parents were missionaries in Basutoland, west of Natal Colony; she was
   many years old before she saw a town.

sented a compromise between the two parent forms, would, as far as
social feeling and courage are concerned, which are common to *both*
parent varieties, be at least as well endowed in these qualities as either
parent variety. But it might not be so. If this law of reversion holds with
human creatures (and we have no reason to assert that it cannot do so);
and supposing that the original type from which in the remote past both
Zulu and Englishman have descended was of a lower order as regards
social feeling and courage, than that to which both Englishman and Zulu
have attained to in the process of ages of development, then their
offspring might revert to that lower type; and the vulgar dictum, that the
Half-caste is more anti-social than either his parent forms would in this
case be naturally and scientifically true.... All that we are qualified to
assert in the present infantile stage of our knowledge is, that there is a
danger, and we are inclined to believe a very great danger, of reversion to
the lower primitive type where two widely severed varieties cross, that
humanity may by that process lose the results of hundreds of years of
slow evolution....

When from under the beetling eyebrows in a dark face something of
the white man's eye looks out at us, is not the curious shrinking and aver-
sion we feel somewhat of a consciousness of a national disgrace and sin?

The Half-caste is our own open, self-inflicted wound; we shall not
heal it by shutting our eyes and turning away from it....

★   ★   ★   ★   ★

To these homeless fugitives [i.e., the Dutch-Huguenot Boers] the
Europe that they had left was as the 'house of bondage.' The ships which
bore them to South Africa were the Ark of the Covenant of the Lord
their God, in which He bore His chosen to the Land of His Promise. As
the Huguenot paced the deck of his ship and saw the strange stars of the
Southern Hemisphere come out above him, like Abraham of old he read
in them the promise of his covenant-keeping God: — "To thee and to
thy seed shall the land be given and they shall inherit it. Look up and see
the stars of heaven if thou canst count them: so shall thy seed be for multitude; like sand, like fine sand on the sea-shore. And when thou comest
to the land that I shall give thee, thou shalt drive out the heathen from
before thee."[1]

And as he entered Table Bay, and for the first time the superb front of
Table Mountain broke upon him, he saw in it his first token from his
covenant-keeping God — "The land that I shall give thee!"...

---

[1] Not an exact scriptural quotation, but a biblical-sounding compound of numerous passages.

Settled on the beautiful Cape Peninsula, and in the lovely Western valleys, where the wild flowers bloom as nowhere else on the earth's surface; where the streams never fail, and the high mountains shut out the parching winds of the north, and where almost every plant known to civilized man will flourish; and where the few Hottentots and Bushmen who had inhabited the land having been easily exterminated or driven away, each man sat (not figuratively, but literally) under his own vine and his own fig-tree, enjoying the fruits thereof; it would be imagined that, at least for many generations, the descendants of the early settlers would have rested, cultivating and peopling their lands along the coast.

But it was not so.

The hand of the Dutch East India Company rested heavily on the people. In some respects a fair government, and sometimes represented by able men, it yet, like all other kindred commercial despotisms, crushed the people where its own interests were concerned under an iron heel...

And so began, one hundred and fifty years ago, that long 'trek' of the Boer peoples northward and eastward, which to-day still goes on with unabated ardour and quiet persistency; and which in its ultimate essence is a search, not for riches, not for a land where mere political equality may be found; but for a world of absolute and untrammelled individual liberty; for a land where each white man shall reign, by a divine right inherent in his own person, over a territory absolutely his own; uninterfered with by the action of any external ruler, untrammelled by any foreign obligation—the Promised Land of the Boer!

As a hundred years ago he stood on the banks of the Vaal and the Orange looking to the lands beyond, so to-day he stands on the banks of the Limpopo and Zambesi; and still looks northward.... Those were the days of hard living and hard fighting. The white man depended mainly on his gun for food. And when the little Bushman looked out from behind his rocks, he saw his game—all he had to live on—being killed, and the fountain which he or his fathers had found and made, and had used for ages, being appropriated by the white men. The plains were not wide enough for both, and the new-come children of the desert fought with the old. We have all sat listening in our childhood to the story of the fighting in those old days. How sometimes the Boer coming suddenly on a group of Bushmen round their fire at night, fired and killed all he could. If in the flight a baby were dropped and left behind, he said, 'Shoot that too, if it lives it will be a Bushman or bear Bushmen.' On the other hand, when the little Bushman had his chance and found the Boer's wagon unprotected, the Boer sometimes saw a light across the plain, which was his blazing property; and when he came back would find the wagon cinders, and only the charred remains of his murdered wife and children. It was a bitter, merciless fight, the little poisoned arrow shot from behind the rocks, as opposed to the great flint-lock gun. The victory was inevitably with the flint-lock, but there may have been times when it almost seemed to lie with the arrow; it was a merciless primitive fight, but it seems to have been on the whole, compared to many modern battles, fair and even, and in the end the little Bushman vanished....

It is easy for *us* sitting at ease in our study chairs to-day to condemn the attitude of the early white men, Dutch or English, toward him, and regret that they did not take a more scientific interest in this little half-developed child of South Africa.... To indulge in philanthropic sentiment is a luxury easily to be enjoyed by the idle and luxurious; to share in generous action towards weaker peoples is a possibility only to those who have sternly set out on the path of self-obliteration; and he who indulges most of the first knows sometimes least of the last.... The Boer fought hard and the Bushman hard; they gave and they asked no quarter; neither can I see that we have any reason to be ashamed of either of our South Africans.

St. Francis of Assisi preached to the little fishes: we eat them. But the man who eats fish can hardly be blamed, seeing that the eating of fishes is all but universal among the human race! — if only he does not pretend that while he eats he preaches to them! This has never been the Boer's attitude towards any aboriginal race. He may consume it off the face of the earth; but he has never told it he does it for its benefit....

The African-born farmer, Dutch or English, who has grown up among the natives, has been nursed by them in childhood, often speaks their language, and knows something of their manners and ideas, may hate them; but always, in his heart of hearts, he recognizes them as men; and his very hatred and bitterness is a kind of tribute to the common humanity that he feels binds them. Man only hates man.

To the newcomer from Europe, on the other hand, who becomes a farmer, or is otherwise thrown into contact with the aboriginal native, he is often an object, not merely of hatred, but of contempt and sport; there is not mere assumption of cynicism when he speaks of the native merely as an object of the chase; he has often no other view with regard to him. We have heard a brilliant young English officer, who had only been a few years in the country, but had been employed in what is called a 'Native War,' dwell with manifest and almost boyish delight on the pleasures of Bantu-hunting. He described the curious delight you feel in finding the mark of a naked foot and tracing it down. 'It is,' he said, 'like the pleasure of the hunting field — with something added!' We have also known a skilful English doctor, a man of singular tenderness and generosity towards persons of his own nationality, who had been only eight years in the country, but had served in two native campaigns, remark that the only two purposes for which natives were of any use were to serve as targets for rifle-shooting and as good subjects for vivisections; while his inhumanity towards wounded and other natives was a matter of common remark among the South African burghers. And a fine young English trooper who had been two years in the country, after hearing our view on the native question, remarked thoughtfully: 'Well, you know, all this is quite new to me; I have never regarded the nigger as anything but something to shoot.' To the South African-born man his light-hearted, callous, sporting attitude is quite foreign. He may take the life of a native, but he takes it sternly, bitterly; it is something much more than hunting down the indigenous black game of the country; he knows in his heart of hearts that the thing he hunts is a *man*, and a strong man; and in his hatred of him there is even an element of fear as well as revenge. This attitude forms a far more promising field for the growth of possible socialized feeling, than any attitude of callous contempt can ever do. Hate is nearer to love than scorn can ever be; and, paradoxical as it may seem, we hold strongly that if, in South Africa to-day, sincere personal affections and sympathies are to be found crossing the line of race, they will be found most often between the African-born farming population, Dutch and English, and their domestic servants. The warmest expressions of affection towards individual natives which we have ever heard have been expressed by English and Dutch farmers towards their old servants....

Our dream of the future of our race is of no John Bull seated astride of the earth, his huge belly distended with the people he has devoured and his teeth growing out yet more than ever with all the meat he has bitten and looking around on a depeopled earth and laughing till all his teeth show and the peoples' bones rattle in his belly: 'Ha! I reign alone now. I have killed them all out!'... Our dream of the future empire of our race is not of an empire over graves but in and through living nations.... We do not dream of our language that it shall forcibly destroy the world's speeches and all they contain, reigning in solitary grandeur, but, as gold in a ring binds into one circle rare gems of every kind and some of infinitely greater beauty than itself, so we dream that our speech being common may bind together and bring into one those treasures of thought and knowledge which the peoples of earth have produced, its highest function being that of making the treasures of all accessible to all.

Appendix D: Historical Documents: Spoils of Imperialism: Gold, Diamonds, and Ivory

[The legend of Solomon and Sheba, from which Haggard takes his title, is found in the Bible, the Koran, and elsewhere. The wealth of the king and queen is for Haggard a symbol of Africa's fecundity, though for his British adventurers it represented the lure of gold, diamonds, and ivory.]

1. The Bible, I Kings 10: 1-13

"And when the queen of Sheba heard of the fame of Solomon concerning the name of the Lord, she came to prove him with hard questions. And she came to Jerusalem with a very great train, with camels that bare spices, and very much gold, and precious stones: and when she was come to Solomon, she communed with him of all that was in her heart. And Solomon told her all her questions: there was not any thing hid from the king, which he told her not. And when the queen of Sheba had seen all Solomon's wisdom, and the house that he had built ... she said to the king, 'It was a true report that I heard in mine own land of thy acts and of thy wisdom....' And she gave the king a hundred and twenty talents of gold, and of spices very great store, and precious stones: there came no more such abundance of spices as these which the queen of Sheba gave to king Solomon. And the navy also of Hiram, that brought gold from Ophir, brought in from Ophir great plenty of almug trees, and precious stones. And the king made of the almug trees pillars for the house of the Lord, and for the king's house, harps also and psalteries for singers: there came no such almug trees, nor were seen unto this day. And king Solomon gave unto the queen of Sheba all her desire, whatsoever she asked, besides that which Solomon gave her of his royal bounty. So she turned and went to her own country, she and her servants."

2. From *Kebra Negast* (c. Fourteenth Century AD)

[The title of this ancient Ethiopian work means "The Glory of the Kings" of Ethiopia. Like the myth of the divine origin of Egyptian pharaohs, Ethiopian kings were supposed of have descended from Menyelek, the son of Solomon by the Queen of Sheba, and were also believed to be divine. Wallis Budge, an early friend of Haggard and translator of the *Kebra Negast* (1922), told him stories of Egyptian archeology and spiritualism (see Haggard, *Days of My Life* 2:30–38).]

And our Lord Jesus Christ, in condemning the Jewish people, the crucifiers, who lived at that time, spake, saying "The Queen of the South shall rise up on the Day of Judgment and shall dispute with, and condemn, and overcome this generation who would not hearken unto the preaching of My word, for she came from the ends of the earth to hear the wisdom of Solomon."[1] And the Queen of the South of whom He spake was the Queen of Ethiopia. And in the words "ends of the earth" [He maketh allusion] to the delicacy of the constitution of women, and the long distance of the journey, and the burning heat of the sun, and the hunger on the way, and the thirst for water. And this Queen of the South was very beautiful in face, and her stature was superb, and her understanding and intelligence, which God had given her, were of such high character that she went to Jerusalem to hear the wisdom of Solomon; now this was done by the command of God and it was His good pleasure. And moreover, she was exceedingly rich, for God had given her glory, and riches, and gold, and silver, and splendid apparel, and camels, and slaves, and trading men (or, merchants). And they carried on her business and trafficked for her by sea and by land, and in India, and in Aswân (Syene)....

And she arrived in Jerusalem, and brought to the King very many precious gifts which he desired to possess greatly. And he paid her great honour and rejoiced, and he gave her a habitation in the royal palace near him.... And he visited her and was gratified, and she visited him and was gratified, and she saw his wisdom, and his just judgments and his splendour, and his grace, and heard the eloquence of his speech.... And of the speech of the beasts and the birds there was nothing hidden from him, and he forced the devils to obey him by his wisdom....

And when the Queen sent her message to Solomon, saying that she was about to depart to her own country, he pondered in his heart and said, "A woman of such splendid beauty hath come to me from the ends of the earth! What do I know? Will God give me seed in her?" Now, as it is said in the Book of Kings, Solomon the King was a lover of women.[2] And he married wives of the Hebrews, and the Egyptians, and the Canaanites, and the Edomites, and the Iyobawiyan (Moabites?), and from Rif and Kuergue, and Damascus, and Surest (Syria), and women who were reported to be beautiful. And he had four hundred queens and six hundred concubines. Now this which he did was not for [the sake of] fornication, but as a result of the wise intent that God had given unto him, and his remembering what God had said unto Abraham, "I

---

1   Matthew 12: 42; Luke 11: 31.
2   1 Kings 11: 1.

will make thy seed like the stars of heaven for number, and like the sand of the sea."[1] And Solomon said in his heart, "What do I know? Peradventure God will give me men children from each one of these women." Therefore when he did thus he acted wisely, saying, "My children shall inherit the cities of the enemy, and shall destroy those who worship idols."...

And ... he worked his will with her and they slept together.... And the Queen said unto Solomon, "Dismiss me, and let me depart to my own country." And he went into his house and gave unto her whatsoever she wished for of splendid things and riches, and beautiful apparel which bewitched the eyes, and everything on which great store was set in the country of Ethiopia, and camels and wagons, six thousand in number, which were laden with beautiful things of the most desirable kind, and wagons wherein loads were carried over the desert, and a vessel wherein one could travel over the sea, and a vessel wherein one could traverse the air (or winds), which Solomon had made by the wisdom that God had given unto him.

3. Anonymous, "The Ophir of Scripture," *The Illustrated London News* (January 11, 1873)

["This is probably the first reference in the West to Zimbabwe" (Edward Bacon).]

Strange stories have been told of late about the Ophir of Solomon having been discovered. The recently-opened diamond mines of South Africa led to explorations further north, which resulted in the revelation of extensive gold-mines. Mr. Hartley,[2] the lion-hunter, and Mr. Mauch, the German explorer, went further, and made known a more northern auriferous district. It is in the last-discovered gold-field that the real Ophir is supposed to have been seen....

The ruins claimed to mark the position of the Bible Ophir are placed in latitude 20° 40' south and longitude 31°40' east. This is certainly in the interior of Sofala,[3] in Eastern Africa, and easily accessible from the sea.

The story goes that a German missionary was told of great mines there; but, as the natives feared to go as guides, the missionary did not

---

1 Genesis 22: 17. Schreiner alludes to this verse in *Thoughts* (Appendix C) to characterize Africa as a gift of God to the European.

2 Henry Hartley (1815-76), a hunter and explorer who was Carl Mauch's guide.

3 Sofala was a Portuguese trading-station just south of present-day Beira from which expeditions were made in search of gold-producing regions to which it gave its name.

visit the place. Mr. Carl Mauch now reveals it, and has sent down specimens of ancient works, with moulding of cornices, and other architectural forms. Recent examination, however, throws the cold shade of doubt over this pretty romance. A geologist discovers the "mouldings" to be a calcareous deposit upon the shale, and asserts that concretions of a similar kind are common in all gold countries.

4. From Hugh Mulleneux Walmsley, *The Ruined Cities of Zulu Land* (1869)

[Based on Zimbabwe's gold-mining history, this fictional account of Egyptians, Solomon, and the lost city of Ophir provided a thematic background for Haggard's adventure into an unknown African interior, as well as details for Haggard's stalactite cave, sorcerer's dance, and sinister chieftain.]

"And why should you wish so strongly to get into the interior?" asked Hughes. "Is your object to found new missions, or are you seeking a crown of martyrdom?"

"Neither one nor the other," replied the missionary, "and I must go back some six hundred and thirty years before the birth of our Saviour, to explain my object to you."

"Go ahead!" said Hughes.

"Well, then, about that period, Pharaoh Necho[1] was king of Egypt, and he collected a large fleet, consisting of one hundred ships, great and small, in the Red Sea, and if he had not done this, you and I would not be talking at this moment on the banks of the Limpololo."

"I don't exactly see what the Egyptian king has to do with the matter. Listen, Wyzinski, there's the lion again!"

"Well, King Necho's fleet sailed right into the Southern Ocean, until winter came with its cold and storms, against which the frail ships of that day could not contend. They then ran for the nearest harbour, and the crews landing tilled the soil until the fine season came round again. Then, reaping their crops, with a well-filled hold they made sail for other lands, and thus those adventurous seamen roamed about the then unknown ocean, passing Aden, Zanzibar, and Mozambique, and on one occasion wintering in a beautiful inlet hereaway to the northward, called Santa Lucia Bay."[2]

"And were none of the ships lost?" asked Hughes.

---

1   2 Chronicles 35:20, 22; 36:4.
2   North of Natal Colony, on the coast of Zululand.

"Some on this very coast," replied Wyzinski; "and their crews, unable to return to Egypt, settled in this land, and it is believed by many, by none more firmly than myself, that the present race of Zulus, incontestably the finest in Southern Africa, sprang from the fusion of Pharaoh's seamen with the then cultivators of the soil. Others go further still, and say that this now almost savage land was the ancient Ophir, discovered by Pharaoh's fleet, and from which at a later period the ships of Tarshish drew gold, cedar-wood, and precious stones. Some of our brethren who have dwelt long in the land tell of a geological stratum promising great mineral wealth."

"Then you are in search of gold?" asked Hughes, with a slight curl of the lip, for he could not help, when gazing on the intelligent face of the man before him lighted up by the fitful gleams of the fire, regretting that a missionary should show such a thirst for gold.

"Diamonds, gold, and precious stones are said to exist, as also vast forests of ebony and cedar trees," continued the missionary, gazing abstractedly into the fire; "but with these revelations came strange tales as to the existence of ruined cities almost swallowed up by giant forest growth; the remains of a mighty but extinct race, said to lie three weeks' journey to the north and west of our settlement at Santa Lucia Bay. It is these ruins I seek."

"And Mozelkatse's[1] pass is necessary to reach them?" asked Hughes.

"Yes! will you join me in the search?" replied the missionary, eagerly, pausing for a while as the other looked moodily into the embers without replying; and then continuing, "I must not deceive you as to the difficulty and even the danger of the search. Efforts have already been made to reach the ruins, and they have ever failed. The jealous care of the native chiefs surrounds them with attributes of sanctity; the terrible tetse fly haunts the country; and the waggons must be left behind. There are danger and difficulty in the path, but it is one which has never yet been trodden by European foot. Up to the present moment all efforts made to penetrate the country have failed, and the old temples and palaces of a once glorious race, if indeed they do exist, serve as a den for the beasts of prey, or a refuge for the hardly less savage Kaffir."...

He struck his hand into the missionary's opened and muscular palm.

"Willingly I will go with you, sharing your danger, your triumph, or your defeat. But what about the pass from Mozelkatse? Did you obtain it?" he asked....

Settling himself in his seat, Mozelkatse looked round the circle, and all

---

[1] Or Moselekatse (or Umsiligasi, Silkaats) (died 1868). One of Shaka's generals, he and his followers treked across the Drakensberg mountains; he was the first King of the Matabele.

at once poured forth a torrent of words, which were those of welcome to the white men who had come to see him, ending with a request that they would settle among and trade with his people. The circle of black warriors applauded, striking their shields with their spears, and as their numbers had greatly increased, there not being less than two hundred and fifty armed men in the enclosure, the applause was noisy enough. As it died away, Wyzinski rose and stood before the chief, his clear silvery voice ringing through the enclosure.

"Some years since," said he, "I was travelling with my brethren far away on the banks of the Limpopo. I saw much of the various nations around, and by chance met with intelligent men of the tribe which calls Mozelkatse king."

The savage bent his head in token of acknowledgment of the compliment, glancing round the circle of his braves proudly.

"I began," continued Wyzinski, "to speak their language, and as I did so became aware of strange stories as to a spot far away towards the north, where stone buildings exist. One of these I was told was as large as Mozelkatse's kraal, having an opening about half its height, through which they who desire to see the ruins must pass. My Matlokotlopo brethren told also of strange figures cut in stone, and of curiously carved birds also in stone. These houses must have once been the dwellings of the white man, and the legends our fathers have taught tell us of such white men, who came many thousand years since from the regions of the rising sun, landing on these shores. To reach these ruins, to prove that our fathers spoke the truth, is our object, and in the name of our ancestors we ask thy protection, chief."

Drawing his robes round him, Wyzinski sat down, and for fully a minute there was a dead silence.

"The broken huts exist," at length replied the king, "though none of us have ever seen them, and none know what far away tribe made them. To reach them my white brethren must pass over the vast plains which lie between the Limpopo and the Zambesi, which the foot of the white man has never yet trod. The elephant and the lion abound there. The savage moohoohoo breed undisturbed, and not less cruel tribes, to whom Mozelkatse's name carries no terror, inhabit them. Let my white brethren stay to hunt, and to trade with us. A party of my braves shall seek the fallen huts and bring back the images."

The rattling sound of the rude applause was once more heard.

"No, chief," replied Wyzinski; "we are not traders. We have turned from our road to ask your aid. Give it, and we shall succeed. The report will go far and wide that through the protection of a great king our fathers' truth has been manifested, and traders will follow in our footsteps. Speed us on our journey, chief."

Mozelkatse did not reply, and for a few moments there was a deep silence. It was broken in a sudden and startling manner. A little man, almost a dwarf, deformed in person and fearfully ugly, leaped into the circle. Executing a wild dance, which he accompanied with shrill screams, he spun round, the warriors crouching down and applauding, not as heretofore with their spears, but by beating on the hard baked ground with their sticks, sometimes altogether, sometimes in an irregular manner.

Stopping as suddenly as he had begun in his mad dance, the sorcerer, for such he was, threw himself violently on the ground at Mozelkatse's feet, breaking as he did so a necklace of bones which he wore round his neck. For the first time the living circle of dusky braves gave way, and all able to do so crowded round the sorcerer, who with fixed and straining eyes was staring at the masses of bones lying here and there, from the position of which the augury was to be drawn. Luckily for the travellers, the omen was tolerably propitious, the seer pronouncing that though there was danger in the path, the white chiefs should return in safety.

The circle was again formed, and a long discussion ensued, in the course of which several of the more noted chiefs joined in, and the result was a mass of evidence as to the existence of ruins somewhere in the neighbourhood of Manica, a country lying to the northward, well watered by tributaries of the Zambesi, all the evidence being however merely hearsay. Eventually the king's aid and protection were promised, and Mozelkatse retired, two braves as he did so advancing, and taking from their sheaths the long glittering knives, performed a curious dance round the strangers, eventually cutting away the grass upon which they had sat, and burying it in a hole under the stone which had served as a throne. This being a ceremony always performed by the chief who wishes to retain the friendship of his visitors, during their temporary absence, was of good augury....

Advancing cautiously, his rifle, only one barrel of which was available, in his hand, Hughes was astonished by the great extent of the cavern. To the right, it soon became black as night, and the sound of falling water was to be heard. This might explain the extreme coldness and clearness of the streams of Gorongoza, for doubtless they took their rise in the heart of these mountains, flowing perhaps for miles in darkness among the caverns. The roof was covered with beautiful white stalactites, but the eye could not penetrate the thick darkness in this direction. To the left a kind of corridor led towards an opening giving on the mountain side, and towards this Hughes turned, glad to get away from the fetid exhalations of the cavern....

Slowly the two moved forward, and as they did so the trees became gradually further apart, the banks of the stream seemed quite clear, even from brushwood. A sharp bend led to the right, and there before them, tumbled here and there among the mighty trees, looking like masses of rock, lay scattered far as the eye could reach, following the bend of the river, fallen masonry.

Both stopped dead in utter astonishment, looking like men at once frightened and bewildered, the missionary's usually calm and impassive countenance growing one moment deadly pale, the next flushing a deep crimson. So great was the shock, so totally unexpected the event—for he had perfectly believed in what the Amatonga had said—that the tears stood in his eyes.

Here, then, was a confirmation of all his theories. Here, the vast ruins among the gold fields of king Solomon; here the source of the Sabe, or Golden River, down whose stream the boats of bygone days floated gold, cedar-wood, and precious stones. An Englishman's first impulse at once seized on Hughes, and, yielding to it, the two exchanged a vigorous shake of the hand.

"What could induce Umhleswa to tell us such an untruth?" were the first words which broke from the missionary's lips.

"Because the ruins are sacred, and these people believe no rain will fall for three years if they be molested," was the reply.

A sense of the danger now stole upon the missionary's mind as his comrade spoke....

There rose right in front of them two massive ruins of pyramidical form, which must at one time have been of great height. Even now, broken and fallen as they were, the solid bases only remaining, they were noble and imposing. Part had come tumbling down, in one jumbled mass, into the bed of the river, while the dwarf acacia and palm were shooting up among the stones, breaking and disjointing then. The two gazed long and silently at these vast mounds, the very memory of whose builders had passed away....

"The day-dream of my life realized. I stand among the ruins of the cities of old; but where they begin, or where they end I know not. The forest has re-asserted her old rights, torn from her by the hand of civilisation," he remarked.

"Look where you will there is nothing to be seen but broken mounds and tottering walls; it would require a brigade of men and years of work to clear these ruins," replied Hughes.

"Yes, the extent of them is a mystery at present. We can but affirm their existence. What a deep dead silence hangs over the spot. Let us go on."

They penetrated the ruined chamber, but hardly had they put their feet across the threshold, when bats in vast numbers came sweeping along, raising, as they did so, a fine dust, which was nearly blinding. The ruins seemed their home, and there they lived, bred, and died in countless numbers. Some were of a sickly-looking greenish colour, and of heavy and lumbering flight, often striking against the two explorers as they came along.... What the building had been it was impossible to tell; but it must have once seemed a mighty pile standing on its platform of stonework, with a flight of broad steps leading to it. These steps had disappeared; but remains of them could be noticed, and from the elevation where the two stood the line which had once been the wall of the town could be traced here and there. There were not any remains of a purely Egyptian character, save a worn arabesque representing the process of maize-grinding; but this was to be seen daily practised among the tribes, and therefore proved nothing, for it remained an open question whether the natives had taken it from the sculptor, or whether he had imitated the natives. Here and there were remains of carvings representing serpents, birds, and beasts of uncouth form, leading to the belief that the building had once been a temple....

The openings of several caves were to be seen, and near one there appeared to have been some fight lately, for blood, evidently quite fresh, was lying about.

To this cave the two climbed, entering very cautiously. Chance had again favoured them, for there lay the leopard quite dead. Bones of different kinds were heaped about, showing that for a time at least it had been the abode of wild animals. It was about twenty feet high, and there were some curious carvings on the walls, the entrance having evidently been scarped down by the hand of man. Close to the doorway were two colossal carvings, as if to guard the mouth of the cave. Each represented the figure of a nearly naked warrior, having a covering only round the loins; and each held in his hand two spears, and not having any shield— in this widely differing from the present race. The faces of these figures seemed of an Arab type. There was no trace of door, but some broken remains would seem to indicate that the entrance had once been walled up, while close by lay a slab of stone bearing a tracing on it of the figure of the African elephant. There were many similar caverns here and there in the mountain side.

"The sun is sinking, Wyzinski," said Hughes. "It will be impossible to retrace our way in the darkness, and the moon does not rise until eleven o'clock; we had better stay where we are."

"I am tired out," replied the missionary. "I don't doubt but that these caverns have once been the graves of the dead belonging to yonder city. This may well serve for ours, only we must contrive a fire."...

The moon rose, silvering with its beams the finely cut leaves of the tall palmyra and the broken ruins, shining on the human figure at the entrance of the cave, and gleaming on the bright barrel and lock of the English rifle; but the soldier slept on his post; the jackals fought over the carrion, the fire burned lower and lower, and finally went out. Day was dawning, when a loud shout close to the mouth of the cavern woke both the soldier and the missionary, but only to find themselves surrounded by a band of the Amatonga warriors fully armed, while the savage eyes and filed teeth of their chief Umhleswa, seemed to give a more vindictive expression than ever to his repulsive face.

5. From Olive Schreiner, "Diamond Fields" (*circa* 1880)

[The daughter of a bankrupt missionary, Schreiner in 1872 joined her brothers as their housekeeper (the "house" was a tent) in the rush to the diamond fields.]

Standing on the edge, and looking down, the mine is a large, oval basin with precipitous rocky sides, so deep that the men at work in the claims below seem mere moving specks, as they peck at the hard, blue soil. Around the edge of the whole mine is the whirl and rush and tumult of many thousand shouts and voices. An eager, hungry, struggling passionate life animates the whole scene. Every man, every wheel, every implement is in motion. At the wheels upon the staging that rises tier above tier along the edge of the craterlike hollow, niggers are turning ceaselessly at iron handles drawing up and letting down the shining buckets which glint in the hot afternoon sunshine. As the blue stuff is landed on the staging, it is quickly thrown down, and in Scotch carts or barrows is carried away to the gravel mounds.... On the top and sides of the gravel heaps that tower like little hills about the mine, sit the sorters; generally white men, for the master does not like to see his nigger at the sorting table. He sits on a campstool or a turned-up bucket, and as he scrapes the gravel off the table with a piece of tin, watches eagerly for the sparkle of the coveted white stones; and yet keeps all the while half an eye on the back men who rock the sieve or break the blue clonts[1] with the heavy sticks.

---

[1] A clont is a measure word in mining, loosely connoting a bowl of material.

6. From Frederick Courteney Selous, *A Hunter's Wanderings in Africa* (1881)

[Selous "was widely believed to have been the model for Allan Quatermain, HRH's disclaimers notwithstanding" (Lloyd Siemens). The incident of Khiva's death in Haggard's story is clearly indebted to the fate of Quabeet in Selous' account. Haggard's novel exaggerates neither the excitement nor the danger of the pursuit of ivory.]

It was whilst they were hunting at "Matja-ung-ombe" that Wood's head Kafir, a man named "Quabeet," from the town of "Inxoichin," was killed by an elephant. I give the story of this mishap as I heard it from Clarkson's own lips.

"Early in September, Messrs. Cross and Wood having taken the waggon to some neighbouring kraals to buy corn, I rode out by myself, and crossing fresh elephant spoor, followed it, and at length came up with the animals themselves — nine bulls, one of them an enormous beast without tusks. As soon as I fired upon them the tuskless bull turned out and went off alone, and I thought I had done with him. The elephant I had first fired at only ran a short distance, and fell dead. Quabeet and another Kafir of Wood's, who carried a gun, wounded and pursued another bull, which also turned from the rest as soon as he was shot. This I noticed as I galloped after the herd. I had just killed my second elephant, and had lost sight of the others, when my gun-carrier, 'Amehlo,' came running up, pointing with his hand, and crying out, 'Sir, sir! there goes another elephant unwounded!' I did not see him at first, but after galloping through the forest for a short distance in the direction in which the boy pointed, I caught sight of him. As I did so, I heard an elephant trumpeting terrifically away to my left, and thought to myself that one of the Kafirs was being chased pretty smartly; however, I did not like to leave the elephant I was near, though had I known what was in reality taking place, I should most assuredly have done so. Well, I killed this third elephant, and then rode back to the one I had first shot, where I found all the Kafirs, with the exception of Quabeet. I then asked whom the elephant which had screamed so fearfully had been chasing, and the Kafir who had been with Quabeet said, 'Oh, he was chasing me!' and began to relate what an escape he had had. I then asked him where he had last seen Quabeet, and he said that when he left him he was still running after the elephant they had first wounded, and that he himself had given up the pursuit because he had trodden on a sharp stump of wood and hurt his foot. We then returned to camp, and Quabeet not making his appearance at dark, we thought he must have missed his way, and would turn up the following day. Early next morning we returned to the elephants, and after chopping out the tusks, retraced our steps to camp, which we reached late in the afternoon. Quabeet was not there; the sun set, and night again shrouded the surrounding forest in darkness, and he was still absent. I now felt sure that some accident had happened to him, and only guessed too truly that the awful and long-continued screaming I had heard whilst I was engaged with my third elephant had been his death-knell. The boys, too, cross-questioned the Kafir who had been with Quabeet, and convicted him of lying. I now determined that on the morrow I would take the spoor of the tuskless bull, for to him I could not help attributing the catastrophe which I felt sure had happened, and as he had turned out by himself when I fired the first shot, I knew I should have no difficulty in doing so.

"At break of day I left camp, and riding straight to where I had shot the first elephant, took up the spoor of the tuskless bull, and had followed it for maybe two miles when I came to a place where he had stood under a tree amongst some dense underwood. From this place he had spun suddenly round, as the spoor showed, and made a rush through the bush, breaking and smashing everything before him. Fifty yards farther on we found Quabeet's gun, a little beyond this a few odds and ends of skin that he had worn round his waist, and then what remained of the poor fellow himself. He had been torn in three pieces; the chest, with head and arms attached, which had been wrenched from the trunk just below the breast-bone, lying in one place, one leg and thigh that had been torn off at the pelvis in another, and the remainder in a third. The right arm had been broken in two places and the hand crushed; one of the thighs was also broken, but otherwise the fragments had not been trampled on." There is little doubt that the infuriated elephant must have pressed the unfortunate man down with his foot or knee, and then twisting his trunk round his body wrenched him asunder. This feat gives one an idea of the awful strength of these huge beasts, and how powerless the strongest of men—even one of "Ouida's" heroes[1]—would be, when once in their clutches.

By examining the spoor Clarkson found that when this elephant charged, Quabeet was following another—doubtless the one he had first wounded—and thinks that in all probability the poor fellow never saw the brute until it was close upon him; and this, I think, must have been the case, as it is astonishing how difficult it is to see an elephant when he is standing still amongst high and thick bush, especially if one's attention is engaged with something else.

---

1   Marie Louise de la Ramée, "Ouida" (1839-1908), a "sensation novelist" whose soldiers performed marvels of strength and courage.

Poor Quabeet! I knew him well, and a real good fellow he was. A Zulu by blood, he was born just before Umziligazi left Natal on his flight northwards, and was still quite a boy when he came to the Matabele country. In the rebellion of 1870, when the kraals of "Zwang Indaba" and "Induba" fought for Kuruman against the present king Lobengula, he took part with the rebels, and received several assegai wounds during the fierce hand-to-hand combat that ended in the defeat of his party. *Requiescat in pace.*[1]

*   *   *   *   *

About 1 P.M. we off-saddled our horses for the first time that day, and had scarcely done so when three heavy shots, fired almost simultaneously, fell in the direction the spoor was taking, and at no great distance. Making sure it was some of Wood's Kafir hunters firing at the elephants we were following, we saddled up again, and cantered along the spoor, but, from the direction it took, soon found that the shots we had heard could not have been fired at the elephants. We now stuck to the spoor without a halt till about an hour and a half before sundown, when, fearing that it would get dark before we came up with them, we took our guns and galloped on, for the spoor was now becoming fresher every instant, and as the elephants were feeding nicely, easy to follow, by the machabel leaves alone, that lay scattered along the track.

I may here say that I was this day mounted on an old horse in very poor condition, which I had bought from Wood, my own having gone lame two days before, and that all our horses had been the livelong day under the saddle, and like ourselves had had no water. Well, we had cantered along the spoor for some distance, when we at last descried two elephants, stragglers from the main body, and then the herd itself. They were moving in a dense mass up a gentle incline on the farther side of a dry watercourse, and as the whole country about here is very sparsely wooded, we had a magnificent view of them. There must have been at least sixty or seventy, great and small, and a grand sight it was, and one not easily to be forgotten, to see so many of these huge beasts moving slowly and majestically onwards. However, as there was now but an hour of sunlight left, we could spare but little time for admiration, and so rode towards them, on murderous thoughts intent. We crossed the dry gully, and passed within a hundred and fifty yards of the two we had first seen, but they never appeared to take any notice of us. Just as we neared the herd, one of the biggest bulls turned broadside to us, and commenced

---

1   (Latin) may he rest in peace; abbr. R.I.P.

plucking some leaves from a bush, offering a splendid shot, of which Clarkson was just going to take advantage, when he saw us, and wheeling round, ran off. As he did so, I noticed that he had a stump tail. The whole herd was now in motion. At first they ran in a compact body and at a surprising pace, raising a dense cloud of dust, and in the confusion one of them, half-grown, was knocked down, and must have been trampled on and half-stunned, for he did not get on his legs until the herd had passed, and then at first ran back, away from his companions; but before long, finding out his mistake, wheeled about, and soon caught up to them again. We now galloped along, even with, and about one hundred yards to the side of the foremost of them, shouting and hallooing, and thus drove them round in a large circle, our object being to tire them before we commenced firing. Though I had killed many elephants, yet having always before this season hunted on foot in regions infested by the tsetse fly, I had had no experience with them on horseback, so, having been told by my friends on no account to dismount, but to shoot from the horse's back, as, in case of a charge, I should have no time to remount, I endeavoured at first to comply with their instructions; however, my horse, worse luck to him, would not stand, but as soon as I dropped the reins, always walked or trotted forwards, thus making it impossible to get a shot. Seeing that if this continued, I should never shoot an elephant at all, I determined to dismount; so, cantering up alongside of the foremost, I jumped off, and gave a young bull a bullet behind the shoulder as he came broadside past me. He only ran about a hundred yards, and then fell dead. After this I quickly killed two more with five shots—a fine cow and another young bull. The fourth I tackled, a bull with tusks scaling about five-and-thirty pounds, cost me six bullets, and gave me a smart chase, for my horse was now dead beat. I only got away at all by the skin of my teeth, as, although the infuriated animal whilst charging trumpeted all the time like a railway engine, I could not get my tired horse out of a canter until he was close upon me, and I firmly believe that had he not been so badly wounded he would have caught me. I know the shrill screaming sounded unpleasantly near.

Just as this bull fell, Wood and Cross came round with what remained of the troop, and I met and turned them back again. The poor animals were now completely knocked up, throwing water over their heated bodies as they walked slowly along, swerving first one way and then the other, as the cruel bullets struck them. A good many had turned out, and made their escape in twos and threes, and as we had been picking out all the best, there were now not many left worth shooting. My friends had fired away almost all their cartridges, but I had still thirteen left; for, owing to my horse refusing to stand, I had not commenced firing as soon as they. As the elephants were now only walking, and sometimes stood all huddled up together in a mass, offering splendid standing shots, I felt sure of killing three or four more with my remaining cartridges, and should doubtless have done so had it not been for an accident that befell me, which happened in this wise. — Having picked out a good cow for my fifth victim, I gave her a shot behind the shoulder, on which she turned from the herd and walked slowly away by herself. As I cantered up behind her, she wheeled round, and stood facing me, with her ears spread, and her head raised. My horse was now so tired that he stood well, so, reining in, I gave her a shot from his back between the neck and the shoulder, which I believe just stopped her from charging. On receiving this wound she backed a few paces, gave her ears a flap against her sides, and then stood facing me again. I had just taken out the empty cartridge and was about to put a fresh one in, when, seeing that she looked very vicious, and as I was not thirty yards from her, I caught the bridle, and turned the horse's head away, so as to be ready for a fair start in case of a charge. I was still holding my rifle with the breech open, when I saw that she was coming. Digging the spurs into my horse's ribs, I did my best to get him away, but he was so thoroughly done that, instead of springing forwards, which was what the emergency required, he only started at a walk, and was just breaking into a canter, when the elephant was upon us. I heard two short sharp screams above my head, and had just time to think it was all over with me, when, horse and all, I was dashed to the ground. For a few seconds I was half stunned by the violence of the shock, and the first thing I became aware of, was a very strong smell of elephant. At the same instant I felt that I was still unhurt, and that, though in an unpleasant predicament, I had still a chance for life. I was, however, pressed down on the ground in such a way that I could not extricate my head. At last with a violent effort I wrenched myself loose, and threw my body over sideways, so that I rested on my hands. As I did so I saw the hind legs of the elephant standing like two pillars before me, and at once grasped the situation. She was on her knees, with her head and tusks in the ground, and I had been pressed down under her chest, but luckily behind her forelegs. Dragging myself from under her, I regained my feet and made a hasty retreat, having had rather more than enough of elephants for the time being. I retained, however, sufficient presence of mind to run slowly, watching her movements over my shoulder, and directing mine accordingly. Almost immediately I had made my escape, she got up, and stood looking for me with her ears up and head raised, turning first to one side and then to the

Works Cited and Recommended Reading

Anonymous. Review of "King Solomon's Mines." *The Spectator* 58 (November 7, 1885): 1473.

———. Review of "King Solomon's Mines." *The Academy* 28 (November 7, 1885): 304-305.

———. Review of "King Solomon's Mines." *The Literary World* (January 23, 1886) 24.

———. "Editorial." *The Book Buyer* (New York) 4 (August 4, 1887): 219.

———. "The Fall of Fiction." *Fortnightly Review* 44 (September 1, 1888): 324-36.

———. "Mr. Rider Haggard." *The Illustrated London News* (December 15, 1888): 710.

Bacon, Edward, ed. *The Great Archaeologists*. London: Secker and Warburg, 1976.

Barclay, Glen St. John. *Anatomy of Horror: The Masters of Occult Fiction*. London: Weidenfeld and Nicolson, 1978.

Bass, Jeff. "The Romance as Rhetorical Dissociation: The Purification of Imperialism in *King Solomon's Mines*." *The Quarterly Journal of Speech* 67 (1981): 259-69.

Bent, J. Theodore. *The Ruined Cities of Mashonaland*. London: Longmans, Green, 1893.

Bolt, C. *Victorian Attitudes to Race*. London: Routledge and Kegan Paul, 1971.

Brantlinger, Patrick. *Rule of Darkness: British Literature and Imperialism, 1830-1914*. Ithaca: Cornell UP, 1988.

Bryce, James. *Impressions of South Africa*. London: Macmillan, 1897.

Bunn, David. "Embodying Africa: Woman and Romance in Colonial Fiction." *English in Africa* 15 (May 1988): 1-28.

Calder, Jenni. *Heroes*. London: Hamish Hamilton, 1977.

Cameron, Kenneth. *Africa on Film: Beyond Black and White*. New York: Continuum, 1994.

Chamberlain, Muriel. *The Scramble for Africa*. London: Longman, 1974.

Chrisman, Laura, "The Imperial Unconscious? Representations of Imperial Discourse." *Critical Quarterly* 32 (Autumn 1990): 38-58.

———. *Rereading the Imperial Romance*. Oxford: Clarendon, 2000.

Clark, Samuel M. "Mr. Haggard's Romances." *The Dial* (May 1887): 5-7.

Cohen, Morton. *Rider Haggard: His Life and Work*. London: Macmillan, 1960.

Crummell, A. "The Culture of the Horrible: Mr. Haggard's Stories." *The Church Quarterly Review* 25 (January 1888): 389-411.

Dalby, Richard. "*King Solomon's Mines*: A Centenary Remembered." *Antiquarian Book Monthly Review* (October 1985): 390-93.

Demoor, Marysa. "Ritual Celebrations as Rites of Passage in Rider Haggard's Dark Romances." *Cahiers Victoriens et Edouardiens*: 39 (1994) 205-217.

De Thierry, C. *Imperialism*. Introd. W. E. Henley. London: Duckworth and Co., 1898.

Eliot, T.S. "*Ulysses*, Order, and Myth" (1923). S. Givens, ed. *James Joyce: Two Decades of Criticism*. New York: Vanguard Press, 1948.

Etherington, Norman. "South African Origins of Rider Haggard's Early African Romances." *Notes and Queries* 24 (October 1977): 436-38.

———. "Rider Haggard, Imperialism, and the Layered Personality." *Victorian Studies* 22 (Autumn 1978): 71-87.

———. *Rider Haggard*. Boston: Twayne, 1984.

Fletcher, Ian. "Can Haggard Ride Again?" *The Listener* (July 29, 1971): 136-38.

Flint, John. *Cecil Rhodes*. Boston: Little, Brown, 1974.

Fynney, Fred. *Zululand and the Zulus*. Maritzburg, S.A.: Horne Bros., 1880.

Green, Martin. *Dreams of Adventure, Deeds of Empire*. London: Routledge, 1980.

Green, Roger Lancelyn. "The Romances of Rider Haggard." *English* 5 (1945): 144-48.

Greene, Graham. *The Lost Childhood and Other Essays*. London: Eyre and Spottiswoode, 1951.

Haggard, H. Rider. "A Zulu War-Dance." *The Gentleman's Magazine* 243 (July 1877): 94-107.

———. "The Transvaal." *Macmillan's Magazine* 36 (May 1877): 70-79.

———. Letter of August 28, 1884, to John Haggard (Lamu, Africa). Henry Rider Haggard Manuscript Collection (Ms 40220E), Rare Book and Manuscript Library, Columbia University.

———. *King Solomon's Mines*. London: Cassell & Co., 1885.

———. "About Fiction." *The Contemporary Review* 51 (February 1887): 172-80.

———. "Preface." A. Wilmot. *Monomotapa (Rhodesia)*. London: T. Fisher Unwin, 1896.

———. *The Days of My Life: An Autobiography*. 2 vols. London: Longmans, Green, 1926.

———. *Three Adventure Novels: She, King Solomon's Mines, Allan Quatermain*. New York: Dover, 1979.

———. *The Private Diaries of Sir H. Rider Haggard*. London: Cassell, 1980.

Haggard, Lilias. *The Cloak That I Left: A Biography of Rider Haggard*. London: Hodder & Stoughton, 1951.

Higgins, D.S. *Rider Haggard: The Great Storyteller*. London: Cassells, 1981.

Hopkins, G.M. *The Letters of Gerard Manley Hopkins to Robert Bridges*. 2 Vols. London: Oxford UP, 1935.

Katz, Wendy. *Rider Haggard and the Fiction of Empire*. Cambridge: Cambridge UP, 1987.

Kebra Negast (The Queen of Sheba). Trans. Wallis Budge. London: Martin Hopkinson, 1922.

Lang Andrew. "*King Solomon's Mines*." *The Saturday Review* 60 (October 10, 1885): 485–86.

Lewis, C.S. "Of Stories," *Essays Presented to Charles Williams*. London: Oxford UP, 1947.

———. "Haggard Rides Again." *Time and Tide* (September 3, 1960): 1044–45.

Magubane, Bernard, *The Making of a Racist State: British Imperialism and the Union of South Africa, 1875-1910*. Trenton, N.J.: Africa World Press, 1996.

McClintock, Anne. "Maidens, Maps, and Mines: The Reinvention of Patriarchy in Colonial South Africa." *South Atlantic Quarterly* 87 (Winter 1988): 147–92.

Monsman, Gerald. "Of Diamonds and Deities: Social Anthropology in H. Rider Haggard's *King Solomon's Mines*." *English Literature in Transition* 43 (Fall 2000): 280–97.

Müller, Max. "Comparative Mythology" [1856]. *Chips from a German Workshop*. 2 vols. New York: Scribner, Armstrong, 1876.

Oliphant, Margaret. "Success in Fiction." *Forum* 7 (May 1889): 321–22.

Patteson, Richard. "'King Solomon's Mines': Imperialism and Narrative Structure." *The Journal of Narrative Technique* 8 (1978): 112–23.

Plaatje, Sol. *Mhudi*. Alice, S.A.: Lovedale Press, 1930.

Pritchett, V.S. "Haggard Still Riding." *New Statesman* 60 (August 27, 1960): 277–78.

Ruskin, John. "Lectures on Art" (1873). *Complete Works of John Ruskin*. Ed. E.T. Cook and Alexander Wedderburn. 20 Vols. London: George Allen, 1903.

Sandison, Alan. *The Wheel of Empire: A Study of the Imperial Idea*. London: Macmillan, 1967.

———. "A Matter of Vision: Kipling and Haggard." *The Age of Kipling*. New York: Simon and Schuster, 1972.

Scheick, William. "Adolescent Pornography and Imperialism in Haggard's *King Solomon's Mines*." *English Literature in Transition* 34 (1991): 19–30.

Schreiner, Olive. "Diamond Fields" (c. 1880). Ed. Richard Rive. *English in Africa* 1 (March 1974): 15–29.

———. *Thoughts on South Africa*. London. T. Fisher Unwin, 1923.

———. *Trooper Peter Halket of Mashonaland*. London. T. Fisher Unwin, 1897.

Selous, Frederick Courteney. *A Hunter's Wanderings in Africa*. London: Richard Bentley & Son, 1881.

Siemens, Lloyd. *The Critical Reception of Sir Henry Rider Haggard: An Annotated Bibliography. English Literature in Transition*. Special Series, No. 5, 1991.

Stevenson, R. L. *Letters of Robert Louis Stevenson*. Ed. Bradford Booth. New Haven: Yale UP, 1995.

Street, Brian. *The Savage in Literature*. London: Routledge and Kegan Paul, 1975.

Torgovnick, Marianna. *Gone Primitive: Savage Intellects, Modern Lives*. Chicago: U of Chicago P, 1990.

Trollope, Anthony. *South Africa*. 2 vols. London: Chapman and Hall, 1878.

Tylor, E.B. *Primitive Culture* (1871). 2 vols. London: John Murray, 1920.

Vickery, John B. *The Literary Impact of The Golden Bough*. Princeton: Princeton UP, 1973.

"Vindex." *Cecil Rhodes: His Political Life and Speeches: 1881-1900*. London: Chapman and Hall, 1900.

Walmsley, Hugh Mulleneux. *The Ruined Cities of Zulu Land*. 2 vols. London: Chapman and Hall, 1869.